THE
BOOK
OF
READING

ALSO BY ERIC LARSEN

Fiction

An American Memory (1988)
I Am Zoë Handke (1993)
The End of the 19ᵗʰ Century (2011)
The Decline and Fall of the American Nation (2013)

Non-fiction

A Nation Gone Blind: America in an Age of Simplification
*   and Deceit (2006)*
Homer Whole: A Reading of the Iliad (2009, 2017)
The Skull of Yorick: The Emptiness of American Thinking at a Time
*   of Grave Peril—Studies in the Cover-up of 9/11 (2011)*

THE
BOOK
OF
READING

A NOVEL

BY

ERIC LARSEN

atmosphere press

For the Past
and
For Our Future

O sacred solitary empty mornings, tranquil medita-
tions—fruit of book-case and clock-tick, of note-book
and armchair; golden and rewarding silence, influence
of sun-dappled plane-trees, far-off noises of birds and
horses, possession beyond price of a few cubic feet of air
and some hours of leisure! This vacuum of peace is the
state from which art should proceed, for art is made by
the alone for the alone, and now this cerulean atmosphere,
which we should be able to take for granted, has become
an unattainable end.

> —Palinurus (Cyril Connolly), *The Unquiet Grave*

Republican senator Arthur Vandenberg told Truman that he
could have his militarized economy only if he first 'scared
the hell out of the American people' that the Russians
were coming. Truman obliged. The perpetual war began.
Representative government of, by, and for the people is
now a faded memory.

> —Gore Vidal, *Perpetual War for Perpetual Peace*
> (New York, 2002)

Q: When did the CIA start?
A: September 18, 1947

> —Google

thousands were watching but no one saw a thing

> —Bob Dylan, *Murder Most Foul*

A NOTE
TO THE READER

Not many things are more intriguing to readers (or writers) than the relationship between fiction and fact, the imaginary and the real, between "story" on the one hand and "real events" on the other. I myself, both as reader and writer, have been involved in distinctions and divergences of this kind for most of my adult life, not least during the time I was writing this present book, *The Book of Reading.*

The Book of Reading is my fifth novel (and eighth book), and I think it's perfectly capable, as it were, of standing on its own two feet. Yet I don't think of it just as a book of its own but also as the fifth installment—or chapter, if you will—of a single extended story.

The writing of this extended five-book-long story has taken place over a long period of time. The first part of it to see the light of day, *An American Memory,* appeared in 1988. That book, however, was composed over a period of approximately seventeen years, meaning that it had its first flicker of life somewhere in or near 1971.

The second part of the story came out four years later, in 1992, under the title *I Am Zoë Handke*. It is, as you might guess, the story of a young woman named Zoë as opposed to being, as *An American Memory* was, the story of a young man named Malcolm. In keeping, however, with the idea that these books are two parts of the same story, I hasten to add that Malcolm *does* in fact have a role in Zoë's part of that longer story, as also does his home town of West Tree, Minnesota.

Now, I haven't forgotten that I opened this note by mentioning "the relationship between fiction and fact" and the fascination that this relationship has for many people. Allow me to go back to that subject now by mentioning that when the third part of this pentalogy of novels came out (in 2011), I began by calling it *The Story of My Life*. Then I changed over to *A History of the Town that Disappeared*. I ended up, however, calling it *The End of the 19th Century*, and in it, once again, are Malcolm Reiner, his home town of West Tree, Minnesota (drawn from the real-life town of Northfield, Minnesota), and even the farm that Malcolm grew up on—a place immediately recognizable to readers of *An American Memory*.

Are such things—places, people, events—real or are they made up? Well, it can be verified easily that there really is a town in Minnesota called Northfield, although the same can't be said for one called West Tree. Curiously enough—as a reading of *The End of the 19th Century* will show—the two places look similar in many ways, with similar streets, a river dividing each into an east side and a west side, and each side harboring a college—St. Olaf College and Carleton College in the real-life Northfield; Old College and New College in the fictional West Tree.

Now, in *The End of the 19th Century*, a singular and major event is that the town of West Tree disappears entirely:

> *Not a trace of it remained. The streets themselves, the*
> *great trees that had lined them, the curbs, sidewalks, and*

*boulevards dating from the earliest years of the Epoch of
Walking—none remained, while in their places stood the
same tall, blossoming, aromatic grass that also grew now
outside of town, where the farm had been, bending over as
the wind rose, then straightening up again as it died.*

Now, some concluding thoughts.

West Tree, Minnesota, disappeared from the map. North-field, Minnesota, didn't.

Which fact, or which phenomenon, holds the truth? Did a town disappear, or did a town not?

A person could answer by saying that both things hold truth, one of them being fictional and one real.

Yes. But here's a question: If Northfield, Minnesota, *had never existed*, is it more likely or less likely that West Tree, Minnesota, could (or would) have come into existence?

The answer, certainly, must be "less likely." In fact, the degree of "less likelihood" would be so great that in the absence of the real-life Northfield, Minnesota, the imaginary West Tree, Minnesota, *would and could never have been created.*

In certain extraordinarily important ways, the two depend upon one another.

A person is reminded of the famous René Magritte painting of a briar pipe, executed in a hyper-realistic manner, with, below the image of the pipe, the statement "This is not a pipe." ("Ceci n'est pas une pipe.")

Of course it's not a pipe: It's a *painting.*

On the other hand, the painting couldn't conceivably exist without the pipe.

Could the pipe exist without the painting of it?

I suspect that most people would say yes, of *course* the pipe could (and would) exist without the painting of it. I myself, however, am not quite so certain. I wonder, for example, whether the pipe—any pipe—would exist *in the same way* if the painting of it had never been made.

Within paradox of this kind lies the Magritte artwork's meaning.

And the same goes for the two towns in Minnesota—or perhaps I must say "in" Minnesota, or in "Minnesota." If you think of one of the towns as the Magritte painting of a pipe, which one would it have to be, Northfield or West Tree? West Tree is the winner, certainly. Now, what would happen if the novel about West Tree were called not *The End of the 19th Century*, but, instead, *This is Not a Town*?

I wonder. West Tree looks just like Northfield. West Tree disappears. Is Northfield changed?

A good question. Worth thinking about.

Now, allow me to say this: The fact that the five novels I'm talking about here are all written in the first person doesn't mean that all of them are about *me*.

And also this: On the other hand, the fact that the five novels I'm talking about here are all written in the first person *does* mean that all of them are about me.

This quality of the paradoxical—in setting, character, voice, action, point of view—is an essential element in the very bloodstream of what we know as "fiction." The truth is that the question of what's real and what's imaginary in a novel or other serious artwork must not only be present at all times, *but it's also a question that must be and must remain unanswerable.*

The minute it does become answerable, the air goes out of the balloon and you no longer have a novel or an artwork. Instead, you're likely to have something that's been reduced to a "message," or perhaps what's known as "non-fiction." Or you might have what we call "fantasy." Or you might end up with an "entertainment," and the question can be asked yet again, "And what's the problem with that?"

Well, there's no problem with any of these. No problem, that is, except that through the experience of none of them—"message," "fantasy," "entertainment"—is a person likely to be *changed*.

On the other hand, if in an artwork the question of what's

real and what's fictional really *does* remain unanswerable—unanswerable, that is, at a deep and not at a shallow level—*then* the experience of reading a novel, seeing a play, viewing a painting may possibly change a person profoundly, and not necessarily in a way that can easily—or maybe *ever*—be expressed in words.

•

Some rudimentary facts: I in fact *did* graduate from college (Carleton College) in 1963, and I did in fact enroll for graduate work at Iowa City in the fall of that year. President Kennedy *was* assassinated that same autumn, on November 22. I *did* allow myself, against my better judgment, to be drawn that same day into a trip out of town, the purpose being to bring encouragement to a fellow student who was suffering from writer's block.

I did *not*, however, find myself transported in time back to 1933, and I did *not* meet and fall in love with a beautiful young woman and literary genius by the name of Eveline Stahl. Eveline is fiction every bit as much, and as little, as Malcolm Reiner is fiction; and every bit as much, and as little, as the couple's long walk from Iowa City to West Tree, Minnesota, is fiction; and every bit as much, and as little, as Malcolm's symbol-drenched and unmanageable father is fiction; and every bit as much, and as little, as the miserably unhappy ending of the story, in spring 2028, is or may be fiction.

EL

4/23/23

PREFACE

I'd been in Iowa City for a month-and-a-half or two months when I discovered that time there existed not in a single plane, as it did everywhere else, but in two parallel planes separated from one another by thirty years.

This was the fall of 1963. I had just graduated from New College and had chosen Iowa City for more study.

The discovery about dual time came on the night of November 20th, a week before my twenty-second birthday and two days before they murdered President Kennedy in Dallas.

Six decades have passed since then. The year now is 2028 and I am forced to cite my age as eighty-seven, a far higher figure than twenty-two. In any case, given my inability to stop growing older, I have an interest in putting down memories—significant ones to me, as I hope they may be to others—before it's too late. These memories, I'm quite sure, will be graspable enough as I present them in the form of scenes, events, and moments. Less evident may be some of the other themes—the true ones—that inform and underlie the memories. Having pondered these underlying themes closely now for a long time, I think of them as being reducible to six. These are love, time, memory, meaning, destruction, and evil.

The themes relate to one another very closely, especially the last three. I say this because, after much thought, I have come to the conclusion that from the moment human beings stop being able to perceive or understand meaning in themselves or in the things and elements around them; from that moment they become incapable of producing anything other than destruction and evil.

Possibly the most vivid example of this truth is the transformation—over the short span of my own lifetime—of my own country from an idealistic though imperfect republic into what is, by every measure, now the leading force on earth for the production of evil.

I'm not so naïve as to expect readers to follow me willingly into the literary thickets I am about to enter. After all, if few people today read much of anything at all, fewer still, it seems, want to read a work touched by the philosophic brush. I, however, have no choice: I've got to go forward now or never go forward at all. I would like company, admittedly, and I welcome it. But, to any who do feel the inclination to come along, I must, after most sincerely thanking you, add these admonitions: Come with eyes open. Fend for yourself. Expect no coherence.

ONE

1

Everything about Iowa City seemed old. The door locks were old, the windowsills were old, the sidewalks were old. The toilets, sinks, showers, and faucets were old. All of the houses on the stately east side of town—the more tree-covered side—were old, and the buildings making up the central campus were especially so. Lawns, hedges, trees, ornamental fences, all were old. Even the shops, stores, diners, and bars that clung like poor relatives around the edges of the central campus were old.

I loved this sense of oldness. I felt at home with it and took comfort from it.

2

For my first semester and most of my second, I lived in the men's residence hall known as the Quadrangle, named in accordance with its shape. It was the university's first building on the west side of the river. Two stories high, of red brick, it formed a large square enclosing an inner courtyard covered in grass and divided by walkways. At each of its four entrance-ways stood a tower rising to three stories.

The reason I didn't remain in the Quadrangle through the end of my second semester is that in the spring I moved in with Eveline Stahl, on the east side of town, in her apartment at 806 E. College Street. In the eyes of the university, however, I remained a resident in my room in the Quadrangle, holding the space. When I did return, without Eveline, I felt I was there merely as a kind of ghost tenant.

3

The bus I arrived on stopped halfway between Washington and Court Streets and stayed there a moment or two, shuddering slightly. Then it gathered itself up and heaved into a sharp left turn. Rocking from side to side, it labored into an alleyway and inched forward until the alley opened up into a wide area inside the block. There, it turned left, crept forward again, and came to a stop with its nose not six inches from the back wall of the bus depot.

This was the last stop on the line. The driver turned off the engine, eased himself out from behind the wheel, stood up, and stretched luxuriously. Then he swung the door lever, went down the three steps, and stood outside as his passengers—ten or a dozen of us—filed to the front of the bus, went down the steps, and set foot on the concrete apron of the back lot.

Not everyone had baggage. With five or six others, I waited for the driver to open the luggage bay. He leaned down, pulled the outside latch and swung up the big door. He set the prop so it wouldn't fall back down, then leaned inside and began dragging out bags. Two of them were mine.

The outside wall of the bus depot was made of weathered red brick and had two small square windows. The door, however, stood open. I went inside. Fluorescent lights hung in rows from the ceiling. There was the smell of stale tobacco. To my right were wooden benches and to my left the ticket counter, with a clock on the wall behind it. Four or five people sat on the benches. All were men, and they sat at varying distances from one another. The clerk had stepped outside and was talking with the driver.

On the far wall was a second door, this one with a round window and hinges of the kind that let the door swing inward or outward. I crossed over, one suitcase in each hand, pressed my back against the door, and went through into the rear of a restaurant-diner. To my right as I faced forward was a counter with built-in stools, and to my left a row of booths. In the space between the two stood a number of tables, both square and round, with chairs.

Seven or eight people sat in the booths, men and women, singly, in pairs, or in small groups. Another four or five sat at the counter. Those at the counter were all men, spaced apart from one another. It was very quiet in the diner. There was no radio or music.

I walked across the room and went out through the front door onto the sidewalk. The sunshine was hot, unbroken, and bright. The intensity of it added to the indelible impression of shabbiness on the diner's side of the street—heaved and cracked sidewalks, cars and dusty pickup trucks nosed unevenly at angles against the curb, the semi-derelict appearance of the storefronts that flanked the diner. On this side of Washington Street there were no trees, bushes, shrubs, awnings, or other source of shade. The only green came from the scrappy tufts of crabgrass at the bases of the parking meters.

Across Washington Street, however, the appearance of things made for a powerful contrast. I was standing at one of the places in Iowa City where town and university butted up against one another without any shading or gradation. Across the street I saw mowed lawns and dense greenery, the entranceways to walks, a glimpse or two of stone buildings—all amid shrubs, hedges, and enormous trees that expanded up in high crowns, where their foliage received the sunlight and filtered it on its way down, leaving what was below in cool and dappled shade.

I picked up my bags from the sidewalk, stepped off the curb, crossed the street, and went in under the trees.

4

Walking from the bus depot to the Quadrangle, I crossed the river for the first time.

From the sidewalk in front of the diner, I crossed Washington Street and entered in on one of the walkways leading into the interior of the old original campus. This was an area consisting of a large rectangle of land situated on the crest of the bluff looking westward across the river. On this bluff were clustered the university's five original halls, forming a quincunx with the oldest in the center, this being the original state capitol building, now the university's administrative headquarters. Surrounded by its outriders Jessup, Macbride, Schaeffer, and MacLean, the old building claimed the topmost elevation and stood facing resolutely west. Taken together, the arrangement created a fine impression—clustered central halls shrouded by trees, accessed by walkways, aproned by lawns, offering to the observer a familiar dignity, weight, and muted splendor.

I walked along the brow of the bluff to a point in front of Old Capitol. There, I turned left onto another walkway, followed it to the bottom of the hill, continued to the Iowa Avenue bridge, and went across.

Once over the river and onto the west bank, I began the climb up the bluff that was counterpart to the one on the east. The walkway took me on a curving route through light growths of trees and past four or five old houses that had been converted into university clinics and offices. Three times I came to forks and bore left at each one, with the result that the path brought me directly into the north entranceway of the Quadrangle.

5

I found my room—I'd requested a single and was lucky to have gotten one—by its number, "B-90." The "B " meant that the room was on the second rather than the ground floor, and the even number meant it faced outward instead of inward across the central yard.

As expected, the room was locked. I set my bags outside the door, returned to the north entranceway, took the stairs down, then walked across the courtyard to the south entrance in order to claim my two keys from the concierge's office. "B-90" was stamped into the metal on each.

I went back to my room, unlocked the door, picked up my bags, and went in. The room was small and narrow, almost twice in depth what it was in width, recalling a monk's cell or ship's cabin. A narrow bed stood against the left wall, and against the right were a table-desk with a goose-neck lamp and a wooden chair. Near the desk stood a small chest with drawers, and beyond that a small upholstered chair with arms. Twin windows were set into the far wall. These faced north so that even though sunlight would never come in, such light as did come in would be steady.

The air was stuffy, close, and dead. I carried my bags in, closed the door with my foot, and set the bags near the bed. I went over to the windows, opened the latches and then turned one crank after the other until each window stood out at a right angle to the wall of the building. Fresh air came in.

I turned around, pried off my shoes without untying them, and lay down on the bed.

6

I woke up an hour and a quarter later, sensing the loss of valuable time that I ought to have spent looking around at this place where I had come to live. My room sported a small sink with a mirror over it, though no toilet. I splashed water on my face, toweled it off, got my shoes back on, went out the door, turned the lock behind me, and took the two half-sets of stairs down into the north entryway. There, I turned left, crossed over the central yard again, and re-entered the south—main— entryway, where earlier I had gone to get my keys.

The south gate was the largest and most important of the four gates, containing as it did the concierge's office, the post office, the entry to a first-floor restaurant open to the public, and the spiral staircase leading to the dining hall in the basement. I passed by all of these and stepped out through the main doors themselves, which were standing propped open to the air. Outside was a portico with columns at its two outer corners and a stairway of half a dozen steps leading down to ground level. I stood on the portico, having no plan other than to wait for five-thirty to come around, when the dining hall would open. I didn't know anyone else in Iowa City and hadn't yet met anyone living in the Quadrangle, so there was no one to look up, visit, or phone. In fact, I had no responsibilities until the next morning, when I was to cross the river to meet with my academic adviser and find out how to begin registration.

For the moment, nothing was required or expected of me. I would therefore do nothing. I would stand there and look out.

There was no indication that I was about to receive the first hint—just a hint—of what I was to learn about the behavior of time.

The street in front of the Quadrangle was named, eponymously, Field House Road, while the street beyond it was the more plainly named Johnson Avenue. In the space between these two parallel streets was an area approximately the length of two city blocks and the width of one. The eastern end of this space had been developed into a semi-rustic park with trees, hedges, walkways, and benches. The western part, meanwhile, consisted of a large open field covered—aside from some worn areas—with grass. In winter, the field was flooded for ice-skating, while in warm weather it served for general recreation, intramural games, athletic practices, marching drills, and the like.

Still farther away, past the playing field and on the far side of Johnson Avenue, stood five or six large and quite stately houses. These were faculty houses, I learned later, inhabited by athletic staff with their families, and by medical and law school faculty with theirs.

Even now, I remember the moment I stood there, on the portico, looking out. The time was getting close to five o'clock. The air, warm and soft, was filled with the pleasant and slightly nostalgic scent of autumn. Sunlight came in at a low angle from the west, right to left, and lay in streaks across the walkways and lawns.

As I stood there, gazing across the park and playing field, there came an unusual change in my hearing that I know could have sent me into a panic if it had lasted longer than it did. But for just a moment—five or six seconds, probably less—my hearing changed in such a way that it seemed there was no difference between sounds coming from close by and those from far away.

At my elbow on the portico, three students stood conversing in normal voices. At the same time, on the playing field across Fieldhouse Road, the all-girl band was ending up its practice, the band members, in rank and file, marching in place as they played.

For the few seconds I've mentioned, the voices from both came to me as if from exactly the same distance away. There was a monotonic sound to them and a robotic quality in their articulation, as if there were no muscular effort behind them. Furthermore, although they were very, very low in volume, I was able to understand them in perfect detail, as if through earphones.

These two sounds were then joined by a third that came from even farther away but reached me with exactly the same qualities as the others.

This third sound came from beyond the playing field and all the way across Johnson Avenue. There, I watched a young boy, maybe ten years old, ride his bike up onto the front lawn of a house, dismount and then step away from it while it was still moving. On her knees nearby, a woman was digging as if with a trowel along the front edge of the porch. The boy said, as he passed her on his way into the house,

Hi, Mom. What's for dinner?

Meanwhile, the band-leader went on making corrections, all in the same low, effortless, robotic voice:

Lift those knees! Higher! Woodwinds! Trombones!

And one of the students at my elbow said,

That's not true. I went out with her myself. Twice. I don't believe it for a second.

Then the moment was over. The students moved away. The band practice ended. The boy disappeared into his house. Sounds from everywhere reached me exactly as they always had.

•

A week or so later, a similar thing happened, this time with no words.

It was a Saturday afternoon (classes ended at noon on Saturdays) and I was in my room reading, having returned there after lunch an hour or so earlier. The sound that came to me this time was the distant roar of voices from the football stadium beyond the fieldhouse.

The afternoon was warm and still, one more in the string

of perfect days since my arrival. My windows stood open and from time to time a current of air whispered in.

The sound, like the others, was distant, quiet, and miniature. And, like the others, it was audible to me without the least effort from me, as if it were coming from halfway around the world and also from a spot right at my ear.

Emerging out of the quiet afternoon, it was an inchoate roar being released simultaneously from thousands of throats. The sound rose suddenly to a peak, held there a moment, then gradually diminished and fell away into silence.

Unlike the others, this sound recurred numerous times. I had little interest in football, but I found the repetitions of the sound, and the irregular lengths of time between them, oddly pleasant. For the rest of the afternoon, as I sat reading, I listened passively and with a certain comfort. One of the seemingly significant things about the sound was that it had nothing to do with me. It required no energy from me, either in my receiving it or in its demanding any response from me. It was simply there—distant, affectless, low in volume, yet also sharply defined and perfectly audible.

An image formed in my mind of an immense area of open grassland reaching from one horizon to the other. Whenever the sound arose, an oblong mound would rise up at one place or another on this prairie. The mound would be perhaps a quarter mile long and half as wide, rising up as if the earth itself—rock strata, subsoil, topsoil, the carpet of sod with its tightly-knitted grassroots—were being pushed upward by some powerful force from below. The mound would bulge up in tandem with the sound's first swelling up. It would continue rising along with the rise in pitch until it seemed inevitable that the earth, soil, and sod would crack into pieces and leave a jagged wound in the surface of the earth. But that didn't happen. As the sound fell back down into silence, the mound followed in kind, lowering down, shrinking, and becoming reconfigured until the surface of the prairie took on the exact contours it had had before.

7

Like everyone else who lived in the Quadrangle, I passed through the south entrance multiple times daily. Except for Sundays, I went in or out six times just for meals, going down the spiral stairs for breakfast, lunch, and dinner, then back up and out again at meal's end. Also, at least once a day and often twice, I went to check my mail, making for six to twelve more trips into the south entrance and back out.

On Sundays there was no mail and no evening meal, so I normally passed through only four times. Still, adding up visits for a typical week, I passed into and out of the south entrance somewhere between forty-five and fifty-two times a week.

And there were other passings-through as well. On my way to classes on the east side of the river, I would leave by the north entrance, but if I wanted to go down the south face of the bluff that the Quadrangle stood on, instead of the north or east face, the south entrance was more direct. Going south had an appeal during warm weather, since by crossing Field House Road and then Johnson Avenue, I would come to an area of large houses, wide lawns, and shaded streets—then, farther on, a small river-view park with benches that made a good place for reading.

Up until the second week of November or so, when the weather finally changed, I paid visits to the little park three or four afternoons a week to read for an hour or so. My trips through the south entrance therefore increased by six or eight a week during that period. Also, I fell into the habit of leaving my room late Tuesday and Thursday afternoons to watch the girls' band finish its practice. This made for four more trips in and out. From the beginning of September through mid-November, I estimate that I made between fifty-six and sixty-four in-and-outs a week, not counting extra trips like coming down at night for a bag of peanuts or bottle of soda from one of the vending machines. Adding three ins and three outs of that kind, my weekly total grew to somewhere between fifty-nine and seventy. Assuming that this pattern went more or less unchanged for four weeks in September, four in October, and three in November, my eleven-week total of trips through the south entrance come out to something between 649 and 770.

I mention these details only to suggest how I could have become sufficiently accustomed to the south entrance that I stopped "seeing" it—so that I began, you could say, taking that part of the Quadrangle for granted rather than actually looking at it. Once this happened, once I began "sleep-walking" through the south entrance, I was making myself susceptible to certain kinds of evidence showing that for some time I had *already* been moving back and forth between planes of time, although I'd been doing it without any conscious awareness at all.

The concierge's telephone is what gave me the proof that I had fallen out of one level of time and entered life in another.

The concierge's office was a bit like a post office or bank in that people did business with the concierge or one of her clerks by approaching either of two windows built into the wall. Like the windows in a post office or bank, these were fitted with a wide counter-top that provided a convenience both for the clerk inside and the petitioner outside.

The windows were fitted with twin coverings fashioned out of wooden slats, like the dust-covers on old-fashioned roll-top desks, except that these retracted not into a desk but up into the ceiling so as to be out of the way during working hours. At other times, they were pulled down and locked into neatly recessed brass receptacles on the surface of the counter. The office was open from 7:00 a.m. to 10:00 p.m. Mondays through Saturdays, and Sundays from 9:00 a.m. to 6:00 p.m. At all other times, the shutters were drawn and the office unattended.

In case of emergency, however, there was still a way to reach the concierge, and this was by telephone. During the day, a telephone stood inside on the counter for the use of the clerk or clerks working the windows. During off-hours, though, it was left *outside* the shuttered window, its cord disappearing back into the office through a small notch cut precisely to make a path for it.

By mid-November, I had had no new hint about the nature of time. Even my experiences from early September—the riderless bicycle, the girls' band, the cheers from the stadium—faded in my memory and no longer suggested the presence of anything unusual.

But then came the incident of the concierge's telephone.

By the last week end of November, the number of my trips through the south entrance had reached something near a thousand. And somehow, if only through habit, laziness, or custom, it seems I had let my eyes fall closed to one plane of time and had allowed them to open up to another, a plane of time that had been there all along, although invisible and unknown to me.

The experience wasn't like gazing off at another location where an alternate plane of time, like a movie, was occurring. Instead of looking on from a safe distance, I had actually fallen—or had been drawn, pulled, transported—through a barrier of some kind out of my own time and into another realm of time entirely.

The evidence revealing this was the concierge's telephone.

Through my weeks of passing back and forth through the south entrance, I had seen the concierge's telephone standing on the counter, day or night, like this:

Then suddenly, at the moment in question, late one night, when the office was closed and the shutter drawn, it was standing there like this:

I wasn't keeping a journal at the time and therefore would be less likely to be able to identify exactly when this incident took place. Two days later, however, as chance would have it, Lyndon Johnson, Alan Dulles, George H. W. Bush and others murdered President Kennedy in Dealey Plaza in Dallas. As a result, I know that the incident of the telephone occurred late on the night of Wednesday, November 20th, 1963.

After they murdered the President, this is how he looked:

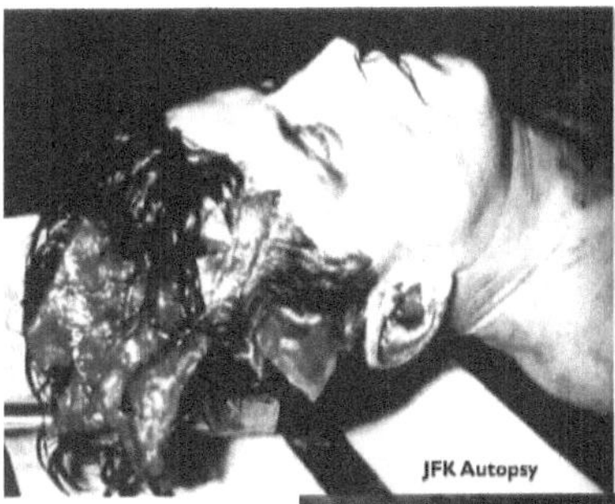

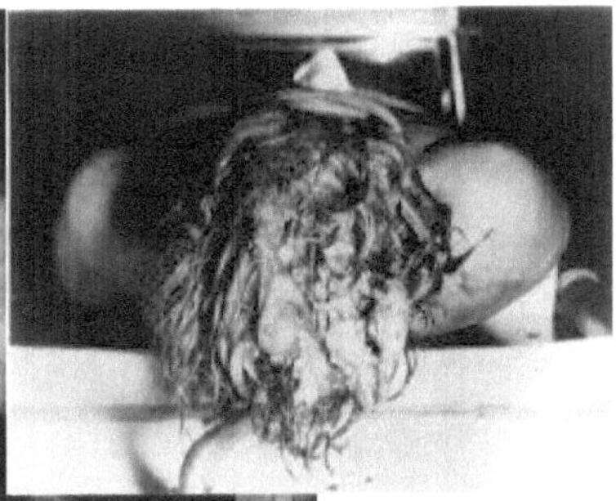

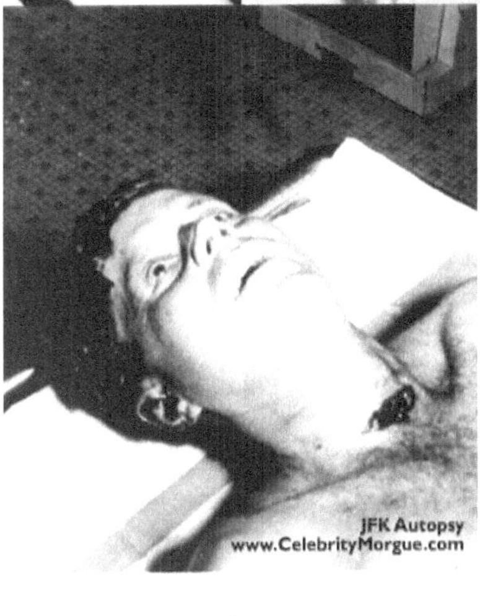

TWO

Initially, the moment of change from one plane of time to another was terrifying. When I saw the telephone, and when I saw that it was now old-fashioned, a true disorientation seized me. I fell into a panic that was extraordinarily intense but, luckily, not long-lasting. Over the decades since that long-ago time, I have experienced enough similarly unsettling moments to know that a briefly disabling psycho-emotional response is natural for someone whose established sense of reality is suddenly challenged, shattered, or withdrawn.

At a week short of turning twenty-two, however, I didn't know this, and the panic I felt came from the certainty that I was losing, or had already lost, my identity, sense of self, and trust in my senses—a sensation not different from feeling that I was going or had gone crazy, or even that I was dying.

If at one moment I saw the telephone this way—

and then at another moment, saw it this way—

—then exactly who was I? Not many hours later I was intensely relieved to learn that this destabilizing question was moot: I was in fact not facing a meta-psychological breakdown, and the truth was that I would remain essentially the same person, whether existing in 1963, on the one hand, or in 1933, on the other. But I couldn't possibly have known this fact at the initial split-second when the force hit me and I was flung three decades backwards. Was it irrational, this immediate fear that I was being torn into two different people no less truly than if an axe were to cleave me, along my vertical axis, from crown to crotch?

The fear came largely from the shock of being no longer agent, but only object: in other words, I myself had not even the slightest choice in guiding or influencing what was happening to me. Further, if disappearing from one plane of time and appearing in another really *did* mean existing as two separate people, two different selves—one of the two would necessarily become dead to the other, no? Or, neither one having consciousness of the other, each would steal *time* from the other, so that great gaps and holes would exist in the memory of each. It would be a prototype of madness. It would be worse than having, literally, two heads. The life of *one* of them—incomplete, incomprehensible, unbearable—clearly, one of those lives would *have* to be stifled, extinguished, eliminated—wouldn't it?

Thank god, nothing about the transformation proved to be so dreadful or extreme as that. Once I had survived the terror of passing through the "barrier" for the first time, I came to find the experience not really frightening at all. The reason for this was, as I learned almost immediately, that someone falling into the past—at least the way it happened to me—would carry along a "memory" of the future that he or she had just left "behind." In other words, when I was drawn back into the 1933 plane of time, I went as a visitor rather than as a native dweller. I kept the same memory and consciousness of 1963 that I was accustomed to, whereas for the people I met or saw *in* 1933, that year was their *only* present time. For them, the years after 1933 still lay ahead, hadn't yet taken place, didn't yet exist. The future held out the same mixture of hope, anxiety, and fear as it would for anyone living in their own "present" time. I, on the other hand, had possession, or consciousness, of both times, even though the two were split thirty years apart from one another.

Another indication that my initial terror was baseless came with the very early realization that my own default "present" time would remain 1963-64 no matter how often I might be dropped back into 1933-34 or how long my visits there—or to other planes of time—might last. My sojourn in earlier planes of time lasted from the autumn of 1933 through the summer of 1934, and it ended, after a jump "forward," in the autumn of 1947. When my era of traveling through time finally did end once and for all, I was returned to a perfectly recognizable month, day, and time in a 1964 that was familiar to me—and I made this final transition "naturally" enough, without lasting harm—other than the experience of *grief*—a grief sharper, deeper, more wretchedly all-consuming than any I had felt up to that time, or since.

That was because of Eveline Stahl, and my losing her.

•

At the beginning of my visits back to 1933—before I met Eveline—I sometimes imagined myself going through the visiting experience *without* intimacy—that is, I imagined simply "walking around" in the past as an observer, unnoticed, making no friends or acquaintances, not falling in love with anyone.

But even just "walking around" and "simply observing" were capable of being filled with unexpected complexity.

As in the case when I saw my father.

On that occasion I did indeed remain silent, and all but motionless, hoping not to be noticed. On the other hand, I certainly *observed*. For a long time, I stared. And stared.

I wasn't born yet—the first cries of my infancy were still eight years away—and here was my father-to-be, of all things, *playing tennis*. Even worse, he was dressed entirely in *white*. His shoes were white, his trousers, his shirt (sleeves rolled to the elbows), even the sweat band around his head was white.

To me, these were extraordinary and astonishing, even enraging, facts. Here was my father, sometime in the spring of 1934, playing *tennis*. Not only that, but he was being watched doing it by his own son-to-be—in whose subsequent life tennis was to play no part, was never to be encouraged, was never to be so much as introduced. The fact is that never—not a single time ever—had I played even a simple game of catch with this father who now, before my eyes, was dressed all in white, was playing tennis, and was doing it very well.

No, these were things wholly out of keeping with the moody, sullen, miserly, angry, selfish, half-responsive and aggressively unathletic father I was to know in the especially damaging years, say, from 1947 or so on through 1963 or 1964.

I had this first sight of my pre-father on a Saturday in the spring, on an afternoon that was prematurely fair and warm. Eveline wasn't with me (although she would be on a later, and more significant, sighting of my father on these same courts). Trying not to draw attention to myself, I walked casually to a spot far enough away as to remain unnoticed but close enough to observe well. There, I leaned against a tree and watched my father's game against his opponent, who, as if in half-imitation of my father, was dressed in white on the top but dark on the bottom. Both were good players, although my father appeared slightly the more confident and perhaps marginally the stronger. Gradually, he earned more points, and it seemed likely that in the end he would win the match.

I stood for a long time watching the game. Standing just behind his own baseline, my father would hit returns, both forehand and backhand, sending balls low over the net and placing them just inches inside his opponent's own baseline. He placed them first on one side of the court and then on the other, and if his opponent grew tired, or if he began to change his position too soon, my father would trick him by sending the ball to the unexpected side of the court and gaining the point. Both players hit the ball squarely, with speed, strength, and follow-through, although my father made fewer errors than his opponent and seemed also to grow less tired.

The fucking bastard.

Or, in words more genteel: The emotions I felt as I stood there watching were increasingly embittering and remarkably strong. Here, one Saturday afternoon in the spring of 1934, my own father was revealing himself to be something that he had never, ever, seen fit to pass on to me, his own son, in the least or slightest of ways.

I had always known that my father once played tennis. But that he had played so proficiently as this—and had done it dressed entirely in white (of all things)—was so little a part of my awareness that the notion wouldn't have come to my mind in a hundred years. I knew that tucked up under the rafters of what we called our machine shed I had found three old rackets, sprung and warped. And that I had found two others in the slope-roofed attic above our farmhouse kitchen. Those in the attic were in wooden presses and less warped, although their strings were dry, broken, and askew. All of them, both the machine shed and the attic rackets, were half-buried in dust.

*To the Reader: A Note
on Method, Subject Matter, and Chronology*

It will be necessary, now and then, to clarify certain technical subjects if hope is to remain of our continuing to move forward together through this narrative.

One such matter is the nature of my father, to be considered first personally, then symbolically.

1

My Father, Personally, Part 1

Admittedly, I spent a large part of my life despising my father. My long period of resentment toward him was activated at the time—I was thirty or so—when I finally allowed myself to realize, first, how unstable, cruel, and selfish a character my father was generally, and, second, how cruelly and selfishly he had behaved toward me in particular.

This long phase in my life, which I call my period of resentment, never really came to an end: I feel it even now, at age eighty-seven, as a distant and not entirely quiescent source of sorrow, pity, and anger. In its acute phase, on the other hand, the period of resentment went on for four decades, from my thirtieth year to my seventieth, far past the time of my father's relatively early death in the middle 1970s. Obviously, the influence one person has on another does not always end, even with the death of the one who most powerfully exerted the influence.

Question: When I saw my father playing tennis that day in 1934—and playing with such sophistication—wouldn't any normal son have felt resentment at the fact that such a thing had not been passed on but had been kept secret from him? Why should a father enjoy such an experience and choose later not to pass it on, or even make it known, to the son?

Fact: I knew from an early age that my father, in good part, was selfish, egocentric, and cruel. Yet never in childhood did I say anything to this effect, never did I fight back, never express injustice or admit to suffering. In all those years, it seemed to me unquestionable that whatever was, *was*. Whatever was my lot, was my lot. It was not a part of me, not a part of my makeup, not a part of my intellectual consciousness to reason *why*, but only to accept whatever came.

Such power exists in fathers.

Still, what forces, pressures, feelings, or fears accounted for so extreme a degree of passivity in me, I don't fully know. I do know, and did know, that my father was very tall and that I was not. I knew that my father was an authority not in any case or event to be questioned. I knew that my father was quick to show impatience, that his impatience if baffled was swift to become anger, that his anger was then transformable most commonly to expressions of disgust. I knew also through miserable experience that to be the target of such expressed disgust was to be shamed, humiliated, and mortified so thoroughly as to make one wish no longer to remain among the living.

My Father, Personally, Part 2

How curious, the way he left events, pleasures, and achievements behind. Things that presumably he once valued and esteemed, things that he achieved with effort and purpose, such things as these he then left rotting and abandoned, trails of garbage left to sink gradually into the earth. In the rafters at the back of the machine shed lay other things in ruins: rods for dry-fly casting; others for reel casting; a broken wicker-work creel; chest-high waders oxidized to the crispness of soda crackers; a canvas hunting jacket with sewn rows of loops for holding shells and immense side-pockets for dead game; in one pocket, an ancient bottle of citronella oil.

None of these things or others like them had I ever seen in use—only the tennis racket and white clothing when I watched my father playing tennis in the spring of 1934.

Two questions, one about me, one about my father.

Question One, about Me:

Why didn't I allow myself to express anger or resentment toward my father until I reached my thirtieth year?

Question Two, about My Father:

Why did my father keep these various elements, activities, and attractions that had existed in the past—why did he keep them secret from me? Or, putting it another way, why did he relegate them to disappearance through secrecy and disuse rather than taking pleasure in his own son's introduction to them?

Answer to Question One:

My fear of his cruelty and anger was sufficiently intense that I created a protective defense consisting of two aspects of denial. That is, regarding the first aspect of denial, I forced, compelled, and coerced myself into believing that my father was *not* selfish and cruel. As for the second aspect of denial, I forced, compelled, and coerced myself into the belief that in *every way* my father was superior to me; and, in a corollary to the first side of my denial, I forced, compelled, and coerced myself into believing that in *every way* I was inferior to him.

So successfully did I internalize these two forms of denial that only near my thirtieth birthday was I able to begin seeing my strategies of denial as prison bars and to begin an escape from them through the achievement of adulthood.

By that time my father was dead.

Answer to Question Two:

Only by the time I turned thirty had I grown mature enough psychologically and intellectually to begin to understand—and dismantle—the defenses against my father that I had put in place decades earlier. That these defenses had necessitated my living intimately within extremes of self-delusion was only one of the reasons that the dismantling of them was so difficult and prolonged. The task I faced was the step by step construction, or re-construction, of a personality—my own—that was in equal parts traumatized and missing altogether. Within this process, prominent among the many questions needing answers were those having to do with my father's abandonment, in the years following my own birth, of various pleasurable elements of his own past that might have brought me joy and fulfillment in my own turn, had they only continued as living things that I could become acquainted with and adopt also as my own. But not so. Why, then, had such things been kept secret from me? Why had my father never so much as mentioned the existence of them to me? And why, just when I myself was emerging into life, had my father disavowed and abandoned them, relegating them to silence, ruin, and decay?

In the end, after decades of pondering these and other questions, I find it impossible to escape from one conclusion. Given the violently self-referential and the violently self-reflective constitution and makeup of his inner self, my father destroyed the past for one reason only: *In order to keep that past from me.*

2

My Father, Symbolically

My father symbolically is the nation I was born into. He is the nation that destroyed its history before my turn came to learn from it and be nourished by it. He is the nation that drove its way west, devouring all living things in its path. He is the nation that is blind to the sight of anything other than itself. He is the nation that visits terror on others and yet believes itself benevolent. He is the nation of torture, killing, threat, and the instilling of fear. He is the nation that eats its young. He is the nation that destroys itself. He is the nation now dying before our eyes. He is the nation infested with vermin.

.

After a time, I left the tree I had been leaning against and walked away from the tennis courts toward the central part of the campus. The sound of the game—the delicious *tock, tock* as racket met ball—faded away slowly behind me.

THREE

I can't deny that I was frightened badly the first time I saw that the concierge's telephone had become an old-fashioned kind. I spun on one foot, left the south entrance, crossed the courtyard, and went straight back to my room, where I flung myself onto my bed and waited, terrified, to see what would happen next.

I must have slept through at least some part of the night. I remember the interminable sense of *not* sleeping, but I also have a clear memory of waking to my alarm clock at the usual time, 6:45.

As for the initial fear—the disorienting panic at thinking I was going through a kind of "dying" or a being "erased," a losing of consciousness of the only self I'd lived in from childhood on—this fear, of waking up "dead," "missing," amnesiac, "whited out"—this fear disappeared in the simple movement and automatic gesture of reaching out and silencing my alarm clock. There was a flood of relief, like the delicious feeling of waking up to realize that a bad dream had been only that, a bad dream.

The relief came mainly from the realization that my memory

was unchanged, fine, and complete. I had apparently lost nothing, including the details of what had happened the night before—my seeing the "old" telephone, panicking, running across the courtyard, flinging myself onto my bed. . . . Not only were these memories perfectly clear, but I also remembered the events and details of the past ten weeks—my arriving in Iowa City, getting settled, registering, beginning classes, and so on.

In other words, what I thought of as my "real" self, made up of its own past and its own present, was not going to be snuffed out, asphyxiated, and left for dead thanks simply to my being drawn into *another* past and *another* present. I was not, after all, going to go insane. And I was not, after all, going to die.

Apparently, I was going to enter into another time simply as an observer. Or so I thought.

•

On that first morning, the light in my room was different. The sun wasn't up yet and wouldn't be for another fifteen minutes, yet my room was lighter than it normally was when my alarm went off. I propped myself on one elbow, looked toward the windows, and saw at once what accounted for the difference: The large box-elder tree that had been standing close up to the north wall of the Quadrangle wasn't there. I went to the window and looked down. No tree at all. It hadn't even been planted yet.

The relief was very great. I was in another time, but I was still the same person.

Still, after I'd climbed from bed, gotten dressed, and stepped to the door of my room, I found myself pausing as I screwed up the courage to turn the knob and walk out into a hallway thirty years in the past.

As chance would have it, the hallway was empty: Not a

soul in it. This in itself wasn't surprising, since breakfast was the one meal of the day for which no observable rush took place, only small trickles of people appearing at any one time.

On my way downstairs, however, I did pass a pair of students coming back up, and, as I crossed the courtyard, I passed another pair, and then one alone, returning from the meal. I didn't recognize any of them, nor would such a thing have been possible. The only two people existing in 1933 Iowa City whom I would recognize would be my father, as I've mentioned, and also, although not yet mentioned, my great-uncle Jakob. I knew perfectly well that neither of them lived in the Quadrangle.

I went through the south entrance, down the spiral stairs and through the door into the dining room, where there were a great many more students—eating, talking, moving from one place to another. Not one paid the least attention to me.

The dining hall was the same one I was used to, unchanged in size, dimension, or layout, yet at the same time it seemed very different. The ceiling, for one thing, was considerably higher than I was accustomed to, and, instead of the long rows of fluorescent tubes, schoolroom globes were placed at regular intervals, hanging down.

These globes gave the dining hall a softer look than I was used to, although at the same time the place seemed darker than usual. The walls—windowless, of course, as ever—were painted dark brown instead of the institutional green—"snot green," the students called it—that I was used to. The food, flatware, and dishes looked the same, as did the tables, both the square and the round, all of them covered with tan butcher paper. The people, however, eating in singles or groups, or those having gotten up to set their trays on the conveyor leading in to the dishwashers—almost all were subtly different from what I was used to. Most of them, for one thing, wore heavy oil or pomade, so that their hair looked glossy and smooth, and they combed it carefully into varieties of curves and waves. Their clothing, also, was different. I saw no denim at all, but instead almost everywhere were trousers of wool, corduroy, gabardine, or the like, almost always cuffed at the bottoms. Perhaps half of these had been ironed or pressed so as to hold a vertical crease, the others not. Everyone in the room wore a jacket. Half or so wore ties.

In college, luckily, I had cultivated the affectation of wearing the same clothing every day, a uniform consisting of a brown corduroy jacket, a white shirt open at the neck, desert boots on the feet, and belted khaki trousers cuffed at the bottom. This sartorial habit, in Iowa City, remained the same as it had been at New College, and as a result I fit in reasonably well and remained largely unnoticed by the students I was mingling with now, in the downstairs breakfast hall, the morning of Tuesday, November 21st, 1933.

•

In the early stages, one of the more disconcerting—or difficult—aspects of moving between the planes of time was the fact of there being no notice as to when the change would occur. So perfect was this absence of warning that I never once, early or late, experienced any consciousness of the change *as it took place*. That is, I never became aware of having been translocated until after the translocation had already happened. Just as on the night of the telephone, I would assume myself to be in 1963 only to find myself in 1933—without the least awareness of the moment when the change had taken place.

My second translocation took place on the Monday after the President's murder. It happened on the Iowa Avenue bridge as I was crossing it for my eight o'clock class.

Just past the middle of the bridge—as I remember it—I became aware not of a change taking place but, as always, of a change *having* taken place. The crowd walking to class along with me remained as dense as before, though countless small details were suddenly different. Once again, there was the absence of denim, as there was also, almost entirely, of sneakers. Also missing were windbreakers and other waist-length outdoor wear—motorcycle jackets, bomber jackets, Eisenhower-style field jackets and the like. Instead, most of the students wore overcoats of one kind or another, varying in length from just below the knees down almost to sidewalk level.

My own cold-weather dress—again, the same as I wore in college—consisted of a wool scarf and belted raincoat, a combination non-descript enough to keep me from drawing attention. I wore nothing on my head, hat or cap. This made me part of a very distinct minority but not a stand-alone.

As you might expect, my translocation this second time around was in no way the frightening experience the first had been—in fact, aside from a brief disorientation at the outset, the second time around brought the first example of a sense of pleasure at returning again to the earlier plane of time—something I will say more about in a moment. First, though, a word about the view of the campus looking east from halfway across the Iowa Avenue bridge—the point where, as it happened, translocations often took place.

The central focus of the eastward view went unchanged in either plane of time, consisting of the five stone buildings atop the bluff that rose up on the east bank—central among them the handsome old state capitol building, facing resolutely west.

When I arrived in Iowa City I didn't yet fully understand the significance of the capitol's placement—why it was situated so as to be entered from the east, or back, side, while its façade gazed immutably across hundreds of miles to the west.

The quincunx pattern was something like this:

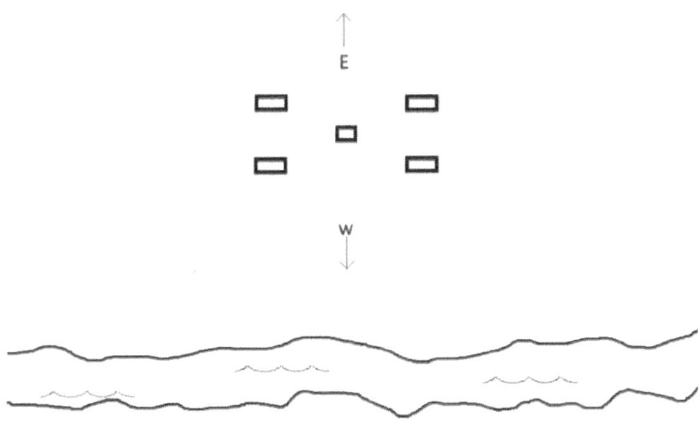

By that time in my life I did understand some of the reasons why churches, say, might be oriented to the east. Why statehouses might be the opposite was something I hadn't thought about, though unquestioningly I accepted the old capitol as a building both stately and perdurable. Completed in 1842, it had stood for ninety-one years by 1933, and for twenty-one years more than a century by 1963, when, newly arrived in Iowa City, I took the opportunity more than once to stroll through its rooms and gaze for long periods out its windows, as if through new sets of eyes.

By the time I returned to the old capitol again—in the summer of 1934—I knew much more about it, thanks in greatest part to my having met Eveline, who came with me when on that return. We walked together through its rooms and, upstairs, stood looking out through its aged eyes.

FOUR

So it happened that when I was halfway across the bridge, the morning of November 25th, 1963, was replaced by the morning of November 27th, 1933. Even then, on just my second translocation, I began understanding that life was going to be very different from now on than it had been so far. Even in my early translocations, curiosity began overcoming fear, and the changes I saw and sensed around me grew less unsettling and quickly became, in a curiously pleasant way, *interesting*.

The interest my translocations held for me, in fact, soon became all-consuming—the more so, naturally enough, after I had met Eveline, and after I had fallen in love with her.

Eveline Stahl. Beloved Eveline. Even now I half believe—or believe—that I was sent back in time precisely for the purpose of meeting her.

But even if that were true, I hear it asked, what would have been the purpose of such a meeting?

Eveline and I were being given the opportunity to undo an immense wrong. If we could succeed, then other and subsequent wrongs, even greater ones, could in turn be avoided.

•

In the weeks following the murder of the President, translocations became even more seamless, until sometimes the change took place so unobtrusively that I remained unaware for a certain time of its having taken place. Suppose that midway across the river on my way to first-hour classes, I should happen to be translocated back to 1933; it was possible that I might cross the bridge and walk all the way to the entrance of Jessup Hall before realizing that the change had taken place. Often, when the experience took place in this way, I relied on certain hints and guides in order to orient myself. For example, inside the main entrance to Jessup were two interior sets of double doors, one to the left and one to the right, and on the wall between them was displayed the building directory. Of the several departments housed in Jessup, the English department was the largest, and, as I came in from outdoors, a glance at its listing would signal to me which year I was "in." If the directory looked like this, I knew I was in 1933:

ABRAMS, J. E.	MCCLAREN, J. P.
BROOK, J. S.	MCGALLIARD, R.
CHASE, W.	REINER, J. A.
CRAIG, H. W.	SHERBURNE, A. S.
FORD, C. T.	SCHIEPS, N.
GODFREY, F. A.	SHERIDAN, P. H.
HENDRON, E.	THORNTON, F. L.
KRUTCH, B. R.	TRUMPENER, C.
KUNCE, L.	WATSON, M. C.
JONES, E. E.	WILLIAMS, E.
LARSEN, J. A.	WITHERS, N

And if it looked like this, I knew I was in my "own" year:

AZAR, N.	POPOLA, C.BALAZS, H. O.
BALAZS, H.O.	RACKOFF, P.
BLOOMGARDEN, I.	RAUSCH, V. I.
BLUM, H. R.	RIELY, G.
CRAIG, H. W.	RIMNER, A.
DARDICK, R.	ROHR, M.
EPSTEIN, Y. J.	ROSEN, M. R.

FERRANTE, K.	SACKHEIM, K. E.
FLYNN, H. T.	SCHOLES, R. W.
FYER, M.	SCHULTZ, B.
GARAFANO, S.	SEPKOWITZ, K.
GOLDBERG, N.	SHIRAZIAN, T.
JONES, E. E.	THORNTON, F. L.
MCCLAREN, J. P.	THAWANI, S.
MUKHERJEE, S. P.	VILLANUEVA, E. R.
NASCIMBENI FERRAN, E.	WEPLER, W. I.
OKOYE, S. W.	YIH, P

Obviously, commonplace details of daily life in either period also served as instant guides as to where I "was," and yet, as with anything, the greater my familiarity with these details became, the less notice of them I was likely to take. Clothing, fabrics, hair, shoes, hats, ties, jewelry, automobiles, trucks—all of these and countless other commonplace things were omnipresent hints as to which plane of time I was in, yet the more familiar I became with all of them, the less instantaneously I took note of them after a translocation, especially if I happened to be preoccupied with one thing or another—a reading assignment, upcoming exam, paper-deadline or the like. Often enough, as time went on, I failed even to glance at the directory in the main entrance and would "come to" only when I was in the classroom and at my seat. There, I would finally notice whether the notebooks I carried were those with sewn bindings or those with spiral metal spines, whether I was carrying a fountain pen or a ball point, whether Eveline Stahl was in the row just in front of mine and one seat to the left, and, of course, whether the instructor who came into the room was McGalliard or Wepler. Significantly, whether in the earlier plane of time or the later one, a great number of things remained unchanged. The season of the year invariably remained the same in one plane or the other, as did also the weather itself in one plane or the other. If I woke to a gray and drizzly day in early December in one plane and was then translocated to the other, the day would come along with me, a gray and drizzly day in early December. The courses I took, the readings, texts, books, even the assignments remained the same as well. In first semester's Old English in both planes, the readings included *The Dream of the Rood, Ælfric's Colloquy, The Battle of Maldon,* and *Judith.* Second semester, of course, consisted solely of *Beowulf.* In the case of *Beowulf,* the class no longer met in Jessup but in the much smaller Meredith Hall, with no English directory inside the entrance for me to glance at. But as always, countless other guides were available, including the identity of the instructor. Another quick device was simply to glance at the copyright page of my *Beowulf* text—something I found especially convenient, for example, if on waking in the morning or before even getting dressed I was curious to know which plane of time I was in. If the plane was 1963-64, the page would show:

COPYRIGHT, 1922, 1928, 1936, 1941, and 1950
BY D. C. HEATH AND COMPANY,

but if the plane were 1933-34, it would show only:

COPYRIGHT, 1922 and 1928
BY D. C. HEATH AND COMPANY

And I could also, of course, simply wait for my classmates, in ones and twos, to come into the classroom and take their usual seats. My own preferred seat was in the third or fourth row, across the room from the entrance, on the aisle. I very much preferred the feeling of protection that resulted—and results—from having a wall nearby. Most people had one sort of preference or another, and once they'd found a seat that felt "right" to them they would stick with it to the end of the term. In my own case, choosing to be on the aisle guaranteed me that no one else would be on my right. If the plane of time was 1964, the person on my left, in *Beowulf,* would be Peter

Cooley, the poet. If the year was 1934, sitting there beside me would be Eveline Stahl.

It was impossible that I could have remained unaware of her. For one thing, she sat in the row just ahead of mine in McGalliard's Old English in autumn 1933-34. For another, I found her impossible not to notice in any case.

I first *saw* Eveline Stahl, then, on only my second translocation in time, the morning of November 27th, 1933. I *met* her two weeks later, when she asked about my great-uncle Jakob. I'd had no idea that she was enrolled in Uncle Jake's Middle English class as well as in McGalliard's Old English, a demanding and complicated pairing of courses that most people would never even think of attempting.

•

Once I'd become more at home with the idea of the translocations, I set out to capture a sight of my great-uncle Jakob. My plan was to lurk in the main corridor of Jessup Hall, where I was quite certain I could catch a glimpse.

I knew from the registration schedule that fourth hour (eleven a.m.) he taught the graduate course in Middle English dialects. I myself had a class the hour before that, but I cut it and not long after ten-thirty began waiting in the first-floor corridor of Jessup. I began by lingering near the tall windows up at the north end. Then I moved closer to the entrance of the English Office itself, midway down the hallway, and finally drifted to the windows at the south end before repeating the pattern. So as not to draw attention to myself, I leaned against a wall on one side or the other and read a few more pages of *The Castle of Otranto*. I was almost finished with it, and in my bag I had a copy of *Northanger Abbey* to read next.

Every five minutes or so I casually changed my location from one part of the corridor to another, with the result that at ten-fifty, when classes changed, I was near the middle of the hallway a cautious distance south of the entrance to the English Office. Up and down the corridor, doors opened and people came out from one room or another and made their way, for the most part, toward the large door under the staircases and out of the building. Others came in through the same door and sorted themselves out either by climbing up the stairs or by joining me in the main corridor and entering any one of its five or six classrooms. The whole time, I leaned against the wall reading my book, or pretending to read it.

The English Office door, I knew, served as the entrance to more offices honeycombed inside, including my uncle Jakob's, and a number of faculty members did emerge from it or return from elsewhere to go back in through it, but my uncle Jakob was not among them. Traffic in the corridor diminished as the hour drew closer, and at a minute before eleven, by my watch, only one or two late-comers appeared, running toward one room or another. Then came the sound of doors being closed, one after another, and I was left alone in the corridor again. Eleven o'clock had come and gone, and still no one emerged from the door of the English Office. Another minute passed. Two minutes. Three. Then, at four minutes past the hour, the door opened and from it emerged my uncle Jakob.

I had had no plan beyond catching sight of him: My thinking hadn't gone further than that. But when I saw him—maybe twelve feet away, coming through the English Office door and crossing the corridor toward the foot of the staircase—it was as though there had been a plan all along that I hadn't even known about. When my uncle Jakob reached the bottom of the staircase, maybe twenty feet away from me, it was as though an invisible string between him and me tightened and drew me after him. I moved away from the wall, following him. When he came to the top step of the first flight, I was setting my foot on the bottom step. By the time he got to the top of the second flight, I was rounding the corner to begin ascending it. My uncle Jakob—he wore a loose-fitting suit of a cream color—left the staircase and entered the second-floor corridor. He walked across it—by this time I was at the top of the second flight—and went in through the open door of a classroom. I heard him say,

"Good morning, lady and gentlemen!" His voice was deep, jovial, and robust, unlike any I had known from my own immediate family, certainly nothing like my father's voice. I hurried to catch up with Jakob, creating slack in the imaginary string between us. But, without looking back, he closed the door behind him as he went in, leaving me outside in the corridor alone.

↓↑↓↑↓↑↓

A Note to the Reader
on Method, Subject Matter, and Chronology

I should point out that what I've just described wasn't the first time I'd ever had sight of my uncle, or, more accurately, my great-uncle, Jakob. I had met him twice before. But, thanks to the nature of time in Iowa City, those meetings hadn't yet occurred when I lingered in Jessup Hall with the aim of seeing him.

That is, the "earlier" meetings hadn't yet occurred vis-à-vis the 1933-34 plane of time, but only vis-à-vis the 1963-64 plane. Even so, I "remembered" those meetings very well, and they went a good way in filling out for me, and validating, the various impressions I had gained of my illustrious great-uncle simply by keeping my ears open to the conversation of adults around me, particularly when those adults included not only my own parents but also Jakob's siblings, my great-aunts Marie and Lutie.

Both of the later, or earlier, if you will, meetings took place in the month of August, although in different years and in different places. Either way, both were sufficiently memorable to me that they found their way into one of my books, the one called *The End of the 19th Century*. In it, for narrative reasons, I changed the name Jakob to "Edgar." Allow me now to change it back again to its real form.

The first meeting occurred at Marie and Lutie's house, on the upper end of Christiania Avenue in West Tree. The year was 1949. The occasion was an afternoon dinner, and here is a segment that includes my uncle Jakob:

The oddity of these movements, along with other arresting details—my mother's large blue earrings, for example, and her yellow summer dress; the billowing of the curtains; my aunt Signe and my grandmother relaying something to one another across the table, moving their lips but using no words; my uncle Jakob leaning back, clasping his hands across his buttoned vest, then with a mischievous expression saying something in Latin; Lutie at that same moment reaching out with a faintly trembling hand to move a small vase (it held a single red peony) an inch to the left on the white cloth—all of these details, along with the general impression of the room and the scene, seized my attention powerfully and yet proved able to hold it for only a short time, the reason being that the horizontal growth of my consciousness arose unexpectedly at almost the same moment and began at once to intensify rapidly.

My second meeting with Jakob took place four years later, at a picnic in the front yard of my family's farmhouse outside West Tree:

Marie and Lutie were also there, for the very last time, and so were their second-youngest brother, my great-uncle

Jakob, and his wife Klara. Like Marie and Lutie, Klara wore a long dress of a dark color, while Jakob wore a light-colored suit and vest. He had hung the jacket from a low branch across the driveway. Hanging there, near our gathering, it looked like something left behind from an Impressionist painting.

Jakob seemed to prefer standing, doing so most of the time behind Klara's chair, although he also moved and stood behind Marie or Lutie's chair, or even behind my grandmother in her wheelchair. He was a big man, tall, with a very high, rounded forehead, traits that I knew had been shared by my dead grandfather. He had a deep voice and an always-ready sense of humor. He was especially fond of making declamations in Latin, which no one understood except Marie and, at least most of the time, my father. Each time, Marie would lean over and whisper in Lutie's ear the meaning of what Jakob had said.

In McGalliard's Old English, before everyone had come in and before class had begun, Eveline Stahl turned around in her chair and tried to get my attention. I pretended to be preoccupied with re-reading the day's assignment. She reached out and tapped my knee with a pencil.

"Say," she said. "I've just got to ask. Is your name Reiner the same as in *Jakob* Reiner?"

"I plead guilty," I said. "My great-uncle."

"You're lucky," she said. "What a pick of an uncle. He's hilarious."

"I know," I said. "I've heard him. A little bit. Not much."

"Every morning he comes into class and says 'Good morning, *lady* and gentlemen.'" She gave a short trilling laugh followed by a very pretty smile. "Because of me," she explained. "I'm the one 'lady' among all the 'gentlemen.'"

FIVE

The afternoon following the president's murder was, for me, banal, flat, and empty. Coming out of Jessup Hall after fourth hour, I saw that people were holding transistor radios to their ears. I tapped someone's shoulder and asked what was going on. The person held his radio a few inches away from his ear and said, "The president has been shot," then put the radio back and went on, frowning with attentiveness. I had no radio of my own, neither in a jacket pocket nor back in my room. But I knew there was a television in the student union, so I walked there, down the bluff, and went inside. People were standing several deep in front of the television. I couldn't get close enough to make out what was on the screen or hear the sound, at least not clearly. An unusually tall fellow next to me was looking over the heads of the crowd and also holding a radio against one ear. I asked him what he was hearing. "It's not believable," he told me. "The president is dead."

Like everyone else, I had no idea what to do. I thought vaguely of going back to my room, but then I heard someone call my name. It was Fritz Dreisbach, talking to a black-haired, gaunt-looking person I didn't know. The gaunt person was wearing a very long raincoat, also black. I went over to them and Fritz said to me,

"I expect you already know."

"Almost nothing," I said. "They shot him. I heard he's dead. I can't believe it."

The other person gave Fritz a soft cuff on the upper arm, said "Later," gave me a sort of wave with two fingers, and turned away. For a second or two I watched him go. His black coat almost touched the floor, like a robe.

"Who was that?" I asked Fritz.

"Condorelli," he said. "You don't know Condorelli? Over in comp lit they call him The Raven, those tight-asses. I like him. A ghost from the Left Bank circa 1900. But listen," he changed the subject. "I'm picking up Peter Hatch and Bob Lehrman. We're going out to Jim Petzky's place. Couple six-packs of beer. Petzky's got writer's block. He's talking about suicide. Have you ever met his wife? A total sweetheart. Come along with."

My initial reaction was to turn him down. All of this took place now very long ago, but I remember it well. I knew I didn't want to be off-campus, certainly not out of town.

By this time, news had gotten out that classes were cancelled for the day, so I had no worries about missing my seminar in narrative theory. It was just that I didn't want to go all the way out to Petzky's. What I wanted was to learn more about the assassination. I wanted to go someplace where I could sit in a corner and listen to what was being said, perhaps a place with a television set. After that, I could move on to another corner, maybe at Kenney's, in the back, where I could watch them play pool and listen to whoever was talking. But I knew I didn't want to leave town. And I knew absolutely that I didn't want to get into a car. The atmosphere of doing either one of those things was totally out of keeping with the complicated way I was feeling.

On the other hand, I had no other close friends, I mean other than Fritz himself and, to a much lesser extent the few I'd met through him—including Peter Hatch and Bob Lehrman.

And of course Petzky, whom I liked very much. On balance, being with other people might offset the negative—the empty—aspects of leaving town.

So I accepted Fritz's invitation, though reluctantly, knowing that I was doing the wrong thing. I knew that for the remainder of the afternoon I would feel out of place, uncentered, above all unprotected, exposed.

Still in the student union, I leaned with my back against the long bank of phone booths and watched people pass by while Fritz called the others and arranged when and where to pick them up. Then I walked with him downriver to the long-term parking lot across from the hydraulic engineering building. His car was in the row farthest away, backed up against the scrub- and weed-grown railroad embankment there. We got in, drove out of the lot, headed uptown, and picked up Peter Hatch and Bob Lehrman as agreed, from the corner where they were standing in front of the Airliner.

Iowa City isn't a big town but it is a coherent one, or at least it was then. What I'm calling coherence was the quality about the town—and campus—that gave me the feeling of security and protection that I'd come to understand, through my first autumn there, as something I craved deeply.

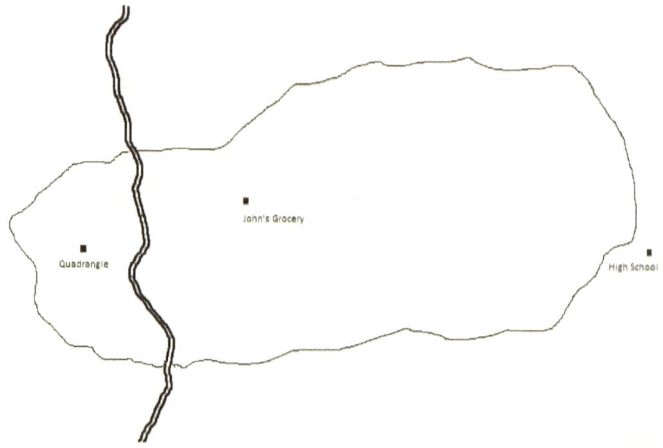

The town was somewhat curiously shaped. Instead of following the river upstream and down, as you might have expected it to, it was formed more like an egg lying with its small end on the west side of the river and its large end swelling out on the east side.

The shell of the egg was the city's periphery. Once you went outside of the periphery, protection ended.

Petzky lived in a subdivision a number of miles east of town, meaning that we would definitely be passing out through the eggshell. A few blocks after picking up Peter Hatch and Bob Lehrman, we stopped at John's Grocery, and I went inside with Fritz. The radio was on at a low volume with news and updates from Dallas. The counter clerk said that Lee Harvey Oswald had been arrested and that a Dallas cop had been shot dead. I know now that this was the beginning of the long and unbroken chain of lies that reaches all the way from then up to this present moment, as I write these words, late one April afternoon in 2028.

Fritz and I came out of John's Grocery with a wooden case of twenty-four beers for John's unmatchable price of $6.20 plus deposit. I held the case while Fritz unlocked the trunk, and then together we set it inside. While we were gone, Peter Hatch had gotten out of the back seat and was sitting now in the front passenger seat, where I had been sitting before. I ignored the move and got into the back. Without turning around, Peter said,

"I hope you don't mind, Mac. It's just I get car sick if I sit in back."

"No difference to me," I lied, or white-lied. Peter was a heavy person, maybe seventy-five pounds over what he should have been. It would have cost him an effort to turn around in the seat. He had double chins, a perfectly oval face, and a mouth whose default setting was the shape of a small letter "o."

Fritz set out on Market Street, took a left on Linn, another left onto East Jefferson, then a right onto Muscatine, after which we just kept on going. There wasn't much of any talking. Beside me in the back seat, Bob Lehrman sat looking out the side window, holding his transistor radio to his left ear. Fritz's car radio was broken.

I wasn't about to let any of them know what sort of discomfort I was going through. They wouldn't understand it, or, more likely, wouldn't believe it. Or would scorn it. They would say—Peter Hatch would say—that if I had fears about leaving town I shouldn't have come along.

I could identify almost exactly the moment we broke through the eggshell. Being aware of this point, where protection and safety ended, required keeping an eye on various other things— the number and density of trees (even when most of them were without foliage), the depth of the lawns leading back to the houses, and of course the size and design of those houses, their age and upkeep, how far apart they stood from one another (inside the eggshell it was as though they were less afraid of each other and made a less foolish pretense of seeming to stand alone), and, of course, the presence of sidewalks. When sidewalks ended, you were outside the perimeter.

We broke through the eggshell as Fritz turned left from Muscatine Avenue onto East Court Street. This was a turn that took us past the wide, low, empty, treeless field of the new Iowa City high school, with its enormous parking lots and cutely meandering "roads." Clearly, we were no longer in town. We were on farmland. That is, farmland that had been adulterated, abused, and transformed. Taken from those who had tilled and dwelled on it previously, it had been stripped, scraped, bulldozed, and re-formed—exorcised of the last vestige of the life it had had before and made ready thus to receive the blandishments of the builders, planners, and financiers who now controlled its fate. What had been a "place" had been made into an "area," something with neither rigor, form, history, depth, mystery, nor dignity, something bland enough to be instantly "likable" to all and as a result wholly absent of overtones of seriousness or authority. No one was expected to find any objection to such an "area." No one was expected to do other than approve of it and, civic-mindedly, be grateful for it. On the other hand, it would never age well. It would never endure long enough to provide the solace of oldness or the unique pleasure that comes from the well-worn. The building and this "area" would never age, but instead they would deteriorate. They wouldn't mature but they would fail to last. They wouldn't age gracefully or with increasing strength, but they would be touched, first in small ways and then in large, by decrepitude. They would become "outmoded" before they became old. The entire project would need "replacement." In these ways, the school represented the values and aims of its nation and era: It was not a project dedicated to dignity or permanence, but it was a project dedicated to plunder.

The men who built this school are the men who murdered John Kennedy.

I said nothing about any of this to the others in the car. None of them would agree with me in any case.

We drove another mile or two past more examples, not of schools, but of buildings, restaurants, banks, show-rooms, car dealerships, home furnishing centers, all of them structures and places whose deterioration was built into their reason for being. My sense of vulnerability and exposure grew more pronounced the farther we went, an unease exacerbated by my inability to find any coherence in the scene. No single thing was related to any other. Flags, banners, and colored pennants flew over a lot filled with cars parked side by side, sale-prices on their windshields, while next to the car lot was a mortuary, next to the mortuary a restaurant called "Ribs 'n Chicks," next to the restaurant a windowless liquor store made of cement blocks, and so on.

It all meant that we were on destroyed farmland. Ever since breaking through the shell we had been on destroyed farmland.

And, of course, the farmland had stood on what was once native prairie.

Petzky and his wife lived in a very small one-story house in a string of half a dozen others like it in what had once been a tiny town but was now a large subdivision called Eden Lake. Their house lacked a curb, sidewalk, or garage, but it did have a driveway. Petzky's car was parked in it, and Fritz pulled up behind it until the bumpers were touching. We got the beer from the trunk and all went inside.

Fritz was right about Petzky's wife being a sweetheart, though that word was too cheap to suit her. Her name, Rhoda, didn't fit her very well, either, a name too big, heavy, old, and round. She should have been named April, Rose, Fawn, or May, although none of those would really have been right, either. It's true that she was small, trim, not slight but almost so, and extraordinarily pretty. At the same time there was a seriousness about her that may actually have been her most pronounced trait. She was far too smart to be missing a sense of humor, but she was also far too smart not to know when to use it and when not to use it. I liked her very, very much.

As for Petzky, I already knew him well—in fact, I knew him better than I did any of the three I'd driven out with, excepting Fritz. Petzky wasn't on the scholarly side of degree-getting, so I didn't see him in Old English, but he was aiming for a degree in fiction-writing, so I did see him every Friday in the seminar on the theory of narrative we were both taking—and where we would be now if it weren't for the assassination.

Petzky was affable and smart, not to mention, with his chiseled face and tight-curled black hair, tremendously good-looking. He came from Fayetteville, Arkansas, where he had gone to the university, and he was modest and quiet, never affected or ostentatious, and above all in possession of an excellent albeit quiet sense of humor. He'd come to Iowa City for the writing program, but now it appeared that he was badly stymied with his fiction and was becoming afraid he might be dropped.

When Rhoda opened the door to us, she said to him over her shoulder and across the tiny living room, "Jim, your rescue team is here."

I'll leave out the greetings and introductions, along with the regrets, comments, and expressions of disbelief about Dallas, though we did turn to Bob Lehrman for the latest update, since only when Rhoda opened the front door had he taken his transistor from his ear and put it in his pocket—and then only for a minute or two. There wasn't any television set in the living room, and, although I thought there might be one in the bedroom, I saw later that there wasn't one there either. After a time, this absence had a certain calming effect on my anxiety and my fear at having traveled outside of the eggshell: being in this tiny little house with five other people and no television. It may even have been that, for a time, I forgot where I was and what day it was. Before long, though, I had to go to the bathroom—the beer—and the earlier feelings came tumbling back. The bathroom was just big enough for a toilet, sink, and shower stall, although it did have a small square window. I stood for a moment looking out through it. Jim and Rhoda's house had no back yard at all, and a farmer's cornfield came up to within a foot or so of the house. By this time of year, the corn had been harvested, and as far as I could see there were only dry and broken stalks. A quarter-mile away or so stood an immense pylon with power lines hanging from its shoulders. Another quarter-mile away was another, and another beyond that. With their immense weight the power lines sagged down low between each tower.

The floorplan of Jim and Rhoda's house consisted of a plain rectangle, with a little more than half of its area devoted to the living room and the remainder split into the bedroom and kitchen, with space cut out of one corner of the kitchen to allow for the bathroom. Except for individual trips back and forth to get more beers, or to go to the bathroom, the group stayed in the living room for the afternoon. A couch stood against one wall, with room enough on it for three people, and, across from it, in a corner, was an easy chair. Diagonally across the room from the front door were the straight chair, card table, and typewriter where Jim spent most of his time. And, once we all got settled, that's where he stayed, though he did turn the chair at a right angle to the table and lean it back on two legs so he was resting against the wall. I sat at one end of the couch, Fritz at the other, and Bob Lehrman in the middle. Peter Hatch had gone straight for the easy chair when we came in, and he continued to sit there, with his mouth in its shape of a small "o." Rhoda brought in a kitchen chair. I offered to trade it for my place on the couch but she said no, she was fine, and, besides, she had to go out before long.

Everyone had a beer, and we made a handful of rather muted toasts. Fritz proposed one to health and then another to hope. Bob Lehrman proposed that we drink to the assassinated president. Afterward there was some more talk about Dallas, although no one knew very much. By this time, on the jetliner, with Jackie standing beside him in the dress that had blood on it, Johnson had raised his big hand and taken the oath of office. None of us, at the time, knew that from that moment we were doomed. With a sigh, Fritz got up from his end of the couch and, gathering empties, took orders for another round. He came back from the kitchen with a bottle for everyone except Rhoda, who announced that if she didn't go shopping she wouldn't be able to feed Petzky that night. There was some laughter. I asked Rhoda where she went for shopping.

"The strip," she said casually.

"Oh, oh, I've got you parked in," Fritz said suddenly. "I'm right up to your bumper."

There was a change in the feeling of things as Fritz went out to move his car and Rhoda gathered up her belongings in preparation to leave. When she was ready to go, Petzky got up from his chair and went out the front door with her. I got up from the couch and went to follow, but the door fell shut on its own and I decided to step to the right instead and look out the picture window. Fritz's car was now parked on the street, and he, Petzky, and Rhoda were standing together at the open door of Petzky's car. At one point they all laughed. Then Rhoda got in and shut the door. She rolled down the window and she and Petzky exchanged a goodbye kiss. Then she started the car and backed down and into the street. The other two, hands in pockets, stood watching until she was out of sight. Then they turned to come back in. Meanwhile, no one in the living room had said a thing. Peter Hatch was still sitting in the easy chair, scowling around the room. Bob Lehrman, not having moved from the middle place on the couch, had his transistor against his left ear, listening intently.

With Rhoda gone, everything felt different, somehow looser and less constrained. Anyone who wanted a beer went into the kitchen and got it for himself, except for Peter Hatch, who invariably asked someone else to bring one for him. Conversation drifted away from the assassination and onto the subject of books and writing—specifically, the subject of Petzky's writer's block. For better or worse, the beer made the conversation flow more easily than it had seemed to before. Petzky was still sitting at the card table, but he sat now on four legs, no longer tipped back against the wall. I remember precisely the words he used once the conversation was fairly well advanced.

"I swear to jesus. I sit here all day. I try and try and try and try. Damn. God damn. I sweat *bullets* trying to get a story going. Rhoda can tell you. I swear, I sweat *bullets*. I'm damn near ready to kill myself."

No one was quite certain what to say or do.

"Write a story about you and Rhoda," Fritz said after a moment. "An allegory. You can call her Sally Forth. And you can be called Holden Bach."

The beer was taking over. No one was really serious any more. Even Peter Hatch stirred himself. Leaning forward in the easy chair, he said,

"No, no. Better yet, give Rhoda the name Manifest Destiny. That's as good as Holly Golightly, even better. Then all you have to do is follow her doings. Damn, that's a story that would write itself."

Conversation broke down. The beer had won. Fritz asked Bob Lehrman what news he was hearing on his transistor radio. I got up from the couch, went over to Petzky, and tried to tell him how awful I thought Peter Hatch's idea was. It was getting close to five o'clock by now. If it hadn't been for the assassination, Petzky and I would now have been ending up our theory of narrative seminar. We often went up to Kenney's for a beer after the class, and then Petzky would head back out to Eden Lake and I would walk across the river to the Quadrangle, where I would make it just in time for dinner.

Petzky stood up from his chair. I gave him a bear hug and said I'd be counting on seeing him next week, or, actually, the week after that, because of Thanksgiving.

It was time to go. I went out into the kitchen and came back with the case of empties, far lighter than before. Fritz had brought his car back up into the driveway, and I stood at the rear of it while he unlocked the trunk so I could set the empties in. Everyone shook hands with Petzky and offered good luck along with thanks and farewells. With nothing said, Peter Hatch got into the front passenger seat. Bob Lehrman and I got in back. Fritz got in last, after saying something more to Petzky. He backed down into the street and we set out. Petzky stood at the top of the driveway watching us go, the same as he and Fritz had stood watching when Rhoda drove off.

No one said anything for a minute, and then Bob Lehrman surprised me by saying, "Jesus Christ, I wouldn't live out here to save my fucking soul."

Fritz gave a big sigh. "I know what you mean," he said. "But I also know it's cheap. Petzky gets that whole little house on the prairie for forty-five bucks a month. Rhoda included."

We had come to a red light that kept us from turning onto the strip. Cars flashed by in front of us, going to the left and right. The light seemed to last forever.

I surprised myself by saying something that I instantly regretted. "I don't see how he could ever expect to write, out here in deadland."

Peter Hatch gave a contemptuous snort. "A person can write anywhere," he said. Then he added, "If they're a writer."

The light changed, thank god, and I was able to ignore the condescension in what Peter Hatch had said, or at least able to pretend I hadn't heard it. But I had heard it. As for me, I had been extraordinarily stupid. Thinking of my friend Petzky, I had said something I actually meant, something I actually thought to be true. But not so to Peter Hatch. It was as if I had slapped down five pounds of bloody red meat in front of a lion. Gone in an instant. It must have been delicious to him, his implicit insult and condemnation of Petzky. Now his smugness and gloating.

I swore to myself that I wouldn't say a word more during the remainder of the trip, not so much as a morpheme, not a phoneme. If need be, I would press myself into the corner of the back seat and pretend to be asleep. After all, imagine what would happen if I actually said more about the truth of my feelings. Not just about Petzky, but what if I actually explained my dread about leaving town, the feelings of uncertainty, vulnerability, and exposure, if I actually told them about the eggshell, or actually said that the high school was intended to deteriorate and had been built in dishonesty, only for plunder, or that nothing was logically related to anything else along the strip, that nothing connected to anything else, that the result was desperation, emptiness, and purposelessness, that the men who had built all these things had built them not for any good but solely for their own gain, investments in plunder, just like the men who offered Johnson the oath of office in exchange for his part in the killing of the president, dooming all of us to the death-in-life that our nation has now inevitably become.

I've drifted far away, I know, from that late afternoon in November of 1963 and the back seat of Fritz's car. At that time, a week away from turning twenty-two, I could never have used words the way I did just now. I couldn't possibly have known what the outcome of the assassination would be. But six decades have passed. And I've spent that time, for the most part, reading and watching. What has happened is beyond terror.

I have never abandoned my concept of the eggshell, although this is the first time I've ever revealed it.

I could feel it when we came back through the eggshall and were on the inside of it again. A sense of relief. Fritz swung by John's grocery, and, as I had volunteered to do, I got the case of empties from the trunk and took it inside for the dollar-twenty refund. Back in the car we split it four ways. We all lived in the Quadrangle, but neither Bob Lehrman nor Peter Hatch wanted to go to the trouble of taking the car all the way back to the long-term lot, so Fritz let them off at the foot of the bridge. I moved into the front seat and we rode to the lot. Fritz parked again as far in the rear as he could. There was a free spot against the railroad embankment, like before, and he backed into it slowly until the bumper touched dirt and shrubs. We got back to the Quadrangle with ten minutes to spare before they closed the dinner line. There was no sign of Bob Lehrman or Peter Hatch.

Fritz lived in a room on first floor south as opposed to mine on second floor north, so after dinner we checked our mail and then split up. I walked across the inner courtyard over to the north entrance. Almost every room I could see had lights on inside the windows. Maybe two or three were dark. In my own room I turned on only the goose-necked desk lamp, bent it down low, and sat down in the wooden chair. Like Petzky, I turned the chair so it was at a right angle with the desk and I could rest one arm on the desktop. I raised my feet up and used the left arm of the upholstered chair for a place to rest them. I was looking toward the two windows. One was cranked open an inch or two; the other was closed. They showed only blackness outside.

The eggshell was a wonderful thing in that you were equally protected wherever you happened to be, so long as you were inside it. Here, now, in my room, at my desk, I was positioned quite far toward the small end, but I was just as secure here as

I would be if I were on the other side of town, so long as I was inside the perimeter.

Everything about it had to do with coherence, with the way things were related one to another, and then one to another again, the way they were intended to be. I had my room, my classes, my books—most of the books were stacked on the two rear corners of my desk. I had classes, hours, schedules, assignments. All of this had to do with the reason there could be meaning and significance on the inside, while on the outside plunder, chaos, and emptiness. I wondered what the others would think of such an idea. Fritz might possibly understand it, but not the others, including poor old Petzky. Certainly not Peter Hatch. But that was all right. None of them was ever going to hear a word about it, at least not from me. It was a secret I would take to my grave.

SIX

The academic calendar at Iowa in 1963 was still the old-fashioned sort, more leisurely than the frenetically quickstep, forced-march calendars in use everywhere today. Fall-term classes started a week or ten days into September instead of in the middle of August, a time that's still the peak of summer to normal people. And Christmas break came before term's end, meaning that a week or so in January would be needed for the completion of fall semester's classes, and at least another week after that for writing exams. Two or three weeks for inter-session meant that Spring-term classes might begin sometime deep in February.

That old calendar, for me, was close to perfect. The more slowly the semesters crept by, the better. In fact, if I could have stopped time altogether; if I could have grabbed it and held it as close as if it were life itself—*then* I might have been happy.

The days immediately after JFK's murder were in few ways normal. Even though no one—almost no one—understood the assassination to have been the *coup d'état* that it was, people were nevertheless shaken by it and some quite disoriented. I knew of none myself, but I heard that a number of faculty members made their own decisions to cancel classes for the following week—though it was admittedly a short week, being only three days long because of Thanksgiving.

I had decided that I wouldn't go home for the holiday but would stay on campus, and I found myself looking forward to the solitude and quiet. Wednesday was a massive cut day, when undergraduate classes were at best half-full, what with so many local or nearby students choosing to head home early. Graduate classes weren't very much affected, since graduate students generally hailed from farther afield, but dormitories became ghost towns after midday Wednesday.

The Quadrangle dining room served dinner during the usual hour-and-a-half window that night, Wednesday. Instead of going at the beginning of that time, however, I held off until the last half hour in the hopes of avoiding Peter Hatch and a few of the others who were usually there near the opening time. I wouldn't have minded meeting up with Fritz Dreisbach, but the danger was too great of the others being along with him. The evening meal was offered between five and six-thirty, and by the time I got there at six, only a few of the tables still had people at them, mostly in small groups. I took my tray to a table near the wall and was lucky enough to be undisturbed. I was reading *Middlemarch* at the time, in a Modern Library "giant" edition. It was an excellent volume for my purposes, since it was supple and pliable and, even when propped up against a salt shaker and a pepper shaker, stayed tractably open to any given page. Because of low attendance, the food service had opened up only half of the space in the dining hall. In the unused half, the tables stood bare, uncovered by the usual butcher paper, and the lights were turned off, leaving that entire area in a shadowy darkness.

A traditional dinner was going to be served on Thanksgiving at one o'clock, though anyone planning to attend it was required to sign up ahead. Without saying anything to anyone, I decided not to sign up, and the next day, at ten or fifteen past one, I left my room, crossed the river, made my way up the hill to Washington Street, and went into the Bus Depot Diner. Since the weather had begun growing colder, I had become a kind of semi-regular there, stopping in two or three late afternoons a week for coffee and a doughnut or slice of pie and some reading time at the counter. On Thanksgiving day, however, it was perhaps only a quarter or a third full, and I took one of the small tables at the front window. I leaned my book up against the sugar bowl and got some more reading done while I ate. Outside, the day was overcast and pleasantly dark. I extended my time by ordering coffee and dessert after the meal.

That night around eight, I left my room, went across the courtyard and through the south entrance to Fritz Dreisbach's door and gave it a knock. He was in, and so were Bob Lehrman and Peter Hatch. The four of us ended up walking back across the river together to Kenney's for beers.

I was glad I'd stayed for the Thanksgiving break, since I was able to make good use of those four days. I thought of them as study-days, and, except for the Thursday night outing to Kenney's, I was able to keep them uninterrupted. It was a pleasure to me, the sense of having so much time that it overflowed, and of having the freedom to make use of it however I liked.

I suppose it was natural enough that out of those unscheduled days I immediately created a schedule of my own. The food service offered breakfast—though only that single meal—over the weekend, and I took advantage of it each morning. Not many others appeared, a fact fine by me. Only a quarter or so of the dining hall, maybe less, was in use, and the rest, vacant and unlit, was lost in a kind of silent gray-toned twilight. If I arrived by eight-thirty, or even eight-forty-five, I was still able to get breakfast, and I was also easily able to find a spot alone at one of the tables along the wall, where I could eat breakfast, drink coffee, and stay for a certain time without interruption, reading my book.

Afterward, usually near ten-o'clock, I went back to my room to get in a few more hours of reading—in the same posture I took up after the trip to Eden Lake: seated perpendicular to my desk, feet on the arm of the upholstered chair, knees raised to make an angled plane for my book, right elbow resting on the desktop, goose-neck lamp adjusted as needed. The dormitory, almost entirely free of undergraduates, was rewardingly quiet, and the windows of my room, for all four days, gave me the same comfortably leaden gray that I'd seen in the sky outside the window of the Bus Depot Diner. It was a sky that would eventually bring snow, although not before the temperature dropped another ten or fifteen degrees.

Around one o'clock I would leave my room and go across the river to find a sandwich somewhere, one time in the student union but after that from a shop or eatery in town, sometimes even the Bus Depot Diner, though I generally preferred keeping that one for later in the afternoon. I spent a good amount of time in the afternoons simply walking, sometimes in and near the campus, but also fair distances through the older, east-side streets of the town. I was glad to be alone—although at the same time, in a certain sense, I *wasn't* alone. The situation I found myself in was oddly confusing. For one thing, recent events seemed unnaturally distant, as though things that had taken place hardly a week before, or less, had in fact happened very far back and very long ago. My first translocation in time wasn't yet even ten days in the past. The assassination had taken place less than a week before. And my second translocation, the one when (where?) I met Eveline Stahl—it in particular seemed unimaginably distant, even though it had taken place only a tiny handful of days before.

It was almost as though it had never happened. Yet I wanted nothing more than to have it back again.

This was the great question over the long weekend: whether I would ever find myself in a 1933 classroom again; whether I would ever see Eveline Stahl again; whether what I called my translocations were real at all, or whether they were imaginary or hallucinatory; or, as I had feared so powerfully on the night of the concierge's telephone, whether—not to put too fine a point on it—I was losing my mind.

On the afternoon of the day after Thanksgiving, I spent two or three hours walking through the streets of the east side looking at the houses there, trying to imagine which ones—most of them—were likely to have been standing in 1933, and in which it was most likely that Eveline Stahl might have rented an apartment or room. I knew that a search of this kind was quixotic, but I continued it anyhow, moving from block to block, house to house, from one lawn or driveway to another. I didn't approach any of the houses or step on any of the lawns, nor did I go up any walkways or drives. I stayed on the sidewalk and looked across front lawns at old houses with wide porches, tall windows, sometimes a turret at one corner, and often twin sets of dormer windows up at the attic level. The afternoon, once again, was overcast and gray, and as darkness began to gather, lights appeared inside windows. Sometimes they shined behind polished glass, and sometimes they glowed through curtains. I would look first at the ground-floor windows, then raise my eyes to the second floor to look for lights there, and then to the very top, where a reading lamp inside an attic window, although a rarity, would satisfy my imagination in a wonderfully lasting way.

It was past five-thirty before I realized how much time I had taken up in this search. I was quite far from downtown by then, and it took me a quarter of an hour to walk back there. In the Bus Depot Diner I was lucky enough to find a place at the same table I'd sat at the day before, by the front window. I would have a real dinner, and possibly I would be able to finish *Middlemarch*, there being not many pages left. In my book bag I had a copy of *Adam Bede*, in case I had need of it.

Once November turned its back and disappeared (I turned twenty-two on its penultimate day), time also seemed to change in a strangely contradictory way. On the one hand, it sped by faster than I had ever known it to before. But at the same time, sprinkled throughout, were pockets of slowness, respite, and languor that themselves hardly seemed susceptible to time. Most of these—all of them—involved Eveline Stahl.

It was all-consuming, my love for her. I have no idea, to this day, how I survived the loss of it.

•

The Monday after Thanksgiving, as I made my way up the bluff toward Jessup Hall, I realized that I had gone through another translocation—and this time the change not only felt effortless, familiar, and natural, but I realized that I also found it extremely desirable. It was taking me exactly where I wanted to be.

In the classroom, Eveline was sitting in the second row, as usual. Both of us were early, and the room was largely empty, with maybe a half-dozen other students scattered here and there. Surprising myself—and yet, in actuality, *not* surprising myself, as if I had already decided to do this—I went across to the window side of the room, then into the second row, and sat in the desk to Eveline's right. It was important that I be on her right, not left, and as close to the end of the row as possible. "Do you mind?" I said.

She turned and gave me the smile I had seen before. "Don't be foolish," she said. "Of course not."

•

When I left the Quadrangle that morning, the date had been Monday, December 2, 1963. When I sat down beside Eveline, it was Monday, December 4, 1933.

SEVEN

December passed quickly and brought a number of changes over a short time. For the first three or four days of that
month, my translocations occurred unnaturally often, sometimes three or four, or even more, a day. Their familiarity led
me to take them almost for granted, and I lost any vestigial
fear that might have remained from earlier on. If I were in my
room late in the afternoon, reading, I would at some point, almost casually, come to notice whether the box-elder tree was
standing outside my windows or whether nothing was there
but open air and early dusk. If the tree was still there, I would,
come meal-time, go down to the dining hall and, by habit, join
Fritz Dreisbach, Peter Hatch, and Bob Lehrman at our usual
table. If the box-elder tree was missing, I would do exactly the
same thing, although my table mates would be Henry Stieff,
Roger Bolin, and Victor Haas.

The next identifiable phase of things lasted slightly under
a week. In this stage, my life was split equally between the
two planes of time, coming in periods of twenty-four hours
each. This would have worked very well in allowing me to go
on seeing Eveline in class each day—but *only* if the alternating

pattern happened to fit the pattern of class days. If, for example, I were to have spent Sunday in 1963, I could have seen Eveline on each of the week's class days, those being Monday, Wednesday, and Friday. Unfortunately, however, that isn't the way things went.

If luck had been with me—if I *had* spent Sunday in 1963, I would have been able to see Eveline in all three classes the following week, like this:

SUN (1963) **MON (1933)** TUE (1963) **WED (1933)**
THU (1963) FRI (1933)

But, instead of spending Sunday in 1963, I ended up spending *Saturday* in that plane of time, with the result that the pattern went awry, and, stuck in the 1963 plane of time on Monday and Wednesday, I missed seeing Eveline for all three class days that week:

SAT (1963) **SUN (1933)** MON (1963) **TUE (1933)**
WED (1963) **THU (1933)** FRI (1963)

Still, as I said, changes that month occurred at a fast pace, and the greatest of them, without question, took place sometime between the end of dinner on Wednesday, December 11, 1963 (parallel to Wednesday, December 6, 1933), and 9:00 a.m. on Friday, December 8, 1933 (parallel to Friday, December 13, 1963). That is, at some point between Wednesday night after dinner (I ate with Bob Lehrman and the others) and Friday morning at nine, when Eveline's Old English class met, my translocations in time came to an end completely and—or so I was convinced—permanently.

In class on Friday, December 13, 1933, when I sat down beside her, Eveline cocked an eye with mock disapproval as if to ask where I had been.

I told her that I could explain everything, but later. And I did. For the rest of the semester, I didn't miss one class. The same was true for the semester after that. I believed, hopelessly, that I was destined to remain in Eveline's plane of time forever.

No matter how long I might have searched for it, I never would have found the house I was looking for—because it wasn't there. Sometime in the decades after Eveline lived in it, the house had been razed.

•

However, around ten o'clock the night of December 8, 1933, I saw it clearly. From the sidewalk. With Eveline. The moon was half full, and in its light, along with help from the street-light hanging over the nearby intersection, I was fairly well able to make out the shape and outline of the house. Three or four windows, here and there, glowed from the inside. It was a big, high, grand old house, its mansard roof sporting twin pairs of tall chimneys.

•

At the end of Old English that morning, I asked Eveline if she would meet me later. She said yes. We each had two more classes that morning. One of them was Eveline's Middle English, and later that afternoon I had my theory of narrative seminar from three to five. Eveline proposed that we meet at six. She suggested we meet at the Bus Depot Diner.

•

When I jaywalked across Washington Street from the campus toward the diner, I could see her sitting at one of the tables inside the front window. It was the same place I had sat the night after I had looked for her house. Eveline's coat, sleeves empty, was drawn around her shoulders like a shawl. She was reading. A mug and a small teapot stood on the table.

•

For a second I was tempted to go up to the window and tap on it to get her attention, but then just as quickly I decided not to. I knew already that she was two years my senior, though I thought of her as even older than that, or certainly as more experienced than I was. So I chose to seem adult rather than playful. I walked in and went over to her table. By way of getting her attention, I said her name. She looked up, said something like, well, hello, and gave me the smile that I had seen before and that I thought was the most captivating sight in the world.

•

In truth, Eveline did have a certain natural authority that other people also sensed and deferred to. At the same time, she was neither imperious nor humorless; in fact, she was almost exactly the opposite of either. She had the infallible indicator of intelligence, a good sense of humor, but also the other infallible indicator of intelligence, the unerring sense to know when to exhibit it and when not. She was trim and unpretentious in dress, manner, and appearance, tending more toward the modest than whatever its opposite might be—the flamboyant, I suppose. The famous words suited her perfectly—"always beautiful but never pretty"—although she couldn't have known them, for the fact of their not having yet been written. As for me, however I might try, I was never able to describe her—the inquiring look I saw in her face, the expression of alertness that almost never changed, the sympathetic quickness of her thinking, the immediacy of her understanding, and the width, breadth, and sensitivity of it. The truth is that during the time I was with Eveline, from start to finish, every aspect of experience was heightened for me, made more rich than I was accustomed to in my "normal" plane of time. This included the sound, sight, feel, scent, texture, even the taste of things. Everything in Eveline's plane of time seemed tighter, more lasting, knit together more closely. Eveline was a window, an entry, a doorway into a world that I had always imagined and dreamed of but had never known before now.

•

It was past nine when we walked out of the Bus Depot Diner onto Washington Street. I asked Eveline if I could walk her home. She smiled and raised one eyebrow. Did I know the way? I did not. We set out, or Eveline did, and I followed. We walked slowly up to Clinton Street at the top of the hill. From there, we continued on Washington to Dubuque, Linn, Gilbert, and then Van Buren. At Van Buren we turned right and, following the ravine with its almost-dry creek, went one block, to College Street. On College, we turned left and continued uphill to Johnson Street and then, on level ground, passed Dodge Street, continued on to Lucas—and stopped.

Well, said Eveline. We're there.

The house was the way I described it before, its three tiers rising up on the northeast corner of College and Lucas. Eveline linked her arm through mine and very gently tugged me the additional few steps to the front walkway, then up the walkway to the immense old house itself. Then she tugged my arm even more lightly, and we went up the three steps onto the porch, crossed it and stood in the darkness at the front entry. Eveline opened the door and pushed it half open, then held it there. Her lips brushed mine and she disappeared inside.

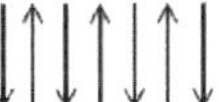

The winter was perfect. The same was true of the spring that followed, and of the summer after that. Never before had I fallen so deeply in love with a place as I did with Iowa City during the months I lived there.

And it was because of Eveline, I know, in greatest part. When I fell in love with Eveline, I felt as though I was connected, through her, to the rest of the world.

•

When my translocations came to an end and I was to live permanently (so I believed; or so I let myself believe) in the earlier plane of time, I gained an unexpected new freedom by merit of being, suddenly, without a family.

Here it was, mid-December 1933. I was living in Iowa City, falling more deeply in love with Eveline Stahl every day—and finding myself free of even the least obligation to parents or family.

It was true enough that my father, at age twenty-four, was himself living in Iowa City at this very time. But the fact is that he wasn't my father *yet*. Nor could he have had the least idea that he would ever *become* my father. To him, I was nothing at all, and I would have been taken for mad if I had managed, or tried, to express any kind of filial gratitude or obligation to him. The same was true of my mother, his fiancée, waiting patiently in West Tree for my father to return for the winter holidays, and then, at the end of the academic year, to return for good.

On the seventeenth of June, 1934, my parents would get married, but even then I would be nothing to them. My age would still be minus eight.

In Iowa City, in the 1933 plane of time, I had no reason to return to West Tree for any part of the winter holidays, a fact that felt tremendously liberating. I had the freedom to remain exactly where I was.

•

Eveline's situation, on the other hand, was much different. She came from a large family with deep roots, and she would be badly missed if she failed to go home for Christmas.

Home was Fremont, Nebraska, where her father, now eighty years old, had been born in 1853. He married twice, both of his wives now gone. Eveline herself was his last child, and she was the third with his second wife. She was born in 1909.

A farmer, Otto Stahl made his first marriage in 1881, when he was twenty-eight, to Elizabeth Bain. Elizabeth gave him three sons close in age, their birth-years being 1882, 1884, and 1885. Then in 1887, a daughter was born, though she lived for only two weeks. Elizabeth died also, shortly after giving birth. The baby had been named Eveline.

Persevering, Otto Stahl continued farming. He built two additional rooms onto the family homestead and invited his own middle sister, along with her husband and their three children, to join the household, in this way making himself able to raise his three sons, with the help of the extended family.

Not until the youngest of the sons reached the age of eighteen, in 1903, did Otto marry again. His wife this time was Victoria Mueller, and she gave him two more sons and one daughter.

The first son came in 1904, the second in 1906. Their little sister was born in 1909.

That baby sister was Eveline.

The children's mother died two weeks before Eveline's tenth birthday.

•

It may seem a bloodless word, but what Eveline embodied and represented was coherence.

It was as though she contained everything within her, and as though all things outside of her were made orderly so long as she was present among them. Eveline: Security, order, intelligence, beauty. To me, it seemed as though everything that had happened—every place Eveline had been, or had known, or had learned about—had become woven into her person, into her being, into the beauty and expressiveness of her face, even into the mellowness and musicality of her voice. I understand now what I felt then—the feeling that history itself had been gathered up in Eveline. Eveline *was* the prairie and the hills, the grasslands and rivers, the farm and the town, the sunshine and the air. Even deaths and births were a part of her—the death of her little half-sister, and of her mother. Then the death, in 1918, in France, of Everett Stahl, Eveline's oldest half-brother. In the same year, of the flu, Eveline's mother died, Victoria Stahl. Eveline was almost ten.

(It was as though she had not one but two families. The first consisted of her two half brothers—ages fifty-one and forty-nine in the year I knew her—along with their wives and their own children, who, though almost the same age as Eveline, were actually her nieces and nephews. The second family was made up of Eveline herself and her own two brothers. As well as their father, of course, the patriarch, central in both families. So it was a much different matter for Eveline, the question of going home for Christmas. I went along with her, in a taxi, to the train station to see her off on her trip to Fremont. I stood on the platform as the train pulled out, then kept standing until the train grew almost too small to see, then finally went around a curve and disappeared. I was quite cold by that time from not moving. Back in the station, I stood at the pot-belly stove in the waiting room. Behind his partition, the dispatcher was sending and receiving on the telegraph. No one else was there except him and me, and the only sound was the clicking of the telegraph key. At last I went back outside and began the walk across town to the campus and my room in the Quadrangle. Never in my life had I felt so lonely.)

•

It was an important time for me, the nine or ten days Eveline was away. The campus was all but deserted, as was the Quadrangle itself. The dining room remained closed, no meals available for the tiny handful of people who had gotten permission to stay in their rooms over the break. The post office in the south entrance still functioned, however, and the concierge's office stayed open as well, although with shortened hours.

I admit that my first night alone was miserable as I wrestled with loneliness and a sense of vacancy and emptiness, sometimes also feeling curious waves of panic. I set the alarm for 6:45 as usual, however, and the next morning, feeling better, determined to make a plan and stick to it.

Having a plan helped a lot, both on the first day and on the following ones. A routine developed such that I would walk across the river for breakfast, usually but not always at the Bus Depot Diner, then return to my room, where I would read—and sometimes write—until one o'clock or so. Then I would go across the river again for lunch—in a place where, preferably, I could stick around for an hour or so of reading. The university library was also open, although for daytime hours only. Sometimes I stopped in to spend an hour or two either in the main reading room or in one of the little side-reading-areas nestled here and there around the perimeters of the second and third floors. Just before Eveline left for Fremont, the weather had turned cold, although without any snow beforehand. Then, the second day after she'd gone, the temperature rose to just above thirty, the sky clouded over, then grew leaden, and in the middle of a dark afternoon snow began to fall, lightly at first, in large flakes coming straight down, stirred by no breath of wind at all. Then the temperature dropped slightly, and the flakes became smaller—and kept falling, heavily, all through the night and until late the next morning. I was in the library the afternoon it began, sitting in an upholstered chair in one of the side-reading-areas, when I happened to look up from the page I was reading and saw through the mullioned window that it had begun to snow. By the time I left the library, not long before five o'clock and closing time, the snow was falling heavily and came already to a depth of an inch or two. I walked along Madison Street to Iowa Avenue, turned left, crossed the river, and continued on to the Quadrangle. In my room I pulled off my shoes and set out my high snow boots so I could wear them instead of shoes when I left the room again in an hour or so. Then I switched off the overhead light and turned on my goose-necked lamp. I turned my desk chair to a right angle with the desk and sat down. I rested my right arm on the desk and raised my feet to the left arm of the upholstered chair. I opened *Adam Bede* and picked up reading where I had left off. I was facing the windows, whose panes showed black. After awhile, I got up and went over to them, putting my forehead against the glass and cupping my hands around the sides of my eyes. The snow was falling even more heavily than before. I could see it coming down through the cones of light from each of the lamp posts along the walkway. The snow was easily visible in the first two or three lights, then less so, until, after a turn in the walkway, there was only darkness.

I had a lot to do, and all of it seemed to me equally important. I laced up my boots, pulled on my scarf, coat, knitted hat, and gloves and set out down the walkway to cross the river again. By now the snow was up to my ankles but my boots were high and I had tucked my pants legs inside them. On the other side of the river, I walked up to the Bus Depot Diner and took the table by the front window where I had sat with Eveline. I opened *Adam Bede* and propped it up against the sugar bowl and continued reading as I ate dinner. When I was finished I ordered a cup of coffee and stayed for another thirty or forty minutes. Only four or five other people remained in the diner by then. A streetlamp hung over Washington Street out in front, and through the window I could watch the snow falling through its light.

I left the diner and followed the route Eveline had taken me on the night she showed me where she lived, now more than three weeks ago. I'd gone this way a number of other times since then, during the ten days that had remained of classes before the start of the break. Now, close to eight o'clock, almost no one was outdoors: Near Clinton Street, and then Dubuque, I saw perhaps three or four people, alone like me, trudging through the snow, but after another block or so there were no more. I assumed the snowplows would come out but saw no sign of them. I went on, from streetlight to streetlight, pushing my way more or less down the middle of the street. It was strenuous, walking through the snow. Whenever I stopped for a moment, all I heard was the sound of my own breathing.

When I came to the intersection of Lucas and College, I felt my way over to the edge of the street, found the curb with the toe of my boot, and stepped up. Like the street itself, the walkway leading to the house was covered by new deep snow. I broke a path halfway up to the front porch and then stopped. Holding my hands against my forehead, like visors, to keep the snow from falling into my eyes, I looked up at the house. It was immense, silent, high, old, and dark. No light came from the windows on any of its three levels. Possibly there were lights I could have seen from the back, but I was not about to make my way around the side of the house, through the bushes and shrubs there, and through the ever-deepening snow. I was here only to look. Just to be. Once my breathing had settled down, it seemed to me that I had never experienced a more perfect silence than the silence then and there. After a time, I realized that I could hear the snow itself, making an almost-silent hiss as it landed on top of the snow already fallen. I listened to this sound and continued looking up at the old house. I found myself making up sentences one after the other, then examining each one logically to determine what truth it contained and what falsehood, and then whether the truth and the falsehood were equally balanced or whether one of them dominated—

> Eveline Stahl lived in this house
> Eveline Stahl lives in this house
> Eveline Stahl is not in this house
> Eveline Stahl is in this house

—and then some of the words for "house" came into my mind, first from the Old English that Eveline and I were studying together, then from dialects of the Middle English that Eveline was studying with my uncle Jakob and had shown me—

> hūs
> hōūse
> hōwse. . .

I was beginning to feel the cold from standing so long, and I turned to retrace my route. The snow had been falling heavily enough so that the tracks I'd made approaching the house were already filled in. No sign remained of my having been there at all. I broke a new track, made my way back out onto College Street, turned right and headed toward downtown. I saw no one else outdoors except for one person, on skis, making long strides and pushing himself forward with poles. Skiing north on Johnson Street, this figure appeared as if from nowhere and passed in front of me like a phantom. I was perhaps thirty or forty feet from the intersection of College and Johnson. The figure went through the light of the streetlamp and then just as suddenly was gone. In my memory, he was dressed in black. I walked across his two fresh tracks and continued along College down to Van Buren, turned right for a block, then left onto Washington. Not a soul was to be seen. The snow continued to fall heavily and steadily. The air was entirely still. I followed Washington past Gilbert, Linn, Dubuque, and Clinton. At the bottom of the hill I turned right on Madison to Iowa Avenue, then left onto the bridge. Halfway across, under the one streetlight there, I stopped at the rail and stood for a time looking down. The river wasn't yet frozen, and I could see the black water below, flowing turbidly. When I looked down, my view was aligned with the direction of the snow's fall instead of cutting across it and there was no need to shield my eyes. I stood for some time and watched the flakes plunging down, away from me, and disappearing into the dark water.

From the end of the bridge, I made my way uphill toward the Quadrangle, passing through one after another of the pools of light from the lamps along the way. The path delivered me directly into the north entranceway. I went in and then up the stairs, where I unlaced my boots and left them outside the door of my room, their toes propped up against the wall. Inside, I went through the same steps I had gone through many times before. I turned on the goose-necked lamp. Then I went back to the door and turned off the overhead light. The room was pleasantly dark, light from the goose-necked lamp pooling over the desktop and falling over its lip. The wooden chair stood at its angle to the desk, the way I had left it in the afternoon. After sitting down, I raised my feet back onto the arm of the upholstered chair, and, holding the verso side of *Adam Bede* open with my left hand and the recto side with my right, my right arm resting on the desktop, I continued where I had left off. *"'Dinah,' he said suddenly, taking both her hands between his, 'I love you with my whole heart and soul. I love you next to God who made me.' / Dinah's lips became pale, like her cheeks, and she trembled violently under the shock of painful joy. Her hands were cold as death between Adam's. She could not draw them away, because he held them fast."* Being one of only ten or a dozen people scattered through the Quadrangle made me feel as though I were entirely alone. The silence was almost perfect. At one point I imagined I could hear the snow falling, or touching up against the windows. I got up to look out and realized that I could hear nothing at all. The snow fell as before through the lamps along the pathway. I went back to my desk. *"He chose this spot, almost at the top of the hill, because it was away from all eyes—no house, no cattle, not even a nibbling sheep near—no presence but the still lights and shadows, and the great embracing sky."* By this time I was within a dozen pages of the book's end: *". . . gradually approaching the foot of the hill. Slowly, Adam thought; but Dinah was really walking at her usual pace, with a light quiet step."* As I went on reading, I began to feel less isolated and more protected, an accumulating sense similar to what I had felt a month before—the night after JFK's murder—on returning to my room after the trip to visit Petzky. Now, in the glow from my reading lamp, I began to feel the way I had felt then, as though, if I simply remained still and went on reading, the sky would gradually become covered over by something capable of offering protection against the zinging and careening, the flesh-destroying evils overhead—and the sky would be covered by a translucent veil of absolutely impenetrable strength, since each line or phrase or sentence that I read would have the effect of causing a translucent but unbreakable filament to appear on the horizon, streak upward, cross the bowl of the sky, then arc downward and anchor itself stoutly to a point on the opposite horizon. This would occur again and again and again with each word, sentence, or phrase—*"so Tristram was I called and Tristram shall I be to the day of my death"*—until the sheer number of filaments springing up from all points on one horizon and anchoring themselves to equivalent points on the other, these transparent tendrils—*"It is a trite but true observation, that examples work more forcibly on the mind than precepts"*—would be woven into an impenetrable—*"upon / a red wheelbarrow"*—barricade against any of the life-destroying forces—*"beside the white / chickens"*—that might otherwise select us as their target and speed downward to transform us into gristle, spilled blood, dead bodies—*"The graves stood tenantless and the sheeted dead / Did squeak and gibber in the Roman streets"*—malevolence and doom the only forces coming to us from above.

•

That night, the night I discovered that a shield for Earth could be brought into existence by reading, was the night of November 22-23, 1963, the night after LBJ and his murderous friends slew the Republic and then picked up the aftermath—not the soul-deprived body of the dead Republic but the blood-smeared muscle-man of new Empire—so as to feed and advance it in the only ways they knew, revered, or were capable of, those being the ways of greed, malignancy, war, spoliation, blindness, ignorance, terror.

There could have been, at this time, no surprise that the sky itself had turned into something dangerous, repugnant, terrifying.

•

The night of the heavy snow was an entirely different thing. The snow fell all night and through the following day, December 21-22, 1933, thirty years before the godless slaughter ended the Republic and gave birth to the Empire. At the time of that snow there was as yet no reason to be afraid of the sky, to fear it as one feared a weapon.

•

The heavy snow took place at the beginning of my year with Eveline. In the world as I began to understand it during that time, through Eveline, the sky was benevolent, defense against it unnecessary, unthought of. The lineaments that were generated from the reading of books, chapters, paragraphs, sentences, phrases, words—as I learned about them through Eveline—these lineaments existed, certainly enough, but, unlike my own, earlier, kind of tendrils, they didn't shoot up to the zenith and dart across the dome of the sky before turning down. Instead, Eveline's tendrils, traveling with the speed of thought, kept to low altitudes, skimming between ten and thirty feet above treetops, prairies, fields, oceans, lakes, waterways, rising up whenever necessary in order to maintain that same height above foothills, flanks, or peaks of mountains, or even above high structures, towers, or entire cities, each tendril or lineament encircling the globe exactly once and returning precisely to its starting point. There, its head would bond with its tail to form a permanent girdle, hoop, or continuous thread that from then on would possess a certain number of beneficial, paradoxical, perdurable characteristics. Foremost among these was the great strength of each lineament, the strength of twined steel cable, while at the same time remaining invisible, totally permeable to light. The invaluable nature of these lineaments, filaments, or tendrils lay precisely in their contradictory qualities: In being real although invisible, powerful although imperceivable. Any who were able to listen properly to the real nature of reading were able also to know the real nature of the filaments and to know that they were there. Those who were able to listen properly knew also that the sheer number of such tendrils or filaments would grow to the near-unimaginable, since the reading of a single line, as for example

God hath sent me to sea for pearls

or

I was never allowed a candle to light me to bed

or even

Last summer, in a season of intense heat

could conceivably generate as many filaments as a single line might contain syllables, or as many as a single line might contain stresses, occasions of consonance or assonance, not to mention other kinds of rhythms, so that "last summer, in a season of intense heat" might generate four filaments alone from the sound of the hard sibilant "s" falling four times with perfect spacing through this gathering of words, and generate another filament in response to the two-part rhythm marked at the point where the comma falls, and yet another, or three more, out of the other rhythmic structure, created by the two long syllables at the start—in "last" and "summer"—the additional two long ones at the end—"-tense" and "heat"—while, in the middle, there's the sprinkling of five shorter sounds, like the tripping of goats' hooves on a wooden bridge ("in a season of"), the mastery and loveliness of the entire phrase thus, in multiple ways, bringing about the creation, arguably, of as many as nine filaments, each one of these moving with the speed of thought in a single trip around the globe, returning then to its starting point and into a bond with the lattermost part of itself to form a circle, ring, or hoop possessing neither a beginning nor an end but instead a salutary, nutritive, benevolent permanence so that, joining its myriad brothers and sisters, some parallel to one another and some crisscrossing one another, it would become one of a near-infinity of invisible threads accumulating in such a way as to "clothe" the earth, thus protecting, serving, and honoring it in exactly the same way as the atmosphere protects, serves, and honors its child, the earth, the filaments differing from the natural atmosphere only in the nature of its origin, earth's atmosphere being a product solely of nature and nature's recombinant forces, the lineaments, on the other hand, being a product not of nature alone but of nature in combination with mind, intellect, and emotion.

●

When I walked Eveline home the night before she left for Fremont, she invited me inside for the first time. We reached the old house, climbed up the steps and went across the porch to the front door. We were holding hands, Eveline gently gripping my right hand in her own left. When she turned the knob, however, and pushed the door open just wide enough to step through, she tightened her grip slightly and drew me in behind her.

Inside was a large hallway that extended toward the rear of the house, all in darkness except for the yellowish light shed by a tassel-shaded lamp on a table halfway down, a table that held a telephone just like the one outside the concierge's office in the Quadrangle. On the left of the hallway was a set of double doors, closed, then farther down a single closed door, just past the lamp. On the righthand side were two more single doors, one just inside from the front entrance and the other across from where stood the telephone-table and its lamp.

To me, the house seemed imbued with the very scent, presence, and ambiance of antiquity itself. It was already December of 1933, but the house had the effect of taking me back more than an additional half-century, to the early 1870s, when people first lived in it. I could smell the old wood all around me, with hints of dust and long-faded furniture polish; I could smell traces of mildew and what I imagined to be heavy and very old draperies hanging in the apartment behind the closed double doors; all of these scents were mingled in turn with hundreds of others, the smells of cooking from half a century before, the walls and ceilings and floors themselves now permeated with the faintest tincture of sauces and oils, of onions fried in 1905, of pork roast cooked in 1914, of sixty winter holidays with pine trees, branches, boughs, and sprigs brought into the kitchen, living room, and dining room where they combined with the scents of cinnamon, ginger, nutmeg, lemon, allspice, herbs of every sort, until the very skin, structure, walls, and floors of the house in some way were made up of this ancient, accumulated, faded wholeness.

Still without a word, and still gripping my right hand with her left, Eveline opened the first door on the right. She went in, drew me after, and closed the door behind us.

The room was dark as black velvet until Eveline slipped away from me, and then I saw her at a desk across the room, where she had switched on a shaded lamp much like the one out in the hallway. She turned back to me where I stood by the door, not having moved an inch. She came up and put her arms around me and we embraced, our arms entwined around one another. Eveline was small, her body firm and strong. I felt her breasts pressing against me. The scent in her hair was of all outdoors, holding the fresh chill of December, but in it also were grass, leaves, rain, sunlight, earth, the scents of every season. She turned her face up to mine—I was only a few inches taller than she was—and she whispered, "This is my place."

We kissed, standing there by the door, for a long time. The kiss was extraordinarily pleasant, even passionate, although at the same time it seemed as though there were no reason to hurry with it, no reason to rush anything. It was less as though we were drawing one another into having sex than it was as though we were authoring a promise and extending it to one another, the promise so powerful and fulfilling and perfect and absolute that it included in itself an entire and unending future time, a future time so entirely guaranteed, so certain and so perfect, that in the present moment, in our long embrace, there was no reason to rush toward the next moment, since all future moments were promised and contained within the unhurried simplicity of this one.

Eveline's rooms, also, were perfect. There were four of them, connected with one another in a chain along the west side of the house. Farthest back was the bathroom, then the kitchen, the bedroom after that, and finally the front room, the one we had entered from the hallway. I have no idea what the function of each may have been when the house was built, but they now served perfectly for Eveline's uses. The front room, whether it had served originally as a smoking room, or music room, maybe a library, served now for Eveline as combination living room and study. There was easily space enough in it for her to entertain guests if she chose. An upholstered settee stood across the tall twin windows on the College Street side, and not far from it stood another chair, as well as, elsewhere in the room, a pair of wicker stools. A low table stood in front of the settee and could serve for holding coffee or drinks, although now it was covered with low piles of books and notebooks. Of greatest importance, however, were the desk and chair that served as Eveline's main study place. These were placed near the side window, on the east wall of the house, and they were angled in just such a way that a person sitting there, if they should happen to raise their eyes from the pages of a book, could gaze comfortably out through the front windows, across the porch, and out to the street, or, by turning their head just slightly to the left, out onto the side yard, a frosted lawn in winter and in summer a grassy expanse with shrubs, trees, leaves, and, climbing up and covering the window itself, vines of blossoming morning glory.

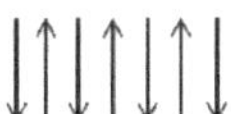

What if it had never come to an end? What if I could have lived with Eveline forever? What if there had never been a Dallas, a Dealey Plaza, a high-powered rifle that blew off the back of the President's head?

Gore. Bone. Blood.

The republic dead. The empire rising.

What if Eveline and I had never begun studying together; or what if I had never come to recognize 1947 as the crucial and pivotal year, when the path was set down that led sixteen years later to the murder of the president and death of the republic?

What if Evelyn and I had never made plans to walk into 1947; to go by foot from Iowa City to West Tree, since there, I imagined, we could dissuade my father from his determined part in planting the seeds that would grow into poison, desolation, loss.

•

But it didn't. I couldn't. There were. And I did.

•

My father was evil. I knew that.

•

I should never have deceived myself into imagining he had a soul that could be reached.

•

That with Evelyn at my side we could do it.

•

Pitiable. Disastrous.

•

These things were to happen:

We would meet him on our farm, on the wide lawn that lay to the west of the farmhouse, where the grass was never cut and the elms reached up eighty feet. September. A warm breeze from the southwest would stir Eveline's hair and press the back of her skirt against her legs.

My father would stand there, tall, looking down, smiling sarcastically. "As lean as a knife and narrow as the blade of one."

But Eveline would not be intimidated by him, no matter what he said or did. She would look up at him and smile, with her disarming, natural, unsolicited smile.

He would turn and begin walking toward the house. Eveline and I, a step or two behind, would follow.

I imagined, wished, hoped that in this way we would change history.

Folly. Beyond folly. Even if elements of it were true.

•

I was wholly in love with Eveline. The very point of life was Eveline. Spring came early that year, and when the first week of genuinely warm days arrived, we did what Eveline told me she had always done during her time in the old house. Her bed was three-quarter size. In the cold months she arranged the room so the head of the bed was against the interior wall, the foot pointing toward the window. But in the summer she turned it around and moved it to the other side of the room so as to take advantage of the window. It was a large bay window rising from near the floor almost up to the ceiling. It was unusually wide, enough so that the head of the bed could be pushed into the breadth and depth it offered. That way, with the two side panels of the bay window raised up, it was almost like sleeping outdoors, or in an arbor, since not only were there a fair number of sizable shade trees on the lawn outside, but pressing up against the side of the house were tall lilac and forsythia bushes that formed a kind of natural curtain or thick green wall. All that summer we kept the side windows open, lying there without a stitch on and yet invisible to anyone outside. In the hottest weather, in the deep of night, it was easy to imagine the old house was stirring, breathing quietly around us, and now and then there would be a muted crack or a distant knock—other students lived in the apartments upstairs—and the silence afterward would be deeper than before. When thunderstorms stole toward us at night, Eveline kept track of their progress by counting the seconds between lightning flashes and thunder. One especially powerful storm approached faster than usual, two miles, one, half a mile, quarter, eighth, then one brilliant flash of light and a tremendous and terrifying crash. A brilliant blue light briefly filled all the windows and I was certain the lightning had struck the house. Afterward, Eveline and I clung together, listening to the thunder as, bit by bit, it grew more distant, while the sound of rain falling on leaves outside the window diminished very, very gradually. Every now and then I would wake up in the small hours to find that Eveline had left me. A faint glow from the front room would lead me to find her there, leaning back in her desk chair, her feet curled under her, reading in the light of her gooseneck lamp. She would be wearing a simple robe, her left elbow resting on the desktop, a book open between her hands, a mug of hot tea nearby. She kept a supply of note cards in one of the pigeonholes on her desk, and she made certain to take some of these with her also whenever she left the house. On them she wrote the phrases and sentences from her reading that especially struck her, particularly when the words grew to be fused with her own memory and senses, and her own memory and senses fused with *them*: This is when they would manifest the energy and permanence transforming them into another tendril that would encircle the earth and, interwoven with myriad others, become a second atmosphere, union of nature and mind, uniquely durable. On one of the note cards, Eveline had written

How orderly the kitchen'd look by night

and on another

Last summer, in a season of intense heat

and another

God hath sent me to sea for pearls,

and

I was never allowed a candle to light me to bed,

and

Ours was the marsh country, down by the river, within, as the river wound, twenty miles of the sea.

and

Down far in the avenue she could hear a street organ playing.

In certain cases the words were more numerous, sometimes almost filling the card:

We lived at the top of the last house, and the windrushing up the river shook the house that night, like discharges of a cannon, or breakings of a sea

or

The snow had somewhat abated; carriages and trades-men's wagons were hurrying soundlessly to and fro in the winter twilight

or

One time there used to be a field there in which they used to play every evening with other people's children, though most were brief, like

Those are pearls that were his eyes

or

O, thou are fairer than the evening's air
Clad in the beauty of a thousand stars. . .

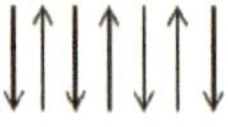

.

I believed Eveline completely. I believed what she said about the tendrils, what she said about their permanence, and, un-questionably, about how they created a "second atmosphere" that protected the earth.

I was young, it's true, and I was in love. But I didn't believe Eveline because I was inexperienced, susceptible, or naïve. I believed her because I thought then—and think still—that what she said was, in *some* most meaningful way, true.

There was another element in my thinking. After all, by going to Iowa City, I had declared my dedication to a life not necessarily of scholarship but certainly of reading—an activity, when undertaken seriously, that seemed to me then, as it does now, one of the most significant, most profound, and, at least some of the time, most constructive activities in the world.

I still think this is true. But at the same time it is a truth that we—now, here, in the bloodlessness and betrayal of 2028—no longer know, see, or practice and have therefore lost almost entirely, and along with it much, much more. . .

.

The night before she left for Fremont—when Eveline drew me into the house, then into her rooms—we did nothing that wasn't perfectly chaste. Exciting beyond the very limits of imagination, yes—certainly so for me—but chaste.

Eveline showed me every room, starting in the back—so that, believe it or not, the bathroom was first—and on our way from the front room to the rear, she made me keep my eyes shut so I would see the rooms only in what she took to be the correct order, back to front.

I would have done anything for her, and keeping my eyes closed seemed like nothing. Besides, she went on holding my hand in her own, and the pleasure even of that much contact reduced me to complete docility. Eveline herself seemed to have been touched that night by some kind of spirit that made her unusually lighthearted. She continued talking as she led me along, giving me one instruction or another, move to the left, there's another step-down here, telling me in the meantime that other men had been in her apartment but only as party guests, in groups of other people, and that I, whether I would believe her or not, was the first man she had invited in alone, which certainly, she went on without a pause, showed the importance and depth of her feelings for me.

I had no choice but to believe her. And of course I chose to.

Eveline guided me through an open doorway and down one last step—I felt the doorjamb on the left with my free hand— and then I sensed that she was moving around behind me, though still holding on to my right hand. I heard the click of what sounded like a light switch, then a doorlatch clicking shut, and Eveline let go of my hand.

"All right," she said. "You can open them."

I did. And there we were, she and I, standing in the bathroom, at the very back of the apartment.

Once again I didn't know what to say. But Eveline arranged it in such a way that I didn't have to say a thing. In a voice as natural as rain, completely unaffected yet at the same time filled with notes and tones of pleasure, she said,

"Isn't this the prettiest room you've ever seen?"

•

There was such a quality of completeness and entirety in Eveline that it seemed as though the usual division between gloom and levity, between the serious and the frivolous, hardly existed for her. As a result, I was able to trust her with an absoluteness I had never experienced with anyone before and never would again. Nothing about her was calculated or presumptuous. She might appear plunged into the deepest, darkest, the most difficult and tormenting of thoughts, but if I were to sit down beside her, she would turn to me with her familiar, unpretentiously cheerful and beguiling smile, all trace of gloom and tension gone. I often asked her, at such times, what she had been thinking about before I came up to her. Once she told me that she had been thinking about the train in "Paul's Case." Once she was thinking about the title of Hemingway's "In Another Country," and once about King Lear, specifically Edgar's lines "The worst is not / So long as we can say 'This is the worst.'"

At other times, however, when she looked thoughtful, preoccupied, or even dejected, her head bent over a book in her lap and her brow furrowed, she would turn to me with her smile, and then read out loud what she had been pondering. Once it was Christopher Smart, whom I hadn't heard of before then. Eveline read to me from *Jubilate Agno*:

> *For I will consider my Cat Jeoffry.*
> *For he is the servant of the Living God duly and daily*
> *serving him.*
> *For at the first glance of the glory of God in the East he*
> *worships in his way.*
> *For is this done by wreathing his body seven times round*
> *with elegant quickness.*

For then he leaps up to catch the musk, which is the blessing
*   of God upon his prayer.*
For he rolls upon prank to work it in.
For having gone duty and received blessing he begins to
*   consider himself.*
For this he performs in ten degrees.
For first he looks upon his fore-paws to see if they are clean.
For secondly he kicks up behind to clear away there.
For thirdly he works it upon stretch with the fore paws
*   extended.*
For fourthly he sharpens his paws by wood.
For fifthly he washes himself.
For sixthly he rolls upon wash.
For seventhly he fleas himself, that he may not be interrupted
*   upon the beat.*
For eighthly he rubs himself against a post.
For ninthly he looks up for his instructions.
For tenthly he goes in quest of food.
For having considered God and himself he will consider his
*   neighbor.*
For if he meets another cat he will kiss her in kindness.

And another time it was

The apparition of these faces in the crowd;
Petals on a wet, black bough.

And another

The yellow fog that rubs its back upon the window-panes,
The yellow smoke that rubs its muzzle on the window-panes,
Licked its tongue into the corners of the evening,
Lingered upon the pools that stand in drains,
Let fall upon its back the soot that falls from chimneys,
Slipped by the terrace, made a sudden leap,

And seeing that it was a soft October night,
Curled once about the house, and fell asleep.

I'm certain that even before I'd so much as spoken a word with her—when it was simply a matter of my not being able to keep from staring at her in Old English (I had to look two or three people to the left and two rows to the front to see her), before the day when she asked about my uncle Jakob—I think that even then I had at least some awareness of the equability in her nature, of the balance in it, the quality she had of being experienced without having been hardened—the qualities that gave her a certain dignity even when she was being frivolous and that allowed her to lower herself into deepest gloom without leaving the sunlight behind. I'm certain—I know—that I was drawn to her not only by her physical beauty, but also by the qualities of self-possession and balance in her character and demeanor—the qualities that gave her the ability to laugh without diminution into silliness, and to stare into the deepest blackness without falling pray to paralysis or morbidity. I loved her overwhelmingly, I was captivated by her completely, and I trusted her absolutely. And yet, without question, she was full of surprises. Who else but Eveline would think that the first room to show her new lover should be, of all things, the bathroom? And yet she was right: It *was* one of the nicest, prettiest, most inviting rooms imaginable, even though most people would likely not make it the premiere presentation, if only out of some kind of presumed modesty or deference to custom. For Eveline, though, whatever was, *was*, and therefore should, and would, be taken as such, at least by her. And it was in fact very nice, this bathroom. It was big, almost enormous, and, whether by day or night, it was filled with light, whether from the glow of a number of cunningly arranged electric lamps, or from the flood of daylight coming through its own floor-to-ceiling window. At one end of the room gleamed a massively white claw-foot bathtub with ceramic-and-silver faucets and spigots. At the other stood a ceramic sink on a highly pol-ished and beautifully grained wooden cabinet, alongside a toilet with seat, lid, and overhead tank of the same gleaming wood. On the wide planks of the floor lay a rag rug in bright colors—yellow, green, red, orange, blue, white—as if it were an Impressionist painting on the floor, while at the window hung four voluminous, leafy, and generously spreading house plants, two hanging from middle height and two nearer the top sill, framing the window in greenery.

I saw Eveline for the first time toward the end of autumn 1933, spoke with her not very many days after that, was led by her hand into these rooms near the onset of winter (on December 20th, the day before she left for Fremont), and yet, excepting the intersession break—I didn't move in with her until four months later, at the peak of a particularly prolix and abundant spring, on the fifth of May the following year, 1934, a Saturday.

I associate her with the seasons, perhaps the more so through having lived with her through only one of each. The warmth of autumn, with its soft air and heartbreaking scent of summer's end until the first rains and the dropping of the leaves; the iron-cold grip of monochrome winter; the sweet and aromatic blessings of spring; and the full, rich, sturdy, profligate gener-osity and abundance of summer.

On the night she first took me in to see her rooms, as I said, Eveline and I did nothing not perfectly chaste. It was true. We went very, very slowly in the beginning. But at the same time something enormously powerful was at work, and the bond that came to exist between us—or perhaps it was there from the beginning—and that held us together rested on strong and deep foundations.

I knew it from the start, or at least from the moment I first heard her voice, although even before then I was already infatuated, beguiled simply by my need to continue looking at her face. She was impossible to resist. I don't know what might have happened, what I would have done, if she hadn't spoken to me—about my uncle Jakob—before I'd conjured up a way to speak to her first. The miracle of her existence, not to mention the greater miracle of her willingness to "go" with me—these colored everything, changed everything, transformed every remaining moment of my life. The night she returned from Fremont—she came back early, two days before New Year's Eve—we ate dinner at the Bus Depot Diner and, as usual, I walked her home. And again, the same as on the night before she left, when we stepped up onto the porch, she took my hand and I followed her in through the door, then through the second door and into her rooms. Things this time weren't as chaste as before, although again, somehow, there was a sense between us of there being no reason to hurry, of there being the luxury—however deceptive and cruel this was—of an unending present. Eveline had no davenport, couch, or sofa in the front room, but only the settee I mentioned earlier, and although we did sit on that—the love seat—for a time, in the half-darkness, in a clinging embrace, before long we started for the next room, and the bed, leaving our coats and scarves on the settee, along with the cloche, knit out of bright red yarn, that Eveline wore in cold weather.

She knew far more than I did about how to carry on with things. We lay down on top of the bed, still dressed, until bit by bit a button here gave way to a button there, a kiss here to another there, until finally the room's cold air on expanses of bare skin made going under the covers desirable, and we lay under them for a long time, talking unhurriedly, almost drowsily, about one thing or another, including our bodies, as we touched or stroked them, or tasted, or kissed. "Don't hurry, don't hurry, don't hurry," Eveline whispered very slowly into my ear, and then whispered it again as I started to enter her. She put her hands on my hips and pushed me away, then drew me in again, then away, saying the same words in a very low voice, "Don't hurry, don't hurry, don't hurry." Her body was firm, sturdy, and extremely powerful. Under me, she arched her back suddenly and raised her pelvis so high that I might have been thrown off if I hadn't had my arms wrapped so tightly around her.

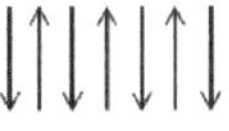

•

From then on, drowning in love and happiness, I ought to have spent every minute in the craven and withering fear that I would be visited again by my translocations and torn away from Eveline and her world, from the security, peace, hope, and pleasure she created and in turn offered to me without reservation.

I *should* have lived in such fear, since that's the very thing that did happen: The translocation returned, suddenly, unexpectedly, brutally—and *finally*. I was wrenched away, absolutely. I never saw, knew, felt, or sensed the existence of Eveline near me again.

And there was something else, something almost as bad, empty, lifeless, and hollow as being torn from her. This was the fact that at the same time I was hurled forward to where I'd begun, into the murderous, bloody, doomed emptiness of 1964.

At that time, Eveline and I were in West Tree, in September, in 1947. So suddenly did the disaster take place that I was allowed not so much as a final lungful of the air from that time, air that still had the scent of promise in it, the scent of past and future joined together.

The air in 1964 was hollow, empty, without aroma—except for a thin scent of blood.

•

If I could have gone back to 1947; if I could still have been with Eveline; if we could have stepped again onto the west lawn of the farmhouse, where the grass was uncut and the elms high—this would be September 15, 1947—a breeze from the southwest stirring Eveline's hair and pressing the back of her skirt against her legs; my father standing, looking down with his scornful, judgmental look; if I could return—even to that doomed moment—I would.

I'd been certain that even my father would be unable to intimidate Eveline. No matter what innuendo, threat, or insinuation of disapproval he might show, Eveline would look up at him and smile with her disarming, beautiful, generous, unsolicited smile.

I was sure that my father would be changed by Eveline, certain that she would temper him, disarm him, appeal to him in such a way as to meliorate his blind egoism, calm his narcissistic rage, dissipate his unholy compulsion to invade and crush others, this father of mine, him, the nation I was born into. I was certain that Eveline would be able to soften his steeled, malevolent heart.

•

Instead, I was bereft of Eveline.

I went with her to 1947. She and I walked onto the lawn of tall grass, smelled the breeze coming sweetly from the southwest. I was certain that Eveline would be able to persuade my father to choose wisdom over greed, selfishness, and ignorance, to persuade him to choose the continuing life of the republic instead of bringing about its death, so that we could alter just that one moment in future history, in 1963, change it just enough so the rifles under the bridge wouldn't be loaded, aimed, fired; the sounds of their reports heard; the assassination committed.

But we failed. And Eveline was no longer there.

And I was no longer there.
Only my father was still there.

•

The nation, cesspool of madness, greed, and egoism that I was born into. My father, cursed by shallowness, ignorance, and grandeur; filled with the seeds of blindness, self-regard, solipsism; my father, who brutalized Eveline before she disappeared forever. My-father-the-nation; the-nation-my-father. The nation that foolishly and willingly, in 1947, set out upon the process of poisoning its own blood; that embarked upon a river of blood; a path that would lead, within the span of my own lifetime, to the republic's collapse and death.

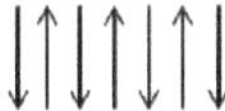

EIGHT

I understood that the world gained meaning, coherence, and order through having Eveline in it.

•

Sometime near three o'clock I woke up, nestled like a spoon against Eveline, her back to my front, each of us on our right side. I waited until I was sure she was not awake and then began to draw myself away through infinitesimal movement after infinitesimal movement in the hope of not disturbing her. We were both naked, and I tried to keep the blankets from following as I moved away so that the cold air wouldn't come in and touch Eveline. I got my right hand out and reached down until it was touching the floor and then began moving my legs. When my left foot touched the floor, I began inching my pelvis toward the edge of the bed, at the same time bunching up the blankets as I slid out from under them and pressing them against the length of Eveline's body, tucking her in. Finally, I was sitting on the floor, my feet ahead of me and knees raised, my weight on spread hands behind me. By this time I was very cold.

My clothes lay puddled on the floor. The light coming in from the street through the front windows was very dim, but it was enough for me to see as I picked up socks, underwear, shirt, pants, being careful not to let my belt buckle make any noise against the floor or bedframe. I tiptoed into the front room, past Eveline's desk, then across to the settee where we had started out. I dressed myself and then pulled on my coat and buttoned it. Eveline's coat and scarf, and her red cloche, were also there, where she had tossed them as we'd gone into the other room. I held her coat up by the shoulders in front of me, pressed it against myself for a moment, then drew the shoulders together and lay it down on the settee, where I folded it into thirds as neatly as I could. I folded the scarf as well, into a neat square, and placed it on the coat. On the scarf I placed the red cloche. Carefully, I moved the whole pile to the center of the settee. Then I went to Eveline's desk, drew out a note card from the stack inside a pigeonhole, and wrote:

Eveline,
May I come back?
I love you with the depth of oceans and in more ways than
there are stars.

I signed my name and then, as an afterthought, added the date:

Dec. 29, 1933

I left the card propped against an ink stand on Eveline's desk. Then I went to the door and let myself out as quietly as I could.

The air outdoors was fresh and extremely cold. It seemed to me unlike any air I had smelled or breathed before. It wasn't that it held traces of pine or hints of woodsmoke, but it was clear and clean and seemed robust when you took it into your lungs or breathed it in through your nose. Freezing and wintry, it smelled of cold, snow, and ice, but it also had another scent so that even inside the brittle, thin, icy smell and taste you couldn't avoid also sensing the most distant hint of sweetness. I walked quickly, the heels of my boots hitting steadily against the cleared sidewalks. The sound was not muffled and yet it was echoless, seeming to have no reverberation. At Dodge Street, I went into the little park, walked diagonally through it, and came out on Washington Street. In my mind, I pictured Eveline in bed, warm and asleep. There was as yet no hint of dawn, no lightness in the sky anywhere, and the streetlights were still brightly lit. As I walked, I began having my first impression of something akin to the earth-shielding tendrils that Eveline was to introduce me to, her brow knit in a way suggesting the seriousness of her vision. As I walked on, it was as if there was a gossamer thread or string unwinding behind me that reached back to Eveline's house, went in through the front door, then in through Eveline's door, then across the first room of her apartment, into the bedroom, and into the bed, where it touched Eveline herself, although I didn't know exactly where, imagining it perhaps on her temple, her cheek, forehead, or shoulder. This thread or tendril lineament was visible to me at certain moments and not at others; if I stopped under a streetlight and turned to look back I was sometimes able to see it, a faint silken line passing from me and disappearing into the darkness, though at other times I wasn't able to see it, while at yet others I was able to see it only if I looked just to the side of where I expected it to be rather than directly at it. The farther I went away from Eveline, the longer it grew, extending between the two of us as I crossed Gilbert Street and then Clinton, then took one of the diagonal walkways across the center of the campus, then past the Old Capitol building, down the hill, across the river, and up the wooded bluff on the west side. I arrived at the north entrance of the Quadrangle, went up the stairs, down the hall, and into my room. I turned on the light and closed the door behind me.

By now the time was close to four and there was still no

sign of daylight. Sunrise wouldn't come until seven-thirty, and not the faintest light would begin gathering in the east before six. The windows of my room were solidly black. I took off my boots and turned off the light. The entire room became dark. I felt for my pillow to make sure it was at the end of the bed away from the windows, then lay down. I closed my eyes and immediately I could see the entirety of the long, diaphanous tendril. It wasn't straight or perfectly linear the way a string would be if pulled tight from each end, but, instead, it moved slightly, undulating slowly here and there, almost as if it were under water, where currents were pressing it one way and another. Again, the entire length of it was visible to me and, as it went down the bluff on my side of the river crossed over the water, rose up again to the height of the central campus lawns and the Old Capitol building, followed Washington Street to the small park, where it went diagonally to College Street and extended from there to the old house, onto the porch, through the front door, then through Eveline's door, across her front room, into the bedroom, and to Eveline herself—who by some extraordinary fact or force I could actually *see*: On the bed, under the covers, on her right side, just as she had been when I left her. Then, however, I opened my eyes, and as I did so, every bit of the vision disappeared and I was left with only the darkness of my room. In a panic, I immediately closed them again—but saw nothing. I opened them, closed, opened, closed, all with no success—until finally I became able, with eyes closed, to see one length or another of the entire tendril— the part crossing the river, or the part going through the small park—but not the whole thing again no matter how hard I tried, and never the segment that let me see Eveline.

I gave up. I pulled a blanket over myself, turned onto my right side, and slept.

•

Loving in truth, and fain in verse my love to show,
That she, dear she, might take some pleasure of my pain,—
Pleasure might cause her read, reading might make her know,
Knowledge might pity win, and pity grace obtain,—

•

That was on the Friday of Eveline's return from Fremont, when we made love for the first time. She had come back two days early rather than, as originally planned, staying in Nebraska through New Year's and returning to Iowa on the second of January. This way, the day after our first love-making was Saturday, and the next day was New Year's Eve.

By this time it seemed as if my whole life was made up of Eveline, her presence, her scent, the feel of her, the sound of her voice, the things she said, the things we talked about. Even when we were apart, her absence was so intense as to be a kind of presence, filling everything.

I was madly, desperately in love with Eveline, who inspired in me a great awe.

It was more than the simple fact of her being two years my senior that made me feel deferential toward her in the way I did. Much more. It had to do also with her family, with the geographical place she came from, with her history and background, with her being named for the infant sister who was lost, with her being the only girl among six siblings, and, for that matter, with the fact of her being the youngest of them all. And then losing her own mother when she—Eveline—was only ten, being left alone with her father and all those brothers. I have often tried to imagine the degree of her self-sufficiency, as I have tried to imagine many other things about her life— after all, what can I possibly know about her, really, about all those days and years before I met her? I know only the things she told me. I know that after her mother died she made almost daily trips to the public library and gained an even wider reputation than she already had for being a "book worm." I know that at the beginning of senior year her English teacher, Hermione Clark, drew her aside and explained that, because she was so far ahead of the other students, she should, instead of coming to class, use that hour each day to go to the school library and continue her own reading, then meet privately once a week to discuss what she had read. Hermione Clark was the one who insisted that Eveline should—must—consider college, something never before done or heard of in the Stahl family. But in September of 1926, when she was seventeen, Eveline entered the university of Nebraska and in early June three years later—she was exempted from a number of classes and also enrolled in every summer session—graduated with a bachelor's degree. Then came what I think of as Eveline's sojourn in the wilderness. She owed her father money, and for two years she worked as a high school English teacher in the distant, flat, open, far-western end of the state, in Alliance, Nebraska.

•

Macbeth. The Mill on the Floss. "The Lady of Shalott." A Midsummer Night's Dream. A Lost Lady. "My Last Duchess." The Red Badge of Courage. Tess of the d'Urbervilles. "Break, break, break." "La Belle Dame sans Merci." "The Darkling Thrush." My Ántonia. . . .

•

Then, encouraged by Hermione Clark, and with the approval of her father and her brothers, Eveline Stahl traveled to Iowa City to begin graduate work in literature. Her first enrollment at the University was in June of 1931, at the start of that year's summer session.

I myself saw her for the first time on the morning of November 27, 1933. I *met* her, and heard her voice, two weeks later, when she asked about my great-uncle Jakob.

November 27, 1933, began, for me, as November 25, 1963. As I was walking to class that morning, the day became November 27, 1933.

And inside that day, where I would find her, was Eveline.

NINE

One of Eveline's friends I especially liked was Ed LaRouche, a graduate student in hydraulic engineering. He was a pleasantly friendly, modestly prepossessing fellow who lived with his wife Audrey in the remodeled attic of a house on East Jefferson, right across the street from the center of the campus. I think what Ed most wanted was to become a jazz drummer. In spite of his clear love for the music, however, I'm doubtful as to whether he ever realized that wish.

But of course I don't know.

I mention him because he and Audrey had invited Eveline over for New Year's Eve—*if* she were going to be in town. And as it turned out, thanks to her early return from Fremont, she was. So she asked Audrey if I could come along too.

A third couple was there as well, a young and very witty assistant professor (and poet) named Paul Evans and his tall and very beautiful wife, who was Austrian (he had met her in England, at Cambridge) and whose name was Roswithe, pronounced Rose-VEE-ta.

I was the youngest person there, quite obviously, but no one seemed to think anything of it. Better yet, Eveline and I were accepted by the others as being a couple ourselves.

The gathering started at nine or so. There was gin, and also wine—alcohol was legal again—and Audrey and Ed had gotten champagne for toasts at midnight. There were bits of things to eat—anchovies and smoked oysters from tins, melba toast to put them on, cheddar cheese cut into small cubes to be lifted up with toothpicks—and conversation grew easier as drinks took effect. There was even some parlor game lightness—people taking turns reciting the opening lines of novels to see if others could name the source, like—

It is a trite but true observation, that examples work more forcibly on the mind than precepts

or

One may as well begin with Helen's letters to her sister

or

Whether I shall turn out to be the hero of my own life, or whether that station will be held by anybody else, these pages must show

or

The family of Dashwood had been long settled in Sussex

—and doing some of the same with lines of poetry, although by that time people were growing less interested in the game and attention had begun to flag.

The LaRouches' apartment was small but also warm and snug, up under the rafters where the ceilings slanted inward. The weather was bitterly cold, and the twin windows that filled the front wall became frosted over more and more completely as the evening drew on. Those windows looked across Jefferson Street right at the old Meredith Hall, odd man out (I didn't mention it before) of the five buildings in the central rectangle of the campus. Not only was it the smallest structure of the five but also the only one of brick instead of more durable quarried stone. As it happened, beginning the next semester, at the end of January, Eveline and I would take Godfrey's *Beowulf* there, going up a creaky staircase to the second-floor and into a room with its own creaky floors. I knew, secretly, that thirty-one years later the building would be gone without a trace, but I said nothing to anyone, not even Eveline, and I myself didn't much want to think about it either.

Ed and Audrey had a small but comfortable sofa and also two compact easy chairs arranged in the front room of their apartment. The sofa stood perpendicular to the front windows. I sat at the window end with Eveline next to me, making me indescribably contented for so long as she and I could remain there, just as we were. Audrey first, and then Ed, were so hospitable as to refresh drinks for us, so it was hardly necessary to leave our seats. I still believe that that night, on that occasion, in that apartment, being there with Eveline, may have been the most perfect night of my life, ever, either before or since. Ed had a collection of Louis Armstrong's Hot Fives and also some of the Hot Sevens, as well as a very small number of Bix Beiderbecke disks. Around eleven o'clock he opened his wind-up Victrola and began playing one record after another—"Muskrat Ramble," "Heebie Jeebies," "Cornet Chop Suey," "Struttin' With Some Barbecue," and then some Beiderbeckes, "Jazz Me Blues," "At the Jazz Band Ball," and the ineluctably beautiful "Davenport Blues." The volume was set low but the rhythm was powerfully infectious, and Ed and Audrey, and then also Paul and Roswithe, began dancing in the tiny floor space available in the little apartment. There was really not enough room for three couples, and, besides, I much more wanted to sit beside Eveline on the sofa than get up and dance. I put my arm around her as if to ask what she would choose, and she leaned her head over onto my shoulder as if to say that staying where we were was best. I never said anything to Ed or anyone else—except Eveline, later on—about my already having listened to all the tunes he played that night. But my own father—whether he was in Iowa City at this very minute or not, I couldn't be certain, but doubted it—loved the same music and collected the first recordings of it, recordings that I then, as a young teen-ager, in 1957, 1958, 1959, listened to over and over again, so long as there was no one else in the house to hear me doing it, since my father's weird disapproval of my taking such pleasure in the music was perversely intense. But this night, in Ed and Audrey's apartment; with the frost thickening on the windows; with the building across the street that would be gone when I first—so much later—arrived in Iowa City; with Eveline beside me on the sofa; with the sounds of the music; with the effects of the gin we were drinking—I think this may have been, as I said, one of the most memorable and treasurable moments in all of my life.

I remember that when midnight came around, it seemed, really, like a moment more soothing and calming than any-thing else. Everyone had a glass, or two, or two and a half, of champagne. Everyone toasted to the New Year, and to each other, and to a handful of things or events or achievements that one person or another wished would come about or be realized successfully in the coming year. But instead of noise-makers, balloons, or confetti—no one had any of these—a kind of relaxed or even meditative atmosphere settled in. The danc-ing came to an end and everyone found a place to sit down, on the sofa, on a chair, even on the floor. I switched back to gin, and so did Eveline. I got up from the sofa and in the tiny kitchen made two new drinks, then came back and reclaimed my cherished spot next to Eveline. Amiable conversation ram-bled on as Ed continued putting one disk after another on the gramophone, which he had muted somehow, keeping the sound even lower than before and in the background. There was talk about how Paul and Roswithe had met, and where she came from in Austria (Salzburg), what Eveline's high school teaching in far western Nebraska had been like, and even, directed toward me, what kind of town West Tree was, with its two colleges, and what had drawn me to come to Iowa City. I made answers the way I always did, by tiny deceptions and inoffensive white lies—Eveline was the only person who, eventually, would know the whole truth—and in this way what remained of the evening went on. I'd had a fair bit to drink, true enough, but what happened to me, I'm absolutely certain, had nothing to do with alcohol, and everything to do with Eveline.

•

The little apartment stayed warm in spite of the arctic night outdoors. Audrey and Ed's sofa, as I said, stood at a right angle to the windows. Facing it across the room were a rocking chair and a small upholstered chair, the two separated by a tiny wooden table. On the floor lay a braided rug, cheerfully colored.

Sitting nearest the windows, from time to time I extended my arm and held a finger against the glass until it melted a small hole through the frost.

Eveline was on my left, where she leaned comfortably against me.

On Eveline's left were Paul and Roswithe Evans.

Across from us, Audrey sat in the upholstered chair, her legs crossed, while Ed sat perched forward on the rocker with his elbows resting on his knees. On the floor was a stack of 78's he hadn't yet played and another stack of those that he had. While one of the sides was playing, it was almost as if Ed were off in his own world, his eyes mostly closed and some part of his body or other moving with the rhythm, maybe a heel, or a toe, a tapping hand or finger, or sometimes his head nodding to the tempo. When a tune ended, he would open his eyes, lift the needle and put it to the side, then lift up the disk and lay it on the played pile, take a new one, center it on the stubby spindle, and set the needle down on the lead-in thread.

I imitated Ed by beginning to close my own eyes when one of the sides was playing, and I began to see something similar to two nights before, when I saw the tendril connecting me with Eveline from all the way across town. This time, she was here beside me, we were together and stationary, neither of us going anywhere. We were both right *there*, centered under the high black dome of winter sky overhead, in the center of Iowa City, snug in this attic apartment—centered within this center: Inside the town, inside the music, inside the conversation, inside the surrounding company of the others.

"Gut Bucket Blues." "He Likes It Slow." "The King of the Zulus." "Big Butter and Egg Man." "Potato Head Blues." "Alligator Crawl." "Oriental Strut." "That's When I'll. . ."

Listening to the music, the voices in the room, my arm around Eveline—I don't know how much time went by before I began seeing a number of unusual things. They came haltingly at first, but then quite clearly and steadily; I was able to see them even though they were outside what would normally be my line of sight. Here we were in the attic, protected by its walls and roof, protected also by the walls and structures of the floors below us, and yet at the same time it was as though the entire house became at one and the same time material and immaterial, so that it continued to protect us but at the same time became transparent, so that I could look out through it and into the velvet blackness of the night sky. And what I saw there were shapes and patterns that changed and grew as I watched them, these being formed out of tendrils, strings, fibers, and even out of very delicate lines that could have been drawn outward with pencil and straightedge. I say "outward" because all of these fibers, lines, or strings originated from a place between Eveline and me, where our bodies were pressed one against the other, and they radiated outward from there in every direction, to every point of the compass, and to greater and greater distances, until they reached the rim of the horizon. The night was like black velvet. All of the fibers, lines, strings, and shapes, however, had the same unusual quality that the long tendril of two nights earlier had had—the quality of being visible, even in complete darkness, or of being visible at some moments and not at others, or even of exuding a very faint blue or green luminescence that might be ongoing and steady as often as it was evanescent.

In addition to the tendrils and lines radiating outward, concentric circles originated from the same point, expanding as they moved gradually outward to the horizon, where they disappeared from view, to be followed by others, expanding in the same way, moving outward so far that they finally disappeared.

•

"Wild Man Blues." "Twelfth Street Rag." "Once in a While." "Come Back Sweet Papa." "Big Fat Ma and Skinny Pa." "You Made Me Love You." "Sunset Cafe S. . ."

TEN

That night, or I should say morning, the first day of 1934, marked the beginning of my intensive course of study in tendrils. In this course, I was the student, or perhaps I should say the novitiate. Eveline was the guide. And, not always, but for much the better part, Eveline's bed was our classroom.

I fell in love with Eveline for what seemed countless reasons: Her disarming candor and her plain charm (there *is* such a thing), her smile, the sound of her voice, her appearance, the way that, in appearance, she was somewhere between pretty and beautiful and therefore without the drawbacks of either—"*May she be granted beauty, and yet not / Beauty to make a stranger's eye distraught, / Or hers before a looking glass*"—I fell in love with her for these reasons and many others, but I had no idea, when I first fell in love with her so entirely, of the reach, depth, range, and quickness of her mind.

The things I'd seen, the tendrils, lines, fibers, and circles, may have seemed perfectly sane and normal during the time I was actually seeing them, but afterward, when I thought about them on our walk home, I found myself hesitant to mention them—even to Eveline—fearful of seeming hallucinatory, off kilter, maybe even a bit mad. But then, with Eveline in her bed an hour or so after we'd gotten back from the Hot Fives party—an hour of under-the-covers love-making in the chilly house—I told Eveline, not in a whisper but in a low voice, into her ear, that the other day, when I left the note on her desk before walking back to the Quadrangle, I had seen a tendril, as if it were being drawn out behind me, connecting the two of us.

We were lying face to face, arms around one another, and I felt her pull me closer in response. She said,

"I know."

I had no idea what she meant and said so.

"Sweetheart. I know about it. I saw it too. So of course I knew it was there."

Again, her arms tightened around me.

"But you were sleeping," I said.

"Yes. I fell back asleep after you left."

"After I left? So you heard me leave?"

"I watched you get dressed and then write the note and then come back over to the bed to see if my eyes were closed."

"And *then* you fell back asleep? After I went out and closed the door?"

"Yes."

"But how could you see the tendril then?"

"Oh, dear Malcolm," she said, laughing lightly. "There are things a person can see without using their eyes."

"I used mine," I told her. "It got very, very long."

She laughed lightly again, stirred in the bed, and reached down. "Yes," she answered. "And *this* has gotten very, very long, too." The rest of the conversation waited for morning.

•

In the morning Eveline and I went over to John's Grocery for breakfast instead of down to the Bus Depot Diner. We could also have made something at Eveline's place and eaten there. She had eggs, coffee, bread, milk. Eveline, by the way, was a very good cook—in her high school years, at home with all those brothers, she often prepared the day's main meal, although the family also had kitchen help.

The front part of John's was the grocery store while the rear made up the diner, with ten or twelve tables of various sizes. There was no counter. Eveline and I went to a table for two in one of the back corners, where being against the wall, instead of out in the middle of the floor, made it feel cozy and snug. We had coffee, eggs, bacon, and toast—Eveline's eggs scrambled, mine over easy—and afterward we lingered over a second coffee.

Breakfast that morning was a powerfully important turning point for me. If my course of study in tendrils had been initiated the night before—by Eveline, who'd as much as said she could see without eyes—it had still amounted only to the slightest crack of the door for me. Now that door was about to be flung open wide.

John's was popular but hardly fancy or chic, and even though the place appeared to be doing a fairly brisk business, there was no line of people waiting, and there were even a couple of free tables. No one seemed to take any notice of Eveline and me staying longer than a second cup of coffee's worth of time, or to take notice for that matter of the way we ended up sitting—both leaning forward, elbows on the table, foreheads touching, my own hands cupping Eveline's elbows, and her hands, raised to my temples, pressing there gently but also very steadily, and quite firmly.

In fact, I don't think anyone took any notice of us at all, there in our corner, but if they had, I'm sure they would have wondered what was going on: This extremely attractive young woman focused *so* intently on giving—*what?*—solace, comfort, reassurance, some kind of help for pain to the young man whose head she was holding in her own hands and whose forehead she was touching with her own.

Pleading, they would have thought. She's *begging* with him about something that has happened.

•

Thinking about things, I'd suddenly gotten scared. I'd suddenly gotten badly shaken. *That's* the thing that had happened. I'd asked Eveline how anyone could see without using his or her eyes, and she had begun describing to me, for the first time, the tendrils wrapping the earth, along with the remarkable idea that they came into existence because of *reading*, and—in a word—she frightened me. For a moment I felt vertiginous and couldn't quite draw a breath. It was as though I had been metaphorically stabbed by the sudden fear that Eveline might be crazy. Might be a witch, say. Or an enchantress.

That's what had happened.

•

"But, Malcolm," she said as she placed her elbows on the table and leaned toward me. "You've seen them yourself, or variations of them. What about the long tendril? You told *me* about that before I told you."

And then suddenly, as if someone had flipped a switch, the fear shifted over to myself. Maybe *I* was the crazy one, delusional, having visions. And that was the moment when I extended my own arms across the table, grasped Eveline's elbows, and leaned forward until our foreheads were actually touching.

"Malcolm," she whispered urgently. "*Relax.*"

I shut my eyes. "And I haven't even told you about the things I saw over at Ed and Audrey's. Why didn't *they* scare me? Why wasn't I *afraid?*"

"Yes, the lines and strings," Eveline said. "The concentric circles expanding outward."

She pressed her hands more tightly against the sides of my head.

"I saw them too, you know. It wasn't just you."

I said nothing. I didn't move. I didn't dare move. I clenched my eyes shut more tightly. For a second or two I felt as though I were falling.

In an intense whisper, Eveline said, "It was very, very nice sitting there together, you and me, wasn't it." She pressed her hands even more tightly against my temples.

Her hands felt reassuring, cool, lovely, wonderful. The same was true of the sound of her voice: Low, earnest, reassuring, beautiful.

But I had been seized in a short, tight, sharply down-plunging spiral of panicky fear. After all, why hadn't it even occurred to me to be *frightened* when I had seen my "visions," first the long tendril, and then the shapes and patterns? Was I crazy, or half crazy, or had I been beguiled into taking things as natural that are in fact anything *but* natural? Had I lost my sense of what's real and not real, so that I couldn't tell the difference any more? How had such a thing happened, or who could have done such a thing to me? Did it go all the way back to my experience of the two telephones outside the concierge's office? *That* had been frightening. And, even if it did go back that far, the question remained of who arranged to make that first disorientation happen to me, the disorientation of the telephones. There had to have been *someone* bringing such things about, *someone* deciding that I should be translocated between the two planes of time, back and forth, and then, even more important, *someone* who arranged that I shouldn't go back and forth any more but instead should stay inside the plane three decades earlier than my own, the plane where my uncle Jakob was teaching Middle English, where Eveline Stahl was his only female student, where Eveline and I would be enrolled in the same section of Old English, and where one day she would ask me whether my last name was the same as his, and I would say yes, that Jakob was my great-uncle, and I would hear her short, light, trilling laugh, see it followed by the very pretty smile, and from that moment on find myself unable to keep from looking at her, beguiled by everything about her, her face, lips, eyes, clothing, hands, slender wrists, the shapes taken by the curls of her dark-brown hair, the way she sat down, crossed her legs, held a fountain pen, opened a notebook, tilted her head, suggesting neither inadequacy nor superiority, and the confident, quiet, alluring sound of her voice whenever it was her turn to recite, her pronunciation and accent invariably poised, effortless, and perfect, and her obligatory translation into modern English unfailingly colloquial, idiomatic, natural.

I knew perfectly well that there were plenty of fervently interested suitors of Eveline, and I could only guess how many *hidden* admirers she must have had—this alluring, attractive, slightly mysterious, unaffected, demonstrably brilliant young woman from somewhere only half known, far away, in the western plains.

And so the question, the question that should have occurred to me well before now, certainly before I'd allowed myself to be tripped up and unmanned by fear—the question that begged for an answer: Did *Eveline* choose *me*? And if so, what did she choose me *for*?

Still holding on to her elbows, my own forehead still touching hers, I tried to get words out in order to ask these questions, but I couldn't get beyond her name before my throat tightened and stopped me.

"Eveline. . ."

I realized that I was trembling faintly, as though from cold.

Gently, Eveline drew her hands away from my temples. She lifted her elbows from the surface of the table, found my own hands with hers and pressed them warmly.

She looked me in the eye. "*Let's go home*," she whispered.

ELEVEN

Classes were scheduled to start again two days after that, on Wednesday, the third of January. But they would continue for only a week, the length of time needed to finish up the interrupted fall semester. Then would come "dead day," the day set aside as study time before the beginning of final exams. Then, after finals, there would be three weeks of intersession before the start of the spring term.

And it—all of it—would be over and done with so quickly that, even now, six—nine—decades later, when I think back on it, I find myself being drawn toward grief at the sense of loss, the yearning to have it back.

•

That day, the first of the year, must have been the most intense day—the most intense day of *learning*—in my entire time with Eveline.

On our walk back from John's Grocery, Eveline behaved with an unusual degree of affection. In general, when we were outdoors together, especially in the daytime, we tended to be quite circumspect. It was as if a kind of shared but unspoken agreement had arisen between us that we wouldn't hold hands when we were walking along in the presence of other people, and certainly we wouldn't embrace, fondle, or kiss one another in public. Yet now, as soon as we had gone down the two wooden steps outside John's front door, Eveline felt for my hand and took it. And then went on holding it. Not only that, but twice on the way back to College Street she came to a stop, turned toward me, and offered an embrace and a kiss. After the first of these times, she buried her face against the front of my coat, her arms around me, and murmured,

"Please. Please."

Then, as we continued walking, she took on a kind of matter-of-fact and efficient tone, describing exactly what she thought we should do once we got "home," a word that thrilled me whenever I heard her use it in a way that included me in it. What we should do, she said, since we obviously had so, so much to talk about, is go into the kitchen, where she would make some hot tea, where the two of us would sit at the table by the kitchen window, and where, however long it might take us, we would set about talking everything through.

And we did.

Eveline's kitchen was large and yet also comfortable, in fact cozy and warm. It was also well-lighted, thanks to its twin-paned window that reached from near the floor almost up to the ceiling. As she had said she would, Eveline filled the water kettle, set it on the range and struck a wooden match to light the gas ring under it. She filled a tea ball, screwed its top back on, and dropped it into a teapot, which she then filled with the hot water once it was up to a boil. She told me which cupboard to open, and I carried two cups and two saucers and put them down at opposite ends of the table, along with two spoons and two napkins. Across the room, Eveline cut a lemon into wedges and put the pieces on a saucer, which she then carried over, also, to the table. After she set down the lemon wedges, she picked up the cup, saucer, spoon, and napkin from the far end of the table, where I'd set them, and moved them instead so that the settings were both at the same corner and much closer to one another. When the kettle whistled, Eveline filled the teapot, replaced its ceramic top, brought it over to the table and set it down on the trivet that was waiting there. She then went back across the room to a canister that stood on one of the worktops, unscrewed its lid, removed half a dozen or so ginger snaps and put them on yet another saucer, which she carried over and set down on the table. Then we both sat down and waited for the tea to steep.

Like she had done at John's, Eveline leaned slightly forward and put her elbows on the table. This time, though, she didn't reach her hands out toward me, but instead she clasped them together and used them for a chin-rest.

She glanced over at me, then looked away again, and said,

"I scared the living daylights out of you. I'm sorry."

It was all I could do to keep from reaching over to her. All I really wanted was to touch her.

"Eveline." I said her name aloud, and then I repeated it, as if the saying of her name could somehow, in any conceivable way, soften or obscure the absurdity of what I was about to ask her.

"Eveline," I said. "Are you *magic*?"

I could see, behind her clasped hands, that she smiled. But then, immediately, she forced the smile away. She shook her head slightly.

"No. Not really."

"Not really."

"Well. . . " One hand moved away from her lips and came toward me, but then she drew it back and clasped it again with the other.

She wanted to touch me as much as I wanted to touch her.

"Are you controlling me, Eveline?"

She whipped her face toward mine. There was a puzzled

look on it, and some anger.

"No. What do you mean?"

"Did *you* arrange it so I saw the telephones the way I saw them?" This time she turned toward me with a look of complete confusion. She looked at me as if I were crazy.

"*Telephones?*" she said.

I was so moved that I started to reach my own hand out to her the way she had done toward me. But then I took it back.

"I'm sorry, Eveline. Forgive me. Please forgive me. I'll explain everything. It's a long story." I saw that I was going to have to tell Eveline in complete detail everything that had happened to me since I'd arrived in Iowa City—and everything that had happened to me *before* I came there.

I was going to have to tell her about my father and how he stole history and then destroyed it. I was going to have to tell her about the president's assassination and what I was certain it was going to bring about. I would have to tell her about the protective eggshell over Iowa City.

"But you *do* see the same things I see. Like the long tendril. And the circles."

Now she wouldn't look at me.

"Anyone can do that," she said in an unusually low voice, "if they want to and if they try hard enough."

"But why see them with me?" I asked.

She still wouldn't look at me but only straight ahead and slightly downward. She had raised her hands now to her temples and appeared to be pressing on them with the flats of her fingers.

"I mean why did you choose *me*?"

Now she turned toward me. She was crying, tears coming but no sobs.

"Because I like you," she blurted out in something almost like a low scream. "*I like you madly.*"

And then, right along with her crying and her wet face, she began to laugh at what she'd said. As for me, I think my heart stopped for a second, with the strength of feeling that went through it, making me feel my own equivalent of crying and laughing at the same time. It was no longer possible for either of us to go on sitting primly, getting on with our conversation "to talk everything through." I pushed my chair back and stood up and stepped over to Eveline. I put my arms around her from behind and kissed the top of her head, burying my face in her hair. Then I pulled her chair back from the table, leaned down to find her elbows, and drew her up. She came up to her feet easily and turned to me. We clung to one another, and clung, and clung. We went ahead and let the tea grow cold.

Eveline took me by the hand and drew me through the doorway out of the kitchen and into the bedroom. By this time it was after four o'clock and the winter dusk was beginning to gather. There were pull shades in the windows of the front room and bedroom, and when Eveline began pulling them down in the front room I helped by doing the same in the bed-room. Eveline then switched on her goose-neck desk lamp and also the small shaded lamp that sat on one of the tables beside the bed. There was no radiator in the kitchen, but Eveline lift-ed the radiator cover in the front room and turned the valve to the fully open position, then did the same in the bedroom. After all of this was done, Eveline opened up the bed and then, before getting in, we began undressing one another.

•

As the year went on, I was to learn steadily more about Eve-line's lack of inhibition in love-making. But about her propen-sity for talk afterward—plentiful talk, significant talk—I knew everything from the start.

It was almost eight o'clock by the time we both realized how hungry we were and got up, dressed, and walked down to the Bus Depot Diner (holding hands, by the way). Eveline's bed, as I think I mentioned, was neither single nor double but closer to a three-quarter size, and, although it lacked any headboard, it was pushed up perpendicularly against the wall so as to allow pillows to be piled up for people to recline against if they chose. And we did. There were times when we lay flat on our sides, facing one another, arms intertwined—at which time whispers or near-whispers were sufficient for almost any kind or length of conversation. On the other hand, we sometimes sat up with our backs against the wall, quite regally, perhaps with mugs of tea while talking in normal voices. After the tea—empty mugs set aside on either of the small tables flanking the bed—it was common enough for us to begin sliding downward, back into the bed, sometimes even for the purpose of sleep.

I think now of that late afternoon and early evening of January 1, 1934—when daylight faded and darkness pressed in around the old house, and while Eveline and I lay together, window shades drawn, with no light other than the glow from small lamps in two different rooms—I think of that night as the real beginning of our bonded lives together. After that night, there could be no going back; we were as close to having been pressed together into one as it was possible to imagine. Eveline explained more exactly what she'd meant by saying she'd seen the same things I had seen, the tendril, then the lines and circles moving outward from Ed and Audrey's apartment. She had seen such things herself, countless times and at certain moments, under certain conditions, at times of feeling certain—almost always powerful—emotions. As for the long tendril, she "saw" it because she had *seen* it, literally, before, on different occasions, under different circumstances. You could almost say, she told me, that something like the tendril was half imaginary and half real, as are many things in the world, and, as with those many things, at certain times the imaginary element, aspect, or energy of it leaps up into the level of the real, and at those times you not only "see" it, with your heart and mind, but you also *see* it, with your eyes. At such times, when something like this takes place, a person doesn't want *anything to change*, since the phenomenon that's occurring wouldn't be occurring in the first place unless things both inside and outside—of that person—were themselves either perfect or close enough to perfect to seem so. Pressing against me, Eveline spoke in a low, steady, and quiet voice into my ear—the wonderfully scratchy hair between her legs pressed against my thigh, her breasts flattened against my chest, her fingers trailing lazily through my own pubic hair—and told me, again, how wonderful and nice it had been sitting together on the couch at Audrey's place, with no need whatsoever to move or get up or go anywhere or do anything else, listening to the conversation—adding to it now and then—and listening to the Hot Fives, sipping our drinks, waiting for midnight to come around—these were conditions like those at other times when she herself had seen the lines and fibers moving outward from what at such a moment felt like the center of the universe—perhaps *was* the center of the universe, for that moment—and had seen the concentric circles moving outward across the lines: So vivid was her memory of having seen them at other times that she *knew* that I was now seeing them—and in fact, in a sense, she herself therefore "saw" them, even if only through association and memory and therefore wasn't lying when she had told me that she knew what I had seen because she had seen the same thing as well.

She didn't ever want to lie, she told me. She despised lying. Nothing in the world was worse or more unforgiveable than a lie. She gave a small laugh and I felt her arms pull more tightly around me. She went on, saying that when, earlier today, in the kitchen, at the table, she had said that she "liked me madly," it was because she hadn't wanted to lie. She hadn't wanted to say anything that wasn't the absolute truth. And so—she pressed her face into the side of my neck—she had said "I like you madly." I lifted myself up and turned onto my right side, facing her, and, with my arms around her, pulled her tightly to me.

•

A good number of students had begun returning to campus, although the following day would see the real rush. Even so, although it wasn't crowded, the diner had more customers than normal over the break. Instead of taking our usual table by the front window, Eveline and I went to a booth in the far back corner, near the swinging door into the bus depot. The booths in the diner were not large and had fairly high backs, so they gave a feeling of coziness and intimacy. We each ordered a hamburger and a bottle of beer, and while we waited for the hamburgers to come I told Eveline more about the long tendril, the way it began to disappear when I looked directly at it, and how it would reappear, but only if I took care not to look directly at it, and how even then only one segment or another would reappear at a time, and never the whole.

We were holding hands across the table. Eveline gave my hands a light squeeze.

"That's because it comes out of both spirit and matter," she said. "The two have to be in balance, and if one of them gets the upper hand, the tendril disappears. It's the same way as with reading. The balance is essential. But with the earth-tendrils that come from reading—well, those you can *never* see. They're always beyond sight. But they're invaluable. And they're *strong*." With the last word, she gave my hands a very tight squeeze and made a comical grimace with her face, her teeth bared.

I was certain that at that moment I loved her more than ever, if that was possible. And yet at the same time I didn't have the foggiest idea of what she was talking about—and said so.

She leaned forward over the table and curled her index finger at me in the "come here" gesture, so I leaned forward too. Into my right ear Eveline whispered,

"I'll teach you. I'll teach you *everything I know*."

I reached my hand across the table to the back of her head

and touched her hair, then drew her toward me, and, forming a kind of bridge over the table, we kissed on the lips.

Of course it was just then, both of us with our eyes closed, that the waiter came over with our order.

"Should I come back later?" he asked.

"Oh, no. Now is fine," I said. The waiter set down our hamburgers and we thanked him and each of us ordered one more beer. After we'd begun eating, Eveline took out one of the note cards she carried with her and wrote something on it, then turned the card face down and pushed it over to my side of the table. I turned it over and read:

After we're done eating, <u>let's go home</u>.

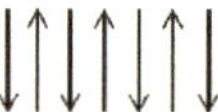

Eveline's earliest conscious awareness of the tendrils began to emerge when she was ten years old, in 1919, following her mother's death that year. Eveline was in fifth grade at the time her mother died, and the young girl's bereavement took the form of her developing an even greater affection for going to school, and for the things she found there, than she had had before. In the fifth-grade classroom she found warmth, light, purposefulness, and security. These were things that she had also sensed in the classrooms of her previous school years, but her mother's sudden death—her mother had been her usual self at bedtime but in the morning was gone—had created in the girl new and heightened senses of precariousness, vulnerability, loneliness, sorrow, danger, and fear both of abandonment and of death.

She had always been good at reading, but now she began to read avidly. An additional pleasure of the classroom was the abundance of books it held, and in addition to its own books, there were also those in the school library. Once each week, the teacher escorted her charges to the library for an entire class period. This was a special pleasure for Eveline, who each week checked out the maximum number of books allowed. It was toward the end of her fifth grade year that others began awarding her the sobriquet "the bookworm." It was not so much that Eveline *read* books, but it was almost as though she inhaled them, absorbed them, ingested them.

The classmates and friends who thought this way about Eveline, or talked this way, were, in fact, unbeknownst to themselves, quite close to the mark. No book that Eveline read failed to become a part of herself. And there was never a time when Eveline failed to leave a part of herself in any book she read.

Her mother had died toward the end of January, so there was a good share of the fifth grade school year left after her death. But days and weeks move quickly, months even more so, and school came to an end much sooner than Eveline could be prepared for. Three months of summer meant that she would be alone a goodly amount of the time. Her father would be at work and her brothers would have jobs. Eveline had friends, of course, although much of the time it seemed that they found Eveline more interesting than Eveline found them. There was the cook/housekeeper, but she and Eveline had little in common, and Eveline found the older woman no substitute for her mother.

So it came about that in June of 1919 Eveline Stahl, age ten, began making regular trips from her family's home to the Fremont Public Library and back. She averaged at least one trip a week, and she often made two in a single week. At this time in her life she made the trip only during daylight, setting out from the front porch of 410 East 12th Street, turning right onto East 12th and walking four blocks to North Broad Street, where she would turn left and go another block and a half, ending at 1030 North Broad Street and the Fremont Carnegie Library.

Borrowers were allowed up to four books at a time, and so

that was the number Eveline checked out at each of her visits. By the end of the summer, when school started up again, she had borrowed, read, and returned forty-nine books. As sixth grade continued, however, she began finding that the offerings in the school's own library were too limited for her, or insufficiently challenging, or books, simply, that she had already read. And so even during the school year, she continued making trips to the Carnegie library, although not as frequently as during the summer. The following year, however, her seventh grade year, brought with it change of a kind beneficial to Eveline. Fremont's educational planners had long before established that grade school was to consist of students' initial six years of study and high school of their second six. This meant that in starting seventh grade and entering "junior" high school, Eveline not only went to an entirely new—and considerably larger—building, but to a building with a considerably larger—and more mature—library.

During her first year in the larger school, and with access to its larger library, Eveline continued reading assiduously—and also continued, on occasion, making trips to the Carnegie library. By the time she reached eighth grade, however, a small number of seemingly minor changes began to take place in her behavior. One of these was that instead of going home at the end of the school day, she would almost as often go instead to the Carnegie library, where, at one of the tables in her favorite room, she would do whatever homework she might have been assigned that day and then turn to her own reading. Another change, more significant than it might seem, was that she would often remain there until after dark. The library closed at eight each evening, and for a large part of the year—the summer months being the exception—that meant darkness would have fallen by the time Eveline, at closing, set out for home.

Eveline—then as now—remained a mystery to most of those who knew her. Even as a girl of thirteen or fourteen, in eighth or ninth grade, she impressed people as oddly contradictory in character. In the company of others, whether adults or young people, she was known for being cheerful and friendly, at ease in conversation, invariably polite, unpretentious, for having a ready and pleasantly melodic laugh, and for being really very, very pretty. At the same time, however, there were things about her that made her seem to others at best unusual or, at worst, unnatural. There was, of course, her reading. Few people—or none—understood how a young girl could possibly be interested in reading to the degree that Eveline was. She was friendly, yes, but at the same time she never sought out friends, or made an effort to find them, or showed any interest, socially, in being a member of one kind of group or another. She was friendly enough, and, yes, she was seemingly normal enough, and yet at the same time she was so very—so terribly—*serious*.

Her classroom teachers quickly noted this trait in her, of course. And they also noted an additional trait, one they mistook as a lack of focus or a habit of day-dreaming—when in reality what they were seeing was Eveline's deep and intractable habit of *thinking*.

Even in the lower grades, Eveline had been seen as a child far more thoughtful than average, but in the months following her mother's death, her teachers felt that she had become even more preoccupied than before, appearing to have grown subject much more frequently to spells when she seemed isolated, distracted, absent, fallen away somewhere in depths of thought, a form of behavior that became worrisome, especially when it manifested itself increasingly often. All of this was taken as being highly unusual, even unnatural, in a child her age. And also, along with these already troubling aspects of her temperament, there continued unabated the girl's seemingly unquenchable thirst for *reading*.

Toward the end of the school year, Eveline's sixth grade teacher grew sufficiently concerned to impel her to request a meeting with the girl's father. Eveline's father by this time had reached the age of sixty-six and remained a fit and handsome man of deep experience, emotional wholeness, and robust common sense who had worked for his entire life, mainly in farming. When the teacher had expressed her concerns about Eveline, he responded by saying,

"Oh, Evie. Evie is a serious one, all right. But she's a good girl. Evie is a fine, wonderful young girl, much loved by us all. I would try not to worry too much about her if I were you."

Gradually, there came to be a general agreement about Eveline's unusual intelligence, but the qualities of her personality and temperament were more difficult to understand or even, for certain people, to approve of. My own belief is that Eveline, from the time of her mother's death onward, was at work on a single great project that absorbed her mind entirely and that demanded almost every bit of her emotional energy. This project had its beginning on the morning Eveline woke up to be told that her mother had died during the night. Eveline went to school, but she was aware that everything—everything *in* her and everything *around* her—had changed. Her mother was gone, and with her mother's absence were gone also not only the love she had given Eveline steadily and with unmitigated generosity for all of the child's life, but also other things that had been certainties when her mother was still alive, things that were never to be doubted and whose absence was never to be feared, universally necessary things like warmth, light, purposefulness, and security.

These things were no longer guaranteed. It was possible they no longer existed.

Two days after her mother's death, and one day before her funeral, it was agreed that Eveline could be taken to the funeral home to see her mother in the coffin she would be buried in. The sight of her dear mother, there and yet not there—there and yet not *anywhere*—was in almost equal parts piteous and terrifying to young Eveline. It was her mother lying there. But Eveline felt as though she were looking not at her mother but at her mother's absence: At nothingness, sorrow, loss, emptiness, at a terrible vulnerability and an unspeakable danger.

•

Death, loss, injury, pain, harm, fear. And, in opposition to all of these, the forces of life and also of beauty. These are the things Eveline became aware of as she stood at the side of her mother's coffin, whether or not she had the words for them. But these are the things she began thinking about in the fifth grade, and the things she then continued thinking about for the rest of her life.

Or at least so I suppose and I can't help but believe. Still, I can't know. What I do know is that she continued thinking about them, brilliantly and boldly and beautifully, for as long as I was lucky enough to know her.

•

Reading made perfect sense to her, since the feelings she was becoming aware of in life were the same as those that lay at the hearts of, and that comprised the subjects of, the books, plays, novels, and poems she was reading. This was true even in the early years, when the feelings were a presence she sensed in her reading even though she may have lacked the experience or vocabulary to express them—and this was a truth that became even more evident in the books she chose and read in the months—and then years—following her mother's death.

In her reading, Eveline invariably found something personal; whatever the subject or setting, or whoever the characters, there was always something that seemed to touch her personally. It occurred to her quite early on that it may have been simply that there, on the page, were words, formed and chosen and arranged by someone else, no matter how far away in time or space, while here—whether in the classroom, or at her favorite spot in the Carnegie library, or in her own bedroom, or on the front porch, or at the kitchen table—here was *she*, Eveline Stahl, age eight, or ten, or twelve—there was *she*, reading the very words that had been put there by another—yes, admittedly unknown—but by another hand, mind, heart, or soul.

In this sense of a connection, at whatever distance, lay the seeds of Eveline's later perception of the earth-protecting tendrils.

The sense of communion or connectedness, the sense of touching another being, person, or soul from even the greatest distance away, was far more immediate to her, far more palpable, meaningful, and valuable, than her teachers' repeated assertions year after year that reading was important because it allowed readers to visit or "go to" foreign lands, places, or peoples. The teachers' notion of travel or of *visiting* held little vividness or appeal for her as opposed to the idea of *touching* another from no matter what unimaginable distance away, perhaps not a physical touching but a spiritual one, the touching of one spirit with another, the touch going both ways, from the reader all the way to the *originator* of the book, and from the originator all the way back to the reader.

When one of her teachers might come upon Eveline appearing especially distant, or absent, or contemplative—those were the times when Eveline was pondering the truly difficult aspects of her experiential idea of touching and being touched. The difficulty had to do also with the nature of reading itself, it being an act that depends equally on both the material and the spiritual, at least if it's going to result in achievements like those sought—and valued—by Eveline. Take any word, before it's even put on paper. It is both spiritual and material, material because it consists of sound waves (material) that are created, propelled, sculpted, altered, and shaped by body parts (material) from the lungs and larynx on through the teeth, tongue, and lips. And yet at the same time the word is able to express, convey, or awaken the most subtle, evanescent, or intangible feelings or ideas, thoughts so fine as to achieve the most incomprehensible element of the spiritual.

True, it is extremely unlikely that Eveline—or any child—at the age of ten, eleven, or even twelve, could, or would be inclined to, take up a project of reasoning as subtle and demanding as this one, let alone bring it to any sort of finished, logical, or pragmatic conclusion. Like any other child, Eveline did not see or experience the world through ideas, but through feeling. As with any other child, feeling led and reason followed.

But the difference between Eveline and other children lay in the unusual extremity and abundance of her intelligence. She may not have had *more* feelings than other children, but she was more inclined than they were to examine, explore, and ponder whatever it was she did feel. She sought not only to repeat feelings of pleasure but also to repeat the experience of fear. She was an explorer of whatever she felt. And then, a good deal sooner than was to happen with the other children, her reason emerged, and she began to *think*.

Reading brought her pleasure, and so she repeated the experience of it again and again. On the other hand, darkness brought fear, and so, in starting to walk home after dark, and when she later formed the habit of going *out* after dark, she repeated the experience of darkness over and over, to the point where she gained a reputation as the strange and lovely girl who walked through the streets of night-time Fremont.

Then, near the time she reached fourteen and went into the ninth grade, Eveline began experiencing sensations of a kind she hadn't experienced before—not sexual, since those were in no way new, but intellectual. "Impressions" or "recognitions" might be more accurate words than "sensations." For the fact is that Eveline was entering into a period of *intellectual* awakening. From now on, her life would not be made up of things that were solely emotional, but it would be made up also of things that were constituted of *thinking*, that themselves were thoughts. No longer would her response to experience or feeling, whether of pleasure or of fear, be limited to the repetition of it. She was becoming aware of a new kind of force, emerging from deep within herself, that allowed her to respond differently from the narrow and re-petitive way she had responded before. Now, she began to realize, instead of simply *experiencing* pleasures or fears, she could actually look at them, study and analyze them, and thereby find a way to react to them that had been unavailable to her before. In a word, she was now gaining the ability to *think* about the things that happened to her.

And there was something else, a thing even more rudi-mentary and profound. If Eveline was now becoming able to think about things, it followed that in thinking about them she was producing thoughts. The remarkable thing is that those thoughts hadn't existed before Eveline had them. This meant that she had created them, that they had emerged from somewhere inside her, that they were hers.

Near this time, in the autumn of ninth grade, Eveline came upon Alfred, Lord Tennyson. The first Tennyson poem she read was "Break, break, break."

September 18th, 1923, was a Tuesday, warm, sunny, pleas-antly autumnal. After school that day, Eveline walked to the Carnegie library, took a place at her favorite table, and did her homework. After that, she opened the volume of Ten-nyson that she had checked out from the school library. It opened to "Break, break, break."

> *Break, break, break,*
>   *On thy cold gray stones, O Sea!*
> *And I would that my tongue could utter*
>   *The thoughts that arise in me.*

O, well for the fisherman's boy,
    That he shouts with his sister at play!
O, well for the sailor lad,
    That he sings in his boat on the bay!

And the stately ships go on
    To their haven under the hill;
But O for the touch of a vanish'd hand,
    And the sound of a voice that is still!

Break, break, break
    At the foot of thy crags, O Sea!
But the tender grace of a day that is dead
    Will never come back to me.

                                    (1842)

In "the touch of a vanish'd hand" and "the sound of a voice that is still," Eveline heard references to her mother and realized also that she herself had created them. Tennyson, eighty-one years before, had provided the phrases, and Eveline herself, now, at this wooden table, by this window, in the silence of this library, had provided the reference. When she had done so, a tendril, a thin and ductile arc, shot out across and through the sky, connecting Eveline with the poem.

She was thrilled by her discovery but said nothing about it to anyone. Sitting there by the window in the library, she realized that the more poems she read that had this same power, the more books, stories, novels that had it, then all the more arcs and tendrils would go out to all the more places and times, starting the process of Eveline becoming connected to everything.

Later that same autumn, in a notebook that she set aside for just this purpose, Eveline began writing pieces of her own. For a year and a half she mentioned them to no one. Then, midway through tenth grade, she chose three or four of the pieces she was most pleased with and asked the twelfth-grade English teacher, Miss Hermione Clark, whether she would be willing to look at them.

•

(At this point I find myself less able to disguise my feelings than I may have been up to now. Even the calendar conspires to create awe in me, and an almost bottomless sadness. I write these words in 2028, a year that falls no fewer than a hundred and three years after Eveline's graduation from Fremont High School—where, by the way, she skipped tenth grade, being considered enough ahead of her classmates to go faster. I can see her, with extreme clarity, in my mind's eye, even though eight more years were to pass before I would see her in person for the first time, in Iowa City, in John McGalliard's class in Old English, second hour, Jessup Hall, the morning of November 27, 1933.

Although she was a young woman in 1933 and still a girl in 1925, I know that she would have been almost exactly the same both times, this extremely attractive young person with brown hair (though faintly lightening in summer toward straw), wearing a white shirt with no jacket (this vision is from September 18th, 1923), a pleated skirt of plaid wool, low shoes, white ankle socks. She is a slim girl and she walks quickly, coming, first, out through the heavy front doors of the high school, then trippingly down the stone stairway, and off in the direction of the Carnegie library, disappearing when she passes under the larch, maples, and elms that in various places lean out over the sidewalk. Books: Eveline carries hers by holding them in the cradle of her arms, pulling them up against her breast.

•

(Three years at the university in Lincoln—all that time living in a single room at the top of a large house on the edge of the campus—great amounts of reading, Chaucer, Sidney, Spenser, Shakespeare, Milton, Donne, Herrick, Herbert, Marvell, Bacon, Hobbes, Browne, Dryden, Swift, Pope, Johnson—learning French— reading European history—Blake, Coleridge, Wordsworth, Keats, Carlyle, Tennyson, Arnold—then also a love affair, begun and ended in Eveline's last year in Lincoln—Hardy, Houseman, Hopkins. The love affair was passionate although not long-lived, ending without rancor.

•

(Alliance, Nebraska. Far to the west. The land a table reaching out to the horizon. The nights dark. The winters long. Power- ful winds gusting from the northwest in the coldest weather, driving snow horizontally to form deep drifts on the lee sides of buildings, fences, and other structures. Eveline lived in rooms on the second-floor of a house three blocks from the high school, where she taught five sections of senior English. The students wrote papers and she read, marked, corrected, and graded them. She assigned novels like *The Mill on the Floss*, *Tess of the d'Urbervilles*, and *My Ántonia*, stories like "Young Goodman Brown," "An Occurrence at Owl Creek Bridge," and "The Cask of Amontillado," and poems like "Ode on a Grecian Urn," "Because I could not stop for Death—," and "A Noiseless Patient Spider." Eveline was generally unhappy during these two wilderness years, and lonely, although she liked her pupils and was frequently invited by their parents to the families' homes for dinner. These were pleasant enough occasions, even though Eveline found that making conversation with the parents was more difficult than with the students, to whom she felt much closer. Still, she discovered something she had already known, that she would much rather read new things than teach the things she already knew, and, overworked by her teaching schedule and its many obligations, she yearned for time to explore new reading on her own. She read the new book, *An American Tragedy*, but it ended up creating no tendrils. As for the subject of the tendrils themselves, those that already did exist, she kept absolutely silent about them, since she knew of no one she could trust enough to confide in. There was another love affair, brief, in the spring of her second year, shortly before her departure from Alliance. It was with a young man who did not interest Eveline but who had a kind temperament and was so completely and utterly infatuated with her that she gave in. She left Alliance with relief and also with a sense of excitement at what might be to come. In letters the two had written back and forth through-out the year, Hermione Clark had urged upon Eveline that she really must enroll for a higher degree, somewhere out-side of her native state, Iowa City, in her view, being the best choice. Eveline had agreed that, indeed, she would look into it. She applied and was accepted. These events took place in 1932. As for me, I would not be born for another nine years, and yet I would meet Eveline in only one more year, closer to two. It seems to me now, looking back across that long arc of decades, that Eveline's activities and movements, beginning in ninth grade and going on through her years in Lincoln and then Alliance and then Iowa City—it seems to me that what she was really doing, unknown to anyone, was preparing to meet me so that we could take up our work together.)))

MARIANA
By Alfred, Lord Tennyson

"Mariana in the Moated Grange"
(Shakespeare, Measure for Measure)

With blackest moss the flower-plots
Were thickly crusted, one and all:

The rusted nails fell from the knots
That held the pear to the gable-wall.
The broken sheds look'd sad and strange:
Unlifted was the clinking latch;
Weeded and worn the ancient thatch
Upon the lonely moated grange.
She only said, "My life is dreary,
He cometh not," she said;
She said, "I am aweary, aweary,
I would that I were dead!"

Her tears fell with the dews at even;
Her tears fell ere the dews were dried;
She could not look on the sweet heaven,
Either at morn or eventide.
After the flitting of the bats,
When thickest dark did trance the sky,
She drew her casement-curtain by,
And glanced athwart the glooming flats.
She only said, "The night is dreary,
He cometh not," she said;
She said, "I am aweary, aweary,
I would that I were dead!"

Upon the middle of the night,
Waking she heard the night-fowl crow:
The cock sung out an hour ere light:
From the dark fen the oxen's low
Came to her: without hope of change,
In sleep she seem'd to walk forlorn,
Till cold winds woke the gray-eyed morn
About the lonely moated grange.
She only said, "The day is dreary,
He cometh not," she said;
She said, "I am aweary, aweary,
I would that I were dead!"

About a stone-cast from the wall
A sluice with blacken'd waters slept,
And o'er it many, round and small,
The cluster'd marish-mosses crept.
Hard by a poplar shook alway,
All silver-green with gnarled bark:
For leagues no other tree did mark
The level waste, the rounding gray.
She only said, "My life is dreary,
He cometh not," she said;
She said "I am aweary, aweary
I would that I were dead!"

And ever when the moon was low,
And the shrill winds were up and away,
In the white curtain, to and fro,
She saw the gusty shadow sway.
But when the moon was very low
And wild winds bound within their cell,
The shadow of the poplar fell
Upon her bed, across her brow.
She only said, "The night is dreary,
He cometh not," she said;
She said "I am aweary, aweary,
I would that I were dead!"

All day within the dreamy house,
The doors upon their hinges creak'd;
The blue fly sung in the pane; the mouse
Behind the mouldering wainscot shriek'd,
Or from the crevice peer'd about.
Old faces glimmer'd thro' the doors
Old footsteps trod the upper floors,
Old voices called her from without.
She only said, "My life is dreary,

He cometh not," she said;
She said, "I am aweary, aweary,
I would that I were dead!"

The sparrow's chirrup on the roof,
The slow clock ticking, and the sound
Which to the wooing wind aloof
The poplar made, did all confound
Her sense; but most she loathed the hour
When the thick-moted sunbeam lay
Athwart the chambers, and the day
Was sloping toward his western bower.
Then said she, "I am very dreary,
He will not come," she said;
She wept, "I am aweary, aweary,
Oh God, that I were dead!"

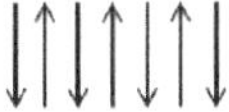

TWELVE

Fall term exams came and went. Intersession began. Winter settled in.

It was a wonderful, beautiful, excellent time, the three weeks of intersession. Almost no one stayed on campus. The residence halls were all but empty again, and even the town itself—or that part of it that pressed up against the campus—seemed sparsely populated, slower-moving than usual, in a pleasant lull. Eveline's house on College Street emptied out. The graduate students from the apartments on the second and third floors—two married couples and three single women in the nursing program—went out of town, leaving only Eveline behind, and, in her own apartment across the hall, the landlady, Mrs. Elisabeth Sladek, or, as she was known to her tenants, Bessie. Bessie was a widow who made a living by renting out the apartments in her house. She was also extremely fond of Eveline, whom she had known now for over a year and a half, from the time of the young woman's arrival in Iowa City. In addition, Bessie was kind and soft-hearted, unusually tolerant, and readily willing to look the other way in matters having to do with what she referred to as "young love." With her implicit approval, and with my addition of a small amount of money to the January rent, I moved in with Eveline for the duration of the three weeks.

We still went to the Bus Depot Diner some of the time, or to John's Grocery, but we also stocked up on provisions and did a certain amount of cooking ourselves. We ate dinner by the light of two candles, at the kitchen table, beside the tall window that would be black with winter night and sometimes frosted over, especially if we'd roasted or baked something in the oven. There was one other change that we made, and that was with furniture. Eveline's reading place, at home, was at her desk, in the wooden swivel chair that also tilted backward. But I had no good place. We wanted to be in the same room when studying, but the settee was too small and constrained for me to read in it comfortably. So, from the used furniture store downtown, we bought a soft, long couch like the one Audrey and Ed LaRouche had. We moved the settee into the bedroom and set the couch across the front windows in its place. I could sit there comfortably to read, either with my feet resting on the coffee table or extended lengthwise on the couch itself while I leaned into the corner formed by the meeting of the back and arm. Through the long hours of winter afternoons, there we sat, each in the company of the other. The couch brought about other changes as well, by way of providing an alternative to Eveline's bed as a place for us to talk. We often went to the couch after dinner, to talk, with a mug of tea each and no light in the room other than what came in from the streetlamp over the intersection.

Eveline never stopped surprising me. I learned immensities from her, many in our long nighttime talks during intersession, the two of us at the far end of the couch, close together the same way we'd been at Audrey and Ed's on New Year's Eve. By this time I was so powerfully in love with Eveline that I found myself, all too often—and not only in moments of passion—blurting out the kinds of things common to lovers everywhere, although in my case they were fraught with risk and potentially even deceitful—for example, that I would love her forever, that I would never leave her, and the like. The fact is that I *have* loved her forever, without diminishment, for the nine decades that have passed, or for the six decades, depending on how you count, since we had our year together. But that I would never leave her—*that* part of it proved immensely, ruinously, untrue, something I should never, ever, have said.

But even then, the immensities, the capacities, the capacious enormities inside Eveline were such that, although she and I *did* fail together, she, like me, was never without the knowledge that a departure between us might be what could, or what would, happen.

However, these were things I hadn't yet learned about her— that she was leagues ahead of me in my own thinking, for example. Consequently, I knew that I would remain tormented, would consider myself (rightly) a liar, unless I told her the whole story, everything, about where I had "come from," about my translocations in time, all of it, including the fact that, no matter how bottomless and profound my desire might be to remain exactly where I was, I might conceivably, at any time, without warning, be torn away.

And so, on one of those winter nights, on the couch in the front room, I told her everything, beginning with my arrival in Iowa City in September 1963 and going on through my first sight of her in John McGalliard's class. The rest, we both knew.

When I came to an end, Eveline found my hand and held it in both of hers. Then she raised it up and kissed it lightly, held it for a second against her lips, and said,

"Yes. I know."

•

Eveline wasn't clairvoyant, but she was powerfully and mightily perceptive. After she had shocked me out of my skin by saying what she'd said—*"Yes. I know."*—we sat up well into the small morning hours, there on the couch, talking. From the start, Eveline had suspected something not quite "normal" about me and where I'd "come from," if only through small details like my never wearing a hat or cap, carrying books at my side instead of in a book bag, and not knowing the other people in my classes the way she did. And there were also my white lies—like the flimsy claim I made that the reason I wasn't going home over the holidays was to save money. She'd seen through that one, too, she said. She turned toward me on the couch, put her arms around me and held tight. I turned too, and held her the same way.

It was perfectly clear that Eveline had unnerved me, and I readily accepted her caresses, which I took as expressing, in part, both apology for having done an end-run around me and as sympathy for my having become rattled, however un-derstandably. Things were easier for her, she said. Or, more accurately, she whispered into my ear that things were easier for her than for me. And the reason was that *she* would never have to leave her own plane of time, the one she had lived her whole life in and was used to and perfectly comfortable in.

All she had to do, she told me, was wait.

I realized that I was holding on to her as if for dear life. Because now, after hearing her say what she had just said, I *did* feel vertiginous, as if, for that moment, I were in freefall. I didn't say anything, but I held on to her, breathing the scent of her hair, a scent of autumn, another of winter, and along with those the most distant scent of some lovely soft perfume.

What she'd said—about *waiting*—meant that now we had to go all the way back to what had happened at the table at John's Grocery on New Year's morning and, even more, to what had happened that same day when we sat down together at the kitchen table to "talk things through." I was dizzy. I clung and clung to Eveline. I was so moved, and frightened, that I felt my eyes stinging with tears.

"Eveline. Did you know *what* you were waiting for?"

She made no answer, but I felt her shake her head.

"So it wasn't me? You weren't waiting for me?"

She shook her head again to say no. But then after a moment she relaxed her grip on me and pulled away just a bit. The light from the street came from behind her so I couldn't make out her face even though we were only inches apart.

"No. But when I saw you I knew that's what it was. What it had been."

"Eveline," I said. "Eveline. Eveline."

I kissed her eyes. They were wet.

"Eveline," I said her name one more time. And then: "We have to talk. I have a million things I've got to tell you."

•

And so there *was* a plan. There *was* something at work that I hadn't understood and didn't understand. I *was* being given a chance to do something important.

It was all true: I had been guided to Eveline.

And Eveline was the key to everything.

•

So I had to tell her about my father. I had to tell her that my father was the nation she and I had been born into. I had to tell her that in 1947 this nation, with my father's influence and approval, would change—*had* changed—from a republic to an empire; and that not very long afterward, in 1963, it had metastasized into an embryonic tyranny.

And here is the rest of what I told her: I told her that it now seemed to me that she, Eveline Stahl, was the only strength, force, being, or presence on earth that could divert my father from the path he had chosen, or *was to choose*, in the year 1947. Eveline and I were being given the chance of a lifetime: she and I could revisit 1947—that is, Eveline could *visit* it and I could *revisit* it—and, once we were there, Eveline could soften my father, could guide him, redeem him.

•

That night in Iowa City, sitting with Eveline on the couch, when I learned that all through 1933 she had been waiting for something, and that that awaited thing had turned out to be me: When I learned these things I also understood something else: I understood that I had been sent to Eveline because she alone, only she, possessed the breadth, strength, accumulated vision, wisdom, and inner goodness to enable her, through meeting my father, to change him.

We would—*somehow*—travel to 1947, where Eveline—*when* Eveline—she alone, would be able to appeal to my father, the nation I was born in, in such a way as to meliorate his blind solipsism, calm his narcissistic rage, relieve and heal his ruinous misunderstandings of history, dissipate his compulsion to crush others, soften the virulence of his disdain for the populations of the world, give breath to the human element in him, open his mind, make a malleable thing of his heart.

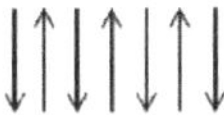

(A job, as it turned out, that would prove impossible. My father, after all, was the nation that destroyed its history before my own turn came to learn from it and find nourishment in it. My father was the nation that drove its way west, destroying and devouring all peoples and elements in its path. My father was the nation blind to the sight of anything other than itself; the nation that visited terror on others and meanwhile declared itself benevolent; the nation of torture, righteousness, destruction, terror. My father was the nation that eats its young; the nation that destroys itself. He was the nation I see dying before my eyes, its carcass infested with worms.

•

(From the vantage-point of 1963, the most destructive year in late American history was 1947.

(From the vantage-point of 1934, the most destructive year in late American history was to be 1947.

•

(And my father had a role in it: A role in making 1947 the year that started the slide toward the death of the republic, the countdown that only sixteen years later saw the murder of the President and, after the unbounded and unqualified success of *that* killing, set up the others to be brought down like tenpins after him, thereby converting the nation once and for all into an instrument whose purpose and destiny henceforth were the bringing about of malice to all, justice to none, and death to the remainder.

(But perhaps, just perhaps, considering what had happened to me so far; and considering what had happened to Eveline so far; and considering the way the two of us had been brought together—just possibly Eveline and I could enter into time through yet another portal; possibly we could find a path into 1947; possibly we could meet my father there; and possibly we could assuage him, temper him, widen his vision, draw him out of his living grave of solipsism, vanity, and desire, and back into the human family, persuade him to alter his role in the making of policy, persuade him to vote *not* for universal profiteering in the currency of blood, *not* for the self-gratification of the nostalgia-blinded or the greed-blinded commanders, but, instead, to vote for the brotherhood of nations, the family of man, the protection of children, the rights of all, the sharing of the future among mankind.

(If we could do this, Eveline and I—*if we could affect just this one momentary change in my father*—then it would follow, I was absolutely certain, that every subsequent event in a chain reaching from September 18th, 1947 through November 22nd, 1963 would consequently be altered also in infinitesimal, indefinable, unimaginably subtle yet cumulatively significant ways—and the assassination of the president, at half past noon, in Dealey Square, in Dallas, Texas, amid the firing of multiple rifles—*would not take place.*

•

(Our destiny therefore had been made clear, and it was up to us—to me and Eveline; me *with* Eveline—to find a way to fulfill it. We must bend every effort, devote every energy, draw on every fiber of our knowledge and will to meet my father, to meet him *in the year 1947*, when we would still have a chance of shaping, influencing, meliorating the role he was to play in deciding the future of the republic.

(I could never conceivably do this alone. But with Eveline, along with the perception and the powers of Eveline, I stood a chance.))))))))

↑↓↑↓↑↓↑↓

THIRTEEN

WORKING NOTES

Course of study:

So it came about that Eveline and I found ourselves inside an emergency. It was not clear how much time was available for us to prepare for what lay ahead, or, for that matter, exactly how we would know when the moment was the right one to begin our trip.

As for the question of when, we would have to wait and watch. Certainly there would be signs of some kind.

As for our preparation, it would consist primarily of study. For me, this was a matter of gaining a practical and true understanding of tendrils—precisely how it is they come into existence, and exactly what the nature is of the good they do for the earth, people, culture, nations.

On Eveline's side, preparation would consist of focusing on a study of the history of the future: That is, focusing on a study of the things, events, and movements that were to take place—or, depending on how you look at it, that *had* taken place—between January 1934 and September 1947.

There were, of course, no volumes in the library to consult for this task, since no books had been written on events that, as of January 1934, hadn't yet occurred.

So it would be up to me to tutor Eveline in the history and events of those years, just as it would be up to Eveline to tutor *me* in the nature, origin, and effect of the tendrils.

•

The importance of 1947:

Nineteen forty-seven was the cruelest year. When WWII came to an end in 1945 with the victory of what were called the Allied forces over those known as the Axis forces, the United States emerged as the world's strongest power. It emerged also as the one nation among the major powers to have had the luck, honor, or fortune to have been the least damaged of all the war's participants, the least harmed, diminished, taxed, drained, ruined, unbalanced, bled dry, or injured.

The United States, in short, emerged from the war in a position to evolve into the world's leader, guide, and example in the development and maintenance of universal institutions dedicated to peace, stability, and welfare; to human progress in medicine, health, education; and, not least, to the protection and maintenance of justice throughout the world.

There might have been the diminishment of hunger, the amelioration of pain, the soothing of loss, the sharing of Earth with the denizens of Earth, the sharing of Earth's fruits with all those themselves who are born of Earth. There might have been respect, fairness, and care. There might have been peace.

But not so.

It was not only that America had tasted blood again and had been reminded once more of the fine piquancy of that particular liquor around the teeth and on the tongue. It was more than that. It was also the deep, unmentionable thrill that came from experiencing the ease with which succulent blood could be transubstantiated miraculously into money.

That is to say, America chose the river of blood.

After 1947, the nation began a moral, intellectual, and spiritual emptying out of its being, doing this with increasing rapidity as the process went on. And into the resultant and ever-enlarging hollowness of the nation, evil poured. Evil had existed in, and inside, the nation before, as its crimes of slavery, genocide, and armed terror testify. But after 1947, the last moment when it could have been avoided, the growth began of a newly merciless spiritual cancer that was bred and afterward nourished by a newly reaffirmed shallowness and emptiness of mind and heart; this omnivorous hollowness of spirit, soul, and mind, as it grew, devoted itself to the promotion, expansion, enhancement, and increased production of those same poisons that brought it into existence and afterward nourished it, so that, over time, growing exponentially, this emptiness devoured more and then vastly more after that, as it will do again after *that*, until it will have devoured the earth, and nothing will be left at all.

My father, for reasons of his own, however ignorant they may have been, chose the river of blood.

FOURTEEN

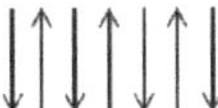

Eveline did much of her thinking through a "flowering model," whereby she first considered seed, then root, then stem, shoot, leaf, bud, and at last blossoming flower. Her study might begin with a single word, continue through phrase, line, sentence, paragraph/stanza and on to an entire work.

The three-week intersession was in no way long enough. Every day during it—and every night—was precious.

For the first two of those weeks the weather remained in the grip of a clear, still, silent, arctic cold. The snow that had fallen so heavily before Christmas was still on the ground, and the sunlight that reflected off it during the middle hours of the day came in through the windows to brighten Eveline's apartment and give it an Alpine feel. During those two weeks we almost never left the house until past noon, and on some days we didn't leave at all. In the mornings, at the kitchen table, we had eggs, toast, butter, and coffee for breakfast, then went into the front room to study. Most of the time, if we were reading, we sat together on the couch, but if Eveline had writing to do she would move over to her desk. As for myself, if I had to do some writing I would go back to the kitchen table, although I was always careful to sit on its far side, since that position allowed me to look out into the front room.

When we did go out for lunch, we went about half the time to the diner and the other half to John's, where the advantage was that we could return from the grocery with new supplies of bread, eggs, butter, and coffee if we needed them, a few bottles of beer and a piece of cheese and perhaps some tinned fish, sardines or kipper snacks, and of course crackers. One time we brought back canned vegetables and beans, two fresh onions, and some potatoes, and Eveline made a pot of vegetable soup that we ate for two nights in a row and then for lunch on another.

During the cold spell, the best parts of outings were the start and the finish, leaving the house and then coming back again. The weather was really very cold, and we wore hats, scarves, and boots, usually with double socks. Even at one or two in the afternoon, the air would freeze the hairs in your nose. At the diner, we almost always took one of the tables in the back corner instead of at the front window. The diner was well heated, so off came hats, scarves, and jackets, to be put back on when time came for the return trip. We walked home not holding hands but with arms around one another's waist. At College Street, we would step up onto the porch and, inside the front door, pull off our boots before going in through Eveline's door and then through the front room into the bedroom, where we would toss hats, scarves, and jackets onto the settee. Then—far from always, though on occasion—we would sit down on the edge of the bed and continue helping one another off with articles of clothing—shirt, blouse, pants, slacks, socks at the end—until none were left and we scrambled in under the covers.

The radiators in Eveline's apartment provided a good amount of heat, but midway through the evenings they would cool down, then remain cold as ice until six in the morning, when pipes would bang with the returning heat.

In those evenings during the intersession, we stayed up long after the heat went off. The couch in the front room was a godsend then, the two of us pressed together at one end, feet at rest on the coffee table—both of us covered from toes to chin by the wonderfully heavy quilt, its patches in various shades of green, that Eveline had brought from Nebraska. Black tea with lemon and honey was a favored drink, and I was the one, invariably, who volunteered to go out to the kitchen to prepare it.

Tendrils. Industriously, I continued learning about them. The requirements for their creation, as Eveline explained to me patiently, were reverent, deep, subtle, and strong.

It was essential, in the first place, that there *be a relationship* between the reader and the thing read.

No relationship, no tendril.

It was imperative also that the relationship be *significant, deeply felt*, and *passionate*.

Neither "deeply felt" nor "passionate," however, meant humorless or somber. In the huge majority of cases, in fact, somberness or the absence of humor in the relationship between reader and thing read would not only fail to advance the germination and generation of a tendril but would jeopardize if not doom both. "Passionate," then, means *strength* of feeling, *strength* of commitment, and it requires a commingling of thinking *with* feeling

Reverence has a meaning different from the meaning of "deeply felt" or of "significant," although it is clearly related to both. It is close to "awe" in its meaning but *not in any way* in the sense of that word when it is—the case far too often—put into the company of the word "dumb," as in the redundant and therefore generally shallow phrase "dumb awe." As associated with the generating of tendrils, "reverence" should be thought of as suggesting the highest form of respect for the thing read combined with a clear and muscular, *not* dopy, sense of wonder at its having been brought into existence, "the achieve of, the mastery of the thing."

Depth, again, has overtones that can be heard in the meanings of some of the other terms and phrases already mentioned, such as "significant" or "deeply felt." Here, however, "depth" has as much to do with the nature of the thing *read* as it does with the nature of the *reader's* intellect or emotion. That is, no tendril will be germinated, generated, or brought into existence if the thing *read* is trivial, slight, meretricious, empty, or otherwise without value of a kind that can and does give it significance. (See the requirement "honest" a step or two further on.)

Subtlety. Like "depth," subtlety has to do both with the reader and with the thing read. Both, understandably, will vary as to the presence, degree, quality, and uses of subtlety in their origin, constitution, and makeup. The value of subtlety is that it allows for the gestation and expression—or the understanding—of meaning at a different level of intensity and significance than is achievable in its absence. *Some* form of subtlety is an essential requisite in any piece of literary art *if* that artwork is to achieve an existence beyond the level of the purely utilitarian and literal—the qualities that are possessed, say, by the phone book. In the achievement of any style or tone possessing the ability to bring a tendril into existence— in any such achievement, subtlety must not only be present, but it must also, in and through the powers of its very nature, do its further work by drawing attention *away* from itself.

And, in the last, or first, place: **honesty**. Without the presence of this final, critical attribute, not even the presence of all the others can suffice to bring about the creation of a tendril. Honesty—in the sense that Eveline meant it—serves as an environment, bond, or glue that alone is capable of bringing the other elements and attributes together and keeping them together in an unbreachable, durable, impenetrable whole. In a word, perdurable.

It must be made absolutely clear, and must be remembered, that this final and necessary element—honesty—has nothing to do with honesty as that word is used in daily life or in common, ordinary discourse. In this use, it has nothing to do with *telling* the truth or with *being honest* in one's personal or business dealings or in one's associations generally. An artwork, in this case the thing read, can "tell" anything, take up, dramatize, or describe any subject or experience whether true or false, real or imaginary, creative or destructive, beautiful or ugly, hopeful or despairing, so long as it remains honest *to* that telling, honest *in* that telling, and honest to *the purpose of* that telling.

Passionate, reverent, deep, subtle, honest.

Passion, reverence, depth, subtlety, honesty

•

Once, I remember, we came upon a man-of-war anchored off the coast.

•

Mrs. Dalloway said she would buy the flowers herself.

•

THOU hast made me, and shall Thy work decay?

•

Safe in their Alabaster Chambers—
Untouched by Morning—
and untouched by noon—
Sleep the meek members of the Resurrection,
Rafter of Satin and Roof of Stone—

•

Be thou a spirit of health or goblin damned,
Bring with thee airs from heaven or blasts from hell,
Be thy intents wicked or charitable,
Thou com'st in such a questionable shape
That I will speak to thee. I'll call thee Hamlet,
King, father, royal Dane. O, answer me!

•

A Litany in Time of Plague
Thomas Nashe (1567-1601)

Adieu, farewell, earth's bliss;
This world uncertain is;
Fond are life's lustful joys;
Death proves them all but toys;
None from his darts can fly;
I am sick, I must die.
    Lord, have mercy on us!

Rich men, trust not in wealth,
Gold cannot buy you health;
Physic himself must fade.
All things to end are made,
The plague full swift goes by;
I am sick, I must die.
    Lord, have mercy on us!

Beauty is but a flower
Which wrinkles will devour;
Brightness falls from the air;
Queens have died young and fair;

Dust hath closed Helen's eye.
I am sick, I must die.
   Lord, have mercy on us!

Strength stoops unto the grave,
Worms feed on Hector brave;
Swords may not fight with fate,
Earth still holds open her gate.
"Come, come!" the bells do cry.
I am sick, I must die.
   Lord, have mercy on us!

Wit with his wantonness
Tasteth death's bitterness;
Hell's executioner
Hath no ears for to hear
What vain art can reply.
I am sick, I must die.
   Lord, have mercy on us!

Haste, therefore, each degree,
To welcome destiny;
Heaven is our heritage,
Earth but a player's stage;
Mount we unto the sky.
I am sick, I must die.
   Lord, have mercy on us!

.

.

. . . any man's death diminishes me, because I am
involved in mankind, and therefore never send to
know for whom the bell tolls. . .

In my beginning is my end.

FIFTEEN

When intersession ended and classes started up again at the end of January, Eveline's landlady thought—she confided this to Eveline, not to me— it would be best if I were to move out of Eveline's apartment, if only until semester's end. She seemed to feel that a certain amount of discretion was somehow more important during the regular term than in the putatively more lax summer session that would follow.

Grievous as it felt (almost like—no; worse than—the trauma of a physical wound), I took my belongings, such as they were (I left as many things at Eveline's as I took with me), and made my way back across town to the Quadrangle. My room there was unchanged, yet in certain ways it seemed altogether different. Instead of giving me the impression of a private place offering comfort and security, as it had all the way back when I first saw it, the room now seemed much smaller, narrower, more cell-like, and without adequate light. I went in and dropped my things on the bed, and quickly enough I realized why the room seemed so much darker than it had before. With my coat, scarf, boots, and hat still on, I sat down—with a deep sigh, I'm sure—at my desk and took the posture I'd used for reading in what now seemed eons back—face to windows, right arm on the desktop, feet resting on an arm of the upholstered chair (though in fact they didn't rest there yet, pending removal of the boots). And I felt as though I were sitting at the bottom of a tub, straining to see over its edge. Three weeks with Eveline, in rooms where the windows came down almost to the floor—that experience made these seem not only absurdly narrow but far too high up in the wall, as if their real purpose were to keep light out rather than let it in, imperil a view rather than offer one.

In short, my little room, which had once seemed perfectly comfortable and, in its own way, simultaneously liberating and offering protection, now seemed like a prison cell. It was as though I had been sent into exile. I felt angry, lost, forlorn, doomed.

Absurd, all of those feelings, among them the unpardonable vice of self-pity. Living with Eveline day and night for three weeks had been an experience wonderful beyond imagination, a gift inexpressible; and who was I to begrudge, despoil, or demean it through an unkempt squall of self-indulgence and bitterness? Silently, I tried to lecture myself, arguing that it was only the shock and suddenness of this unwelcome change, of being separated from Eveline so abruptly—this is what gave me my despairing sense of finality, a finality that in fact wasn't there at all. Eveline had promised me everything I could conceivably ask, wish, or hope for, a fidelity to the love between us and a promise that nothing would change—*except* that for the time being we would have to stay in separate places. Everything else—*everything*—would remain the same.

•

And it was true. Or at least it was true that we met every day and that we were still unqualifiedly in love. But everything else was changed. Completely.

Intersession, in Eveline's apartment, a warm nest in the middle of a frozen January, had been like the Garden of Eden, the Bower of Bliss, and we could as well have been the primordial couple, more completely married than statute, oath, or church could have made us. And now? Now it was as though we were two college kids, not really independent at all, a couple, yes, but merely known as "going steady."

We met and met and met, but our time together seemed never to be private, intimate, and deep the way it had been before. The only class we had together was McGalliard's *Beowulf*, which met at eleven o'clock three mornings a week. Neither of us had class in the hour preceding it, and so on every *Beowulf* day we would meet for breakfast at the diner, where, for some reason never spoken about between us, whoever got there first would sit at the counter instead of in one of the rear booths or at "our" table by the front window. I've tried hard to remember how this change began, or *who* was the first to choose the counter, although I'm almost absolutely certain it must have been Eveline. The counter was less private. Conversation was far more likely to be overheard, so the counter was a sort of natural guard against intimacy. I remembered Eveline, at John's grocery, whispering to me, *"Let's go home,"* and then saying the same thing again in the back booth here at the diner. And we did. We went home.

Now, the only place for us to go was Godfrey's *Beowulf*.

The steps to the door of Meredith Hall were worn into smooth depressions from the scuffing of a half-century of shoes. These steps were of stone, the building's exterior of softened red brick, while everything inside was of wood, dark, creaking, dry, ancient. The floors groaned and so did the stairs as I followed Eveline up to the second floor and into the southwest corner room. Three windows stood in each of its two outside walls, so plenty of light came in, including direct sunlight on clear days. The brightness had the effect of heightening the antique appearance of the room, making only more visible the worn wood floors, the chips and gouges on the student desks, the scuffed walls. Professor Godfrey himself added a kind of brightness. He was short, with a round face and head, the latter with very little hair left on it. He was jovial, friendly, and, for a stout man, notably quick in his physical movements. He was fond of pacing back and forth at the front of the room during recitation and lecture, both hands supporting the open book in front of him. Often when he came to one side of the room and pivoted there in order to reverse course, the round flat lenses of his glasses would glint in the light.

•

That was the room where we gathered for fifteen weeks to recite, translate, correct, and analyze the text of *Beowulf*.

Eveline and I sat in the second row on the righthand side of the room (the side opposite the windows), my own seat on the aisle and Eveline's to my left.

And, for the first two or two and a half weeks, I couldn't rid myself of the dreadful, sickening feeling that something was wrong.

I would have had trouble saying exactly how, but it seemed as if there were a distance between Eveline and me. It was something unspoken but there nevertheless. Or it seemed as if we—both of us—had somehow become self-conscious, slightly uncomfortable, at being seen by other people in this new way, not just as a "couple," but as a couple who were behaving, who were doing *every*thing in only the most conventional, predict-able, commonplace ways.

We weren't being true to ourselves, neither of us, but I was afraid to say anything. Had I in one way or another done some-thing to displease Eveline? Had she changed? It seemed so, but *why* such a thing might have happened, I had no idea. At the diner, our conversation consisted, astonishingly, almost solely of small talk. There was something self-conscious and chill be-tween us—not icy, but also not flowing, normal, and intimate the way it had been until now. In an attempt to get around this awkwardness and feeling of artificiality, we got into the habit of quizzing one another on Old English vocabulary, especially verbs. Eveline was twice as quick at memorizing as I was, her memory twice as capacious. Now and then we managed to get some laughter going—at my expense—and it seemed a thaw might be taking place. But then afterward, on our way to class, Eveline would begin to grow quiet again, or she would fall into the new way she had of seeming almost proper, slightly distanced, strangely *polite*.

We limped on this way for a week, then for another after that. It had come to seem almost impossible for the two of us to talk in a way that felt normal or natural or intimate or even just personal. I began to feel rudderless, uncentered, almost as if I were going mad. I thought I'd known how much Eveline meant to me, and how much I depended on her. But now I wondered whether I had over-estimated my feelings, or hers.

On the Friday at the end of the second week, as we were about to get up from the counter, something happened. I didn't know I was going to do it, but I suddenly reached over, took her by the wrist, and leaned in close. "*Eveline,*" I said, and I must have sounded more anguished than I'd thought. "*What's happening? Where have you gone to?*"

She looked down at the counter in front of her. I let go of wrist. She reached over, took my own hand, and squeezed it firmly. She turned her face toward mine and just looked for a second. Then she kissed me, on the lips, hard.

Some guy behind me, at the counter, whistled.

Outside, we went across Washington Street and started toward Meredith Hall. But Eveline stopped me and we stood there face to face.

"I'm going to cut class," she said. "But you go. Everything is all right."

"But what's *wrong*, Evie?" I asked her.

She smiled and gave her short laugh, with a trill in it.

"I just said everything was all right. Everything *is* all right."

I knew better—or I think I did—than to say anything more. Eveline began turning away but stopped and gave me the strangest orders.

"Don't sit where we usually do. Be sure not to sit in your regular place. Go off somewhere toward the back."

And she was gone.

•

I wrote to her that night. I thought of calling but quickly put that thought aside. There were no phones in the rooms in the Quadrangle, so I would have to go downstairs to the concierge's office, or else out to a phone booth. But Eveline had no phone, either, at least not inside her apartment. There was only the phone out in the hallway, and whenever that one rang it was understood that Mrs. Sladek would get it. All much too public, difficult, and cumbersome. So I wrote. By this time it was past ten, closer to eleven, on Friday night, and I would have to carry the letter—if you could call it a letter—across the river and to the post office if it were to reach Eveline in the morning. The only light in my room was from the goose-neck desk lamp. On a sheet of paper, on the desktop, I wrote:

February 16, 1934
Quadrangle, B-90

Beloved Eveline,

I know that something is wrong, and I need to find out what it is. I love you more powerfully than I ever imagined it possible to love another. And I am worried sick about you.

If I lose you, I will lose absolutely everything.
Tell me what to do.
My love ever, and beyond—

M.R.

I folded the note, put it into an envelope that I'd already addressed—

Eveline Stahl
806 East College St.
City

—then sealed and stamped it. Boots, scarf, coat, gloves, hat. It was by this time almost midnight. The snow cover had settled down into itself and no longer had its fresh look. The streets and walkways had been shoveled and cleared, their edges lined with the rough ice and worn-looking snow that had been tossed there. I went down the hill under the string of walkway lights and onto the bridge and across the river, then up the hill past the university buildings, over to Washington Street, across Dubuque and then Linn, until I got to the post office. I pulled open the heavy front door, went in, crossed the totally empty lobby, and dropped my envelope into the slot marked "local mail."

When I went back out I stood for a minute at the top of the steps. The night was absolutely still, not the least stirring of a breeze. I saw no one else anywhere. No car passed.

After a minute I went down the steps and turned left. I continued along Washington until I crossed Gilbert and Van Buren and got to Johnson. There, I crossed the little city park on the diagonal and came out on College, went another block and crossed Lucas. There was Eveline's house. I followed the sidewalk up to where the front walkway began. Then I stopped and just looked.

Here I was again, outside, staring at the house, just as I'd done during the heavy snow, when Eveline was in Fremont. Two months ago. It felt like two years. Eveline hadn't been in the house at that time, but more than three hundred miles away. Now was different. She was inside. She *must* have been inside, in bed, asleep. Unless she had decided to sleep on the couch, inside the front windows, rolled up in blankets.

It occurred to me to tiptoe onto the porch and peek in. But that would be insanity. An immense mistake. A monstrous, overwhelming, unforgivable violation. I couldn't believe the idea had even occurred to me. As if whipped from one side, I turned abruptly, back toward downtown, and started walking, fast.

•

Saturday was an excruciatingly lonely and empty day. The sky hung low in a monotone gray and, although the temperature hovered somewhere in the middle thirties, the moist air was penetratingly cold. It was a day that begged for the warmth and security of indoors, for hot tea, blankets, shawls, a fire-place. I wasn't able to arrange any of these, except for the indoors and hot tea, though tea at the diner counter delivered less in aroma and steaming comfort than I would wish for. Like everything else, it would have been altogether different if enjoyed in the company of another. It wasn't yet noon by the time I finished the tea, but I had little interest in a midday meal and even less in visiting the Quadrangle cafeteria, where I would doubtless run into the awful Henry Stieff or the less offensive Roger Bolin. Or perhaps I could dodge them and manage to find Victor Haas, the best of the batch. But even with Victor I wouldn't want to talk about Eveline—and with-out any question he would ask. Well-intended as he might be, I wasn't about to confide in him the least whisper about tendrils or about Eveline's otherworldly genius or about our plan to meet my father in 1947 and soften him into being a guardian of the republic instead of one of its violators and destructors. I could too well imagine, if I were to start in on the least part of these things, what Victor's reaction would be—a polite enough interest at first, then a rising eyebrow, the failing attempt to repress a smile, finally the twirling of a finger at the side of his head. Impossible. It was imperative that I stay away. If nothing else, Victor would wonder why I was in the dining hall instead of with Eveline. Anything I might answer would be a lie—ex-cept, that is, "I don't know." But even saying that would feel like talking behind Eveline's back, a betrayal of the confidence between us that I held as an absolute.

I had enormous amounts of reading to do. Maybe later I would feel hungry. I left the diner and went on Washington down to the library. I went inside, then up the stairs to the second floor and through the stacks to my favorite spot for reading. This was one of the reading-lounges on the Washington Street side, a private-feeling place with three or four upholstered chairs and a small table. Stacks pressed in on three sides, and on the fourth side were the mullioned windows where, back in December, I'd watched the heavy snowfall begin.

Luck was with me and no one else was there. I set my books on the table and chose one of the chairs with a good view of the windows. I draped my coat over the back of the chair, sat down, and got to work. I took up my long assignment in Arnold but soon enough, finding it hard to concentrate, turned to *Sartor Resartus*. I could have switched to *Beowulf*, where there was always work to do, but *Beowulf* would only fill my head with more thoughts of Eveline, every time I came to a verb I had to look up but that she would already know. I stayed with Carlyle for another hour, then switched to Dreiser and an hour with *An American Tragedy*. By this time it was a little past five and the windows were dark.

When I stepped out of the main door, the air felt colder and even more moist than it had earlier in the day. I wondered whether there would be snow. I pulled my knit cap down further over my ears, tightened my scarf, raised my coat collar in back. Then I set out on Washington Street up the hill. As I went past the diner, I looked in. Neither of the small square tables inside the front window was occupied. The counter was maybe half full. I continued along Washington across Clinton and then kept going until I passed the post office, after that went on to Johnson, then cut diagonally across the little park and went on to College. This time I crossed to the far side of the street, directly across from Eveline's house, and came to a stop. There were lights shining dimly from inside three or four windows. One of them came from inside the front room of Eveline's apartment. Of course I wondered what she was doing. I wondered if there was another light on in the back of the house; maybe she was in the kitchen, making something to eat. Or maybe she was at her desk. Or on the couch, reading. Or maybe she wasn't home at all. Maybe she had left the light on just to make it seem as though she were home. Maybe she was out, maybe with someone else.

This was agony. Everything felt gloomy, empty, and dark. Purposeless and hopeless. The night was cold and dank, and I was lost and confused. I turned back toward downtown, walking slowly. When I finally got to the diner, I entered and went down to the far end of the counter, to the last seat. I had *In Our Time* with me. I would read it over dinner.

•

It was late, somewhere between one-thirty and two. Everything seemed as though it were absolutely silent. I was in my room, at my desk, reading, as I had been for most of the evening. Earlier on, at the diner, I had more than taken my time. I'd ordered something and eaten it slowly, nursing a beer on the side while also reading my book, propped up in front of me. After the meal, I asked for a mug of tea. I took my time with that too and afterward asked for a refill.

When I finally paid up and left the diner, I had finished all but forty pages or so of *In Our Time*. By then it was nearly eight o'clock. The night outside was absolutely still. When I had walked down the hill from the diner and gotten halfway across the bridge, I stopped and looked down at the river for a while. Along the shorelines, there was a good amount of ice, but the strong current kept ice from forming in the middle. The water was turgid and dark when I looked down into it.

Back in my room, I took my boots off and, even though

they weren't wet, left them on the newspaper near the door. Coat, scarf, and knit cap I hung on the hook waiting for them just inside the closet. The little room was comfortably warm. I took my usual place, sideways at my desk.

I decided to keep the remaining pages of *In Our Time* as a treat for later and to take up Matthew Arnold where I had left off that afternoon in the library. An hour or hour and a half of Arnold, then back to Carlyle. The same for him. Then finish up with Nick Adams and his trip on The Big Two-Hearted River. By then it should be late enough for bed.

But it was difficult getting back to work. I felt empty, miserable, hollow, doomed, lost. I had no idea where to turn or what to do. Even my room felt like a prison.

I had managed, somehow, to force myself through my plan of dedicating a sweep of time to the critical asseverations of Matthew Arnold, then another—now done, at last—to Carlyle's tirelessly prickly philosophizing. I was in the act of picking up my copy of *In Our Time* in order to have some of it as a nightcap—the time was by now close to two—when I heard a sound so absolutely unexpected as to make me think for a moment I had imagined it. But it came again, three slowly deliberate raps at the door, slightly muffled, as if there were a glove on the hand doing the knocking.

The usual questions raced through my mind—who, so late, wrong door, certainly not for me—as the three knocks were repeated for a third time.

It's possible that suddenly I did understand, and knew it was Eveline. In any case, in one motion I jumped up from my chair and tossed Nick Adams on the bed. Two steps took me to the door, a twist of the knob let me draw it open, and standing there was—a very young man wearing a flat cap pulled low over his forehead, a waist-length brown padded jacket, knickerbockers, leg socks, and leather gloves. In one hand he held a yellow telegram. He held it out to me, saying nothing. At the same time he raised one gloved finger to his lips and, holding it there, glanced down the hall first one way and then the other. Then, after the faintest curtsy-like dip from the knees, he stepped lightly inside.

•

It was no different, really, from sitting ourselves down at a corner of Eveline's kitchen table to talk things out, or from sitting together under a blanket at one end of the couch so we could whisper for hours and hear one another perfectly—except that this time the location was my room in the Quadrangle (and my bed, mostly), and except that this time there would be powerful repercussions if we were to be "caught." If Eveline were to be caught having "entered" the men's dormitory, and if I were to be caught having "entertained" her there—the repercussions would consist, first, of expulsion from the university for us both and, second, of every degree of humiliation, woe, shame, sorrow, and regret that would be attendant upon the simple facts of the expulsions themselves. We lay in my narrow bed together, naked and still. Pieces of clothing were strewn around the room, mimicking the scene of their hasty removal—Eveline's flat cap hanging from the doorknob, her panties dangling from the switch on the side of the gooseneck lamp, shoes kicked into various corners, my shirt and pants across the back of the upholstered chair. We'd slept for a while, maybe half an hour. The only light came from the gooseneck lamp, and it was turned facing the wall. I could feel Eveline as much as see her. She was awake and looking at me. Just as she had done at the door, she brought one finger up and put it across her lips, then whispered, "Did we make too much noise?" I gently moved her finger to the side and kissed her on the lips. "No," I whispered back. But then I realized that I wasn't at all sure. "Well, maybe too much. A little bit too much." Eveline gave a big sigh. She got her arms around me and pulled me more tightly against her. Then she started tugging at the blankets so as to get them pulled up higher around our necks. I helped her. She gave a passing shiver at the pleasure of being warm and snug. I kissed her on her forehead and on the bridge of her nose. Then I lowered my head to the pillow and lay there, facing her. Our noses were almost touching. I was too close to see her in focus, but I saw her as if by feeling, by the warmth of her skin, the faint stir of her breath. She arranged her legs in such a way that one of my own was clamped tightly between both of hers. She pulled me still more tightly against her. She whispered, and I could hear her perfectly.

"Now. Let me explain everything," she began. "But only in whispers. We don't want to get caught. My god, we mustn't get caught. That would be awful. Dreadful. Horrible. We could lose everything." I started to make a reply but she dug her fingernails into my back, hard, and said "*Shhhhh*. No talking by *you*. No talking by you until I'm done explaining. I owe it to you. Please receive it. First. You wonder why in damnation I came to see you *here* if it's so dangerous. The reason is perfectly simple. It needed to be someplace private. As absolutely private as possible. It could have been in plain sight if no one would notice. But they would. But not here. They wouldn't think of looking here. We can be invisible, so long as we're quiet. I'll be quiet. I promise. And we can stay here as long as we want. At least until the cleaning service comes on Monday. You do have the cleaning service? Don't answer. Just nod. Maid service. Maid service, for godsakes." At this point, again, she dug her fingernails into my back, but just for a moment. Then again. "Malcolm, Malcolm, Malcolm, please, please, please forgive me. Forgive me for becoming so chill, and distant, and mean. I was going crazy. Sweetheart, sweetheart"—the nails—"I felt like I was going crazy. I felt like I was losing you. I *was* losing you. You must have felt it, too. It was embarrassing. It didn't have anything to do with *us*. It all had to do with *them*, with all of *them* sitting there, the big lump of them, defining us and judging us and thinking of us in *their* terms and in *their* words and in *their* imagery, transforming us into 'Mr. Joe College' and his 'Going-Steady-Now,' how pretty and cute, his perfect 'Miss Co-ed,' dumping over us every fistful of cheap tinsel, every banality, every meretricious clot of unearned imagery regurgitated from their basement-brains. . ." She paused. My arms were around her as hers were around me, and I could tell, not from any sound she made, but from the faintest movement in her shoulders, that she was *weeping*. She had put her chin down, and I reached down to raise it up gently, turning her face toward mine, and kissed her wet eyes. She cried harder for a minute and then began to stop. Her arms tightened around me. I felt her fingernails again. "Thank you for the letter," she said, still in a whisper. She paused. "But I would have come even if you hadn't sent it. I was already planning how to do it. We needed someplace where we could be absolutely invisible to everyone else, and this was the only one I could think of. For now, I mean. I'm going to talk to Bessie. I'll bring her around. I *know* we won't have to wait all semester before we can move back in again. At my place. We have to be alone. I only want privacy. I only want you and me." She was getting drowsy. "That miserable twerp in the diner yesterday, actually *whistling* at us, for the love of god." She gave a slight shiver. Then she fell sound asleep.

•

For an hour or so, perhaps longer, we both slept. When I woke up, the gooseneck lamp was still burning, the windows still dark. Everything around us seemed to be entirely, wholly, absolutely silent.

Eveline seemed not even to be breathing, she was so still. Then she stirred. She rolled over onto her back and arched up into a brief stretch. Then she rolled back onto her left side, the way she had been before, facing me.

"We have to talk," she murmured.

Tenets of Eveline, Part 1

For love to be intense, dynamic, and durable, it must also be private. Love is the lovers' only and no one else's and must therefore be kept as invisible as possible.

This tenet originates not from an impulse of pride, selfishness, or superiority but from a conviction that the honesty of something can best be served through its being defined by itself alone and not by reflections in it of the shaping thoughts and emotions of others.

The rose reaches loveliness through qualities of its own, not through the admiring words of those who declare it a thing of grace, color, beauty, and poise.

•

To be most effectively in control of their pleasure, lovers must appear, so far as possible (especially to strangers or near-strangers), not to be lovers at all. The lovers know the truth of the state they are in. The fewer beyond them who also know, the better.

•

Holding hands in public; walking with arms around one another's waists; kissing in public or engaging there in explicitly amorous physical behavior; for those who study the matter closely, these forms of behavior are indications not so much of the uncontrollably fervent impulsiveness of young love as they are suggestions of immaturity, lack of depth, absence of self-knowledge and also of true seriousness. Furthermore, and sadly, these behaviors are often harbingers of love affairs more likely to be short-lived than long, likely to be intellectually and emotionally sustaining through fewer rather than more decades in the lives of those who inform them and are informed by them.

This tenet originates not out of prudishness, timidity, puritanism, fear of sex, or any revulsion to it in any of its abundant normal and natural forms. Instead, the tenet arises, first, from an understanding that in the romantic sexual relationship, when honest, genuine, and fully realized, lies the key to the growth of the greatest social, republican, intellectual, and aesthetic strengths achievable by and through human beings. The tenet arises, second, from the twin understandings, one, that sexual intimacy in its pure form creates love in the first place and can exist only inside of love; and, second, that its creation of love—a parallel to the creation of a work of art—can be achieved only in solitude and only by a sole artificer.

Sexual love must by its nature remain a lonely thing, since it can be communicated only by one lover to another and can be shared only by one lover with another. It can, however, and through its very nature does, produce immensities far beyond itself, these being of a knitting, sewing, healing, generating, consolidating power and goodness. From the intrinsically unshareable, from the purely local, private, hidden, magnificently secretive phenomenon of sexual love between two people—from this universally significant yet absolutely private experience and from nothing else come, first, new life, and then, accordingly, family, this accompanied by the overwhelmingly powerful and binding love that welds parent and offspring together, then family; and then, after the creation of family, there will be brought into existence also the increasingly larger units of life: community, region, state, nation, and at last the world itself, this almost inconceivably vast immensity comprised of myriad infinitesimal parts that are and must be, every one of them, knit, sewn, and woven together with at least one other being, and perhaps many more than one other being, by the countless invisible threads and tendrils connecting each particle of created life with that life from which *it* was created, on the one hand, or, on the other hand, with that life to which it has become bonded through sexual love.

This type of connecting tendril, bond, thread, or filament, then, is the type that allows (or causes) humanity to live in ways that are familial, orderly, and social. When tendrils of this kind are broken, sickened, ignored, destroyed or otherwise caused or allowed to die, we live no longer in order, hope, and light, but in darkness, ruin, impotence, want, and war.

Lost, o lost, are we then.

•

The remaining category of tendril is the one that, while not serving to bring coherence to the social life on earth, serves instead to protect and ennoble earth itself and therefore, accordingly, to protect and ennoble all of life that exists upon it.

A clarification is necessary before we go further in discussing this category of tendril.

The importance of the tendrils in this category can be suggested in part simply through nomenclature. The category can accurately be named the "psycho-aesthetic" category of tendril, and with equal accuracy it can be called the "intellectual" category. Finally, it is also the "quantum" category of tendril.

•

Now, despite the correctness of the terms just mentioned, it must be understood absolutely that this category of tendril does not lie solely under the auspices or control of the human. It lies in fact under the control of three powerful forces, all of which are, if you will, super-human. First of these is the inestimably powerful force of earth's geological life. Second is the force of earth's flora in its entirety. And third is the immense force that comes from the existence of the animal kingdom, in its entirety, that also inhabits the earth.

Without any question, the "psycho-aesthetic" tendril is inextricably related to the human mind and therefore to human existence and behavior. But the dual point that must be made is, first, that prototypes of this tendril existed on earth millennia before the emergence of homo sapiens, and, second, that these same "prototypes" continue to exist even today.

•

Long before the emergence of human beings, there already existed these "caretaker" tendrils. Their purpose, then as now, was "to protect and ennoble earth itself and therefore, accordingly, to protect and ennoble all of life that existed or might exist upon it," as well—of vital importance—the life of earth itself.

Earth heals, forms, and ennobles itself through the shaping, evolving, and rejuvenating energies of its own geological forces and principles. It does the same, sculpting and enhancing itself, through the evolving energies of its indigenous vegetation, flora, or biota. And it adorns itself, equips, readies, fulfills, and expresses itself through the multitudinously complex gestation, growth, and expansion of its almost infinitely varied animal kingdom.

Earth before human beings was breathtakingly fecund, glorious, generative, self-healing, an unparalleled wonder of the universe.

Tenets of Eveline, Part 2

In order to tend to the earth's well-being, and to gain some understanding of the imponderable mystery of his own existence on the surface of that earth, man invented and developed philosophy and the arts.

That is to say, he did two things peculiar to no other animal: He thought about his existence, and he studiously and ritually created objects that lacked any obvious utilitarian value.

•

Exceptions existed, but, outside of a rare few, almost no human beings had any awareness whatsoever of earth's needs, or of its abilities, or of its delicacy or susceptibility to injury or harm, or, above all, any awareness of the myriad subtle and near-miraculous balances that existed between its various elements, features, powers, regions, engines, and forces, these being the countless balances, more subtle and intricate than the workings of a vast cosmic clock, by which earth nurtured, tended to, promoted, and maintained its own health and well-being.

But it was slow in this process of self-maintenance, and in time man began to overwhelm earth. With man's exponentially growing pace of reproduction—rodent-, lemming-, or rabbit-like—and with his way of spreading himself, his dwellings, and his accursed array of fierce behaviors ever more widely and broadly across the face of the planet—given these factors, it was obvious that injuries and offenses to earth were not only to become increasingly common, widespread, and severe, but also that they would occur, and continue to occur, faster than earth could cure or repair them.

And so, near this point in the later development of life on earth, tendrils began coming into existence.

•

Among certain elites, a sense of concern and alarm began to arise, gradually at first and then with increasing urgency. These elites consisted initially of magicians, seers, chieftains, gurus, magi, shamans, medicine men, and priests, and in later and then still later times there came to be included among them alchemists, astronomers, metallurgists, historians, philosophers, artists, sculptors, writers, musicians, and poets.

As time went on, figures such as these, along with others like them, formed what came to be known as the intellectual, academic, professorial, and artistic classes within human society. And their highest responsibility, albeit gradually, came to be the creation of tendrils that could heal, protect, and ennoble earth itself and therefore, accordingly and also, heal, protect, and ennoble all life that existed on earth.

These tendrils would spring into existence through the interactive relationship that exists between mind and matter, a relationship that, when approached honestly, dutifully, earnestly, and correctly, results in the release of an inventive energy sufficiently powerful to create a tendril of the kind described, and to keep it in existence forever, outside of time.

With the creation of an idea, as in the case of the philosopher or alchemist; or with the creation of sounds, as in the case of the musician or composer; or with the creation of significant objects, as in the case of the artist: Each of these created things is meaningful *because it has been created through the interactive relationship that exists between mind and matter*. This is why the resulting tendril can be placed in the category of the "intellectual" tendril, or, somewhat more accurately, in the category of "psycho-aesthetic" or "psycho-material" tendril, or, most accurately of all, in the category of the "quantum" tendril, it being most at home in this last category because the tendril does not in fact spring up into existence *until* it is "observed" by the experimenter, thinker, or artist; or, one might say, *until* it is "conceived" or "felt" or "thought" or "imagined" by the thinker, investigator, or artist.

The tendril, in other words, cannot spring up into existence until such time as there has actually been a union, however brief, between mind and matter, between psyche and earth, between the mind that ponders and the thing that is pondered by it. This "union" may be thought of as an *intercourse*, in a great many cases infinitesimally brief yet capable of generating energy, light, strength, and permanence sufficient for the creation of an ennobling, protective, and healing tendril.

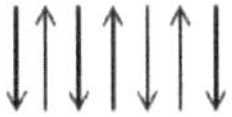

Tenets of Eveline, Part 3

(Each moment of the experience of correct reading calls for the greatest possible seriousness in the reader and the most intense possible concentration. These two qualities, mingled with one another, are capable of helping bring into existence the simultaneous narrowness of focus and breadth of vision necessary for the creation of an energy sufficient to allow the interpenetration of mind and matter, letting each of these for a certain time dwell inside the chambered presence of the other.

("The greatest possible seriousness" is almost certain to be misunderstood or misconstrued. The truth is, however, that this degree of seriousness has no relationship at all with that which is somber, joyless, or gloomy. Nothing just now said negates, rules out, or forbids lightness, laughter, hilarity, or whimsy, any more than, say, a consideration of the body would rule out the sexual body, the body and the sexual body being one and the same. Possibly the greatest evil to have befallen thinking humanity is the evil that comes from the mistake, made again and again and again, of believing the part to be the whole. When the part is believed to be the whole, the part is then not true. The whole, on the other hand, when seen and believed to *be* the whole, is true. Those who assume that joy must be banned from the high task of generating tendrils are like those who ban laughter in church or joy at birth or chimes in cathedral spires. War itself would melt, thaw, and resolve itself into a dew if the half-truth were shamed and forbidden, expunged from the canon of mankind. Every man is a piece of the continent, a part of the main. . . . When Raskolnikov throws his coins into the waters of the Neva, he is seeking communion with all humanity, for all humanity is connected, from one side of earth to the other, by water. (In the future, when I meet Malcolm's father, it won't be on water, for Malcolm tells me we will meet on the lawn west of the farmhouse, where the grass stands unmown and the elm trees rise in stately rows. There will be a September breeze from the southwest pushing the fabric of my dress against the backs of my legs as I stand there, no more than a foot or two away from this man who personifies the doomed nation Malcolm was born into and who now, for me, will personify something worse, a nation teetering on the edge of its yet greater doom, about to slide precipitously, swiftly, profoundly, into the abyss of sin, loss, criminality, and grief that awaits it. My task will be to prevent this cataclysmic ruin, this poisoning of the muscle, fiber, flesh, and soul not just of the nation but of earth itself, the task being to prevent this calamitous horror, this boisterous ruin, to keep it from taking place. It will be up to me to approach, calm, and soothe the destructive father, get him to come sit with me, perhaps on the porch, perhaps on the lawn, perhaps to stroll together under the high elms. It will be difficult but necessary, a matter bursting with urgency and necessity. It will be my task to get him to listen, and then to introduce to him the grave error of believing the part to be the whole, a sin that in those who are the more evil is a sin created out of will, desire, and blindness, while in others, those misled and lied to, who from birth have been nour-ished by their mentors and superiors on a diet of falsehood, error, and untruth—in these, although the sin is no less a sin, it remains a sin originating only in ignorance, which, unlike blind will, is a condition that can be attended to and cured.

(This father, this stiff, angry, sealed, righteous father whom Malcolm is relying on me to temper, mollify, and soften—will he prove to be a sinner who has been shaped through the power of his own will and unseeing design, or will he prove to be one who dwells in the condition of sin only as a result of the depths of ignorance that have been foisted upon him throughout life by countless mentors, guides, instructors, countrymen, leaders?

(No, certainly not. It can't be possible that Malcom's fa-ther is a man of ignorance. He is educated, a reader of books. But once read, what did he do with them? He played tennis and then cast aside the accouterments, habiliments, and para-phernalia of the game, letting them fall into disuse and decay. He fished in lakes and streams and then cast aside the gear, equipment, and trappings of the sport—disgusted by them?—causing them also to decompose and fall into tangles of ruin and decay. What, then, did he do with the *books* once he read them? Did he cast *them* aside as well, repudiate them, throw them out through doors and windows into the long wet grass under the groves of trees, where, swollen up, they served as sustenance for several years' worth of mushrooms while them-selves decomposing and being transformed gradually into earth?

(I must learn, study, know. In the time remaining before I meet him—this man who will be standing on the west lawn, who will be smiling sarcastically down at me, who will be "as lean as a knife and narrow as the blade of one"—before I meet him, carrying with me the yearning hope that I will be able to turn him from the path I know he is poised to take, the path that will turn the nation toward an ever greater darkness,

ruin, crime, mayhem, and slaughter, transforming it into a
thing without soul, beauty, or hope, without any possibility
of redemption—before I meet this figure, the man who will
come out from inside the old farmhouse, the man on the wide
lawn, under the high trees, I must discover what kind of evil
lies inside him, otherwise give up all hope of taming it.)))))

The gooseneck light was still burning, throwing its light against
the wall behind my desk. The windows still looked as if they
were covered with black felt. My watch read 5:35. The only
thing I wanted was to stay with Eveline, or to have her stay
with me. It was Sunday. I told her that there was no maid
service or room-cleaning on Sunday, that no one would ever
know we were here. I could get things to eat from the diner and
bring them back. But she wouldn't have anything to do with it.
She kissed me and kissed me, threw her arms around me and
whispered things into my ear. But no. Too soon there would be
daylight. She had to get back before Bessie noticed she'd gone.
It was imperative to be absolutely fair with Bessie; she was on
our side, and soon enough she was going to be so good to us,
in the spring, when I would come back to the house. Meanwhile I was helpless, able to do nothing to keep Eveline with
me. I was equally unable to convince her to let me come along
with her. She laughed. Absurd, she said. Just what a Western
Union boy needs, a *date*. Transfixed, I watched her as she got
dressed—as I watched her disappear. Tantalizingly, she sat on
the edge of the bed to pull her leg socks up over her knees
even before she stood up to pull on a pair of cotton panties.
Her brassiere came next: wearing it backwards, she adjusted
it to the very tightest hook, then twisted it around and drew
the cups up over her breasts. After that, the long-sleeved shirt,
buttoned all the way up. Then the knickerbockers, the shirt
tails tucked down under its waistband, its belt pulled up tight.

Then the waist-length brown padded jacket, buttoned from bottom to top. And, the very last thing, her hair. She pulled on the flat cap, at the same time tucking her hair up under it on all sides, then pulled the visor down low over her forehead to reveal herself transformed as—a boy. My heart broke. This boy picked up the folded piece of yellow paper he had arrived with, drew open the door, listened carefully, peered both ways out into the hall, then slipped out and drew the door silently shut behind him.

I was alone.

SIXTEEN

And so during spring term we prepared for our trip. The academic load itself was heavy, and both of us worked hard. We each had Godfrey's *Beowulf*, of course (where we now sat apart, I at the back and Eveline toward the front). On top of that, Eveline was taking my great-uncle's Literature in English before Chaucer; Non-dramatic Literature of the Elizabethan Period; Literature of the Augustan Age; and The Romantic Period from Gray to Byron. I wasn't up to carrying so heavy a load as Eveline, so I enrolled in only four courses instead of five, although I was also taking German—for a single credit—with an eye to passing another of the reading-for-research requirements the following summer (I had already passed the one in French).

Then on top of the usual academics came the "second curriculum," the added project of preparing for our trip and our meeting with my father. This preparation was arduous and demanding. It seemed to me that there were two major parts to it. The first was to identify the precise nature of my father's psychology in the form it had reached as of September 18, 1947. And the second, equally important, was to identify those historical influences that had been most consequential in shaping that psychology.

•

I need to be very exact. I need to proceed with extreme care.

•

The fact is that throughout my life—a life that has taken me now into my eighty-eighth year—I have done little else, really, other than study, ponder, and grieve over the psychology of my father. A lamentable thing. But I have had no real alternative. He, him, the nation I was born into. So visible was he, so dominating, calamitous, that there was little hope for escape. Here I am, still at it—worrying, fretting, poking into the character, constitution, and psychology of my long-dead father. If by some strange twist it hadn't been back in 1934 but instead right now, in 2028, that Eveline and I were preparing to meet him—then for textbooks I could offer her the books I myself began to write once I reached my forties and began feeling at least some release from the bondage of my long period of resentment, the time when I begin to feel at least some sense if not of release at least of resignation, enough to begin writing. And in the books that came, one after another, there appeared inevitably—my father. On those pages, as in life, he was for the most part silent. On those pages, as in life, he was willful, ruthless, plotting, secretive—and, in the end, calamitous. The nation I was born into. I could no more get away from him than from the air I breathed. There he was, living inside the sentences, paragraphs, chapters. I would see him, a tiny figure hanging from the top of one page or leering around the dog-eared corner of another. He would bore wormlike through the thickness of two hundred pages and form a cyst inside one of the stiff covers, making a tiny tomb where he could remain, dry, poisonous, and silent, forever.

•

My father was impenetrable. My father was incorrigible. My father, in the end, was irredeemable.

•

Until a week or ten days into March, the freeze remained fierce, hard, and cold. Then came a long period when everything remained gray, moist, chill, with a low and monotone sky. The temperature would rise seven or eight degrees above freezing in daytime, then fall the same number of degrees below it at night. Melt-water on the sidewalks turned to ice at night and made walking hazardous. This period after winter and before spring felt more oppressive than winter itself had felt, and people's desire almost universally was to stay indoors. For Eveline and me it was a difficult time, since finding places where we could be together with one another wasn't easy, especially when Eveline didn't want us to be seen as a couple any more than was unavoidable.

We didn't meet at the diner any more, and in fact, except for the three mornings when Godfrey's *Beowulf* met, we wouldn't see one another at all until late in the day, past four o'clock, when even my own late afternoon classes were over. Saturdays were another matter, since classes ended at noon, but the question invariably remained as to where we could go in order to have a certain degree of privacy and, not least, be relatively comfortable.

The library turned out to serve as a retreat for a good part of the very dreariest weather. I remembered the side-lounge where I had spent time reading back on the day when the heavy snow began, and then again later, just before Eveline sneaked into the Quadrangle and my room. There were a number of reading areas like that one, tucked into the edges and corners of the floors that held the main part of the collection. My old reading spot had been on the second floor, but I passed it by and climbed the stairs to the next, and top, floor in hopes of finding something even more private and remote. And I did. Tucked away in the far northeast corner of the third floor was a small area, like a notch cut out of a corner of the stacks, with two upholstered chairs instead of four, its own small table, and its own twin mullioned window. Ours. I told Eveline about this spot and began going there every afternoon when I was done with classes for the day, even if we hadn't made a plan to meet. But Eveline was as familiar with my schedule as I was with hers, and most of the time each of us knew the whereabouts of the other. In the beginning, Eveline tended from time to time to sneak up on me by coming through the stacks without a sound—as silent as a fox or doe—then peering at me from the edge of the forest before moving closer and, from behind, putting her hands over my eyes.

We began smuggling in food so that we could stay through the dinner hour and not leave until closing time. Eveline brought a thermos and we drank coffee out of the nested metal cups that screwed onto its top. Sometimes I brought sandwiches from the diner, and at other times Eveline made them at home and brought them in. She once surprised me with oatmeal-raisin cookies. We had to be careful not to bring in anything that was warm—except for the coffee—because the aroma might be noticed. I was fastidious about cleaning up before we left, making sure we left nothing behind, not even crumbs.

Our life with one another during this time was very different from what it had been during intersession. Then, we had also lived secretly, not having any classes to go to or appointments to keep, just living in Eveline's rooms as privately as possible, but also freely. When we wanted to go out, we went out with little or no sense that other people were observing, or monitoring, us. Once classes began, though, the situation was different. It went badly in Godfrey's *Beowulf* class, for example, when we quickly came to be seen as an "item" and were judged accordingly by those who pigeon-holed us in one way or another, as being "cute" or "sweet on one another" or "a good couple" or something of the sort. The truth is that I liked it as little as Eveline did, and so we went into seclusion, with our third-floor corner of the library as hideout. When the weather finally grew more moderate, we looked for alternatives, but in the weeks of bone-chillingly cold winter and in the following, although fewer, weeks of cold, damp, monotone gray, the library served almost as a home. In our two chairs, with our feet resting on our shared table, we read for hours, took time off to quiz one another on *Beowulf* passages—and then, an hour or two before closing time, when the windows were black as night, we would, in preparation for our upcoming journey, turn to history.

Thanks mainly to New College, I had a fairly decent grasp of contemporary history up through 1963, while what Eveline knew, naturally, ended thirty years before that. If we were going to be prepared to confront my father, it would be helpful for Eveline, too, to have a basic grasp of what had gone on up to 1947.

Over several weeks that winter and on into the spring, I recollected for Eveline as much as I could events that were to unfold between 1934 and September 18, 1947. Certain important things were already appearing, or *had* appeared, in newspapers—Hitler's capturing the Chancellorship, for example, the Reichstag fire, and the Enabling Act. For an hour or two every day, in the library at first, then in various locations around town (once the weather got warmer), and finally back again in Eveline's College Street apartment, I told Eveline as much as I knew about history-to-be. Spring that year was splendid, rich, balmy, and warm, rife with blossom and growth. A week into May, I moved back in with Eveline on College Street (with Bessie's tacit approval and her coquettish charade of looking the other way), and it was then, just before final exams, that we finally came out from the near edge of the Second World War and not so long afterward reached 1947, finding ourselves face to face with that year's grave importance and the corrupting decisions that were to be made in it, by my father, with others.

•

By the end of May 1934, then, we had worked our way up to autumn 1947. By then, as I said, I had moved out of my room in the Quadrangle—but kept my key—and carried such possessions as I had with me in Iowa City—two suitcases' worth, slightly less—over to Eveline's apartment. Our reunion in the old place felt like much more than just a coming together again. It wasn't joyless—by no worldly measure could you say it was joyless—but at the same time there was something different about it from before. It was in no way somber, but there was something about it, felt by both of us, that made it seem more serious than before. More stable, deeper, more set. There was still laughter, and there were still games, jokes, and various kinds of play. There was still sex—in fact, more than ever. As for the feeling of change, I don't know how much time passed before it found its way into words. Who spoke first I don't even remember. It hardly matters. But we found ourselves admitting to one another that it felt now as though we were married. That this wasn't literally true—legally—didn't make any difference at all, either to the way we felt or to the way we might think or behave. It was all settled. We were married. We *would* marry.

In the meantime, we continued reading. And we went on studying in the other ways too.

I remember when Eveline asked me, very seriously, why we should stop with 1947. After all, she said, didn't I know things up through 1963?

•

Godfrey's final exam in *Beowulf* was at one p.m. on the fourth of June. A Monday. The day before the exam was perfect for studying—a gentle spring rain lasted all day, ending around six in the evening. At that time, the clouds opened up in the west and the sun came in at a low slant, transforming the scene outside each of Eveline's windows into a separate Monet painting.

But for most of the day, when the rain was still falling, we sat on the couch trying to come as close as possible to memorizing the last two thousand lines of *Beowulf*. Godfrey had given the class an enormous boon by announcing that on the exam he would choose sight-reading passages from only the second two-thirds of the poem. So Eveline and I scoured those two thousand lines, then scoured them again, then again. Each of us had written hundreds of interlinear marks and notes in our own copies of the poem in order to identify meanings, cases, past participles, and the like, and we had each come as close as possible to memorizing these. Sitting on the couch, we took turns, one of us reading four lines in the Old English, then the other attempting to translate by ear. It was late that afternoon, and we were working along—

> *Ða se gæst ongan   glēdum spīwan,*
> *beorht hofu bærnan,   brynelēoma stōd*
> *eldum on andan;   nō ðær āht cwices*
> *lāð lyftfloga   læfan wolde.*

—when I heard Eveline ask, at my ear, in a voice scarcely above a whisper: "Why do we have to stop *there*? Why do we have to stop In 1947? Why can't we keep going to 1963?"

Unlike me, Eveline seemed to have little or no trouble thinking about more than one thing at a time, or, for that matter, doing more than one thing at a time. Here she was, memorizing *Beowulf* and at the same time thinking about pushing farther into the history of the future. There on the couch, Eveline was extending thoughts three decades forward into the future and at the same time ten centuries back into the past.

Imagine the tendrils being sent out during such a time, one after another, circling the earth, linking entirely different eras one with another, strengthening everything by strengthening the wholeness.

When the clouds broke and the sun came out, taking a break was irresistible. We pulled on our shoes. I dropped our two *Beowulf* volumes into my bag and slung it over my shoulder. And we went out. Stepping onto the front porch was like going through a museum wall and finding that you had stepped into a world-sized version of one of its paintings. Everything around us was light, color, nuance, loveliness. And scent. All of outdoors held the perfume of rain, grass, leaves, blossoms, and earth.

We set out along the wet sidewalk in the direction of John's Grocery.

I took Eveline's hand.

I would never leave her. Ever.

SEVENTEEN

It was necessary for me to think as carefully, precisely, and thoroughly as possible. So much was going on—everything at once—that not being able to keep one thing clear from another was a path toward certain failure. Yet at the same time it was equally necessary to remain aware of the oneness and singularity of the entire project—of the relationship between the whole and each of its parts, and, in the other direction, between each of those parts, however small, and the whole.

We worked hard at cultivating each strand, identifying its relationship to the others, then tying them together to provide the whole with true strength.

•

I couldn't have known that we were doomed.

•

The *Beowulf* exam was Monday, June fourth, as I mentioned. On the preceding Friday, Professor Godfrey kept up tradition by throwing a dinner for his students, or for his "scholars,"

194

as he called us. The event was to be at seven o'clock, in the mezzanine dining room of the Burlington Hotel downtown. The Burlington's dining room was quite spacious, with a row of tall windows facing west. As Eveline and I came to the top of the stairs—we were the first to arrive—and looked in through the double door, there was Professor Godfrey, on the far side of a long center table, bending forward and reaching out to make one tiny adjustment or another to the place settings. When Eveline said, "Hello, Professor Godfrey," he looked in our direction and the light from the windows glinted in the circles of his glasses.

•

Does that image have anything to do with anything else, connect anything with anything else?

The suppleness of Eveline's mind made me think of a fly fisherman, who stands in a stream and, with a flick of the rod, sends a fly to a certain point over the water, and in that way joins fisherman and fish.

•

It was a pleasant tradition, the *Beowulf* dinner.

By the end of the meal, the windows looking to the west were dark.

•

It was necessary to hold incompatible thoughts in your mind at the same time and not let their incompatibility dissuade you of the validity of any of them.

I took Eveline's hand.

•

Huge areas of knowledge stood waiting. So far, we had covered the major events that took place through what was now universally called the Second World War; but we had agreed, beyond that, to continue on through my own last known year of 1963. Then there waited also the massive and multi-disciplined field identified generally as "Studies in the Nature of My Father."

The studies were challenging not only in their magnitude but also in the difficulties posed by the necessity of identifying such methodologies as were appropriate and necessary for the mastery of them.

Of critical importance in our efforts was the all-important necessity that we must allow no identifiable truth to invalidate any *other* identifiable truth, lest we make ourselves guilty of misidentifying the relationship between the part and the whole.

If such a thing were to happen, we would be left without the least shred of hope for averting the nation's pivot to bloodshed, emptiness, terror, depravity.

•

SELECTED NOTES FROM EVELINE'S AND MY STUDIES

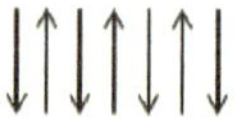

War

(1933, Chancellor. Night of the Long Knives. Nuremberg. Italy. Ethiopia. Anschluss. Goering. Sudetenland. Appeasement. Kristallnacht. Czechoslovakia. The passenger ship *St. Louis*. Poland. The Low Countries. France. Vichy. The Draft. "Arsenal of Democracy." Operation Barbarossa. Pearl Harbor.

Italy. Stalingrad. The Siege of Leningrad. Majdanek. Treblinka. Berlin air war. Dresden firestorm. Hitler's bunker. D-Day. Paris liberated. Death of FDR. V-E Day. Pacific Theater. Pearl Harbor. Coral Sea. Bataan. Midway. Guadalcanal. Tarawa. Iwo Jima. Leyte. Okinawa. Los Alamos. Manhattan Project. Fat Boy. *July 26ʰ 1945, Potsdam. Hiroshima. Nagasaki.* V-J Day. Surrender on deck of the *USS Missouri*, signatory table draped with a robe of green.)

My Father, My Nation

He was born into a family of religious believers from whom he worked steadily to distance himself, although he never succeeded in this project of severance with a completeness sufficient to free himself entirely from the *habits* of religious feeling, thought, or imagination. Even when he was a young man—and, as such, proud of demonstrating his independence from the family through any of the various means available to him—even then he would backslide regularly. Prepossessing in appearance, well above average in height, he was a young man of obvious intelligence, invariably a good student, widely read in history and literature. He very much wanted to be taken for a non-believer, for an educated man of secular habits, liberal beliefs, and sophisticated practices, and he acquired numerous affectations to encourage his being seen in these ways. He was highly conscious of the clothing he wore, fastidious both in its correctness and in its care, and aware of the fashions of the day. He was highly conscious of his own physical movements and took great care never to move too quickly or too slowly, but always to maintain the impression of being self-possessed, unflappable, incapable of being surprised. In a word, my father set out to cultivate for himself a bearing, image, and stance that would be taken as cosmopolitan.

This plan of self-actualization—as it might be called—was undertaken consciously by my father in his early adolescence as part of his plan to distance himself from the doctrinaire— they were sophisticatedly hidebound—members of his family. By the time he entered high school, however, it had grown into something else altogether—this once-conscious collection of stances, attitudes, and poses had been transformed into an ingrained set of mannerisms that were as unconscious and involuntary to him as breathing. The assorted airs that my father had consciously set out to practice in adolescence had been transmuted into the veritable descriptors and uncon- sciously held agents of his adult character.

And so this pattern of character formation, put into mo- tion as a means of achieving distance from the religiosity of his parents and siblings, may have ended up, for my father, being an escape from religious *doctrine*, but it proved to be no escape at all from the *habits* of religious feeling, thought, or imagination. My father may no longer have been trapped inside the wooden dogma of German or Norwegian Luther- anism, but certain elements in his character and qualities in the nature of his thinking kept him in the narrow prison of religiosity albeit without the bars of dogma.

The persona he had invented in order to show himself aloof from the religiosity of the others had the ironic effect, over time, of breeding in him the same air of being one of the elect that he so much disliked when he saw it in them. He powerfully disliked the airs of pride, smugness, and self-sat- isfaction shown by those who knew themselves to be among the saved, unlike the legions of lost souls living outside the faith. But no one who knew my father at any time in his life from late adolescence onward could fail to see in him salient qualities of self-satisfaction, superiority, and aloofness, the ironic legacies of his successful breaking away from faith.

There was one additional and extremely deep irony in the history of my father's rebellion. The expulsion of dogma from his heart, mind, and intellect had left behind a void, and, as everyone knows, no void can long endure but must be filled by *something*. In the case of my father, what took the place of dogma was self. Dogma had made it obvious that god was the center of the universe. Along with the eschewed dogma, however, god is also gone, and what replaces god as the center of the universe is self. In short, my father had been transformed into a Romantic, and, as a result, the universe now radiated outward from *him* as the observing center. What my father *saw* was what *was*. Reality was *whatever my father saw*.

By this path my father reached the very center of Romanticism, or the very height. Both metaphors—of the pinnacle on the one hand and of the center on the other—function accurately as descriptors of Romanticism of this kind and this degree of completeness. God has been replaced by the Romantic Self, and as a result that self occupies the pinnacle previously occupied by God. Similarly, the Romantic Self, as God once did, now resides at the center of the universe and is in fact the creator of that universe. When the Romantic Self looks out from inside its own self (we may think of this as the Self looking out through its own eyes, though in actuality this Self looks out through its own *mind*), those things that it *sees* are those things that *become* the universe.

The universe, then, is created not by a superior or external divinity but instead through the process *of being observed by* the Romantic Self, much as, in Quantum Mechanics, events in the realm of small-particle physics are *changed or even created through being observed*, and much as, in Jungian thought, psychological reality is changed *by the projection of one's shadow outward onto another*.

In its most fully developed instances, the Romantic Self is capable almost equally of bringing about toweringly humane accomplishments and of behaving with extraordinary selfishness, thoughtlessness, and cruelty. The reason for this extreme duality is that the Romantic Self by its own inner nature is at one and the same time visionary and all but blind. As creator of the universe, it is filled with joy, delight, promise, expectation, vision, and wonder. And yet at the same time, being at the *center* of the universe—and therefore being, literally, *self-centered*—it inclines naturally toward narrowness and even solipsism, possesses a diminished sense of otherness, and, perhaps most important of all, remains faithful to concepts, objects, phenomena, or other beings or minds only during the brief time when these might be, as it were, directly in front of its eyes. Once any such phenomena drift away or move off to one side, the Romantic Self—again, being *self-centered*—will cease to value or even think about them but instead, since they no longer have any immediate relation to the Romantic Self *itself*, will drop them altogether. This quality of the Romantic Self demonstrates its perfect suitability for being *the American self*, since the two of these, indeed, are one and the same.

Whether these two sides—the visionary and the all but blind—of my father's own psycho-religio-aesthetic-politico make-up were evenly balanced, I don't know. But I do know with certainty that the difference between the two was sharp, vivid, and extreme. The difference was clear, rigid, and complete.

The part of my father that resided precisely at the center of his own self was the part by far the more evident to me in the long years of my growing up. This was the part of my father, as I have explained, that caused him to be cruel, cold, unaware of others, and selfish. The experience of history for this side of my father was an experience pure, acute, essential, and intense—but it was also an experience, paradoxically, very close to instantaneous. For this side of my father's self—not the myopic side but the *mono-opic* side—the experience of history was the experience of separate *moments*. These moments were almost always intense, brilliantly lighted and colored, and quite, quite engrossing to the centric part of the Romantic Self. But they also passed quickly. And just as quickly they were abandoned altogether, forgotten, and left for dead. Americans do not remember history; they only remember the self as it felt or existed inside separate moments. The reason for this is that it makes the eternally recurrent pattern of affairs, however horrifying it may be, at least understandable. This part of the Romantic Self, residing at the center of the universe and thus also at the center of its own Self (again, *Self-Centered*), distills itself into an evermore pure state of solipsism and, in that increasingly pure state of internalness, loses all awareness of the myriad other things, beings, minds, selves, or consciousnesses that exist, may exist, or ever did exist. As a result, this side of the Romantic Self has neither any awareness of the existence of a historical past nor any concern for such an existence. The sole true reason for preserving the past, for preserving history, after all, is to be able to hand it on, or hand it down, to others. In the absence of awareness of others, this side of the Romantic Self knows only one feeling or idea, and that feeling or idea is its contentedness to relegate history to the dustbin, ignore it, let it die.

•

Study Questions

Study Question 1: What did Malcolm find curious about his father's behavior?

Answer 1: He found it curious the way his father left events, pleasures, and achievements behind, things presumably once valued and esteemed, things achieved with effort and purpose, now left rotting and abandoned, old trails of garbage sinking into the earth. In the rafters at the back of the machine shed lay other things that were broken and in ruins: rods for dry-fly casting; others for reel casting; a broken wickerwork creel; chest-high waders oxidized to the crispness of soda crackers; a canvas hunting jacket with sewn rows of loops for holding shells and very large side-pockets for dead game; in another pocket, a small, ancient bottle of citronella oil.

Study Question 2: What question did Malcolm ask himself about his father's behavior?

Answer 2: Why did his father keep these various elements and attractions of the past a secret from Malcolm, or, putting it another way, why did he relegate them to destruction rather than see his son introduced to them?

Study Question 3: What did Malcolm conclude about the nature of his father after analyzing his father's behavior?

Answer 3: Malcolm's conclusion, in his own words: My father is the nation I was born into. He is the nation that destroyed its history before my own turn came to learn from it and be nourished by it. He is the nation that drove its way west, destroying or devouring any and all life in its path. He is the nation that is blind to the sight of anything other than itself. He is the nation that visits terror on others and believes itself benevolent. He is the nation of torture, killing, and fear. He is the nation that eats its young. He is the nation that destroys itself. He is the nation now dying before our eyes, its decaying body infested with vermin.

EIGHTEEN

Exam results and term grades began appearing on the professors' office doors. Attached to Professor Godfrey's door were two sheets, one showing the final exam scores and the other showing overall grades for the term. Eveline's was the highest score on the *Beowulf* final, and her overall grade was "A." All of her grades were at the top. The final exam scores were posted also for Literature in English before Chaucer. Eveline's score there was the top one, too.

Everything we did that spring and summer consisted of one form or another of reading, study, research, memorization, planning. One major aspect of this work consisted of my tutoring Eveline as best I could in historic events and political affairs from 1947 through 1963. Most of the time we approached this task by taking our usual places on Eveline's couch and doing our listening and lecturing there. Spring remained warm, mellow, burgeoning, aromatic, loud with birdsong. We kept all the windows open, from the one in the bathroom on up to the twin windows in front, and the scents of spring drifted through the apartment like airborne balm.

I used the words "listening and lecturing." I should explain what I meant.

I didn't lecture, but I talked, reminisced, tried to remember everything I could from the years in question. Eveline in turn would ask about one thing or another that I may have said, remembered, read about, or alluded to. Sometimes she wanted clarification, sometimes more information, and sometimes she simply wanted to know the *atmosphere* of a place and event.

During this time, the necessity remained that I must *not*, as mentioned before, fail in being able to hold incompatible ideas and feelings in mind without allowing alteration or damage to any of them. At the start I didn't confide in Eveline about this challenge (although not long afterward I did), partly because I couldn't—yet—understand it myself. But a number of things were becoming more clear to me. One of these had to do less with contradictions than with a certainty: my new certainty that there was no need for us to wait thirteen years for 1947 to come about, but that *we could travel to 1947 at any time we felt we were prepared and equipped to make the journey.*

I felt confident that we could be prepared for our departure in time to arrive in West Tree, after a comfortable pace of travel, shortly before September18th, near the end of this coming summer.

As it happened, Eveline and I never so much *searched for* the portal to 1947 as, rather, we prepared for it, studied for it, readied ourselves for it—and then set out, hoping it would reveal itself to us. And it did—albeit, in the end, with catastrophic results.

NINETEEN

Evelyn was avid and indefatigable in her desire for knowledge. The more she learned, the more she wanted to know. She would read, study, scrutinize, observe, listen, and question, calling no halt until she felt as certain as possible that she had gotten at least a rudimentary grip on the nature and meaning of a subject, idea, or thing. Only then would she feel free to go on to the next.

Sitting on the couch, I set out to chronicle everything I knew—or everything I remembered—from 1947 through the following sixteen-plus years. In the same way that Eveline had told me about her years growing up in Fremont, I told her—tried to tell her—about my years growing up in West Tree.

Especially, she wanted to learn everything she could about my father, since he remained the center of our study.

•

The spring air wafted through the rooms of Eveline's apartment. As we sat on the couch, the windows behind us were wide open, as was the window next to Eveline's desk. Mid-afternoon. We had hours and hours and hours of time at our disposal.

I described as much of the history of the future as I knew. As for my father, I told Eveline about his nostalgia for the Second World War and his regret that the war had come to an end. The conflict had presented itself to him in such a way that he found the entire experience as much an adventure as a trial, not so much destructive and deadly as bracing and invigorating, personally fulfilling. I told Eveline the treasonous thought I had about my father—that when as many as 85 million people died because of the war, my father's intense nostalgia for it might be thought to indicate an emotional and intellectual outlook less inclusive, sensitive, principled, or humane than it might have been.

When he joined the Navy, he began in Tucson, Arizona, where he was to be trained as a junior officer. As it turned out, he enjoyed the training as much as he had ever enjoyed anything before. He loved about it, above all, the company of the other men. Beyond that, he loved the order, symmetry, rigor, and the camaraderie. He loved the humor that was shared among his fellows. And he loved the weather, the dry heat during the day and the cool air at night.

Furthermore, he loved the clothing. He loved the khaki worn for work hours as much as he loved the dress uniforms, the whole panoply of khaki, blue, and white being a delight to him. He loved the circular flat-topped hats with their shiny visors and their metal badges of wings and anchors in bas-relief. In every case, he loved the fabric the uniforms were made of, pressed, starched, crisp. He loved the jackets; he loved their epaulets; and he loved their gold buttons embossed with miniature anchors.

When training ended and he went to sea, my father loved everything about that part of the experience as well. He loved the ships and he loved being aboard them. They—and life aboard them—satisfied his sense of order. He loved them because they were clean, tidy, neat, and trim. He loved them for the necessity they posed for economizing on space and using it ingeniously. Furthermore, he loved being on the open sea. His fleet was once overtaken by a typhoon that went on for three days, with waves sixty feet high. My father loved every minute of it and wished it would never end.

•

Although he was often on the far outer edges of action, he was never in the midst of it. One time his ship passed over an area where a PT boat had been attacked from the air and sunk. There was an oil slick. On the edge of the slick five sailors floated, wearing life jackets that caused their heads to be thrown back. Their mouths were open, and so were their eyes. They stared up into the sun.

•

Aside from that occasion, I don't know that my father saw blood during the war, or death.

The dead sailors had been machine-gunned from the air. In spite of the bullets having penetrated them, their life jackets remained buoyant, being filled with kapok instead of air.

•

It was a highly partial view of the war, the one gained from my father's experiences, a view, as it were, through rose-colored glasses. For my father it was powerful, memorable, profoundly influential.

War was so extremely attractive in so very many ways.

President Truman didn't want it to end because then the economy would slow and the profits would dwindle.

My father, like Truman, didn't want it to end either.

•

(Eveline wrote the number in her notebook and then turned to me with a skeptical, faintly accusatory look. Her face was endlessly expressive. I found her stunningly beautiful.)

"Eighty-five million? That many will die?" she asked. Then she added, with certainty, "That can't possibly be correct."

•

Words written in 2002, on the subject of the war that never ended:

". . . [S]ince 1947 America has been the chief and pioneering perpetrator of 'preemptive' state terror, exclusively in the Third World and therefore widely dissembled."

—Arno J. Mayer, professor emeritus of history at Princeton University, in the newspaper Le Monde, quoted by Gore Vidal in Perpetual War for Perpetual Peace (New York, 2002)

•

(Up in the library, in the northwest corner of the third floor, our two upholstered chairs stood beside one another. Even so, from time to time Eveline would get out of hers and come over and climb up to share mine. I would move to one side to make as much room as possible and Eveline would lie on her side more or less on top of me, her knees flexed, arranging herself in the shape of a large letter "s." When she did this one night, I put my arm around her. Her head rested comfortably against me, her lips almost at my ear. "Take me along, then," she whispered. "With two of us we certainly can do it.")

•

More words written in 2002, these regarding the events of 1947:

"Fifty years ago, Harry Truman replaced the old republic with a national-security state whose sole purpose is to wage perpetual wars, hot, cold, and tepid. Exact date of replacement? February 27, 1947. Place: White House Cabinet Room. Cast: Truman, Undersecretary of State Dean Acheson, a handful of congressional leaders. Republican senator Arthur Vandenberg told Truman that he could have his militarized economy only if he first 'scared the hell out of the American people' that the Russians were coming. Truman obliged. The perpetual war began. Representative government of, by, and for the people is now a faded memory."

—Gore Vidal, *Perpetual War for Perpetual Peace (New York, 2002)*

•

My father was in the White House Cabinet Room that afternoon, among the others who were preparing to betray us. He returned to Washington again on September 18th of the same year, 1947, to offer his approval to the proceedings of that day as well.

•

(What Eveline meant when she whispered in my ear was this: Certainly together we would be able to soften my father, make his heart sympathetic and his judgment humane, and in that way persuade him to choose the good health of the republic rather than embrace its ruin.)

•

Words written by me on February 25th, 2028:

I can only thank god that I didn't know, then, when I was with Eveline, that everything was going to end in blood, death, emptiness, ashes.

The merciless, unforgiving, unbearable fact of knowing it now.

•

Keep in mind that when I was with Eveline, I knew nothing that had happened, or that was going to happen, beyond the end of 1963 and the first month or so of 1964.

•

The weather was so warm that spring that we had already moved Eveline's bed across the room and turned it so the head extended into the bay window. With the side sashes raised up, sleeping there was like sleeping outdoors, or in a tree house, what with the tall, lush greenery pressing in on three sides.

•

This was near the time when the thunderstorm came and made me think the house had been struck by lightning. As perhaps it had. The sound was instantaneous, terrifying, immense. Every window in the apartment turned from black into a bright sky blue. Involuntarily, Eveline and I sprung together and clung to one another like magnets. One more enormous crash followed, almost as loud although with much less light. After that, we lay there listening to the storm move gradually away. We were left with the sounds of dripping and trickling water outside the windows until we both fell asleep.

•

Ed LaRouche and Audrey held a party to celebrate the solstice. It was almost an exact duplication of their New Year's party six months earlier, even down to the guests, who again included Eveline and me along with Paul Evans and his wife, Roswithe. The drinks were different—gin and tonic this time—but almost everything else was the same, although now, instead of frost thickening on the twin front windows, the sashes were raised and in front of them an oscillating fan stood wafting air into the room.

There was conversation, a literary parlor game or two, and after everyone had had a couple of drinks Ed began putting on the Hot Fives and Hot Sevens at low volume like before. He set up a small rubber practice pad on a three-legged stool that he held between his knees and with his drum sticks quietly rolled, tapped, and riffed along with the music.

Still, the feeling of the party, for me, was much different from what it had been before. Eveline and I sat on the couch like before. The feeling I got simply from being there with her was wonderful, like before, but this time it was even more wonderful, so much so as almost to be uncontainable. It was because no one knew our secret. No one knew about our project. No one knew about our studies, or about the history of the future, or about my father, or about how we were to meet with him, or about the enormity of what was at stake, to change the direction of the nation's history. Eveline and Audrey talked with one another across the coffee table. When I touched Eveline's hand, she squeezed mine back. I got up and went into the kitchen and returned with two new drinks. Thanks to the small size of Ed and Audrey's apartment, everyone ended up being part of the same conversation. Paul reminisced about his time at Cambridge, where he had met Roswithe. He drove an MG while he was there, courted Roswithe with it and wished he could have brought it to the US. While I listened to him, I thought: *Eveline and I. Our secret. No one else knowing. How much I loved her.* The sun went down at a quarter of nine. Not long before that, I looked out at Meredith Hall across Jefferson Street; the sun, shining on it horizontally, softened and mellowed its weathered old bricks. I couldn't see the room on the far corner where Eveline and I had had *Beowulf*. I sat back down beside Eveline and we all went on talking, though much of the time I mostly just listened. There was a moment, like the last time, when the roof rolled up and away on hinges and the walls fell outward on other hinges, noiselessly, leaving us exposed to the immensity of the night, like soft black velvet, radiating outward to the horizons, while in the enormous dome inconceivably high up above us, up *there* were lights, up *there* were stars, up *there* were myriad worlds, incalculable in number, incalculable in size, incalculable in distance, strewn in an incalculable absoluteness of abundance, and in an incalculable absoluteness of mystery. But what I failed to see—lower, on the horizontal plane of the night—were the fibers, lines, strings, the tendrils that I should have seen emanating from a point on the couch between Eveline and me and reaching outward from us to the horizons, and neither did I see concentric circles that began as single points emerging from in between Eveline and me and widening into circles that moved concentrically outward from us, until at last they fell away over the curve of the earth and disappeared. A little before midnight we said our farewells and left for home, and on the way I told Eveline about the absence of the fibers, lines, and circles, the tendrils. She stopped and turned to me. "Oh, they're there," she said. "You might not see them. But they're there." The gin and tonics had gone to my head, and I suspected they might also have gone to Eveline's. She was looking up at me. I bent and kissed her on the lips. Then we held one another tightly and I told Eveline that I loved her, that I loved her and would always love her no matter what. She surprised me by laughing lightly. Then she looked up and I kissed her again, for a long time. "Me too," she said afterward. She pressed the side of her face against the side of mine. "I love you too. Madly." Her arms were around me and she pulled them tighter. "We're both crazy," she said. And after a half-second she added, "Thank god." Eveline took off her sandals and, following her example, I took off my own shoes and socks and we walked together in the dewy grass between the sidewalk and street, making slow progress not only because we were slightly drunk but because each of us had an arm around the other's waist plus a pair of shoes hanging from two fingers. At the house we sat on the top step of the porch, put down our shoes, and leaned together and kissed for a long time. I had had more to drink than I realized, and as for Eveline there was something mischievous going on with her. She put her lips to my ear and whispered the word "tendrils" two times, three, "tendrils," then pushed her tongue into my ear and I thought I might faint from the pleasure. Eveline stood, drew me up by the hand, and we went in through the door, shoes left behind.

TWENTY

Near this point, we set out more consciously on what Eveline and I called the geographical aspect of our studies. Our project was still the study of history, with the aim of influencing an event that lay in its future. But that meant the necessity also of undertaking the study of time.

It is impossible for history to exist outside of time. Imagine the absence of a present. Without a present, the past and future also disappear. This is to imagine the absence of everything.

If history is synchronous with time, it is also synchronous with territoriality, area, regionality, and space.

In other words, history needs a place to happen. It cannot happen nowhere. It can only happen somewhere.

The "whereness" of history is as important as the temporality of it.

Where it has happened; where it *does* happen; or where it is *going* to happen: In each case, these matters have an influence on *what* happens.

•

Another element in the geographical aspect of our studies concerned the contiguity of particles, these being the particles that constitute matter.

On the sensory level, all particles can be thought of as being connected to all others. That this idea might be challenged on the molecular, or quantum, level does nothing to negate the experience known to us all on the physical, sensual, or tactile level. The near end of the playing field is connected to the far end, the center to the edges. The east edge of a continent is connected to the west edge. The south pole is connected to the north pole, the tropics to the equator, and the equator to everywhere. The unity achieved by particles of rock, stone, earth, soil, clay, and loam is also achieved by bodies of water, where every particle of water is contiguous with every other; a hand immersed in New York harbor touches a hand immersed in the harbor of Shanghai.

•

Two or three times a week, Eveline and I went on treks as part of our plan of study—a plan that had now evolved into a study of the unity of history, time, and place. In our program of trekking, we stayed inside Iowa City at first, although soon we advanced into the town's immediate environs, then later ventured out farther, more deeply into the countryside. As an additional aspect of this project, we agreed that we would read American literature, or as much of it as we could in the time available, which meant almost all of June (beginning June fifth, the day after the *Beowulf* exam), all of July and August, and then the first seventeen days of September, for a total of one-hundred-and-four days. It seemed the best use of this time—in effect doubling it—could be accomplished by Eveline's and my reading *different* books and sharing them with the other. So Eveline set out with William Bradford and Anne Bradstreet while I turned to Edward Taylor and Cotton Mather, or I might take up Jonathan Edwards and Benjamin Franklin while Eveline turned to Thomas Paine and the Federalist, all to be shared later.

On trekking days the reading program had to be set aside, especially when we were still inside town; later, when we went farther afield, we would find stopping places where we could settle in for a handful of reading hours before our return—and later still, when we began staying out for entire nights, we naturally could make time for long stretches of reading.

Washington Irving, James Fenimore Cooper, Ralph Waldo Emerson, Nathaniel Hawthorne, Edgar Allan Poe, Henry David Thoreau, Herman Melville, Emily Dickinson (*"Men die—externally—/It is a truth—of Blood—/But we—are dying in Drama—/ And Drama—is never dead—"*). . . .

•

It was important, if they were to be worthwhile, that our explorations be to places that held an innate interest of some kind and that were able also to benefit the students' awareness, knowledge, and understanding in a way contributing to the overall plan of study.

It wasn't possible for every outing to fit these criteria, but all in all we were fairly successful. We began with seven or eight treks, as I mentioned, that kept us inside the city. Two of these were of greater impact and significance than the others—our trek to, and through, the Old Capitol building, and then our trek to the entrance of the main library in order to watch my father playing tennis.

Both of those early treks had a shared characteristic—each drew our consciousness an immense distance outward from the initial viewing point. They weren't alone in having this effect, but they *were* alone in the dramatic intensity of it.

A memorable although less dramatic trek was the one taking us to the location still inside the city limits but simultaneously *the farthest possible* distance from Kenney's bar.

Using a map, we identified the spot seemingly best qualified. Then, after spending the morning at home reading, we set out to find it.

The city limits were very irregularly shaped, as I have shown before, and they also reached much farther "out" than either of us had realized before we had studied the map. The spot we aimed for lay at the extreme northeast "corner" of the area that was still city-zoned, and it took us easily half an hour to reach it—but once we got there, how interesting it was. After leaving College Street, we walked in the right direction until the sidewalk ended and we were forced to switch over onto the street. After a time the street itself came to an end and was taken over by a simple gravel road. Some distance on, that road traded itself for wheel-tracks worn in long grass. We followed these tracks until they brought us to the edge of a very wide field planted in rows of young corn. *There*, at the near edge of that field, the city limits came to an end.

We stood there, Eveline and I, looking out over the corn rows, our toes in the field and our heels in town. The corn was three feet high or so, deep green in wide-set rows that went up over a low hill and disappeared on the other side. The farmer was driving his tractor back and forth from one end to the other, dragging a harrow to loosen up the soil between the rows. When we first got to the field, he was on the far side of the hill, coming toward us, and we watched as first the upright exhaust pipe of the tractor became visible, then the farmer's hat, then his shoulders and arms, and finally everything, including the tractor and its big driving wheels fixed with angled iron cleats. The farmer was looking back over his shoulder to be sure he kept the harrow away from the corn plants, so he didn't see us at first. But when he came to the edge of the field near where we were standing and turned the tractor around in the narrow space, he saw us. He raised an arm in greeting and we did the same.

•

It took much longer for us to reach Kenney's than it had taken to get to the city limits, since our starting point on College Street had already been far closer to the cornfield than Kenney's was.

We followed the wheel-tracks back to where they became a gravel road again, then the gravel road until it became a macadamized street, the street until sidewalks reappeared, then sidewalks downtown to Kenny's. The weather was perfect, the vault of sky a steady blue right down to the horizons, the air as gentle as a lover's breath. Before long we were far enough back into town so that the maples and elms, planted in the last century, rose up above us again from both sides of the street and joined their arms overhead. We walked in dappled shade until the trees grew smaller as we neared downtown, then disappeared almost entirely, so that sunlight fell steadily and shadowless along the streets.

•

Inside, Kenney's was quiet and pleasantly dark. The front door stood propped open, and now and then the afternoon air came in and drifted toward the back, where a handful of customers were scattered along the bar. Up front were booths, and Eveline and I took the second one back, closest to the air from the door. We sat together on one side of the booth, facing the street. I wanted a roast beef sandwich, and when I ordered it Eveline decided she would like one also, so we got two, and a beer each. The sandwiches were good, and after finishing them we had a second glass of beer each. It felt perfect, sitting there with the air coming in, now and then hearing a tag of conversation or a bit of laughter from the back. One more beer each, though when we finally left I'd drunk not only mine but half of Eveline's too. At home, we did some reading for an hour and a half or so, but in easy things, Mark Twain, Bret Harte, Ambrose Bierce, Stephen Crane, Hamlin Garland. I began having a heightened sense of the interconnectedness of things and when I asked Eveline whether she had the same feeling, she said, "Yes. Of course." She rested a hand on my knee, I put an arm around her shoulders, and we read that way for a while longer. In my mind, I retraced our steps and thought of us returning to the tree-shaded street we'd come on, continuing to the place where the sidewalk ended, then to where the macadam ended, then to where the gravel ended, and then to where the wheel tracks ended, at the very edge of the cornfield. I wondered if the farmer was still there, on his tractor, drawing his harrow back and forth across the field, row after row.

Without any doubt we were a bit tipsy on leaving Kenney's, but it made the walk home a greater pleasure. The air seemed even more balmy and sweet than earlier, the quality of the light under the shade trees more subtle and inviting. Even the mundane sounds of things going on around us were appealing—the clopping hooves of the ice man's horse, the shout of a young boy to his friend across the street, the almost silent whir of the lawnmower that a man, a little bit like the farmer, pushed across his front lawn back and forth, from one end to the other.

Home again, in the aromatic and somnolent gathering of the long summer evening: James, Dreiser, Adams, Robinson, Frost.

TWENTY-ONE

There was so much to do. The preparations seemed mountainous if we were to get anywhere near ready.

One of our treks out of town was to Eden Lake, fifteen miles or so east of Iowa City. We got up early, a little past five, and left the house at twenty before six. Fifteen minutes of walking on Muscatine Avenue got us near the city limits and to the point where the avenue became Route 6. From there, we hitched. Two people with backpacks made for a space-consuming pick-up, but Eveline's being beautiful made getting rides easier. (She had a gold ring that had been her mother's, and, to help avoid raised eyebrows, she'd slipped it onto her left ring finger before we left the house.) We got our first ride almost right away from a salesman who had to turn off just half the way to Eden Lake. We waited almost half an hour for our next ride (quite a few farm trucks went by, but the truck beds were full-up with grain or hay, and there was only one empty seat in the cabs), but it was a beautiful morning and the waiting time seemed short. We were in the midst of farmland that rolled out in every direction across low hills. Seemingly from everywhere came the music of birdsong, mourning doves, meadowlarks, bobwhites, now and then the call of a grouse or pheasant.

Our next ride, from a middle-aged farm couple on their way home to their farm near Eden Lake, dropped us off just outside town. We walked in to look around before going out to the lake to find a campsite.

The little town was quiet, small, pleasant, quaint, the main street was scarcely more than three or so blocks long. Cars parked with their noses diagonally against the curbs. Among them were many farm trucks like the ones we'd seen on the highway.

Eveline and I stopped in at the town diner, set down our packs near the door, and sat at a table by the front window. The place was a near-replica of the Bus Depot Diner in Iowa City. We each ordered a plate of eggs, potatoes, toast, and bacon, with coffee, since we hadn't eaten breakfast before leaving College Street. The waitress was friendly but didn't ask anything about who we were or where we were going until it was time for her to clear the table and bring us the tab. That gave us time to get a story together beforehand. We were, of course, married, as Eveline's ring showed. Both sets of our parents lived in Denver, and we were students at Iowa City, hitch-hiking our way back from Colorado in time for the second summer session and, after that, the fall term. I placed the waitress at about age sixty, on the plump side, with a conventional grandmotherly appearance. She seemed well enough satisfied with our tale and wished us good luck with the rest of the trip. She gave us a smile and said,

"Well, at least you don't have much farther to go now, do you."

Neither of us liked leaning on fabrications, but it seemed a practical thing to do. Still, it was a relief to leave the diner and make a point of turning left—as though we were heading for the west-bound highway, although in fact we were heading for the lake, a short way north of town.

For a while we addressed one another as "dear," just for the fun of it.

At the west end of Main Street we turned right onto North Third and continued along the sidewalk. Frame houses with mown lawns flanked the street for a block and a half or so. Then smaller houses took over for another block and a half, replaced in turn by small unpainted structures made of weathered wood and looking like toolsheds or woodsheds, perhaps now and then a one-car garage. Near this point, the sidewalk ended, and so did the pavement, and we were out of town, going along a trail through brush and long grass. The lake was a quarter mile or so farther on, evident at first thanks to the stands of trees that flourished around its shores. Closer to the water and looking down at it, we could see that here and there were small beaches, it often (like at the place where we now stood) requiring a fair climb to get down to them. I took off my pack and went down first—a four- or five-foot decline. Then Eveline handed my pack down to me, and after it her own. Then she herself climbed down, backwards, like coming down a ladder, with me reaching up to steady her.

The day was getting hot, the sky still an unclouded blue, the breeze light. We walked clockwise around the lake to what was more or less the southwest point on the shore and settled on a spot there to camp. It had an attractive little strip of beach that was more sand than soil, inviting us to take off our shoes and socks and go barefoot for the rest of the day. We even went in wading, up to the knees. The bottom was firm and the water clear enough so that we could see, with each step into deeper water, the flash of a hundred tiny fish as they turned tail.

I had decided to wait until we were settled in before telling Eveline why I'd wanted to come to Eden Lake. Or why I'd wanted to come "back" to Eden Lake.

At the spot we'd chosen, the embankment that rose up from the beach was very steep, almost vertical, though grass-covered a good way up from its base and held in place with thick growths of brush higher up. At the top, where the level ground stretched away from the lake, stood a considerable gathering of trees, among them a half-dozen extremely tall elms that made me wonder whether at one time a farmhouse had stood nearby.

It was very pleasant, really. Instead of putting up our tent, we lay it out flat, for the time being, as a ground cover, then spread our blankets on top of it in such a way that we could sit on them and lean back comfortably against the grassy embankment. By now it was somewhere between eleven o'clock and noon, and as the sun moved west, our spot became covered in shade from the trees above us. We spent more or less the first half of the afternoon reading, then decided to take a break by going on a walk along the shore of the lake. The idea came up of going all the way around in a circumambulation. I guessed the whole distance around might be two miles. We put our shoes back on and set out, not hurrying but just strolling comfortably. Plans to circle the lake changed, however, when we got to a point maybe a third of the way around. There, the embankment gradually became lower and then disappeared altogether, so that the land outside the lake was on the same level as the surface of the lake itself. Here, extending right up to the water's edge were dense growths of bushes, shrubs, and dark brambly thickets of one sort or another. Extending a good distance beyond them out into the lake itself was an area where the water looked green and was clotted with reeds, fronds, and lily pads, and with vegetation that looked partly like floating moss and partly like half-submerged lily pads the size of dinner plates.

At this point, neither of us really wanted to go farther. I suppose we could have turned inland to look for a spot dry enough so that we could step across the rivulet, or brook, or spring, or marsh, or whatever it was, and then turn back again to the lake. But to get to a dry place away from the lake we still would have had to go across the soft and wet part alongside the thickets, reeds, and shrubs. I tested it by setting one foot on the wet area and then adding my weight. My shoe went straight down and I was barely able to pull it back up, with a sucking sound, before sand, water, and muck flooded into the hole it left behind. Thoughts of quicksand came to mind, and Eveline and I agreed to turn back. Also, the afternoon light was beginning to change, softening a bit and growing more mellow as the sun moved west. I was surprised when a glance at my watch showed that it was already four-thirty. We sat on a fallen tree to take off our shoes and socks—one of mine was sopping wet inside, after all—then turned to walk back, side by side, each with shoes dangling from two fingers like the night after Ed and Audrey's party. Deciding to turn back from the overgrown place made me think of one of the books I'd brought along, when Nick Adams decided to go back to his camp with what he's already caught instead of going down into the swamp to fish there.

Back at our spot on the shore, things were just as we had left them, our packs sitting there and our blankets smoothed out. Two or three books lay stacked on Eveline's side where she had put them, and two or three others on my side. From one of the packs I got out our bottle of wine and opened it with the corkscrew on my jackknife. We'd brought two collapsible cups and drank from them, sitting on our blankets like before, leaning back against the embankment. The scene was quiet, still, bucolic. A dog barked three or four times from some-where, then stopped. There was birdsong, though diminishing as the afternoon drew nearer an end. A squadron of ducks pad-dled near shore a certain distance away, and across the lake we could see a flock of black crows fluttering down clumsily to congregate in the tree tops, and we could hear them too, although faintly, from across the water.

The wine was pleasant, but we would have to be careful to go slowly with it. The time now was between five and six o'clock. There would be plenty of daylight until eight o'clock, then enough for doing certain things until nine, although by that time we would probably want to be asleep, or near it. The night wouldn't be long. In the morning the sky would start growing light after four, and at five-thirty the sun would come up—certain to wake us, since it would rise straight across the lake from camp and would be right in our eyes.

We had decided we wouldn't make a fire and wouldn't cook. For dinner we'd brought along bread, cheese, kipper snacks, apples, and even some oatmeal-raisin cookies that Eveline had made.

All of this meant that we still had time to enjoy our wine for awhile before turning to other things, dinner among them, but also setting up the tent so we wouldn't be soaked with dew by morning. Against the deepening blue sky high up above the lake a hawk was riding a thermal, soaring in wide circles. Its great wings were outspread and all but motionless as it looked down, searching for prey.

Sitting together, side by side, looking out over the scene, I began telling Eveline about my previous—later—visit to Eden Lake, on the day the president was murdered.

I described almost everything for her, how I'd come out of class to find students walking around with transistor radios pressed to their ears, and about my asking someone what they were listening to, then going to the student union and bumping into Fritz Dreisbach. By then there was no longer any question that the president was dead. I told Eveline about Fritz wanting to drive out to see Jim Petzky, who lived with his wife out in Eden Lake. I told her about Fritz saying that Peter Hatch and Bob Lehrman were coming along too and adding that I really, really ought to join them. After all, classes had already been canceled. There was no reason to stay in town.

But Fritz had no idea, I told Eveline, of the way I felt about leaving Iowa City, of the way it felt to me like going out from underneath a protective dome and being exposed to every sort of harm and danger and risk and threat. And yet, still, I went along. And Eden Lake was awful. It had turned into a highway strip-mall with heavy traffic, gaudy throw-away buildings, and parking lots. Even the house Jim and Rhoda lived in was tiny, flimsy, cheap, and bleak.

(I poured another cup of wine for Eveline and one for myself and went on describing what Eden Lake had been like, and what the visit to the Petzkys' place had been like, and telling about the beers we drank and the drive back to Iowa City. I told Eveline how I had never really liked Peter Hatch and had never really trusted him. And I told her about dropping the case of empties off at John's Grocery, then dropping Peter Hatch and Bob Lehrman off at the foot of the Iowa Avenue bridge, and about me going with Fritz to park his car again and how he and I still made it back to the Quadrangle with ten minutes to spare before they closed the dinner line. I described what it was like when I got back to my room, how I felt safe again once I was finally there, and how I realized that that feeling of being safe, everything about it, had to do with coherence, with the way things were related one to another, and then one to another again. How I had my room, my classes, my books, hours, schedules, assignments. I explained how all of this had to do with the reason why there could be meaning and significance on the inside, and on the outside plunder, chaos, emptiness, and ruin.

((Together, we put up the tent while there was still enough light to see by, and the bottle still had wine enough for a half cup each. Between us we had four blankets, two of wool and two lighter, of cotton, and that was plenty for weather as warm as this. We put them down in such a way that we could lie on them and still have enough to pull over on top of ourselves if we chose, and we rolled up one of the lighter blankets to serve as a pillow. We decided to sleep naked because of the warm weather and also to avoid getting tangled up in clothing. I brought our packs inside and put them at the top of the blankets, where they were also good for leaning against while we went on talking. In my pack, I had stashed a half-pint of whiskey, and we shared taking sips from it, followed by water from one of our canteens. Except for the background noise of crickets and frogs, the night was quiet and still, though now and then we would hear something splash in the lake. My other trip to Eden Lake was on November 22nd, 1963, and three days later I saw Eveline for the very first time, in McGalliard's Old English class, in Jessup Hall, on November 27th, 1933, when I knew immediately that I had never seen a more beautiful girl, and that I would never see a more beautiful one again, ever. Eveline fell asleep before I did, and after a little while I reached across and drew the excess of blanket up over her, the woolen one, then, moving as little as possible, I reached behind on my own side and did the same for myself, so that I was also covered loosely by the wool. It felt good. In spite of the hot weather and the sun all day, this light covering was very nice. I felt more naked lying under the blanket, our limbs entangled, than I had when both of us were completely uncovered. Intimacy. Warmth.

(((The scent of Eveline's hair, holding every scent of the outdoors. Lying with her there, the weight of us bearing down on the earth, separated from it only by the tent floor and the thickness of two blankets, I found myself being less and less certain of which I loved more, Eveline or Eveline's world, Eveline or the world of Eveline, Eveline or the world imbued by Eveline, and it began to seem, feeling her limbs against mine, and feeling the smoothness and warmth of her flesh, it began to seem as if she and I were becoming intermingled, that we were becoming a single thing, and then, as had happened so many times before, it became more and more clear to me that Eveline and I were touching not only one another, not only the blankets and tent floor under us and the earth below those, but that we were touching everything everywhere, since every molecule touches the molecule next to it, every molecule of every kind, whether earth, air, water, rock, clay, loam, vapor—or flesh, bone, organ, blood—so that Eveline and I were touching every molecule in the universe, and every molecule in the universe was touching *us*, and therefore, because history can occur only if it has a place to occur, which is to say, since history is locational, Eveline and I were also therefore being carried along inside history, and therefore we were being carried along also inside time, inside time and inside place—Iowa City Fremont Eden Lake West Tree—and then, in the dying flicker of final consciousness, Eveline beside me and night all around me, I saw the truth and knew it to be the truth, as certain as death, the awful truth that my father was going to betray me, was going to betray Eveline, was going to betray both Eveline and me and the entire nation she and I were born into.)))

TWENTY-TWO

It became clear that my own field of study, however I might resist the fact or wish it otherwise, was going to consist of study in the river of blood. Each day pushed me more deeply into the knowledge that there was no escape from this abysmal end and no alternative to it. Only one condition existed that could have allowed escape from it or that, even, could have allowed *preparation* for escape. That condition was that I be allowed to remain with Eveline for the remainder of my life. No, of *our* lives.

•

The truth is that I still don't know with complete certainty what it was that broke Eveline and me apart. I know that she and I failed miserably in our appeal to my father—or, to put it another, equally true and perhaps *more* true, way—I know that my father failed miserably in *receiving* Eveline's and my appeal.

Sheltered, naïve, vain, inexperienced, monstrous in his ignorance, solipsism, and desire: My father chose the river of blood.

•

He turned away from us and went down the drive, walked along the road into West Tree, went by bus to St. Paul, train to Chicago, train again to Washington, D.C., then to the White House and the Cabinet Room.

•

Even then, even given the enormity of his betrayal and the absoluteness of his abandonment, I still believe, if only Eveline and I had been allowed to remain together, that we could have exerted a meliorative and humanizing influence on the course of blindness, greed, and hollow opportunism that my father chose. But she would now soon be taken from me entirely and all would be lost. She would be gone, out of my reach absolutely, and I would experience the most horrible thing that had ever befallen me and that has ever befallen me since.

TWENTY-THREE

The river of blood had been there from the beginning. *We* knew that. Eveline and I both knew that. But we also knew that the river of blood had not been the *only* river. In the four-hundred-fifty-five years leading up to the fatal turning point, there had been other rivers also. There had been the river of grass, the river of the seasons, the river of planting, the river of harvest, the river of hope, the river of birth, the river of poetry. There had been the river of apples, the river of music, the river of others, the river of desire, the river of song, the river of firesides, the river of home, the river of union, the river of medicine, the river of care, the river of kindness.

But after the fatal turning point and the start of the collapse, there was only the river of blood.

•

As Eveline and I worked on the history of the future, I did what I could to keep either of us from becoming frightened, or at least more frightened than absolutely inevitable.

Time was passing too quickly. Summer was almost half gone. Time now stretched in almost equal lengths back to the

Beowulf exam and forward to our meeting with my father.

And, in our studies, without question, the coming three decades included horror tripping on the heels of horror, all audible in words, names, numbers—Bataan, China, Leningrad, Stalingrad, 16,825,000 dead, Crimea, blood, 20,000,000 dead, Dresden, Berlin, Mauthausen, Auschwitz, Dachau, 6,000,000 dead, blood, suffering, more suffering, Little Boy, Fat Boy. . . Inexcusable, diminutive nicknames of things undiminishable, nicknames that put a flip irony in the place of terror, death, loss, agony, torture, the inhumane.

I would prefer not to. . . .

•

Eveline changed. Grew quieter. Remained pensive for longer periods of time.

•

Still we continued our program of reading. Sandburg, Frost, Robinson, Lowell, Eliot, Aiken, Millay, Hemingway, Anderson, Cather, more Dickinson (*"I willed my Keepsakes–Signed away / What portions of me be / Assignable–and then it was / There interposed a Fly– // With Blue–uncertain stumbling Buzz– / Between the light–and me– / And then the Windows failed–and then / I could not see to see–"*)

•

In our reading we were able to find some respite, some of the time.

TWENTY-FOUR

We allowed just under four weeks for our trip to West Tree. Part of the plan was that we would complete the journey without using fire, at least not fire of our own making. When we stopped in one town or another and decided to eat in a restaurant or diner, then of course we used fire, or the cooks did, for their grill or oven, or for brewing coffee or tea and the like. But it wasn't fire of our own.

Eveline and I decided to approach the trip in as leisurely a way as possible, to think of it as a vacation of a certain kind, and the decision not to make fires was one way of keeping things simple. We weren't interested in "roughing it" or in making a hardship journey as penance-through-rigor of one sort or another. In fact, the aim was almost the opposite. We had no way of knowing what waited for us at the end of the trip, evil or good, happiness or horror. That gave us all the more reason for making the trip itself as pleasurable as possible.

In fact, as things turned out, our long trek was almost entirely perfect. The weather, for one thing, was absolutely splendid as August gave way to a calm and beautiful September. Almost the entire walk took us through low rolling hills of long-grass prairie that was punctuated by stands of trees along the waterways, conveniently identifying the places where we usually made our camps. Before leaving Iowa City, we bought a new tent, very small, and, along with it, two sleeping bags that could be configured in different ways. Each could be used as a large blanket or ground cover, or as a single sleeping bag, or, if zipped together in a certain way, as a sleeping bag for two. All of our gear was tidy, compact, and economical, everything about it efficient enough so that we had plenty of extra space for carrying books. I had a compact little tool kit and also a hatchet good for pounding in tent stakes and also sharpening new ones if need be.

The land was open, immense, spectacular, and—although the word may seem odd—kind. On the entire walk from Iowa City to West Tree we passed no farm, climbed no fence, and crossed no plowed, tilled, or planted field—although a certain number of such fields did exist, but they were invariably grouped and clustered around or near the perimeters of towns. As for the towns themselves, no two were quite alike and yet all were of a type. Each had a single main street or avenue, with the length of this street being an indicator of the size of the town. All aspects of commercial life took place along this corridor, while residential streets reached out from it on one or both sides. The number of these streets varied in accordance with the size of the town's population, which might be as small as three to five hundred or sometimes, if rarely, as high as four or five thousand, although we never came upon one larger.

One of the most notable and possibly most significant things about these places is that in each of them there was always, without exception, something noticeably *pleasant*. The residents we happened to meet, for example, although few in number, were invariably affable, friendly, and eager to please. The food in the towns, as well, while never pretentious, fancy, or in any way aimed at either the gourmet or the gourmand, was invariably fresh, varied, honest, nourishing, and tasty. Most of the time, we went into a town once a day, this for the purpose of obtaining food that we would then take with us to whatever place was to be our next camp. Sometimes, if it happened to be quite early in the day when we went into a town, we would stop for breakfast in a local restaurant or diner before shopping for provisions to take along with us on the next leg of our journey. At other times, if we happened to go into a town near the middle of the day, we would stop for lunch before continuing on. In addition, one time each week, we made a point of going into a town in or near the later part of an afternoon, on which occasions we would take a room in a hotel or boarding house and stay the night. On such stay-overs, of course, we would enjoy having dinner in town, and, next morning, breakfast as well. These weekly sojourns provided benefits enough to make them well worthwhile. For one thing, sleeping in a bed was admittedly a pleasure after six nights in the tent, no matter how accommodating our camping gear might be. And, not least, Eveline and I were both happy at having an opportunity to give ourselves a good soapy washdown and rinse.

In each of the towns where we stayed overnight, we made certain to locate and explore the public library. Even if only an hour remained before closing time, or sometimes less, Eveline and I would take places at one of the wooden tables—fixtures and furniture changed very little from library to library—and read for a time, either something taken from the shelves or one of the books that we were carrying along with us.

Never were there more than a small handful of other people using the library, scattered here and there, and they, too, were invariably quiet, preoccupied with whatever it might be they were reading. At such times I found myself thinking of Eveline's days as a schoolgirl in Fremont and what she had told me about them. Here we were, Eveline and I, at a point in our walk from Iowa City to West Tree, one afternoon in August of 1934, in the library of a small town somewhere in Iowa. Those facts were true enough. But it seemed to me that simultaneously we were also back in Fremont, on an afternoon in 1922 or 1923, in *that* Carnegie library, with the same afternoon sunlight flooding in at an angle through the windows, *here* having become the same as *there*, *then* having become the same as *now*. I found myself lulled invariably into a feeling of contentedness and pleasure by moments such as those, since in effect they gave me more of Eveline, more time with her. From almost the very moment I fell in love with Eveline, I found myself tormented by the awful desire that I could have known her *before* then, that I could have been part of her life even *before* I knew her, that I could have had her in *all* time, to touch, hold, embrace, and have.

Those moments in the libraries were perfect. The sunlight coming through the windows was perfect. The quietness was perfect. Eveline was perfect. Eveline, sitting across from me, reading.

•

For the duration of the trip, the towns along our route remained invisible until such time as we had need for one of them. Now and then a town would appear with no more solicitation than the fact of Eveline's and my having spoken with one another about its being time for a stop. At other times, simply the fact of one of us having *thought* about its being time for more provisions would result in the appearance of a town. From time to time, although rarely, it did happen that a town would fail to appear in spite of our having spoken or thought about needing one. In those cases, we would simply turn forty-five-degrees away from our route, either to the left or right, and continue walking. Within five minutes, or inside a distance of not more than a mile, a town would make itself visible, allowing us to enjoy the pleasures and benefits it offered.

In every case, it was not so much as if the towns hovered quietly just below the horizon and then rose up into view; it was more as though they were *there* all along, in their normal places and positions, but existing in or on a part of the light spectrum imperceptible to our eyes. Only when subtle change caused a town to become manifest, or when a town manifested itself at a visible place on the spectrum, would we be able to see and enter it.

It was impossible not to think of this phenomenon of the shy or retiring towns as a gift or gesture of some kind prepared intentionally for Eveline and me on our journey north. Or perhaps we ourselves were causing the effect, somehow bringing it into existence, since it was difficult not to think of it as related in some way to Eveline's concept of the protective, earth-encircling tendrils generated through reading.

I admit to a certain skepticism at first as to the similarity between the disappearing towns and the encircling tendrils, since, while the tendrils were clearly protective, it was more difficult to see how the retiring towns could be the same.

But then I saw the link. It came to me while I was gazing at Eveline walking along in front of me.

We almost always walked single file, usually with me in the lead and Eveline following. But now and then we switched places so that I walked behind Eveline, and this particular afternoon was one of those times. The day was glorious, calm, and still, the sky a cloudless blue, the air sweet, the temperature a perfect mix of late summer and early autumn. If I could have fallen in love with Eveline all over again, I would have done it then, simply from watching her walking in front of me, as if without effort, upright, straight, supple, strong, with a grace and naturalness of step as her feet, one after the other, appeared and then disappeared in the long-grass we walked through, while the sunshine polished her gorgeous brown hair and highlighted the yellow bandana tied loosely around her neck, adding the perfect mark of jaunty loveliness.

•

We stopped for a while, set down our packs, and took a rest. This was in a small copse of silver maple trees. I sat down leaning back against the trunk of one, and Eveline sat in front of me, facing the same way and leaning back against me.

So many things were obvious, even though I may never have thought of them before. I thought now, for example, about the towns. I realized that in their way of remaining hidden and then manifesting themselves, they were providing for us, offering us protection.

As I mentioned, one of our treks inside Iowa City was an exploration of the Old Capitol building, the iconic structure at the center of the campus, where it stood with its face gazing west.

Entry was possible only from the back, where a person climbed up six or eight outdoor steps and went in through the double door set into the rear wall. Entering the old building required that a person go from east to west.

Inside the old building: Offices. Closed doors. Silence.

In the very center of the structure was a circular staircase, wooden railed and impeccably painted, that rose up to the floors overhead.

We had chosen a Sunday afternoon for our visit, and so far as either of us could tell we were the only ones in the building. Everything inside had a look of being extraordinarily clean and polished, including the windows, their tall panes without streaks and crystal clear.

Eveline and I climbed up the staircase to the next floor, then the next, and on to the top. Up here, the silence seemed even more absolute than it had downstairs when the front doors had fallen shut behind us. Up here, it was as though the air were filled with invisible cotton and was no longer even a *medium* for sound. Sound was not only absent, but sound *was* an absence. Neither of us said a word, but together we moved toward the row of tall front windows, chose one, then did nothing more than stand there, side by side, looking out.

These were the windows that I had come into the old building to see earlier, or later, at the start of fall term 1963, before I had met Eveline or knew she existed. "I took the opportunity" to visit the old building, I wrote, "to stroll through its rooms and gaze for long periods out through its windows as if out through new sets of eyes."

Now, looking out through them together with Eveline, these sets of eyes revealed far more than they had then. Eveline looked. I looked. And the ancient eyes of the old building looked. In addition, it was as though I were looking out not only through my own eyes but simultaneously out through Eveline's eyes, and as though Eveline were looking not only out through her own but also out through mine, so that both of us saw with some extraordinary kind of lucid amplification everything that the windows had looked out on for the past ninety-two years, seeing everything that had happened across those thousand miles of plains to the west, unable *not* to see whatever that was or whatever it had been. . . A vastness. An expanse of westward-reaching land across the river, past the Quadrangle, beyond the farthest buildings that housed athletics and law, across the western border of Iowa City, farther west than Eden Lake was to the east, all the way across Iowa to the Missouri River, past Omaha and past Fremont, beyond the western boundary of Nebraska and the town of Alliance where Eveline had taught, across Colorado, Utah, Wyoming, past Idaho into Nevada, Oregon. . .

And, appearing across the width and depth of this map-like immensity of low, rolling, dry-grass-colored land were marks, or smudges, or stains, most of them widely separated from one another and yet some of them sufficiently clustered so as to blend together almost into one—low-lying marks, darknesses, or stains that had the appearance more than anything of being pools of dried blood, darkened areas like bruised flesh—there, and over there, and up there, through there, out there, down there—marking the places where people had been encircled, surrounded, attacked, assaulted, slain, violated, tortured, massacred, men, women, children, the old, from one decade through another, and another, and another in a program of ferocity and rage until those peoples and nations slain, crushed, and no longer living on the plains included the Wichita, the Arapaho, the Blackfoot, the Otoe, the Assiniboine, and the Kiowa, until they included the Comanche, the Crow, the Ponca, the Gros Ventre, Lakota, and the Lipan, the Cheyenne, Quapaw, Omaha, Apache, Ojibwe, Sarsi, and Nakoda, the Tonkawa, Arikara, Dakota, Hidatsa, Iowa, and Kansa, the Kitsai, Mandan, Missouria, Osage, Pawnee, the Cree. . . .

Eveline turned away from the window. She pressed her hands over her eyes.

•

So then I did see the link, and what led me to it was the memory of Eveline in the soundless old building that day, when she turned from the window. Neither of us spoke, said the least thing, or touched one another. After a second or two, Eveline walked to the top of the circular staircase and started down, slowly, her right hand gliding smoothly along the impeccably painted balustrade.

•

Now and then a light breeze rustled through the copse of silver maples. Neither of us moved or spoke. It was too pleasant just sitting there, too restful and perfect, me with my back against the tree trunk and Eveline with her back against me. We slept for perhaps twenty minutes, maybe thirty. I thought back to Eveline starting down the circular stairs. If now, under the trees, I hadn't been so comfortable, half-asleep, I would have—*should* have—reached out and dragged my pack over, gotten out a notebook and pen, and written down "August 30, 1934, 2:35 pm, Iowa," and then:

Memory from 7/1/34. Old Capitol. Eveline turning from window. Kurtz, Heart of Darkness, what he saw. Ophelia, what she saw: "Oh, woe is me, / T' have seen what I have seen, see what I see."

•

Eveline turned away from the window.

•

Kurtz said: *The horror! The horror!*

•

Then suddenly I *did* understand: The disappearing towns were part of something much larger. They were part of a greater plan being managed by who knows what power, spirit, or mind located in who knows what part of the earth or sky—a plan whose purpose was to let Eveline and me see that such atrocities as had taken place over a span of more than twenty decades—in *Iowa City-Fremont-Eden Lake-West Tree*—would lead now to the final acts of ruin, loss, horror, and depravity that I know—watching from a window of my apartment in this present year of 2028—are flinging themselves against the very doors and walls of humankind's home.

TWENTY-FIVE

Resting under the silver maples, I realized that something very strange had happened. Eveline and I were now—and had been since leaving Iowa City—in an entirely different plane of time from before. This fact explained a number of things, dominant among them being the reason why Eveline and I were *walking* to West Tree. We had never said much about it after having decided to do it. The truth is that we hadn't given much thought to it; it had seemed natural, a kind of logical variation on the treks we had been going on all summer.

I sat up so that I was no longer leaning back against the tree and put my arms around Eveline; tightening them slightly, I drew her toward me. The yellow bandana was still tied around her neck. I took in the wonderful scent of her hair, the scent of all outdoors, and gazed across the landscape rolling out gently to the horizon from the slight elevation our copse stood on.

Our new translocation in time explained almost everything—including the strange lapse in Eveline's and my powers of observation, or, if not exactly *that*, our curiously heightened susceptibility to the changes around us on the one hand and, on the other, in our blithe willingness to accept them virtually without question.

I suspected that Eveline was awake but I wasn't certain. I whispered in her ear and asked. She nodded yes.

"Evie," I said, and then spoke her name again. I tightened my arms a little.

"Something has happened," I said.

Once again she nodded yes, but more vigorously this time. She was having the same understandings and recognitions as I was.

The absence of roads, farms, fields, fences, houses, cattle, sheep, chickens—the absences, which both of us had simply accepted, almost instinctively, now made sense logically.

Eveline set her palms against the ground and pushed herself up. She turned toward me.

"Where do you think we are? I mean, when do you think this is?"

I told her.

"I think it's before Columbus. Before the Europeans. Before the white man. Before *us*."

Eveline nodded again and looked out over the landscape. The sky was blue right down to the horizon.

"That's what I was thinking too," Eveline said, very quietly. "Before *us*."

•

My watch said it was getting on toward four o'clock, and we decided to walk farther until we came on a good place to camp. We had plenty of food for now. The next morning, we would find a town, perhaps have breakfast there, and re-supply ourselves.

Things felt different, with the new understanding of where we were, or of *when* we were.

I found myself looking at the hills, sky, trees, leaves, grass, streams—feeling that I was seeing all of them in a new way.

We decided to camp at a place where a grassy slope went down steeply to the east and leveled out a few yards from the edge of a stream. We would be snug there, protected by the slope if any wind should come up out of the west, although that wasn't especially likely. In the morning, when the air would be cold, we would get the benefit of direct sun. We set up our tent and got settled in, then lay down on the grass Roman-style, each propped up on one elbow, and made an early supper of our remaining bread, hard sausage, and cheese. After eating, I went over to the streambank to refill our canteens. The stream was about a foot deep at that point, with a firm, steady current. The water was perfectly clear and, looking down through it, I could see a dozen or more trout, pointing upstream, holding themselves in place against the current.

We lay on the grass outside the tent for a time, watching the light change. Our side of the bank was already in deep shadow, but on the other side of the stream there was still sunlight on the far hills reaching away to the east. Then gradually the valleys and low places became gathered into shadow and only the hilltops remained sunlit, then grew yellow-golden, after that more and more red, until they, too, disappeared into shadow.

Inside the tent we got into our sleeping bag—zipped so as to make it a double—and for forty-five minutes or so sat side by side, leaning back against our packs, taking turns reading, this time aloud. The book was Emily Dickinson, like before—the poet was easy to carry and lasted a long time. We traded the reading back and forth; I would read a stanza and then hand the book and the little flashlight to Eveline, and so on. Especially considering where we were, reading the poems was a strange experience, the more so reading them aloud, with only the nighttime for audience, if it chose to be so.

I read first:

*"There's a certain Slant of light, / Winter Afternoons–/
That oppresses, like the Heft / Of Cathedral Tunes–"*

Then Eveline, then I, then Eveline for the final stanza:

*"When it comes, the Landscape listens–/ Shadows–hold
their breath–/ When it goes, 'tis like the Distance / On the
look of Death –"*

We were both a little bit frightened that night and lay holding each other until sleep came. Outside, the night was loud
with the sounds of crickets and frogs and the call of owls, and
every now and then we would hear something splash in the
stream.

•

In the morning the sun woke us early. We struck the tent,
packed up, set out again, and, after an hour's walk or so began
thinking about finding a town. The town that appeared was
named Waterford and, as we made our way from the perimeter in toward the main street, we were translocated again into
the year 1934.

The main street was like the other main streets. There was a
plain but pleasant diner where we each had a plate of scrambled eggs, pork sausage, toast, home-fried potatoes with onions and green peppers in them, and plenty of coffee. After
breakfast, we walked farther down the street and at a grocery
store got more hard sausage, bread, and a block of cheese.
Camping without making fires was an excellent way to travel,
but it was possible only if you had access to towns the way
Eveline and I did. In my journal, I kept a list of the towns
where we stopped, a journal that I still have, even though it's
now ninety-four years old—that is, if you begin with 1934 and
count up to 2028. I treasure this compact journal, with its

sewn binding, as much as any possession I have—and I also remain astonished that it (it and my little volume of *Howl*) came along with me when the blackness closed like a lightning bolt without light, negative light, and everything in the universe went silent and I "woke up," as it were, in September 1964 in the deepest state of loneliness, sorrow, disbelief, despair, and regret that I had ever experienced up to that moment or that I have ever experienced since.

That was when Eveline was gone. That's when everything was gone. That's when my father had destroyed everything, when he had left me with ruin, emptiness, and death.

•

After breakfast, and after our visit to the grocery store, Eveline and I walked to the end of the main street and continued on from there back into the countryside—and also back into the year that by now I had begun thinking of as 1464. If I had the year correctly (and who could know, really?), this meant that Eveline and I were now leaving Waterford and walking back out into the countryside almost exactly five hundred years before my first arrival in Iowa City. And that in turn meant, adjusting for my translocation into 1933, that it was now four hundred and sixty-nine years before I saw Eveline for the first time, in McGalliard's Old English classroom, on a morning in November that was exactly thirty years minus three days before the red line reached Dallas, slew the President, and destroyed the republic.

Which is what Eveline and I wanted to undo, or, more exactly, prevent.

•

Here, from my tattered old notebook, are the twenty-eight towns that Eveline and I visited during our roughly month-long trip to West Tree. The list of the towns follows the order of our visits to them. Therefore, by finding Waterford's place you can see how far along on the trip we were at that time we visited that town:

Albion, Faulkner, Isanti, Pine Center, Osage, Taopi, Gilead, Scio, Lakota, Waterford, Elmsford, Cloverdale, Stanton, Elgin, Watermill, May City, Archer, Hartley, Gayville, Paulina, Marshalltown, Makaton, Black Walnut, Garrison, Vernon, Bock, Watoma, Bassett

•

Between the end of Godfrey's *Beowulf* class at the close of spring term and the day we set out for West Tree, Eveline and I went on a total of nine treks. Five of these were inside the city limits and four, like the one to Eden Lake, outside the city. In some ways the most unpleasant trek—not counting the trip to the inside of Old Capitol—was the trek to go watch my father playing tennis.

The courts he played on were right across Washington Street from the main library. So the place we chose to watch from was our old winter hideaway in the corner of the library's third floor, tucked into the extreme northeast corner of the stacks.

As it happened, he was already playing when Eveline and I walked by on our way to the library. From College Street we had come by the usual route, cutting across the little park at Dodge Street to get over onto Washington, then continuing straight down Washington all the way to the library door.

It was a warm and sun-filled afternoon at the end of June, and as we got halfway down the hill from Clinton Street past the Engineering School and to Madison, we could hear, from the pleasant *thock* sound of tennis balls being hit well and squarely, that games were being played. The four courts were laid out in a large square behind mesh fencing, and my father—I saw as we drew closer—was playing in the court closest to where Eveline and I stood watching, and in the court, as it happened, that would be most directly in view if a person were to look out one of the windows in our old corner of the library.

The spot where Eveline and I stopped to watch—on the library side, looking across Washington Street—gave a view of the court from behind one of the base-lines instead of from the side. My father's opponent, his back to us, was playing in the end nearer to us, while my father was at the other end, facing us.

So there he was, absolutely unchanged from the other time I'd watched him play on this same court: My father, twenty-four years old, totally unsuspecting that the young man watching from across the street—me—was anything but another stranger out of countless strangers, another student out of thousands. Furthermore, I hadn't been born yet—and wouldn't be so for another seven years. Even if that weren't the case, even if by some miracle my father *knew* that I existed, that I was twenty-two years old, and that I was a student in Iowa City—he *still* would never in a million years have taken *me* for his son: *Me*, huddled in my five feet and ten inches in comparison with his own towering and elegant six four?

No, my tall, lean, handsome father wouldn't even have *seen* me; he would have looked right past me, or through me; wouldn't have had the least conceivable reason to imagine himself being *related* to me.

I was totally incognito. Entirely unnoticeable. Or would have been, *if it hadn't been for Eveline.*

A break came and the two players proceeded to change courts. My father's opponent walked away from Eveline and me and around the west side of the net to the far court. At the same time, my father came toward us, advancing around the east side of the net. He paid no attention to me, but he noticed

Eveline immediately.

He smiled and at the same time raised his racket in the air as a means of waving at her.

My father's smile: This was the smile I had seen a hundred thousand times, though directed only at others, not at me; simultaneously subtle, complex, disingenuous, and sinister, it was a triple-purposed smile of greeting, flattery, and seduction.

"Hello!" he called out to Eveline. "Why don't you come over on this side and watch the game?"

So even when concentrating on the game he had watched us—he had watched *Eveline*—watched Eveline watching him.

Instead of resuming the match at once, my father rested his racket casually over one shoulder and came up to the fence, where he put the fingers of his free hand into the mesh, letting his elbow hang down, and continued to smile at Eveline.

He was extremely handsome, though his smile had something distantly sinister about it, perhaps because it was asymmetrical and revealed teeth, the canine and those flanking it, on only one side.

And also, the unrelenting whiteness of his clothes created a hint of something circus-like. My father's partner wore black tennis shoes, brown shorts, and a blue shirt with the sleeves rolled up. A rolled red bandana tied around his head served as a sweatband. But my father's tennis shoes were white. He had on white slacks, pleated and cut very loose, and a white polo shirt. Even his sweatband was white.

Hardly two seconds had passed.

"No?" my father asked. Then he added, "But you're certainly pretty in any case," and turned to go back to the game.

I looked over at Eveline. Her face was immobile, her expression fixed, serious, intense, puzzled, and inquiring all at once.

I said her name, but at first she didn't look at me. She kept staring across the street.

"*That's* him? That's your *father*?" she asked. A second or two went by before she looked at me, locked eyes, and added,

"Are you *sure?*"

I don't think I ever loved Eveline more than I loved her at that moment. Her brow was furrowed, her eyes wide, her expression imploring, pleading, disbelieving.

"Yes," I said. I added: "Only too sure."

You could hear the sound of the tennis balls again, being hit back and forth. Eveline reached for my hand, grasped it tightly, and turned toward the entrance to the library. I followed her up the steps and in through the door.

Saturday afternoon and a beautiful summer day meant that the library was all but empty. Still, Eveline had a plan.

"I want to go to our corner," she said. "But we have to go separately. You go first, but look for something in the card catalog before you do. Then go to the second floor and dawdle there a bit before you go up to our corner. I'm going to go look at the out-of-town papers. For ten minutes. Then I'll come up."

She squeezed my hand, turned away, and went off toward the periodicals room. I did exactly as Eveline had told me. At the card catalog, I looked up Hamlin Garland, Robert Frost, and Willa Cather and jotted down a call number or two for each. Then I took the stairway to the second floor and walked into the stacks there. I think I may have been the only person on that floor, or at least it felt that way. I followed the Dewey decimal guides and, at the right place, took down a copy of *Main-Travelled Roads*. Standing there, I read the first three or four pages of "The Return of a Private," then re-shelved the slim volume, made my way to the stairs and, as if casually, went up to the third floor. There, I walked through the stacks to the northeast corner. Our two chairs were there but not Eveline. I went to the window and looked down to where my father was still playing his match. Even though a few small branches with leaves obscured him when he played from behind his own baseline, it was generally easy to follow him because of his being all in white. I watched him hit long low shots into a corner of his opponent's court and just short of his base-line, placing the ball there again and again before switching unexpectedly to the other corner and leaving his opponent out of position to make the return. As I was watching, Eveline came up silently behind me and put her hands around my waist. Her hands felt so good that I didn't want to disturb them, and so I didn't turn around. Then she leaned against me from behind, and that felt even better. When she moved her hands around to my stomach, I covered them with my own hands and held them there. We stood pressed together like that for a time, both of us looking out the window watching my father play tennis in his white clothes.

Eveline's face was pressed against the side of my own. After a while, she kissed my ear and then whispered, "He's a really arrogant bastard, isn't he." I moved my hands from hers and turned just enough so I could kiss her on the lips.

"Yes," I said afterward. "And at the same time basically naïve. That makes it worse."

We stood looking out the window again. Eveline moved behind me again the way she'd been before and put her arms back around my waist. She asked me, "Are you afraid of him?"

"I've been afraid of him all my life," I said.

It was so quiet inside the library that even through the closed window, very faintly, you could hear the sound of the tennis ball when one of the rackets hit it.

"I'm afraid of him, too," Eveline whispered. "I really don't like him."

Once more I turned toward her and she moved forward so that I could kiss her again on the lips. After that we stood holding one another, as tightly as possible, and I told her how much I loved her, saying it over and over.

After a moment or two, Eveline whispered,

"Do you want to go home?"

I whispered back, into her ear,

"Yes and no. Do you?"

I felt her head nod quickly a number of times as if she

meant to say yes, but instead of saying yes she said,

"Yes. Yes and no. Yes. Yes and no."

The window was less interesting than before. We turned away from it and walked into the stacks until we came to what seemed the quietest, deepest, and most remote spot, a place no one else on earth would ever visit.

TWENTY-SIX

Outside of the towns, wildlife was everywhere, although we saw signs of people only once.

Rabbits, gophers, pheasants, prairie hens, prairie dogs, squirrels—both on open land and in among trees, groves, or woods—deer, fox, antelope, elk, pronghorn, songbirds in immense numbers, and of course bison. Many days could pass without our seeing them, and then, two or three grass-covered hills away from us, we might see a herd of thirty or forty, their immense heads held down low as they grazed. Only once did we see a truly enormous herd, made up of what must easily have been two or three hundred of the huge creatures. They were somewhat farther away from us this time, the entire herd moving slowly. There were so many of them, and they walked so closely together, that from a distance they looked almost like some form of brown, shaggy ground cover.

•

We were about another day's walk away from West Tree when we saw people.

On our next-to-last morning the town we visited was Watoma, and the morning after that we would visit Bassett, the final town, as it turned out, before West Tree. The day between Watoma and Bassett was beautiful, fine, fair, and still. And the walking itself was pleasant, through grass-covered hills that rolled away to the horizons, looking as much as anything like low waves on a dry sea.

It was close to four o'clock when Eveline and I decided on a break, took off our packs, set them down next to each other, then sat down ourselves and leaned against the packs. Eveline tipped her head back to let the sun fall over her face. She shut her eyes. I leaned over and gave her a kiss.

We agreed that the next creek or stream we reached would become our camping place for the night. I was certain we would find such a place in another hour or so, as usually happened. Only once on the entire trip had nightfall been quicker than we were, forcing us to put up our tent right on the open face of the prairie, without so much as a valley, stream bank, hillside, or embankment to give us at least a feeling of shelter.

As we were reminiscing about that night and agreeing, pleasant as it was, that we shouldn't let our rest continue much longer, I saw something against the sky to the northwest of where we were sitting. It was smoke, three frail, ropy columns of smoke rising up from the far side of a hill that was smooth-crowned and treeless but quite high.

Cookfires. Three of them.

I touched Eveline's shoulder, then shook it the slightest bit. She opened her eyes.

"Look," I told her. "Up against the sky. Coming from the far side of that big hill." Absurdly, I realized that I was whispering.

Eveline made a sharp intake of breath and gripped my forearm. After a moment, she said,

"What should we do?" She was also whispering.

How strange, but that was exactly the question I had. Without really thinking, but by a sort of instinct, I found myself saying, "Well, I think we should just go on our way. They're neighbors. And so are we." Then I found myself adding, still in that urgent kind of whisper, almost as if I were talking to myself, "Amazing. This experience is incredible."

We got up, hefted our packs, and continued on our way, though with frequent glances to the left and up the big hill. When we had gone perhaps twenty yards I saw something that made me stop cold and turn to face the hill. Eveline all but collided with me from behind, but then she turned also to look up the hill. At its crest, a figure had appeared and now stood there, motionlessly, looking down at us. Then, as we watched, a second figure came up over the crest, appearing bit by bit, first the head, then shoulders, torso, and the entire person. The two stood there, just slightly apart from one another, looking at us.

It was intensely exciting to see them, indescribable.

My mind was roaring. All I wanted was to do no harm.

"I'm going to wave at them," I whispered to Eveline. The idea, crazy or not, tore through my brain that raising only one arm might seem threatening because of its resemblance to the raising or throwing of a spear. So instead, I raised both arms straight up over my head, opened them slowly into the shape of a "V," then continued lowering them until they were perfectly horizontal and held them there for a moment before dropping them to my sides and then repeating the whole motion. I did this three times. Then I waited, for how long I don't know. And after a minute or two, the figures on the crest of the hill made exactly the same motions with their own arms. They did this three times, then stopped.

Eveline and I turned and continued on our way. I felt as though my heart might burst out of my chest, it was beating so hard from excitement and from something I could identify only as sheer joy.

TWENTY-SEVEN

I knew we were near West Tree when we came on what I was to know centuries later as The Wagon River. From the point where Eveline and I came on it, the stream flowed north-northeast almost straight to West Tree. All we had to do was follow where it led us.

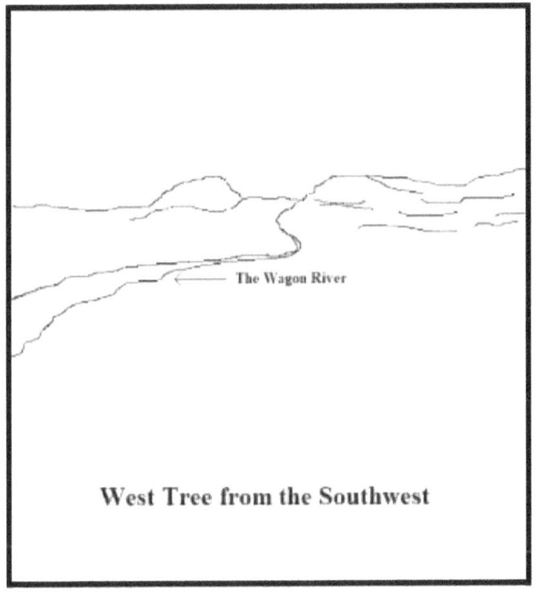

West Tree from the Southwest

We'd provisioned ourselves well that morning, in the town of Bassett, so there was no real need to go into West Tree before the next day. The weather, furthermore, was glorious—warm, fair, still, autumnal—and the idea of putting our tent up on the riverbank and spending the night was appealing. And so we did it, right where we were. Morning would be soon enough for us to begin taking care of things. Soon enough for us to walk the mile or so out to the farm and begin looking for my father.

•

I went down to the river and looked in and saw trout, in their plentiful numbers, pointing upstream and holding themselves against the current.

•

In the morning, as it happened, we did go into West Tree, but through no conscious will of our own, since when we woke up on the riverbank everything was quite different from the way it had been when we'd gone to sleep. It turned out that we had made camp inside what would become the city limits of the town, so that when we woke up the year was once again 1934, in place of 1464. You can imagine the differences. We had gone to sleep along a trout-filled prairie stream but woke up on the bank of a millpond. Fifty yards or so downstream from our camp stood the dam responsible for holding back the water to form the pond. It had a drop of perhaps seven feet, and beside it, on the west bank, stood a boxy mill building four stories high.

The center of downtown appeared to be across the river from the mill. A sort of traffic circle over there enclosed a small park with, at its center, a stone monument dedicated—as Eveline and I would soon discover—to the memory of those who had perished in the Great War.

To cross the river we had the choice of a bridge upstream from our camping spot and another downstream, both about the same distance away, not much more than a block. We chose the downstream bridge and made our way around the mill to reach it. Once across, we went over into the little park in order to read the inscription on the monument. For some reason I imagine us there as someone in the town might have seen us: A man and a woman, each wearing a canvas-colored backpack, bending forward in order to read the words cut into polished stone.

In the Ideal Café—a restaurant that would still be there thirty years later, during my college years—we had a breakfast of eggs, potatoes, bacon, toast and coffee, and then on our way out of town—on the west side of the river again—we stocked up on another day's worth of provisions at a National Tea store. The provisions were simply cautionary. I had no way of knowing whether we would find my father right away, on this first day of our visit, or whether it might take longer than that to locate him. So I wanted us to be prepared for more camping out if we should need it.

The morning promised to be another in the string of perfect autumn days that had been ours for the entire trip, and this fact, along with knowing we had all but finished our journey, gave us both a certain feeling of light-heartedness, or maybe relief, and a pleasant realization that we had a certain amount of extra time to make use of if we chose. It was no longer necessary for us to hurry.

"Well, then," Eveline said. "Why don't we drop these someplace and walk around a little bit? I mean, we're in your home town. Show me around."

By "these," Eveline meant our backpacks. We were still on the sidewalk in front of the National Tea, where we had just been shopping. I gestured with a thumb toward the store and raised an eyebrow at Eveline. Eveline raised an eyebrow at me, and together we went back in. Halfway to the rear, the manager had one of those half-walled offices tucked up under the ceiling and accessible by a small set of stairs. He agreed to hold our packs for a few hours, so I carried them up, came back down, and Eveline and I went back out into the holiday-seeming morning.

It was an interesting and unusual experience for me, walking around in my own home town and birthplace, although seven years still had to pass before I would be born. It felt very nice, almost celebratory, the airy feeling of walking around without the weight of our back packs. I thought I would take Eveline to the campus of Old College first, then back through downtown, past the house where my family lived at the time of my birth in November 1941, and then to the campus of New College, where I would graduate, or where I had graduated, in 1963, just before I went for more study in Iowa City, experienced there my translocation in time to 1933—and saw, met, and fell in love with Eveline Stahl, herself walking now at my side, in September 1934, on an impeccable autumn day, through the streets of West Tree.

From the main street we turned west onto Christiania Avenue, a route that took us past the house, built in 1921, where my great-aunts Marie and Lutie lived, then to the foot of the hill that Old College stood on. The walk was pleasant, and the lighthearted feeling I mentioned earlier stayed with us both. At some times during the walk, we held hands, while at others each of us put an arm around the waist of the other. At some points, we stopped, embraced, and exchanged a kiss. To me, it didn't matter at all whether anyone saw us, since I was still minus-seven years old and no one could possibly recognize or identify me. As for Eveline, although she was now twenty-four years old, she had been born hundreds of miles away in Fremont, Nebraska, and no one in West Tree would conceivably identify or recognize her.

Our privacy was a pleasure and even, in a certain way,

exciting. I pointed out Marie and Lutie's house to Eveline as we passed it, and also, on the south side of Christiania Avenue, the Old College Café, a favorite haunt of my parents in their own student years. The ascent on the roadway up the hill was steep at certain points, but we went slowly and rested when we chose. On the top of the hill, the panoramic view to the west was extraordinary, a vision of low rolling prairie reaching outward for what seemed a hundred miles. We turned east and went past the various campus buildings, including the old two-and-a-half-story clapboard house where my great-aunts had lived for two years until their own new house was completed for them, in, as I said, 1921.

I took Eveline to First Hall, which, as its name suggests, was the original Old College building, dating from 1854. Unlike Old Capitol in Iowa City, First Hall faced east rather than west. From its hilltop, it gazed out over West Tree, eastward to the far side of the Wagon River, where it locked eyes with its counterpart, the slightly younger first building of New College, which stood on the crest of its own hill, gazing west across the same river, and across the same town.

One facing east, one facing west. I wondered what that meant.

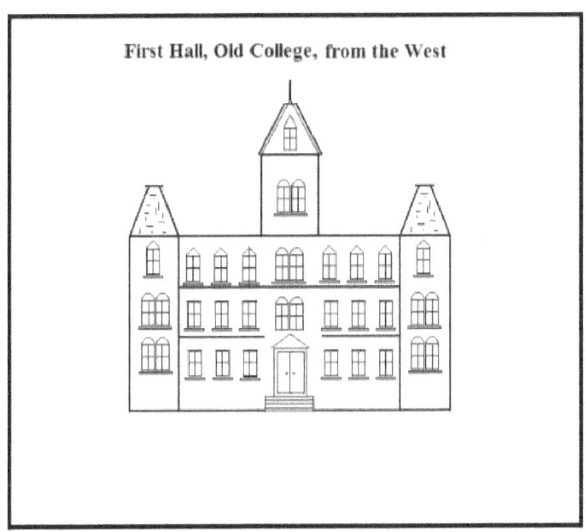

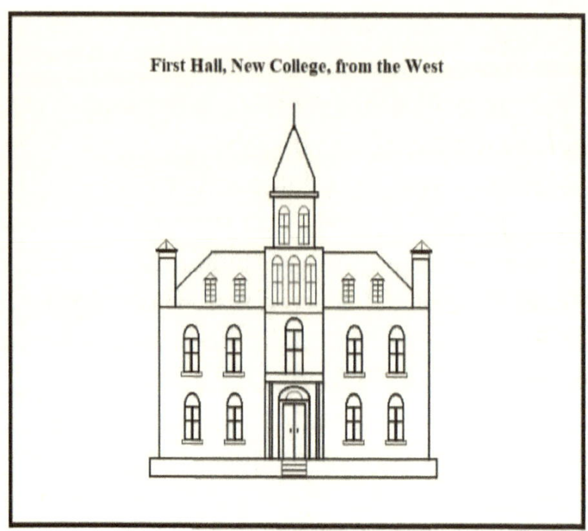

First Hall, New College, from the West

TWENTY-EIGHT

As usual, the moment we crossed the city limits going out of West Tree, we also returned again to 1494.

I wasn't able to resist the desire to look back, if only because, of all the towns Eveline and I had visited and subsequently departed from, this was the only one well known to me. I paused and turned around. So did Eveline. I took her hand. Then for a moment we stood and looked.

The millpond was gone, the dam was gone, the mill was gone. The streets were gone, the National Tea was gone, the Ideal Café was gone, the war monument was gone, the main street itself was gone. And the colleges, also, were gone, both of them, entirely. But the hills they stood on were still there, one to the east and one to the west, the river running between them.

•

I knew the way out to the farm so well that I didn't need a map, guide, or aid other than the guidance of the land. The thing most like a road, of course, was the river, and Eveline and I followed it for three-quarters of a mile, to the place where it turned, although not sharply, toward the north-north-east. I knew that from that point on, the river would take us farther away from the farm rather than closer to it. It was time to leave the river and continue straight north.

This meant a little bit of climbing, since the eastward turn in the river took place due to the water's being rebuffed by a low but rock-filled bluff that ran there along a good length of its left bank. We faced a climb of perhaps fifteen feet, not a steep climb but prickly, since the bank was crowded with shrubs of wild blueberries and raspberries. At the top was a wide and deep expanse of grassland rising gently toward a low ridge perhaps another half-mile away from us. When we had walked a third of that distance we stood on a spot that would put us on the center-line of the state highway that would later run there, more or less parallel to the river below. Eveline and I pushed on, and when we came to the top of the low ridge I set down my pack and helped Eveline off with hers. We were standing at a place that, when I was to live on the farm, I came to think of as offering as perfect a vantage as any other outlook nearby. Across the river directly to the south you could see the hill that New College would later occupy, and to the southwest the same was true of the hill that Old College would rise up on. Between the two, looking down the bed of the Wagon River as if it were a road leading south, your eye could follow the twin rows of prairie trees as they lined the banks of the river for a good distance measurable, certainly, in miles. But, at least from this spot, the view to the southeast was the most splendid of all. The low hills surrounding West Tree, and reaching like a rolling sea far away into the southwest and west—those hills differed from the terrain to the southeast, where the hills by and large were oblong in shape rather than circular, and lay alongside one another like felled logs, while their tops tended to be more flattened than roundish. The view in this direction, like that to the southwest, was unobstructed, and the dozing hills carried the eye countless miles away. The grasses covering them must have been more varied than those covering the tawny hills to the west. Early in summer mornings, but even more vividly in the hour or so before dusk, the low-angled sun was capable of drawing out faint tones of purple, violet, green, even softened rust, from the flanks of those hills and from the areas half-gathered in shadow between them.

So those were the views from the low ridge looking toward the south. The view to the north was quite different. The grass-prairie rolled away from us in that direction for a distance of probably another three-quarters of a mile. At that point the northward view came to an end, stopped by another rise of low hills that were stretched out in an east-west direction, similar to the crest that Eveline and I were now standing on. And exactly there, due north from where we stood, on land just this side of the hills' southern flank, was the site where, centuries in the future, the farm I was to grow up on would lie.

There it was: Our destination; the place we had traveled so long and so far to reach; the place where we would locate my father, if that were possible; where we would reach out to him through his insolent armor of arrogance and naiveté, if that were possible; where we would implore him not to leave the farm, not go to the Cabinet Room, not choose the republic's destruction, not extend the red line, not incarnadine the tawny prairies and the surrounding seas, not make of earth itself a place and thing of insult, sorrow, suffering, and death—if any of these were entreaties that could possibly succeed.

To me—for me—my father was formidable, dire, cold, treacherous, poisonously innocent, possibly mad, my father, the nation I was born into. If there were anyone on earth who could reach him, soften, change, tutor him, find a way to lure him into listening, hearing, responding, that person was Eveline.

Everything depended on Eveline.

•

Fear began gathering inside me at this point. It was almost undetectable at first, like the earliest hint of an illness, extremely faint and so little out of the ordinary as to make you uncertain whether it's there at all. I tried to hide my awareness of it—from Eveline, certainly, whom I didn't want to frighten as well—but also from myself, in the vain hope that through my ignoring it the fear would go away.

On the other hand, being in this particular place was itself all-consuming, being granted the experience—privilege—of setting foot on this particular "square" of prairie four centuries before it was to be declared a homestead, then gradually a farm, a possession to be handed down—having become *property*—from owner to owner over the decades, until the members of my own family were to become the ones who lived in the two-story house with white clapboard siding that was built in 1882 and that had stood ever since, companion to the weathered barn of unpainted wood and to the few additional outbuildings and sheds of the same gray wood never touched by paint.

·

That is, the house stood until 1947, until almost the end of September, until Eveline's and my visit and our confrontation with my father. After that, it still stood, but only literally, since from that point on it was filled with emptiness.

TWENTY-NINE

We waited three days without a hint that change of any significant kind might be in the offing.

For the first time, it seemed possible that all of our preparation, including our long walk from Iowa City to this particular, singular, bucolic spot on the prairie outside West Tree—it now seemed possible that every bit of it had been for nothing, that my father would never appear, that we would never have the chance to divert him from his determined course.

Still, our three days of waiting did turn out, in actuality, to be quite splendid. The weather, for one thing, was unsurpassably beautiful, the sky immense, deep, and azure, the temperatures perfect, the breezes bringing with them a bouquet from the autumn prairie, aromas of drying grass and of earth itself mingled with the sweetness of wildflower blossoms and—once or twice, very faintly—the scent of woodsmoke.

I was familiar with the contours of this spot, which in four centuries or so would become the farm I grew up on, when I would all but memorize it. In any case, we set down our packs and strolled around through the tall grass while I pointed out to Eveline what it would be like after all that time—that the house would stand there, the barn there, the pump house, chicken coop, tractor shed there, there, and there. We decided to put up our tent on the long, gentle eastward slope just east of where the barn would later stand, while farther down the same slope would be the old apple orchard, and, farther still, the creek that ran through what would one day be Tom Ridley's land—the creek that would disappear later but that would provide us now with a place to fill our canteens.

On the second day we walked back to West Tree, waited on the outskirts while the town manifested itself into materiality, then went in. We were like old friends with the waitress who brought us our breakfast at the Ideal and with the counter clerk at the National Tea. They'd seen us with our packs the day before and both asked now where we had set up camp. Eveline and I said we had chosen a spot by a creek about a mile-and-a-half straight north, an answer that had the merit of being the truth, although both of us did avoid mentioning the centuries-long difference in time.

After a stop at West Tree Hardware for flashlight batteries, we crossed the bridge at First Street, turned right on the west side of the river, and followed that branch of the main street north until we crossed the city limits—and went back again five hundred years, as before. This time, instead of following the river, we stayed on the upland until we reached the point where we had climbed up from the river the day before, and from there continued to the low ridge with its splendid views, and then on to our camp spot overlooking the creek.

Really, there was nothing for us to do except wait—nothing else we *could* do. Our camping spot, on the eastward-declining slope, turned out to have been an especially good choice. In the chilly mornings, the abundant sun from the east made for welcome warmth, and in the late afternoons, when the heat of the day had built to its peak, the crest of the rise behind us cast a shadow eastward that gave off a coolness as if we were reclining in a grove.

We continued, as we'd done throughout the trip, getting in

at least two or three hours of reading each day. On our departure from Iowa City, we each carried six books in our packs, so that over the month, if we were able to read them all, each of us would have read the equivalent of twelve. I was now on my fifth, as was Eveline on hers.

On the third day we went into West Tree again, but we stayed somewhat longer since, as we'd done in other towns before, we stopped in at the Carnegie Library to spend some time there.

When we left, the time was somewhere between twelve o'clock and one. The weather again was almost indescribably lovely—sun-filled, warm, bright, gorgeous. Neither of us was inclined to hurry on our return trip, and once or twice, at a particularly appealing spot—under a copse or on the peak of the low ridge—we stopped and sat down, or lay down, propped on elbows, for half an hour or so of reading.

I wanted to take Eveline to what had been one of my favorite places on the farm—its point of highest elevation—when I was growing up there. So instead of going back to our camping spot, I guided us to the northwest. Walking through the high tawny grass, we went over one low hill and into the valley beyond it, then up the long southern slope of the next and larger hill until we reached its top, where it leveled out onto a plateau that continued for a distance of perhaps a mile off to the north. But we didn't follow the plateau, since we were already as high up as it would take us. Instead, we stopped. I told Eveline to close her eyes, then took her gently by the shoulders and turned her until she was facing the direction we had just come from. The view was wonderful. We weren't high up in comparison with the elevations far out to the west, but we were just high enough in comparison with the land south of us to offer an immense panorama. Just as we'd done from the low ridge (we were almost once again as high as we'd been on that ridge), we could look miles and miles off to the southeast across the sleeping backs of the oblong hills, and again we could do the same to the southwest, where the grass-covered hills with their rounded tops of every size, rolled away, again, to the horizon.

After a minute or two, Eveline said, "So you came up here a lot, as a kid?"

"Sometimes," I answered her. "Well, pretty often, I guess. I mean, when the weather was nice."

"I see," she said. She looked at me, smiling in a certain way. She cocked one eyebrow slightly. "For the view."

It was impossible not to catch her meaning.

"The grass was really short then," I teased. The grass now reached high, above waist-height. "There was hardly any. It was all mowed down. There was nothing right here but wagon tracks."

"And now there's nothing here but nice long grass, and sunlight, and a soft warm breeze. And you and me. No one else. Anywhere."

We kissed, embraced, held tightly. Then we continued slowly. We took every piece of clothing off, slowly helping each other in turns with each button, shoestring, snap, or sleeve, until we were completely naked. The sun, the breeze, everything felt different then, on bare skin. We spread the grass apart and tromped some of it down. Then we lay down our various pieces of clothing to make a kind of bed, then lay down on that. We lay on our backs at first, side by side, stroking one another lightly. Then on our sides, embracing one another, urgent with kisses. Then I changed my position, and so did Eveline, and I went inside her. There was birdsong around us—meadowlark, chaffinch, goldfinch, a pheasant calling from somewhere. Eveline crooned softly, as she so often did, "Don't hurry. Don't hurry. Don't hurry."

•

We slept, although it couldn't have been for long. I'd fallen off of Eveline and woke up to find myself lying by her side, on my back. For a few moments I watched the tassels of the prairie grass above me stir in the breeze. The tassels were well lit by the declining sun, and their rich tawny-brown stood out beautifully against the deep blue of the sky.

I must have fallen asleep once more after that, and when I woke up, I sensed a change, a subtle alteration in the color of the sky that wasn't due simply to the sun's having fallen farther west, but that had to do with the blue having become very slightly less blue, very, very faintly milky, almost as if there were a high, thin, all but invisible layer of cirrus spread across it.

I knew immediately what it meant. My father was returning. From wherever it was he had been.

The fucking bastard.

Now, everything would be changed.

I bent over Eveline. I kissed her on the temple, then on the cheek, then on the lips.

She stirred, stretched, sighed, opened her eyes, and looked at me.

I whispered endearments to her, calling her by a string of pet names, intimacies, love-names. Then I said,

"My father is coming back. Come and watch."

We got up on our knees, as naked as newborns, and looked out over the top of the tall grass. Everything was changing, and it was changing fast. As we watched, what had been a vast, undulant sweep of sunlit drying grass as far as the eye could see was changing into rectilinear parcels, squares, and rectangles, some quite large and others less so, most with fence running along their edges. Such a fence rose up suddenly almost at my elbow, wooden posts strung with barbed wire, while across this fence, in a sunken roadbed, railroad tracks appeared—and I found myself, in spite of the roadbed being sunken, looking down at the sunlight reflecting off the polished tops of rails. How could that be? Shouldn't the tall grass that Eveline and I were nested in—shouldn't the high grass be standing between me and the gleam of sun on those sunken rails? I looked eastward, to the left, and straight ahead, to the south. No wonder I could see the sun down on the roadbed—the grass that would have obscured that view was gone, missing, it was nowhere, hundreds and hundreds of thousands of acres of the tall waving grass were gone, and there we were, Eveline and I, on our knees in the middle of a field of stubble, as naked as jaybirds, there for anyone to see who might happen to look.

Most likely no one would look, or be likely to look, but just knowing that it was a possibility once again, that farm people were back in the landscape, and that one or more of them *might* see us—the feeling was unpleasant, shaming and withering. After all of our time alone, it felt like an unfair intrusion.

In an attempt to be both protective and gallant, I stood up, keeping my back to the south, and held my own shirt and pants up as a kind of screen for Eveline to dress behind. The only farmsteads where people might have a view of us were the Tom Ridley place, straight to the south just across the road (the road had also reappeared), and the Shuha farm, a quarter mile to the east, between Ridley's place and our own. The Bill Ridley farm, to our northeast and over the crest of a hill, had no line of sight that would allow anyone there to see us. In any case, the point was that the *feeling* of things was suddenly changed and altogether different. When Eveline had her underwear, skirt, and blouse on, she sat down to put on her shoes and socks. At that time, I took my own turn to lie down beside her on the ground—on the stubble—where I wrestled on my underwear, pants, and then shirt, and buttoned everything up as quickly as I could. After that, my own shoes and socks. And we were ready.

Eveline and I stood up and looked around. The changes were amazing. There was nothing to see that we hadn't seen many, many times before, but nevertheless, after our trek across the virgin prairie of 1464, to see the swift, sudden, abrupt return of the characteristics, qualities, details, and manifestations of 1947, and seeing how they had pushed aside the simple, unified, unbroken grandeur that Eveline and I had become accustomed to—this was an astonishing and even shocking experience. Our own farm was now clearly recognizable as having the form of a perfect rectangle—a road running along its south boundary, the railroad along its west, post-and-wire fencing along its north and east boundaries. Eveline and I stood in the very northwest corner of this large rectangle, looking down and all the way across to where the five-acre "homestead" occupied its own perfect square, tucked into the southeast corner. We watched as its smooth cover of long, waving prairie grass shriveled and then disappeared entirely (our tent was visible, exactly where we had set it up), then as the barn took form and rose up (the tent going out of sight on the barn's far side), the same with the manifesting of the farmhouse, then of the pump house, chicken coop, corncrib, tractor shed, each precisely in its place there, there, and there. Fencing appeared around three sides of the square that constituted the homestead (the side along the road remained open), and more fencing took form to set off the barnyard (but not to enclose our tent), while a row of lilac bushes grew up along the road (although not in front of the farmhouse), accompanied by a row of fruit trees, and, further in from the road—but there our view was obscured by the appearance of thick growths of windbreaking trees to the west and northwest of the farmhouse, including the majestic row of elms, planted in 1887 and now, six decades later, holding their arms seventy feet in the air.

•

So our nest in the tall grass disappeared and left Eveline and me standing on the pair of dusty wheel-tracks that paralleled the rail bed and led down to the gravel road that ran east and west along the south border of my father's farm and the north borders of Tom Ridley's and Harve Shuha's farms. Although Eveline and I had approached our nesting spot by walking diagonally across the grass prairie, we now followed the wheel-tracks straight down to the gravel road, since the fields no longer invited walking, one of them being already plowed and another thick with rough drying stalks of tall corn. At the road, we turned left and set out on the half-mile, or slightly less, that would take us to my father's driveway. When we passed Tom Ridley's driveway, I heard a dog barking out at us but saw no sign of life. Farther on, Harve Shuha's wife Bess was in the side yard taking sheets and towels in from the clothesline. When we went past, she raised an arm in greeting but gave no sign that she might have seen us up on the hill, standing there naked.

The weather hadn't changed with the change in centuries. The sky remained blue and clear, the air balmy and soft, while the breeze out of the southwest carried with it the pleasant scents of autumn.

We didn't continue all the way to the driveway leading in to the farmyard but turned off the road before we got to the drive, stepped through the drainage ditch that ran beside the road, climbed over a fallen tree and through a bit of under-brush and then came out onto the wide green lawn that sloped away gently from the west side of the farmhouse.

That's how it came about that we met my father.

And that's how, as Eveline and I stood there, it came about that the warm breeze from the southwest stirred Eveline's hair and pressed her skirt against the back of her legs.

And that's also how it came about that my father ("as lean as a knife and narrow as the blade of one"), when he had walked halfway down from the house, and when we had walked half-way up toward it, stood looking down at Eveline, smiled sar-castically, and said,

"Why do I feel as though I've seen you somewhere before?"

"Oh, I don't think so," Eveline answered. "I don't think that's possible." She looked up at him and smiled with her dis-arming, beautiful, unsolicited smile.

My father said nothing for a second or two. Then he turned his back to us and set out toward the farmhouse.

"Well," he said, "since you're here, come in."

He hadn't so much as looked at me, acknowledged me, or greeted me.

I could have predicted those familiar omissions. The remarkable thing, though, something I would never have predicted: He was wearing his naval officer's uniform, his summer dress whites, complete with white shoes, pressed pants, white tunic, and flat circular hat with its black visor and metal badge in front.

I gave a quick glance over at Eveline. She put a wry expression on her face, tilted her head, raised an eyebrow, and twirled a finger at one ear inquiringly. I quickly kissed her on the lips. Then we followed my father up to the farmhouse.

THIRTY

In spite of our efforts to deter him, my father, late on the third day after we had met him on the lawn, set off for the Cabinet Room, in the White House, in Washington, D.C., where he joined a number of powerfully influential and like-minded others in abandoning the republic and ensuring that a program of keeping the river of blood at flood level not only be agreed upon but be awarded the highest importance among the aims and affairs of the nation.

As much as I may have hoped and wished otherwise, my father was unreachable. An unspoken and inexplicable inner conviction, an inward zeal, drove him. He was impossible to deflect from a direction once he had settled on following it. I believe now, in looking back, that he was mad, if only in the sense that once he was fixated on a single feeling, image, or idea, it kept his attention away from a focus on any others. Turning to the river of blood ended up being that idea. "Republican senator Arthur Vandenberg told Truman that he could have his militarized economy only *if* he first 'scared the hell out of the American people' that the Russians were coming. Truman obliged."

•

During those three days of waiting for my father, it remained a matter of crucial importance that I maintain the ability to carry certain numbers of incompatible thoughts in my mind without ignoring any of them and without letting any one of them detract from the validity of another.

For example, there were—there *would* be—the contradictory facts that I loved my father and yet despised him. Add to those the contradictory facts that I envied him and yet at the same time disapproved of him to the point almost of feeling disgusted for him. For most of my life I had wished devoutly that I could confide in him, a desire contraindicated by the feeling that I could trust him no more than I could adders fanged. The primal truth was that I must not harm or damage my father, my progenitor and my very creator—but this truth was contraindicated by the truth that I wish devoutly I had stricken him dead for the wrong he did me, for the wrong he did himself, for the wrong he did to the nation I was born into, the wrong he did to Eveline.

•

I may have mentioned the matter of my father's stature in comparison with my own. In any case, he towers a great deal over me, his six-four and one-ninety being well in excess of my own five-ten and one-sixty-five.

But it turned out there was a strength in me I hadn't known about. I wouldn't have thought myself capable of immobilizing my writhing father for several minutes, then lifting him up from the floor—and dropping him off the edge of the open and stairless doorway.

He landed on his feet. From there he set out for Washington.

•

There were a number of ways to enter the old farmhouse—a front door (almost never used), a second front door that opened directly into the "parlor," two "back" doors, one on each side of the big kitchen, and a "rear" door that led from the house into what eight decades earlier had been built as a garage but was now a windowless shed filled with tangles of old, broken, cast-off, abandoned wreckage.

With the back of his dress whites conveying the faintest hint of yellow from the setting sun, just now gliding above the horizon, my father crossed the driveway, climbed three steps up onto the small side porch, and went in through one of the two open doors to the kitchen.

Eveline followed. Then me.

Both of the kitchen's doors and its two windows were open wide, and a pleasant movement of air from outdoors passed through the room. A large round table stood in the middle of the floor, with four chairs placed around it. My father sat down on the far side of the table, leaned back comfortably and flung an arm across the back of the empty chair to his right.

"So what brings you here?" he asked. But he spoke as if it were a declarative sentence rather than an interrogative one, so that it came out,

"So what brings you here."

Eveline and I sat on the two chairs across from him, next to one another but a foot or so apart.

"Well," I said, with the faintest bit of lightness. "This is where I live."

My father made no response and didn't even glance in my direction—mannerisms, or the lack of them, that in their familiarity swept me back to my decades of boyhood and youth. Almost everything about him was hyper-familiar to me. His usual way of sitting, with one arm across the chair next to him, put a strain on his tunic, so—as I could have predicted—he took a moment to undo its five buttons and let it fall open. A loose white undershirt was revealed. On the jacket, where its left lapel would be if it had had one, were pinned twelve or fifteen service ribbons, making a broad stiff rectangle of small but brilliant colors.

"I'm sure I've seen you before," my father said, speaking not to me but to Eveline.

Eveline smiled with her simple smile and gave a musical bit of a laugh.

"I don't think so."

"I do." My father showed no interest in reacting either to Eveline's lightness or to her humor. He continued looking at her with a level gaze across the table.

"Tennis," he said flatly. "Iowa City. May or June of 1934. I saw you. You were with someone."

Eveline and I looked at one another. Somehow I conveyed to her the equivalent of a nod or a "go ahead" in a way that I hoped would be imperceptible to my father. In any case, he was looking at her, not at me.

"Well. I suppose that could be," Eveline granted. "It's true, I was in Iowa City then."

"In front of the library," my father went on. "Just across that narrow little street that runs there. Not even a street, really."

Eveline raised her eyebrows and shrugged her shoulders as if to say "who knows." Every response or movement she made, every gesture or word, made her seem only more infatuatingly beautiful to my father.

"The guy you were with was hopeless. Small. Drab. Glasses. Not up to *your* standard at all."

I could hardly let that pass without losing every bit of leverage or credibility I either had or might hope to gain. I glanced at Eveline, then looked back across the table at my father.

"That little drab guy," I told him. "That was me."

My father remained absolutely still. Nothing about him moved except his eyes, and those only enough to show that his gaze had shifted from Eveline's face to mine. His head itself remained absolutely still as he looked at me, his expression stern, implacable, stony. He was scowling. As usual at moments like this, I was afraid of him, of his volatile and unpredictable anger. But after three or four seconds passed and nothing had happened, I sensed that he wasn't edging toward anger but that instead he was puzzled—*or* that he was pretending to be.

"And who are you," he asked, with slight emphasis on the "you."

"I'm Malcolm. That's why I said I lived here."

My father actually smiled, although sarcastically, his lips thin and not parted. He straightened up in his chair and raised his arms, put his hands behind his head with their fingers interlaced, his elbows sticking out to the sides.

"You're not Malcolm," he said. "Malcolm, if I may inform you, is six years old. Not even a lad." He brought his hands down as if to emphasize what he'd said, placed each of them palm-down on the table top and used them to push himself up to a standing position. He stood for a moment, looking down at Eveline and me, first one and then the other. He was very tall. Out of what impulse, I don't know, but he pulled the sides of his open tunic together and, almost demurely, buttoned two of the five buttons. Then he went around the table and toward the refrigerator, which stood in a corner of the room behind Eveline. The light coming in through the west door had by now grown red from the sunset, and my father's uniform took on its color.

"It seems," he announced, with a kind of oratorical in-flection, "to be time for a drink." He opened the refrigerator door. At the front of one of the shelves inside, placed shoulder to shoulder, trim and at attention almost as if for a parade inspection, stood three stemmed martini glasses, full to their brims. My father picked up one, brought it over, and set it down on the table in front of Eveline. He did the same with the second, putting it in front of me. He then took the third and, having shut the refrigerator door, brought it over, put it down at his own place, and seated himself once again.

He raised his glass and said before drinking, "To you. Whoever you are."

"And to you," Eveline and I both responded, drank, then set our glasses down.

"This is very nice, and so thoughtful," Eveline said after a second or two had passed. Then she added, "But I don't understand. How did you know how many drinks to make? I mean when you didn't know how many of us there would be—or any at all?"

My father made a sound something like a grunt. He was comfortably sprawled in his chair again, one arm resting on the chairback to his side like before. He had undone his tunic buttons again and the grunt he gave made his lean belly move.

"No, not thoughtful," he answered Eveline. "Not at all. I made these for myself. These were intended to be my first three drinks for the evening."

Eveline gave a little laugh, a raised brow, and a big smile. "*First* three?" she said.

My father actually smiled at her, although in a thin-lipped way and very faintly. "Take it or leave it," he said. "That's the way it is. Now tell me who you are and why you're here. Both of you."

I took a deep breath and stood up in order to move my chair closer to Eveline's. After that, I sat down again.

"All right," I said. "Now listen closely." Normally I would have used one or another form of address from my old—self-defensive—collection of terms useful in addressing my father. I used to call him things like "Captain" or "Commodore" or "Skipper" or "Boss," sometimes "Pater" and at others ironic variants like Pappy or Pop—anything, in short, but the conventional and wholly unarmored "Dad." To call my father "Dad" would be like calling Mephistopheles "Phil" or a rattlesnake "Ratty." The routine policies in my life with my father had been (and were), first, never to get too close to him, second, never let my guard down, and, third, never to trust him—especially at six inches less in height and ten times less in imperious manner.

But the reason I used no form of address was that none of my usual old forms would have made any recognizable sense to him—that is, *if* he really, truly, genuinely had no "memory" whatsoever of people, places, or events between 1947 and 1964.

That is, *if* he wasn't testing me; *if* he wasn't talking to me by speaking in silence; *if* he wasn't showing his power over me by diminishing me—in this case, shrinking me out of existence.

How could I be sure? I knew that in November of 1963 he had *seen* the river of blood that he'd voted for in 1947. But now it seemed as though the future—the time between 1947 and 1963—had disappeared from all of his senses.

For me, it was crushing. It felt as though the nation I was born into was blind, had no eyes.

•

I braced my voice and spoke.

"All right," I said. "Now listen. It may be hard for you to believe, but I really am your son Malcolm. I swear. I'm not sure why you don't remember. But this is where I was raised, here, this farm. When you left for the Navy I was too young to realize what was happening and too young to remember it. But I do remember your homecoming and I remember all the years afterward, the second half of the 1940s and the whole of the next decade and the start of the one following. I finished New College in 1963 and then went to study in Iowa City. That's where I went through a translocation in time. It took me back thirty years. That's where I met Eveline. And where I've been living ever since."

It was getting quite dark in the kitchen, but I could still easily make out my father across the table. He was slumped low in his chair, an elbow braced on one of its arms and the point of his chin resting on one fisted hand.

I waited a second or two. Then he said, making it sound as

much like a statement as a question,

"You're married, you two?"

Eveline answered in a completely matter-of-fact tone:

"Oh. Yes. Of course," she said.

No one said anything for a moment. It seemed like a very long time. Then my father pushed his chair back.

"Well," he said as he stood up. "I don't believe you. I don't mean the married part. Who cares about that. But the rest of it." He flicked a switch on the wall behind where he'd been sitting and the light over the table came on. It hung on a cord from the ceiling and reminded me of the light over a pool table. The thought occurred to me that it would be a good card-playing light. It wasn't excessively bright and in fact it was somewhat cozy.

My father collected the three glasses and set them in a row on the drainboard of the kitchen sink. Then he opened the refrigerator again and this time slid out a large ice container. He put two big cubes of ice in each empty glass, returned the ice container to the refrigerator, then went back to the glasses and filled each one with water, over the ice. Then he turned and stood with his back to the sink, leaning against it. He was imposingly tall. Only one button, now, held his tunic closed. He crossed his arms over the front of it.

"You can't prove a thing," he said and gave a small, curiously self-satisfied smile, as if he had just scored a point in a debate against an opponent for whom he felt only scorn. "Yes, it's true that I was in Iowa City in 1933, actually 33-34. But I can guarantee that as sure as Satan *you* weren't there, Mrs.—"

"Oh. Eveline. Please."

"—that *you* weren't there, Eveline, unless you went to college at the age of six or seven, seeing that now, what, thirteen years later, you couldn't pass for a day older than nineteen, maybe twenty, no matter how hard you tried. You're a true beauty."

He turned back to the sink and tossed out the ice and water from each glass, then went to the refrigerator and took out a very large pitcher made of fluted clear glass. From it, he filled each of the three glasses and then put the pitcher back in the refrigerator. He brought the glasses to the table and put them down the same as before.

Once he'd sat down again across the table, we raised our glasses and drank.

"Well, thank you," Eveline began, but my father interrupted her.

"There's no need for thanks or no thanks in a matter of beauty like yours. A fact is a fact. And your fellow there, whatever his name is, he's one very lucky guy."

"This 'fellow' is Malcolm," I said, and then I added, in a tone as sarcastic as I thought I dared risk, "*Dad.*"

"Those are two premises you're going to have a very, very hard time proving, my lad. Little Malcolm is around here someplace, I don't mean necessarily on the property, but someplace. Most likely off with his mother. Sometimes they're gone for days at a time. But when she brings him back you'll see for yourself that he's him and you're you—whoever you are."

"But the real reason we're here, Mister Reiner," Eveline began, but then broke off and added, "I'm sorry, but I'm afraid I don't actually know how to address you."

"Call me Harold," my father told her. "That's my name."

"Well, the real reason we're here, Harold, is because we want to talk to you, or I want to, no, we both do, We want to talk to you about your trip to Washington that's coming up."

I could see my father stiffen slightly and begin to lean forward in his chair before he relaxed back again.

"My what? How do you know about that?"

"Oh," Eveline said as if taken aback. "Well, Malcolm told me."

"Malcolm told you," my father parroted. "You don't have the faintest idea what you're talking about, either of you."

"Oh, but I think we do," I said. "And I think you do, too, except that you don't seem to be recalling very well right now."

He gave a certain laugh, one that I knew only too well. It

was the laugh he gave when he knew he was cornered and *should*—but wouldn't—have the decency to capitulate instead of fight. It was accompanied by a peculiar gesture of the mouth, a closed-lip smile that seemed to be struggling with itself not to be a smile. It was asymmetrical, like the smile he gave Eveline at the tennis court. But *that* was his predatory smile. *This* was his retreat smile, and it showed no teeth.

"And just where are you getting your information, if I may ask."

"Oh, there's plenty of information," I said. "I'm just surprised that you don't seem to have it as well."

Eveline put in, "Really it's just a matter of how you think you're likely to vote. That's what *I* want to talk about, and I know, I'm sure, the same is true for Malcolm."

I nodded that yes, it was.

My father pushed his chair back and stood up. "Time for number three," he said. Instead of letting him collect all three glasses, Eveline and I stood up also and took our own glasses to the sink, where my father went through the same process as before. Two martinis is a great number of martinis for the unpracticed, let alone three—or more, since three, for my father, was only the number he'd planned to start with. Eveline and I exchanged a glance, almost a little pantomime, part of which was an eye-roll and part a simulation of someone in deep water going down for the third time.

We all went back to the table, sat down, and continued with the conversation. I had no idea of how things were likely to develop with my father—whether he would end up angry and do something familiar but unpleasantly drastic—dash a glass, or maybe two, into the sink and storm off, for example— or whether the drink would soften him up, turn him slow, nostalgic, and wistful so that he would maunder increasingly and end up asleep at the table with his head on his arms.

It turned out to be a combination of the two. He did go away and disappear (for two days, in fact), but not in a towering rage. And he did get increasingly sleepy, slurred, and muddled before the end. I counted his drinks—I don't think he did—and he was on number eight, which never quite got finished, by the time we closed up shop.

•

Eveline did all she could to reach my father, to connect with him—and, in a pitiful way, I think that that very effort, in good part, became a catalyst for the wretchedness that followed. I already knew that deep down my father was a blustering and incontinent child, needy and fixated on himself, though I learned it in a dozen new ways through Eveline's and my long encounter with him that night. With each drink, the boundaries of his philosophic and personal world revealed themselves to be growing narrower, as he himself became the more hopelessly entangled with his own wants, feelings, and desires—while the immensities everywhere else, reaching to the edges of the continent and then around the world to join one another on the other side—these fell by the side and went unnoticed.

That my father was to some degree deranged and to a very great degree a solipsist I have known for a very long time, but all the way back then—whether it be 1964, or 1934, or 1934 cum 1947—I knew only what I saw of his behavior, and I hadn't yet achieved a way to name or label it; I hadn't yet found the keys I needed, the revelatory shortcuts of words, terms, and clinical identifiers to make sense of what I saw.

My father, I knew perfectly well, thought of himself, or wished very much to think of himself, as an urbane and experienced observer of the world, at home wherever he might find himself, a man at ease, sophisticated, cosmopolitan. But there was something in him much too vain, needy, and self-referential to allow for his vision of the world, or of his role in it, to remain as he might imagine or wish it to remain. He was too judgmental, for one thing, and too obsessed by desire, for another.

Things, ideas, people, or modes of behavior that my father saw and disliked he rejected out of hand, not infrequently with vehemence and expressions of revulsion or disgust. Tolerance was not part of my father's natural makeup or native disposition, but, on the other hand, desire was very much so.

Alcohol highlighted and intensified these qualities in my father's intellectual and emotional makeup. The use of alcohol caused a rapid, unstoppable narrowing in the focus of his intellectual attention and, along with it, a powerful surge in the passion and desire he might feel for whatever it was at the time that remained corralled inside that small magic circle of his consciousness.

•

About the journey, he was adamant. Nothing that I was able to say, and nothing Eveline was able to say, made even the least inroad into the rocklike solidity of his determination to go. That part of our plea, then, was clearly hopeless, impotent, and doomed. And conceivably that was for the best: Conceivably, the more important thing was to influence what my father would do once he was already there, once he was already *in* the Cabinet Room. The figures assembled there, after all, each in his own way also a father of the nation we were born into, these assembled figures were going to take a vote, and the vote they took would determine whether the republic lived or died; whether the river of blood would be widened and extended on the one hand or drained and diverted on the other; whether a virus would be implanted into the body of the republic, sending it on its long and irreversible path into blood, sickness, murder, war, death; or whether the fathers could be reached out to and encouraged to vote for wholeness and harmony, for the health of the republic and its children, of all the people born in it and of it, all of them deserving the protection of its earth, water, and sky.

•

I implored my father, pressing my belly against the edge of the table, leaning toward him, my hands extended, "You *saw* what happened. You *saw* them do it. You saw it happen. You saw them make the kill. But now we're back here, sixteen years before it happened, and in fact before the group that did it has even been created. That means you have a chance to do something so that it *won't* happen. You have a chance to make it *not take place*. You have a chance to help make that group *not* come into existence. *Why won't you take that chance?*"

•

Night-sounds coming in through the windows and doors. Background orchestra of sawing crickets and pulsing frogs. Call of an owl. The lone bark of a dog far off. Once, frighteningly nearby, so that all of us jumped, the high piercing shriek of something being killed, then a handful of muffled wingbeats before silence again.

•

"I don't have the faintest idea what you're talking about," my father said. "I have no idea who you mean. Someone killed someone?"

Can there be amnesia when a person goes back in time? Can there be amnesia of the future? Can it be the same kind of forgetting as when a person moves forward with the pace of time and gradually loses a grip on the past, sees it drift away and dissolve, no longer knowing what it was, or even *that* it was?

•

On the day of the assassination, after Fritz Dreisbach and I had finished dinner, I talked to my parents. I called them from the phone outside the concierge's office. A collect call. There must be a record of it somewhere, even though by now it would be over sixty-five years old. Nevertheless, called them and we talked. They were shocked, of course, like everyone. My father, drawing a few words from his literary side, said that the assassination had sent us into the heart of darkness.

•

"Someone killed someone?" he said now. He said it off-handedly, as he would do if asking about something that held little interest for him.

•

As the alcohol continued to take greater effect, my father's range of attention grew more narrow. His attention went back to World War II, to the Navy, to the Pacific Theater. Nothing Eveline or I said or did could restrain him or keep him from returning there.

In my father's view, and in his memory, those days in the Pacific were of an almost unblemished perfection. Life inside them was clean, robust, honorable, purposeful, firm, and hale. Those many days, and the daily life within them, were dignified in their orderliness, poise, organization and detail, above all in the calling they served. Their purpose was to ensure the conquest of good over evil, honor over infamy, civilization over depravity, glory over shame, courage over cowardice, light over darkness, right over wrong. In the gradually narrowing eye of my father's memory there appeared the image of an officer, handsome, lean, and tall, standing on the flying bridge of a medium cruiser on the open sea. Everywhere, sunlight. The officer looks out over an immensity of south Pacific. The wind is brisk. It flips up a corner of the officer's shirt collar, then lets it fall again. The cleanliness, scent, and warmth of the air, all of these are memorable and perfect. My father wants to return there. He wants to stay there forever.

·

He was a sensualist, nostalgist, and sentimentalist. These traits, by merit of his being additionally a solipsist, achieved a grip over his personality even more powerful than it might otherwise have been. It seemed to my father self-evident that such feelings as he himself experienced must without question be experienced also, universally, by everyone.

·

Late that night, the walls of the kitchen, quietly and unnoticeably, fell outward, as if on the signal of an invisible stagehand, the same one who caused the ceiling to lift up and away as if on hinges of its own, then to disappear altogether.

It was the same thing that had happened at Audrey and Ed LaRouche's apartment, except that here it felt altogether different. It brought with it no sense of charm, wonder, reassurance, unity, or pleasure. This time there were no faintly illuminated lines, shapes, tendrils, or circles radiating outward to the horizon—but instead we were surrounded by absolute darkness, an entire world of velvet blackness. I imagined how we would look if seen from a distance away. A lighted area, like a scene in a play, appearing as if suspended in the midst of nothing. A linoleum floor. Three people at a round table, two sitting close to one another, facing the third. An overhead light hanging from the ceiling even though no ceiling is there.

Above all, my father's spotlessly gleaming white naval uniform.

·

When the walls fell away, a chill came in from the night air, drifting over us.

•

I had a clear sense, at the moment I imagined seeing us in that way, from far off and surrounded by darkness, that everything was lost. As it was. The way it turned out, Eveline and I were to have one more day together and most of a second one. Then my father would return to the farm and it would be the end.

If I had known with absolute certainty that the end was going to come, and that it was going to come *then*, and that it was going to come in the way it did, I think I might have found a means, somehow, to kill myself. I would have explained to Eveline; I would have pleaded with her, begged and implored her to understand. After all, her return would take her back to 1934, and in spite of the world's immense storage-lockers of grief, depravity, murder, and horror waiting to be split open so that their poisons could spew forth, few of those things and little of their effect would reach all the way to her, especially if she remained near her home and went on reading, and studying, and weaving protective tendrils around the earth. Starting out again in 1934, she would have thirteen years of at least a relative openness, industry, and freedom before the year 1947 came, by which time she would be thirty-eight years old, and very, very possibly she could by then, or would by then, have found a life, a position, a place and a home that would at least for a certain time protect her from the worst of the ruinous, demeaning, depersonalizing, lacerating and privacy-destroying forces that had been unleashed by my father's decisions in the Cabinet Room, first on February 27th, 1947, then again on September 18th of the same year, a single day after Eveline was sent back to 1934 and a single day after I was sent forward to the mean, thin, vacuous, atmosphere-less, criminal, depersonalized year of 1964, where I was forced to live alone, by myself, without Eveline, wracked by memory, desire, sorrow, loss, regret, and a thousand associated feelings that together drew me into paroxysm of grief and self-pity so deep that I doubted whether I would be able to return to anything resembling a sane or normal or coherent life again.

I was wracked, tortured, ruined, flung into weakness and sickness by the suffering I went through from the loss of Eveline, the wanting of her, the wanting and wanting and never having, she being by then only an absence that I nevertheless craved, and craved, and craved, until I was mad with craving.

•

War. Wartime. Conquest. Profit. Conquest. Profit. Repeat. Equation: W+W+C+P+C+P+=War Machine.

•

"Republican senator Arthur Vandenberg told Truman that he could have his militarized economy only if he first 'scared the hell out of the American people' that the Russians were coming. Truman obliged. The perpetual war began. . . ."

•

♩"What a war it was! What a war it was! What a war it was to win, good old, good old World War Two!"♩

•

Keep it going! Keep it going! Keep it going!

•

It was past midnight when my father stood up from the table for the last time, not in order to make another drink, but to bring the evening to a close. At first, he looked quite unsteady, unsure on his feet, swaying noticeably, as if his height would certainly overwhelm his ability to balance, making a fall inevitable. But what shocked me slightly was his face. Its flesh was flaccid, loose, and sagging, almost like the face of someone asleep or, worse, like a death mask. But my father did a strange thing at that point. He leaned forward from the waist and, with his elbows straight and his hands a good distance apart from one another, placed the extreme tips of his fingers on the table top, all ten of them, well spread out from one another, as if the intent were to provide the most efficient support with the least possible contact with the table. As he did this, he stopped swaying and his face began to get back its familiar shape and appearance, complete with one eyebrow raised faintly and mouth once again asymmetrical, slightly higher on its left side, in the expression I thought of as his predatory smile, lips parted only on the raised side, the faintest glimpse of a canine visible behind them.

He pushed his chair back and started around the curve of the table toward Eveline and me, one hand remaining in contact with the tabletop, palm held high, fingers spread out as before. When he came quite close to Eveline and showed no sign of stopping, she pushed her own chair back noisily, stood up quickly and took two steps backward, away from the table. But my father simply diverted his own course in order to continue toward her. She took two more steps back. When I saw what was happening—obviously every word that Eveline had spoken to him all night had been like a call to his heart even though his mind had accepted not a syllable—I got up and stepped in front of my father, so that I was between him and Eveline, and stopped.

For the first time in my life, the thought passed through my mind that my father, at heart, might be a coward. When I stopped in front of him—we were hardly three inches apart— his face changed instantly into an exaggerated look of surprise and alarm, the sort of thing you might expect on the stage of a backwater theater at the climax of the sorriest melodrama—the mouth an "o," the eyes widened in fear—but that you would never quite expect to see on a real person, in real life, in a real situation. The chiseled good looks, the calculated, faintly taunting hauteur, were gone, and the face left behind was soft, flaccid, cowering, and—if it had been anyone other than my father—pitiful.

Or perhaps it *was* pitiful even so. It's perfectly conceivable that, until this moment, he had never believed I was real, or had never *had* to believe it. Or perhaps only now had he realized not only that I was real but that I was actually his son. Distantly conceivable, although unlikely. It's also possible that I was merely seeing the wreckage caused by eight martinis.

I reached a hand back to make sure Eveline was still right behind me and that I was still in between her and my father. Then I said, stepping out of his path and gesturing for him to pass,

"Okay, Pops. Bedtime."

THIRTY-ONE

I don't know where he went and I never will. The night was black as pitch, made all the darker in contrast with the soft— and quickly dimming—hanging light that continued to illumi- nate the kitchen table and the small area immediately around it. Hand in hand, Eveline and I set off in the direction of our tent, and after we had gone hardly more than a dozen steps the lamp dimmed abruptly, held on for a second, then disap- peared altogether, as though it were a candle that had just finished drinking its wax and guttered out. I knew the con- tours and slopes of the ground by memory and, even though flying blind, I simply continued on, although more slowly and with a tighter grip than before on Eveline's hand. The wooden barnyard fence was directly in front of us, perpendicular to the direction we were walking. We came to it and followed it east—I kept one hand on the top rail—then went around the corner with it, to the north, and then, after half its length on that side, off to the right and just a small way down the east- leaning slope, to our tent.

We crawled in through the flap and found our way to the tangled pile of sleeping bags and blankets that were exactly as they'd been when we'd left the tent that morning for our walk into West Tree, an event that now seemed weeks ago. But now, in the absolute darkness, we lay clasped tightly together, my arms around Eveline and hers around me, as she, poor Eveline, sobbed and sobbed and sobbed, overwhelmed and seized by fear and anger and sorrow and a sense of what was to come.

At long last the cruel iron around her heart loosened, and we slept, in the ocean of all the chirping, trilling, and singing night sounds, until dawn.

•

For almost a day we'd had nothing to eat, not since our trip into West Tree the morning before this one. We unpacked the things we'd bought on that trip and lay in front of the tent in the morning sunlight like ancient Romans, propped on our elbows, and dug into the bread, salami, cheese, and olives from the day before.

•

Because I know when it was that things came to an end, and how they came to that end—and because that knowledge darkens, warps, and colors everything else—I find it all but impossible to recapture, or even suggest, the feeling and quality of that day, Eveline's and my last full day, and the night that followed, and the morning after that, a day that included our last walk into West Tree, and our last breakfast there, at the Ideal Café, and our last return out to the farm.

Our plan was that if my father hadn't returned by then, we would get up early, pack everything, and set out again on our return trip to Iowa City.

We would have begun that trip, then, on September 18th, 1947. But my father came back mid-afternoon of the 17th.

•

Chronology:

September 14th, 1494: Eveline and I arrive at the pre-farmland outside West Tree.

September 15th, 1494/1947: We walk back into West Tree for breakfast and provisions and then, on our return from town, go up to the land's highest point and make a love nest. My father returns to the farm. As he does, 1494 disappears and is replaced by 1947. We meet my father on the west lawn. A warm breeze comes out of the southwest. In the kitchen that evening and into the night my father drinks eight martinis and frightens Eveline by approaching as if to molest her. He then disappears.

September 16th, 1947: Eveline's and my last full day together.

September 17th, 1947/1934/1964: My father returns to the farm. In the kitchen, he goes further in his attempt to molest Eveline. I pull him away from her, immobilize him, then drop him outside the kitchen door. He throws words back at us and sets off for the nation's capitol, where he will do his part in poisoning the nation, guaranteeing the assassination of President Kennedy, and bringing on the death of the republic.

I never see Eveline again.

THIRTY-TWO

I think it may have been the most beautiful day of the year, sky cloudless and blue, temperature balmy, air soft, filled with every pleasant scent of autumn. Most important, however, the very first thing, was to ascertain that my father had gone. We went up to the house. The kitchen was still without its roof or walls—the kitchen light still hung over the table, attached to nothing—but the rest of the house was intact and normal. From the kitchen, we walked through every other room, dining room, living room, even the bathroom, then went upstairs to the bedrooms, two large and one small. No one was anywhere in the house. Everything was neat and tidy, nothing out of place, the beds neatly made and trim. And quiet: It was museum-like and ghostly in its quietness. Except for two or three nights over the past month, Eveline and I had been outdoors almost always, night and day. I had forgotten how quiet it can be behind windows and walls, under a roof.

But no sign of my father whatsoever. It was a relief, like being granted a whole day with the promise of no rain. Eveline and I took a leisurely walk into West Tree for provisions, and when we came back stowed them in our tent. We'd been lucky, on that first night, in 1494, in deciding where to put our tent: Another six or eight feet higher on the grassy slope and we would have been inside the barnyard. As it was now, the cattle would come up from time to time and gather along their side of the fence, at the point nearest our tent, almost as if they wanted some company. They would scratch themselves against the posts and against the thick heavy planks that served for the rails. Once or twice we went up ourselves to socialize, with the fence between us and them. It was nice to pat their big drum-like sides and hear the hollow sound, or to pet their powerful foreheads.

If you followed the fence to its southeast corner and then turned with the fence and continued toward the barn, you soon came to a place where the fence broke off for ten feet or so while in its place rested the stock tank, itself serving both as fence and as watering hole. Made of formed concrete, the ten-foot tank was approximately four feet wide and deep enough to hold close to three feet of water.

It was a favorite place of mine, and Eveline and I stopped there for a while. I climbed up and sat on the top rail of the fence. Eveline, below me, leaned with a shoulder against the fence, one hand hanging from the top rail, one from the middle rail, and one foot hooked onto the bottom rail.

A half-inch pipe at very low pressure perpetually fed water from the barn into the tank, and just now it was brimful. A thin sheet of water rolled over the mossy east lip, it being ever so slightly lower than the now-dry west lip. After a time the cattle came over toward us, as if they'd decided to have a drink before returning out to the pasture. There was room for three at a time at the tank, or four with some crowding. They put their noses down into the water to drink, and when they did, Eveline reached out and patted their big, rocky foreheads. You could sense their contentment. Sometimes they would close their enormous long-lashed eyes, and now and again one of them would pause for a moment and give a big sigh. You could see the water level go down as one group finally moved away and another came up.

We were in no hurry, really, of any sort. I was certain my father would be gone for at least this whole first day, and, without him anywhere nearby, it would be a pleasure to show Eveline around the farm a little bit.

It was a pleasure and yet admittedly also a strange one, thanks to the various planes of time that were spinning around. *And* thanks to my father's presumed amnesia. I was still confused in the aftermath of our evening with him, and yet again I tried to make sense out of it.

Here I was, after all, in 1947, showing Eveline the farm I had lived on from the time I was five all the way up to age twenty-one, when I went to Iowa City, was transported into 1933—and met Eveline. In some ways, it was almost too much to keep straight, too many facets to hold in mind at once. Earlier, I had wondered whether or not Eveline and I would become older in coming from 1934 to 1949, but from my father's reaction to Eveline's youthfulness, it seemed clear that she and I were still 22 and 25. But that answer, as usual, gave way to other questions. My father, for example: Was he thirty-eight (that is "now," in 1947), or was he actually his "real" age, that is, his 1964 age, which would be fifty-five?

There wasn't any argument, really: As I think I said, my father clearly looked the fifty-five that I remembered him as being. So there's an answer, but, as always, an answer followed by questions: Why, for example (again), did my father recognize Eveline but not me? Unless, of course, he was faking, just as he may have been faking about his memory, or lack of it, of anything from 1947 through 1964.

Well. He didn't recognize *me* that day at the tennis courts for the perfectly good reason that he'd never seen me before and I wouldn't be born for another seven years. Furthermore, I was nondescript, "the small guy, drab, with glasses." But my father certainly remembered Eveline, beautiful Eveline, with her dark hair, powerful eyebrows, strong cheekbones. . . .

But there had to be more to it than only that. There had to be something more to explain my being invisible, at least to my father, as well as his black-out of the years (and therefore also of *me*) from 1947 to 1964, *if* the black-out was real.

"Eveline," I said. "I can't figure it out." This was when we were still dallying at the stock tank, I sitting on the top of the fence and Eveline leaning against it below me.

"Do you mean his memory?"

"I guess so. His not remembering me, at least. Or so he says. His not *acknowledging* me."

Eveline heaved a big sigh. She leaned over the tank and reached for an ear of the nearest drinking cow. She ran her fingers over the length of it three or four times, from the base to the tip, going with the lay of the hair. When she let it go, the cow flicked it back and forth. The ears were huge.

"I know. I don't understand either. *You* remember West Tree. And growing up. And high school. And New College. And I expect to remember—at least I *hope* I'll remember—all of *this*—"she gestured with a toss of her head—"when we get back to Iowa City."

"I love you, Ev," I said and jumped down from the fence. She turned to face me. It's true that she was extraordinarily beautiful, dark eyes wide enough to fall into. I put my arms around her and we stood there for a moment or two holding on to each other.

"I hope you can forgive me," she said, in little more than a whisper, in my ear. "For my lie. That we're married."

I laughed and held her more tightly.

"You took me by surprise, I'll admit," I said. "But I wasn't about to give it away. And I like the way it sounded."

She pushed me away a little and looked up. "Do you think he believes it?"

"Ah, the sixty-four dollar question," I said. "I have no idea." Then I added, "Probably not." She pulled me close again.

"And forgive me for something else," she whispered.

This time I held *her* a little bit away to see her face, but she pulled back to me.

"There's nothing else," I said. "In fact there's nothing in the first place."

"Yes there is," she replied. "I was awful. Miserable. I wasn't any help at all. I didn't even make a dent in him. You'd have been better off without me."

I held her and we swayed together slightly for a minute or two.

"Eveline," I finally said. As I spoke, I felt an almost over-whelming surge of emotion, and I wondered whether I would be able to go on speaking these words—words that I had never so much as *thought* of until right now, right here, this minute. "Without you, Ev," I heard myself saying, "I wouldn't even *be* here. Without you, I wouldn't have had a snowflake's chance in hell even of realizing the possibility that maybe I *could* come here, that there might be a way to get here, that it was even a *concept*." The words tumbled out, making perfect sense—in spite of the fact that I had never so much as imagined them before this very minute, let alone thought them through. They made me feel as though I were speaking in voices, as though I were in the grip of some force I couldn't identify or name or recognize but that, even so, felt absolutely natural, true, ac-curate, and right. I remember everything about that moment in absolute, perfect, photographic detail. I can see it, feel it, recall it, recreate it in every detail—I remember noticing, as I held on to Eveline and went on talking, that the cows had slaked their thirst and one by one had turned away from the water tank and were gathered together now in the middle of the barnyard waiting for their leader to start them off on their amble back to the pasture. It amazes me that I noticed them at all, since the only thing that mattered was holding on to Eveline, pressing my face into her hair, and going on with my words until every last one of them was out.

Whatever invisible power was generating the words went

on generating them, and I said to Eveline, "Without you I wouldn't be here, *we* wouldn't be here, and there wouldn't have been any chance at all to sway my father. So it's you who've done everything. You have nothing whatsoever to apologize for, sweet Eveline. *Nothing.*"

And that's when I realized that Eveline was weeping again, no, not weeping, sobbing, just as she had done the night before, in our tent.

I didn't know or understand what I had done. The fact is that I hadn't done anything, I hadn't said anything other than the absolute truth. It *was* all because of Eveline. Without Eveline, I know for certain that there would have been nothing, no program of studies, no trip to West Tree, not even a *chance* to alter my father's path and to allow the true past, the past Eveline embodied, to flow naturally through the present and into the future instead of that future being throttled in its crib by greed, zeal, desire, solipsism, ego.

What I failed disastrously to see, what I failed to understand until far too late, was that Eveline saw—she knew—much, much more than I did. She already knew the outcome: saw it, sensed it, perceived it, probably even understood it, *certainly* knew that it was inevitable, and just as certainly knew that we were doomed. She knew what was going to happen, and this knowledge plunged her into grief and despair. And that was what she was trying so hard to keep from me, to protect me from.

We leaned against the fence and I held her and held her. In time Eveline's sobs grew fewer, and soon she was left only with some hiccups and a very, very tear-streaked face. With cupped hands I got water from the stock tank and helped her wash away the tears. Then, filling her hands from the little feeder-pipe, she drank in order to help with the hiccups.

After a time, she looked up at me, eyes still moist but with a brave smile, and said,

"Let's go walking in the grass. Let's go up on the hill and walk in the long grass."

•

And we did. We went out through the pasture and up the far hill to the east-west property line. A fence ran there, with tall grass growing on both sides of it, making it into a kind of grass wall running along the top of the ridge. Halfway toward the railroad tracks was a spot I had always especially liked, a lone apple tree right on the fence line, so that I used to imagine the tree belonging half to us and half to the Bill Ridleys. It wasn't large at all—maybe twelve or fifteen feet high—but very old. It blossomed in spring and did produce apples, although they were very small and gnarled, enjoyed mainly by such insects and birds as might happen by. I laced my fingers together and offered Eveline a stepping platform so she could reach up into the branches. She brought down five or six of the little apples and we made our own sitting place, leaning back against the trunk of the tree, and sampled them. Their flesh was sweet, although there wasn't very much of it, and caution was needed to avoid taking in such small worms as might already be dining there.

The area covered by grass was wider around the base of the tree than elsewhere, enough so that we could settle down in it. And the grass was tall enough that, when we were sitting down, we couldn't see over the top and across the fields down to the county road below. It was another secret love nest, and we stayed there for a good amount of time. Now and then a breeze moved over the grass, making the tassels bow and nod, and we were serenaded off and on by a pair of meadowlarks perching nearby on the top strand of the barbed wire fence.

"We could build a house up here," Eveline said at one point, sleepily, and I wondered out loud whether there might already have been a house located there, long ago, with the apple tree the only sign of it left behind.

•

By this time it was ten-thirty or eleven o'clock in the morning, and the rest of the day seemed to go by with an almost unnatural quickness, the way days off from work go by, or vacation days. It was all pleasant, a good day, and also a desirable one, but at the same time both of us knew that something was going unsaid between us, something obviously important, and yet something that neither of us wanted—or dared—to bring up. I know now—and doubtless I knew it then too, deep down—that it had to do with the certainty that we were going to fail in our attempt to tame, recover, civilize—oddly, the word "harvest" also comes to my mind—my father. But even to mention this subject felt impossible, seemed inconceivable. That subject had become the unspeakable.

Eveline *knew*. As for me, I had doubts, and those doubts were unnerving, debilitating, and deep. But, unlike Eveline, *I didn't know*.

Imagine the pain and horror she was going through in knowing what was going to happen.

I am, as I write these words, a very old man, age eighty-seven, recalling an event that took place—well, eighty-one years ago if you count from 1947. On the other hand, an equally good case can be made for counting from 1934, in which case my loss of Eveline, and our loss of the republic, took place all of ninety-five years ago. Or you could count from 1964, in which case the event I'm recalling took place sixty-four years ago.

The choice of any of those dates is as justifiable as any other, since all of them are part of the story I'm recounting—and, in one sense or another, all of them are a part of it. I don't for an instant believe that history comes into existence in perfectly sequential one-second increments ticked off by some kind of divinely appointed world-governing clock. Eveline Stahl, studying in Iowa City in late fall 1933, was living inside the history of 1933 but also had an immense influence on the history being lived in late fall 1963; otherwise, I would—or could—never have been taken back thirty years to a drafty classroom in Jessup Hall, never have seen Eveline, heard the music of her voice, fallen in love with her, and, through her, made a sacrificial effort to save the republic from being destroyed by the glory-and-greed-driven men whose simplicity, infantilism, clinical naiveté, as well as ignorance both of history and of the civilizations of the world, caused them to ignore the essence and soul of what made the republic a humane and living thing—and to crush it as a boy would crush a robin's egg fallen from a nest onto the lawn.

History is everywhere, existing at once in all times, just as any living body is a thing mortal not only in *some* but in *all* of its parts, so that the entire body merits and needs the physician's healing care, not just one part. When Eveline was born, in 1909, the nature of what happened to me in November of 1963 was changed, altered, transformed. Her mother's death, in 1919, Eveline's tenth year, touches not only on Eveline's learning about the creation of the connecting tendrils, which she continued weaving throughout 1924, 1931, 1933—but her mother's death reaches as far as 1947, and 1963, even as far as 2028, where it touches lightly and almost invisibly on my desktop as I write these words.

THIRTY-THREE

For the whole day, the sky remained the same cloudless blue it had begun with. The temperature rose to something over eighty, but, with very low humidity, so that the warmth was a pleasure, even in the direct sun.

In spite of the uncomfortable—and silenced—fear and anxiety that lay under the surface of every moment, this day of waiting *was* ours to do whatever we wanted with. And the decision, which emerged as we came back across the pasture from the north hill, was that we should idle, meander, and do whatever might come up. That meant a walk in to West Tree for lunch, but first a look back inside the farmhouse for some reading to take along with us. Most of my father's bookshelves were in the living room, although there were some also in the west bedroom upstairs. The house had the same near-muffled silence as before, and there was an airlessness about it that I didn't remember from our earlier visit. Neither of us wanted to stay inside for long, so we simply picked two books from the downstairs shelves and went back outside. We tossed them into the bag that I was carrying over my shoulder. Eveline's was the Harriet Monroe poetry anthology, and mine was Peter Negoe's *Storm*.

It was good to be back outdoors. A good walk in the open air helped clear the head. Instead of going on the highway, we took what I always called "the back road." It was a little longer than our old cross-country route but it made for a pleasant walk. It took us west across the railroad tracks before turning south and leading more or less directly into West Tree.

At that time there were only two farms along the stretch of road after it turned south, one not so very far from the turn and the other closer to West Tree. The farmhouses and buildings of both of them stood on the west side of the road, and almost midway between the two was a large area of swampy lowland with a deep woods behind it. On summertime nights the sounds from the swamp were mysterious, rhythmic, deep, almost thunderous.

The walk to West Tree took something like forty-five minutes or so. We went straight to the Ideal Café and were lucky enough to get the second booth from the front, the best place to benefit from the air coming in through the open front door. We ordered a green salad each and a sandwich of roast beef on rye. The waitress, Veronica, knew us well enough by this time and held off bringing coffee until after we'd eaten our sandwiches. She didn't mind if we sat for a time afterward, reading. Even so, things felt different from usual. I reached my left hand across the table and Eveline met it with the clasp of her own right hand. As always, I was stirred by touching her. Simply seeing Eveline was one thing, the mere fact of being with her, but touching her was something altogether different, a magnitude of difference, the difference between looking at the surface of a still blue lake as opposed to jumping into it.

The book I'd chosen didn't hold my interest, but watching Eveline as she read her own book held it powerfully. The tilt of her head, her dark hair, the exquisite, perfectly balanced sculpture of her forehead, eyebrows, nose, lips, chin, things mundane in the listing but unsurpassably beautiful in the observing—I gazed, no, I stared, at Eveline's face. She sensed my looking at her and raised her eyes. Her face was poised, beautiful, imperturbable—until she cocked one eyebrow ever so slightly, alluding to everything she and I shared, everything we had shared, everything we *would* share, a love-message that, if we'd been alone, might have led to things of a kind impossible to fulfill in a public place, in the second-from-the-front booth of the Ideal Café, the afternoon air coming in through the open door.

Eveline and I held hands across the table. Eveline went back to her reading while I watched her. My own book lay facedown on the table beside me. I found myself thinking back to our trip, now long ago, our walk from the farmer's cornfield all the way to Kenney's bar downtown, where we also sat at one of the front booths, near the open door, the summer air drifting in.

Things now should have been the same as then, but they weren't. Eveline and I were the same, and everything else should have been the same too, but it wasn't. Veronica came over with seconds of coffee and I asked for our check. There was no hurry, but on the other hand I realized that there was a sense of something missing, and if that something were still here, it would have been meaningful to stay. For a short time I couldn't identify it, but then I did. The sidewalk and street outside the open door, with the sun falling across them, and then the sidewalk on the far side, with its buildings standing there shoulder-to-shoulder—the missing thing was that it didn't feel as if this town were able to take me farther, it didn't feel as if it were actually situated in any particular place, or that its particular place was connected to other places radiating outward from it, and to others beyond those, and even more beyond those—so that being here, in this town, on this street, in this café, would give a person the feeling not only of being *some*where but that that *some*where was connected in a million delicate, subtle, yet unbreakable ways with what lay beyond it, and then with what lay again beyond *that*, and then still further beyond, so that by sitting here in this booth in this café, or by standing here on this sidewalk, a person would know, sense, feel, be aware of the interconnectedness of all things that exist between the seas, which is to say that a person would be aware of the republic, would know that the republic in one place is the same as it is in another place, and would know that the republic is not a unit but a singularity, a multitudinous and varied plenitude of places, peoples, climates, languages, freedoms, songs, ideas, feelings, landscapes, desires, all held together by a million woven tendrils that are delicate and invisible and yet as strong as braided steel *for so long as the ghost and guiding spirit of the republic, spoken or unspoken, written or unwritten, remains dedicated to the nation's original and foundational principles of freedom, fairness, and dignity, and to the continuing of a nurturing kinship and harmony with all other peoples, places, and republics of the world.*

I realized that that's what was missing, that that's what was absent. One thing was no longer connecting with another. The republic had begun dying.

It could mean only one thing: My father was coming back; he was getting closer to West Tree.

·

Out of the wish not to trouble her, I said nothing to Eveline—although I am now certain, as I have said, that she knew full well what was coming, and *had* known ever since the night of the martinis. I'm certain that she had sensed for herself the un-cohering of the land, and certain that she understood, even before I did, what it meant.

·

Lost, o lost.

·

It went unspoken that something was not right. Both of us knew it and neither of us mentioned it.

•

thousands were watching no one saw a thing

•

I can't remember whether it was Eveline's idea or mine, but we decided to return to the farm the "old way" instead of returning by the road again. First, though, we stopped for more provisions, including two bottles of red wine, and got everything safely stowed in my canvas bag. Then we set out the way we'd gone the very first time we'd headed out to the farm, back when West Tree disappeared piece by piece behind us and *we* went back into 1494.

The river this time was considerably changed, although its condition was better than I was to know it in the future, a decade or two decades after 1947. The water was no longer crystalline, as it had been in 1494, but it was a light brown, although colored only by soil runoff and not yet by fertilizer and chemicals and untreated waste. For a certainty, it no longer held any trout.

Just before climbing up from the river we passed the ruins of Baxley's Mill. The building was roofless and only two of its walls were standing, at right angles to one another, like two hands that held between them a large but low mound of brick, mortar, and stone.

Once we'd climbed up from the river we made our way sixty or seventy yards along the level edge of a cornfield, went down into the drainage ditch and up again to the edge of the highway. Once across the asphalt, up a driveway leading to a loose cluster of three houses (which of course hadn't been there before), and past the houses along a nearby fence line, we started up the incline to the high ridge where, before, we'd stopped for the immensity of the views. Off to the southeast you could still see vestiges and remnants of the oblong hills with their flattened tops, although farms were now sprinkled among them and the thick groves of trees around each home-stead gave the scene a much different look from before. As for the southwest, there was now no view at all, it being obscured by a large stand of woods half a mile square or more.

To the north, however, the view was wholly unobscured. We looked out over three-quarters of a mile or so across low hills covered now half in grain stubble and half in drying stalks of ripening corn. And there, at the far end of this view, was our farm, miniature and distant. There was the gabled shape of the white clapboard house and, on its west, there were the high elms casting their shade on the lawn where Eveline and I had met my father, a memory that now seemed weeks ago, though in fact it was just yesterday.

•

It seems now as though things moved at an unnaturally fast pace between our return from West Tree and the end of every-thing. And I can't rid myself of the idea, either, that it was as if that short time held within it no real dramatic rise or shape, as if it were made out of nothing but a short string of mechanical reactions brought about by tiny, unimpressive joints, gears, levers, and springs.

High, despairing, world-altering events from trivial, mean, lowly sources and causes.

•

Eveline and I went to our tent, stowed our provisions there, then crawled in after them, made ourselves comfortable in the soft tumult of our bedding, and fell asleep for an hour, maybe longer.

•

When we woke up, the day no longer seemed so much like a free thing full of opportunity, the way it had before. There was now a feeling of its slipping away too quickly, even of its already having gone. As a restorative, I suggested a walk up to the railroad tracks and back, along the road. It turned out to be a good idea, as a way of clearing the head. By this time it was past three; the sun was still forty-five degrees above the horizon but its light was already beginning to change, or maybe the change was simply that shadows were beginning to draw out eastward.

We followed the road on its rise in elevation of twenty feet or so up to the level crossing. At the crossing itself were no gates, bells, or lights, but only two upright posts, one facing each way, each with the classic two boards crossed in the shape of an X and showing the words RAILROAD CROSSING. Growing up on the farm, in the years to come, when I had time on my hands, there were countless occasions when I would come up to the crossing to poke around, explore, dawdle, smell the creosote, see how far I could throw pebbles down the tracks, look for railroad spikes to add to my collection, and, with luck, watch a train go by. Eveline and I did more or less these same things, including seeing a train pass by, a northbound freight with 104 cars, not counting the locomotive, coal car, or caboose.

We could have watched the Twin Star Rocket rush by. That would have been a pleasure, but it would have meant waiting until almost a quarter past five, nearly half an hour, and neither of us felt like doing that. We set out on the way back instead, walking slowly along the left hand side of the road. The sun on our backs felt good. Our shadows, by this time, stretched out well ahead of us.

I wanted to shake off the sense I was feeling, an unnamable mix of anxiety, melancholy, and foreboding. That, in any case, is how I think *now* of what I was feeling *then*. There's a problem with keeping myself absolutely honest, however, and that problem lies in the immense difference between what I know now and what I knew then, that warm afternoon, Eveline at my side, as she and I came back from the railroad tracks, our shadows leading us on.

It was commonplace for me to have some degree of foreboding in dealing with my father, however mundane that dealing might be, since a person never knew whether anger might bark in him or tolerance purr, whether he would be chill and disapproving or, for once, pliant, amenable, and plain. I doubt very much that even he knew which of his caged selves might manage to snap the lock and rush out.

I do know, however, that the chief keeper, the keeper of *all* the locks, was the *desiring* self. And I also know—in fact I remember putting down these words—that when the desiring self looks out from inside its own self (that is, out through its own eyes, though in actuality out through its own *mind*), the things that it sees are those things that *become* the universe.

And what he desires, he is malevolently helpless not to take.

•

So much to think through. To accommodate.

•

Devastation, loss, wreckage.

•

And Eveline. The profundity of her courage. Being in terror and not saying a thing.

•

At least she didn't know my father would jump her like a tomcat.

•

Neither did I, the fucking bastard.

THIRTY-FOUR

I suggested to Eveline that before we got to the driveway, we should turn off the main road and continue by way of what we called the field road. This wasn't really a road at all, but just a pair of wheel tracks worn by tractors and wagons on their way out into the fields. The tracks ran along the west side of the five acres that made up the homestead property, then forked, one fork going into the fields, the other following the north edge of the homestead plot. After we left the main road and took the dirt wheel-tracks, the fields were spread out to our left while on our right were the thick growths of trees that had been planted long ago for windbreaks and that were now clogged with underbrush.

Walking on the field road was easy, but the pace changed at the point where I decided we should turn right and climb through the windbreak. First there was a barbed-wire fence to get through. Then came a distance of eight or ten feet dense with brambles, deadwood, prickly bushes, burrs, and under-growth (I pushed through backwards to break a path, hold-ing Eveline's hand so she could fellow me), but then, beyond this rugged borderland, came the interior reward: A long-grass "meadow" that at midday was sun-drenched but that now was home only to narrow streaks of light coming in low from the west. Overhead, meanwhile, around the meadow's edges, stood the mature trees, high and old. Many were evergreens, excellent for climbing, with branches that extended horizontally like the spars of a ship.

It was a pleasant and private place, this hidden meadow, and the air was still warm in spite of the sun's getting low. The grass that covered this secret area wasn't like field or prairie grass but instead it was like the grass on the west lawn, lying over on its side. There was something near the middle of the opening that I wanted to show Eveline. We strolled over there, and I spread the grass apart with my foot to reveal the ancient, bleached skull of a cow nestled down almost among the roots of the grass. I told Eveline about how I had first discovered it there as a young boy, back in my first life during 1946 or 1947, how I kept it a secret from everyone but checked it from time to time to see whether anything about it had changed. It was still there, unaltered and untouched, when I left for Iowa City in 1963, and I know that it was still there the last time I set foot on the farm, one cold spring day in 2001, when I stopped by to pay my respects to the young couple who had then become the farm's new owners.

"But whether it's still there, I have no idea," I told Eveline. We happened to be holding hands, and I felt her grip tighten suddenly, and then tighten further. Then we were in an embrace, and then we were kissing hungrily. I felt moisture, and, holding her by the shoulders I gently but firmly pushed Eveline away. Her face was squeezed up pitifully, almost like a little child's, in her effort not to break into sobs again, while her eyes brimmed over and tears ran down in streams. It was almost more than I could do to keep from breaking into tears myself. I held onto her so tightly that I became afraid I might hurt her. In a moment, somehow, I turned us so that we would be free of the skull and began lowering us down, until we were lying together on the long soft grass, where I went on holding

Eveline, cradling her head, kissing her eyes, until after some unknown length of time calm began coming back to her.

We lay there for a while, not moving, just holding one another.

When we began to negotiate how to sit up, then how to get back up onto our feet, there were things we said to one another, apologies, reassurances, intimacies, promises, pleas that I won't try to re-create. Moving and intimate, they felt profound and significant in ways that I could never suggest if I tried to replicate them now.

Walking from the little meadow in the direction of the farmyard was easy going, since there was no band of undergrowth to push through. A slight incline led up toward the farmyard, and the long lying-down grass covered perhaps half the distance. Then, as if there were some sort of designated property line, the rougher growth took over, milkweed, nettles, and stalky grasses. None of these were tall, however, and pushing through them wasn't difficult.

The point where we came back into the open farmyard was behind the barn and a little bit to the northwest of it. I led Eveline over, just for a look. An earthen ramp led up to the north wall of the barn with its huge double doors that allowed entry into the hayloft. Suspended on rails, the doors were easy to slide open to any width, enough to allow a tractor—or team of horses—to go in onto the barn floor even with a full wagon-load of hay behind.

I pulled one side of the door open just enough for Eveline and me to slip inside.

On first stepping in, it seemed dark, silent, gloomy, somber. But after a moment or two sounds began to return, along with a certain amount of light, as your eyes grew accustomed to the dimness. Pigeons lived in the tin cupola up at the very peak of the roof, and, after falling silent for a time upon our entry, they began to resume their cooing sounds, getting on with their teatime socializing. Over the decades, people had made the cupola into a shooting target from outdoors, and the last sunlight from the west now came in through the bullet holes that had been left behind in the tin and created a faintly reddish light that seemed to transform the cupola into a kind of lantern. Both to the left and right of the barn floor where we stood, twin mountains of hay rose up, making the barn not silent but, instead, muted as if with expectation.

For a moment or two we simply stood there, breathing the perfumed air.

Then Eveline curled her finger to indicate that I should come close. She put her lips to my ear and whispered two words:

"Hungry. Thirsty."

•

The air remained balmy enough, and the daylight sufficiently abundant, that we could spread our sleeping bags out like a single blanket in front of the tent and indulge in another leisurely meal in the Roman style. Earlier in the day, I had come upon a yard-long piece of dry, weathered board and set it aside with the thought that it might be of use. Now, I lay it down on the blanket in between us to serve as a kind of table top, since the blanket itself was too soft to hold things like cups upright and was made only softer by the long grass lying underneath it.

Together we set out a tin of kipper snacks, another of liver paté and one of sardines, and opened them all. Our firm loaf of pumpernickel I cut in half, returned one of the halves to its waxed bag and roughly cut the other into chunks with my jackknife. Eveline took our block of cheddar out of its own waxed wrapper, and with my knife we were able to break off chunks as we wanted them. I opened one of our bottles of wine and poured a tin cup's worth for each of us. I toasted to Eveline, and Eveline toasted to me. Everything else went unmentioned.

Our little dinner was a pleasure, and, although neither of us said anything about it, you could tell that we were both making it go slowly, drawing it out in order to make it last. I was glad that we had the wine. I was afraid that without it we might very well have begun feeling fearful and become gloomy. As I've said probably too many times, I'm absolutely certain that Eveline knew, saw, sensed what was going to happen, but that she was just as absolutely determined to say not a word about it. Superstition? Conceivably. Fear? With no question. Determination, strength, and dedication? Without the least shadow of a doubt.

And despair?

Ah. . . Despair.

Yes. I'm certain. Despair.

When we'd finished a second cup of wine I made Eveline promise to rest right where she was and let me clear the "table." I put back in their wrappers the things that could be saved and stowed them again in the bottom of my pack. What couldn't be saved, empty tins and the like, I put into the oilcloth bag we had for that purpose and sealed them in, to be thrown away in the morning.

I moved the weathered old board from where it had lain between us and put it behind me instead, where it could function as a bar. There, I poured a third cup of wine each. Daylight now was almost entirely gone. Before I lay down beside Eveline, I went into the tent and from my backpack brought out our small lantern-style flashlight. In another fifteen minutes the very last vestiges of daylight faded away entirely. There was no moon. In the darkness, Eveline said,

"If he doesn't come tomorrow, do you really think we should leave?"

"I do," I said. I couldn't see her. I leaned closer until I could smell her hair and the scent of her skin.

After a minute, she said,

"I wish that's what would happen."

I spoke her name softly, two times. Then I said,

"It might happen that way. I wish for it too. But I doubt it."

"Well, then, maybe we should just run away. Just get up at the crack of dawn and leave."

"But then we wouldn't even have *tried* to stop him," I answered. "Then there'd be no hope at all of changing what happens. No hope of *keeping* it from happening." I stopped. Then I found her hand, held it, and went on. "Evie." My voice was so low that even I almost couldn't hear it. "That's the whole reason I met you. The whole reason I got moved back to fall semester 1933 in order to *find* you. I know that anything can go wrong. It might not work. Maybe nothing can change him. But don't we still have to try?"

I realized that she was crying. But she was doing it so quietly that you could hardly tell. She was desperate to keep it a secret from me if she could.

I didn't let on. I let her keep her secret even though it broke my heart not to reach over and embrace and comfort her. I waited as long as I could stand it and then said,

"There's a little more wine. Enough for a bit each. Should we have it?"

Eveline nodded her head vigorously. I could feel her doing it.

I would need to turn on the little lantern in order to pour the wine. Before I did that, though, I asked Eveline for her cup and touched her on the shoulder. "Here's my hand," I said. I didn't want to turn the light on until I was looking the other way, to let her keep her privacy about the crying.

I held the two cups in one hand, picked up the lantern from the blanket with the other, and rolled away from Eveline. Then I switched on the light. It was a small light, but in the pitch darkness it produced a remarkable amount of brightness. I set it down on the rough board, placed our two cups in its beam, and then, all with one hand, worked the cork out and poured as steadily as possible in spite of lying elbow-propped on my side. The last of the wine made for two cups almost full. I left them both on the board in the beam of light and rolled over onto my back so I was supported by both elbows against the ground. Then I sat up, reached back for one of the cups and handed it over to Eveline. I made a point of not looking at her. I reached back for my own cup and raised it in her direction.

"Santé."

"Prosit."

Her voice sounded steady. I was careful not to say anything about it.

I was wearing my usual light-canvas safari-style jacket, and rolling back and forth on the blanket during the wine-pouring had reminded me—because I felt it there—of the little paperback stuck into one of the inside pockets. I'd put it there that morning after finding it in the bottom of my pack—to my surprise, since I'd altogether forgotten about having brought it along. Still, it had been a good choice, being tiny and thin but also gloriously readable, especially aloud. It was *Howl*, one of the two or three books that had come along with me when my 1963 room in the Quadrangle became my 1933 room—probably because I'd had it in my jacket pocket then, too.

The light was off and I was lying on my side again, leaning on one elbow, facing Eveline. I couldn't see her, really, at all, the night was so purely dark. But I could touch her, although not with a hand, since I was leaning on one and holding my wine with the other. But I bowed forward the slightest bit and found my forehead touching Eveline's. She gave me a light bump by way of greeting.

"I've got this book," I said. "I forgot I had it. Want to hear some of it?"

Naturally enough, Eveline asked what it was, and I told her. I explained who the Beats were. I wouldn't be able to read, though, until I drank some of my wine, having no free hand. So I drank some of it, then felt around behind me for the rough board and set the cup there. I managed to get the little book out of my inside pocket, then felt around on the ground for the light and switched it on. And there was Eveline. I kept the beam pointed down, but it gave enough light so that I could see her face again. It had an expression that I hadn't seen before. It wasn't happy, certainly, and on the other hand it wasn't sad. It wasn't expectant, and not bored. The most unusual thing is that it didn't have Eveline's thoughtful or pensive look. The truth is that, more than anything else, it was the expression of someone having no expression.

It frightened me, in fact it frightened me badly, but only for a moment. I leaned forward and kissed her on the lips, very lightly.

"Can you feel the wine?"

"Yes. Some."

"Are you getting cold?"

"Nearly."

It was almost more than I could do to keep myself from asking something like "Are you all right," or "Is something wrong," or "Is anything the matter." Inane and stupid questions whose answers were no, yes, and yes. Lunatic questions in light of the immensity of the things that were wrong.

"This one is called 'America,'" I said.

America I've given you all and now I'm nothing.
America two dollars and twentyseven cents January 17,
    1956.
I can't stand my own mind.
America when will we end the human war?
Go fuck yourself with your atom bomb.

"Read that one again," Eveline told me. Her voice had a touch of life in it again. Not expression, but a promise of expression had returned to her face.

"'Go fuck yourself with your atom bomb,'" I read again, putting the slightest bit of emphasis on "fuck." Eveline's smile was followed by a short trilling laugh.

"Carry on, monsieur," she said, and I read some more.

I don't feel good don't bother me.
I won't write my poem till I'm in my right mind.
America when will you be angelic?
When will you take off your clothes?

"Now I'm getting cold," Eveline said.

"Me too," I said. "It's getting chilly."

I stood up and took off my safari jacket, then leaned down and draped it over Eveline.

"Let me sit up first," she said. When she was sitting up, I arranged the jacket over both of her shoulders. I gave her the light.

"Hold this," I said, "while I get the sleeping bags." Eveline shone the light while I folded up one edge of the spread-out sleeping bags, a foot or two worth, then doubled that and doubled it again until I was up to where Eveline had been sitting and was now getting to her feet. She stepped off the blanket and I made the last fold. Eveline went over to the tent and shined the light near the entrance so I could drag the blanket in. Then she shined the light behind me, aiming it into the tent, so I could spread out the blanket and put various things in order.

When everything was ready, we walked down the fence a fair distance and took turns peeing, one holding the light when the other needed both hands. On the way back, it seemed as if Eveline was herself again. She leaned against me a little as we walked back toward the tent. She recited,

America when will we end the human war?
Go fuck yourself with your atom bomb.

And then added,

Malcolm when will you be angelic?
When will you take off your clothes?

Both of us laughed. Eveline's laugh was far the better one, quiet, expressive, and melodic.

Inside the tent we did take off our clothes, doing it sitting down since there was no room to stand up. From the roof pole I had fastened a string and tied a loop at its lower end for hanging our light. Eveline and I sat under it, our arms around one another, and together read aloud from the book. We were like William Blake and his wife reading naked together, except that they were reading *Paradise Lost* and our book was *Howl*:

> *Moloch! Solitude! Filth! Ugliness! Ashcans and unobtainable*
> *Dollars! Children screaming under the stairways! Boys*
> *Sobbing in armies! Old men weeping in the parks!*
> *Moloch! Moloch! Nightmare of Moloch! Moloch the loveless!*
> *Mental Moloch! Moloch the heavy judger of men!*

• • •

> *I'm with you in Rockland*
> *in my dreams you walk dripping from a sea-journey on the*
> *highway across America in tears to the door of my cottage*
> *in the Western night*

THIRTY-FIVE

In the morning we got up early, neatened the camp to make it nice and orderly, and then packed some things to take for breakfast under the apple tree on the north hill. By the time we got up, the cows had already come in from the pasture and had had time to drink their fill at the tank. Gathered in the barnyard, they watched us somewhat lazily as Eveline and I followed the outside of the white fence to its northeast corner, turned toward the barnyard gate, ducked under the barbed wire fence there, and set out on our walk across the pasture. After a slight delay, as if they needed some time to think about it, the cows moved one by one toward the gate and followed us out into the pasture, as if we were all on our way to enjoy it together. The day was warm and calm, just like the day before, but what had been a blue sky then was covered now by a pale, high, almost steel-colored layer of hazy cloud. The cloud layer was thin enough so the sun almost but not quite broke through. If you looked up, it was easy to see the exact position of the sun. But on the ground it cast no shadows.

•

By the time we came back across the pasture from our breakfast and climbed over the fence into the rear of the farmyard, my father had returned. Eveline and I stood there, by the fence, silently, pondering what to do next.

I don't know for certain how I knew he was back, but I did. There was something in the air, in the atmosphere, in the unnatural silence of the place. Normally, the pigeons in the barn would have been making one of their flurries up in the cupola, scratching and cooing as they jockeyed for space. Or a crow would have cawed, a chicken come out into the drive to scratch around, a dog trot by, a cow moo, even a cat slink around a corner of the tractor shed and come toward us slowly, with that unhurried gait of a cat that isn't hungry.

But there was nothing. No bird in the sky, no animal on the ground, no sound anywhere. Not even a breeze stirred. There wasn't so much as a breath of wind.

I reached beside me for Eveline's hand and then, thinking better of it, I turned, threw my arms around her, and held on as tightly as I could. I realized that I was terrified. I realized that I was terrified both of what might be going to happen and also of what might *not* be going to happen. As I've said before, it was always this way with my father. One approached him invariably in a state of fear for the very good reason that it was impossible to know what might be about to happen. You never knew whether he was about to meet you with kind feelings and good manners or, an equal likelihood, with a chill, dismissive scorn. Sometimes he would reward you with sympathy and understanding but at others, altogether unpredictably, you would be victim of his withering distaste or even explosive rage.

In the silence, Eveline and I walked across the grass past the high, imperturbable west wall of the barn, across the turnaround, past the tractor shed and granary, and along the driveway beside the house until we got to the side entrance into the kitchen. I was certain that's where we would find him, in the kitchen. Eveline and I went up the steps.

Just as with our visit two days before, the windows and both kitchen doors were standing open, although this time the air was still and no breeze came through. My father sat where he had sat before, on the far side of the table from the door where we came in. He was wearing his white dress uniform again, like before, and he looked even more trim and polished this time. He even had on his flat round hat with the visor. I don't know whether I've mentioned before that during World War II my father began sporting a mustache, certainly not pencil-thin but nevertheless carefully trimmed. By no means did this mustache function the way a mask would, or even a full beard, as something to hide behind, but it did have a certain kind of related effect. It managed somehow to make my father's mouth look smaller than it otherwise might have, and thus to help disguise, or alter, the expressions conveyed by that mouth. My father, as I've mentioned, had an idiosyncratic smile in which the left side of the lips rose but not the right. The mustache had a way of exaggerating the asymmetry of that smile, but also, just as noticeably—perhaps merely by contrast—the right side of the mouth had become more enigmatic as well, and even when my father's face was at rest, it seemed impossible for his expression not to convey a certain skepticism as to the openness and truthfulness of whoever it might be he was in conversation with.

Through all my years of growing up, it had been necessary for me, as a means of self-protection, to guess as best I could what emotion, mood, or attitude it might be that was waiting behind the expression on my father's face.

I never guessed correctly.

•

On the table in front of him, beside a coffee mug, was a book, lying open. As Eveline and I came in through the door my father put in a marker to hold his place and closed the volume.

Even before I was close enough to read the title, I was able to identify the book. Everything about it was familiar—its heft, design, typography, degree of wear, even the muted rust-red of its cloth cover. *The Fifth Column and the First Forty-Nine Stories*. Published 1938.

•

My father didn't say anything when we came in, so Eveline and I spoke first.

"Morning, Pop," I said.

"Good morning, Mr. Reiner. Harold," Eveline said.

My father may—or may not, hard to tell—have nodded his head very slightly in greeting. Either way, he asked,

"Have you had coffee?"

"No," I said, and at exactly the same instant Eveline said, "Yes."

We looked at one another and laughed, while my father remained expressionless, having decided for reasons of his own to disregard our amusing bit of awkwardness. Looking at him, I realized how comical he looked, like a character in a play, sitting there in his white uniform, complete with the round, flat-topped hat. Suddenly, the hat struck me as absurdly enormous, especially in comparison with my father's somewhat smallish head.

I drew a chair out for Eveline, the same chair she'd sat in last time.

"Do you mind if we sit down?" I said. Instead of answering, my father gestured with his chin, very slightly, toward the stovetop. "Coffee there if you'd like it."

This oddly elusive, or deflective, behavior of my father was the result of a certain mood he often got into whereby he pretended to wish that no attention at all would be paid to him, or that he might prefer being invisible, since then he would be free from the onerous burden of making even the least imaginable social or personal responses to those around him.

I just said "he pretended," but of course I was wrong in the choice of those words. I fully realize that the effects this visiting mood had on my father may have been quite, quite real, and that he may have pretended nothing whatsoever. But most of the time it was impossible for me to believe that it wasn't a pretense, that it wasn't a way for my father to gain and keep control. After all, didn't his way of not answering a question—"Do you mind if we sit down?"—in effect logically suggest the non-existence of the person asking it? And didn't it furthermore create a test impossible for anyone to pass? If those who ask the question but get no answer *do* sit down, they not only get the test "wrong" but also show presumption. If they do *not* sit down, they give approval to their own non-existence, make themselves risible—and invisible—and are demeaned, lorded over, cast away.

•

Eveline and I sat down, but with our chairs angled to the table so that we each had only one elbow on its surface and were facing one another as much as we were my father.

In the many years of living with my father, the technique I developed as a defense against this particular mood, his "deflection and silence mood," was to ignore it as completely as possible and to go on talking as if the conversation were normal.

So, once I had ascertained that Eveline really didn't want a cup, I went on as if my father had actually responded to me.

"We've been drinking a lot less coffee than usual lately," I said. "Mainly because during our trip we didn't make any campfires. Did no cooking. Made no coffee. So we had coffee pretty much just once a day."

No response from my father other than to sit looking at us, at me and then at Eveline, back and forth. His hands weren't folded, but they were placed on the table in front of him, one covering the other. He had pushed his officer's hat back on his head farther than normal. The circle it made looked like a stylized halo.

"Usually we got up around six and struck camp, then went along our way until nine or so and started looking for a town. When one materialized we'd go in and have breakfast at a restaurant or diner, usually diner. Then buy provisions for another day and be back on the road. Except of course that there weren't any roads."

I was enjoying it, thinking back on our journey, reminiscing. On an impulse, I reached over and took Eveline's hand, the one that was lying on her lap, then let it go and sat back.

"And sometimes we'd stay over. Evie, how many times did we stay over? Was it four? Or only three?"

"My memory is four," she said. "Once a week, roughly. It's in the little journal, with the names of all the towns. It was nice having a shower," she added as an afterthought.

"The little journal. It's in the tent. I know right where it is," I said.

"Well, don't go for it now," Eveline told me.

"I'd like to remember the town where we stayed in the library so late that one afternoon."

"The library that reminded me of Fremont," Eveline said, with a bit of wistfulness in her tone. Then, as if just having thought of something, she added, "Oh. Your father's books."

"Right." My canvas bag hung from the back of the chair I was sitting in. I reached around, drew out the Harriet Monroe and the Peter Negoe, set them on the table and pushed them an arm's-reach toward my father.

"We borrowed these yesterday," I said. "To take on our outing to West Tree."

Throughout all of this, my father still hadn't said anything, but his expression made it look as though he were listening. I nodded toward the book on the table in front of him.

"*The First Forty-Nine*," I said. And then, "Which one were you reading just now?"

He drew the book toward him and opened it to the marker, looked for a second, then closed it again and pushed it slightly away.

"'God Rest You Merry, Gentlemen,'" he said.

"Oh, man," I said. "The one about that poor sixteen-year-old kid."

"You remember it?" Eveline asked me.

"I do," I said. "If you'd read it you would, too. Especially if you were a boy. When you read it, you'll remember it."

At this point my father spoke. Just one word. He made it sound as if it were both in italics and in quotation marks, also followed by a question mark.

"*Materialized?*" he said.

I glanced at Eveline, then looked back at my father with what must have been an inquiring look.

"You said the towns '*materialized*,'" he repeated.

"Oh. Yes. Yes, that's right," I said. In the second it took me to say those five words, I made the decision not to change so much as a detail but to describe every detail exactly the way it had happened. Besides being the truth, this plan felt the most natural. It was akin to my tactic of talking normally when my father was in his silence-and-deflection mood.

"Yes," I went on. I reached over and took Eveline's hand again, then again let it go.

"When we left Iowa City, things felt mainly unchanged. We'd walk for most of a day, camp for the night, and sometime in the next forenoon stop through a town to re-provision. But then there were changes—no roads, no fields, no fences, no farms, just the land. And no towns—that is, not until we had need of one. When we started thinking about a town, one would— like I said—materialize. We'd enter at the outskirts and walk into the downtown, have breakfast, shop, and then head back out."

I paused and looked over at Eveline.

"Am I getting it right, Evie?" I asked. She nodded her head

in the same quick way I'd felt her do it the night before.

"It sounds exactly right so far. We went in and out of different times." She looked at me, then at my father, then back at me and gave a sign that I should carry it on from there.

"We left Iowa City on August 18, 1934. Then we gradually realized—with the lack of farms, roads, fields, and so on—that we were walking in the year 1494. The towns that materialized for us, though. They were all existing in 1934."

My father tucked his chin down a very little bit while keeping his eyes fixed on me. This small change in posture gave him a faintly scowling look, an effect heightened by slightly squinted eyes. He looked only at me and not at Eveline.

I felt surprisingly calm in spite of the moment's inevitably reminding me yet again, and vividly, of the literally countless times I had been tricked, traduced, shamed, silenced, or demeaned by this person, my authoritarian and ever-unpredictable father. The difference now, the enormous difference this time, was that Eveline was with me, that Eveline was here, and that I was with Eveline.

She had given me, she gave me, the strength that I had always needed in the decades before and that I now inwardly triumphed and rejoiced at having. This was the strength that came from the simple truth. I had learned it from Eveline. Simple truth *was* the strength.

How amazing it was—amazing, I mean, that it was so similar to the way I had learned just to go on talking normally when my father was fighting the world, and me, inside one of the deep caves of neurosis that were carved out behind his eyes.

I put my hand on Eveline's hand and went on.

"They were all real and actual towns, Iowa towns and then Minnesota towns, once we crossed the state line—or what would become the state line four hundred or so years later. I have all their names written down. We kept a little journal. I'll get it later and show you. Anyway, except for the towns, during the time we went into them, we spent the whole trip in 1494. When we got close—coming along the river—West Tree materialized and we stopped at the Ideal for breakfast, got some provisions at the National Tea, looked around town, then started the walk back here. Of course, nothing was here but the land. We put our tent where it is now and waited for you. When you finally arrived, the time changed to 1947."

There was a silence. For a moment no one moved. Then my father pushed his chair back from the table, stood up in the most leisurely of ways to his full height, and walked slowly over to the refrigerator. When he opened the door I saw inside what looked like a forest of beer bottles. He took out three, carried them the step or two over to the sink ledge, picked up a church key, and began prying off the caps, tossing them into the sink one by one. With each toss he said one word.

"You. Are. Insane."

He carried the bottles over to the table, put one in front of Eveline, one in front of me, and, when he got there, one at his own place. When he was seated again, when he had raised his bottle in our direction, and when he had taken a swig, he finished his statement.

"If I may say so," he said.

Laughter—actual laughter, not just a polite titter—came from me. Not a guffaw, not anything condescending or belittling or falsely exaggerated, and not a signal of embarrassment, either, but just a short honest bit of real laughter. Along with my self-determined diktat to talk normally went its corollary: to laugh normally.

Turning to Eveline, I raised an eyebrow and shrugged, but so slightly as hardly to be noticeable from across the table. Then, in a normal voice, purely conversational, I said to my father,

"By the way, where's Mother? I'd really like her to meet Eveline."

To this my father made no response. Instead, he looked

straight at me, again with his chin tucked down, and said,

"How tall are you?"

"Pardon me?"

"How tall are you?"

"Ah. Well, I'm five-ten," I said.

He pushed his chair back again, angling it to the table so he had room to cross his long legs.

"You're no son of mine at five-ten," he said.

"No room for an aberration?"

Again, no response.

"You know, here's the truth," I said. "I came up along with Eveline for a visit because I thought you'd be impressed by her, the way I've been, and am, and that she could be persuasive in suggesting ways for you to see in a different light what it is—well, what it is you're going to Washington to do."

Predictably enough, again there was no response. Instead of saying anything, my father arose, went to the refrigerator, took out three more bottles and did with them exactly as he had done with those before—although without saying again that I was insane.

"I understood you'd be leaving tomorrow," I said.

"Yes. But I might leave earlier. The way things are going. Maybe today."

He didn't look at either of us as he said this. He had assumed a new posture, leaning somewhat forward in his chair with forearms on the table. Slowly, he was peeling off the wet label from his beer bottle.

Eveline spoke up.

"It's just that Malcolm and I wish you would do something that would help change history," she said. My father raised his eyes, but not his head, looked across the table straight at her, then lowered his eyes again. He peeled at the label.

In a minute I said,

"We talked about this the other night too."

My father made a sound of acknowledgment that sounded

something like "mmmph." Then he said,

"And it didn't make a bit of sense then either." For some reason saying this caused him to glance at his wristwatch, then back at his progress with the beer label.

"You know, Pater," I said, "I can prove that it makes perfect sense. There are things in your memory—there've got to be— that make it make sense. I know for a fact that you knew that they assassinated Kennedy, and when. I called you up from Iowa City, you and Mom. That evening, after dinner. I even know something you said. You said the assassination had sent all of us into the heart of darkness."

The look he gave me sent a chill down my back. I mean this literally: I felt my hackles rise. Whether I reacted in any way physically, whether I flinched or the like, I don't know. I don't think so. But I do know what I felt, what I wanted. I wanted only to jump up from the table, grab Eveline, and run for our lives.

But I didn't. I should have seized Eveline and run. Everything was about to end.

•

So, so many things to explain.

Foremost among them, what was there in the look my father gave me that terrified me so badly? And, for that matter, why hadn't I felt the same way before, on the night of the martinis, when he had said the same thing, that he had no memory of what I was talking about, when he said, "Someone killed someone?"

True enough, he hadn't given me a look like the one he gave me this time. He hadn't given me *any* look, perhaps thanks to the martinis. After half a dozen of them, with two more on the runway, things like facial expression and eye contact may not have been exactly in full operation.

But the reason I'd had no breakdown that first night, the reason I'd felt no terror, was simply that I hadn't believed a word he was saying.

I'd thought he was leading us on. I'd thought he was fibbing. I'd thought he was telling a whopper.

My father—my old man, as he'd be known if he were cast in *The First Forty-Nine Stories*—wasn't always to be entirely trusted when it came to perfect leveling. It often took some waiting to get the truth out of him, or certainly to get the *whole* truth. He enjoyed finding out what he might learn from the other party if he himself kept his own hand well hidden.

But I'd read him wrong that night. Every bit of his performance was authentic.

He'd lived through the assassination but it was as if nothing had happened.

Thousands were watching but no one saw a thing.

Something was wrong with my father. Deeply, powerfully, rudimentarily.

He deceived me, but Eveline saw him for what he was. He was a man without memory.

That's the reason she wept so piteously, that night and the night after.

She may not have seen its first meaning: That after all our effort, after my being brought into the past, after my meeting her, after all our care and long preparation, we weren't going to be able to prevent Kennedy's murder after all.

Perhaps not. But she did see all too clearly the second meaning: That she and I were going to be split apart from one another.

In this, I was the blind one. As a result I was about to be stunned in a way I could never have conceived possible.

•

He was not a man of sufficient principle to *have* memory. Desire and wanting trumped memory.

The look he gave me held piercingly difficult personal ramifications for me, naturally enough. These, however, were overshadowed and diminished by other, infinitely greater implications of breathtaking historical significance.

After I recounted the fact of having phoned my parents the night of the assassination, my father didn't say a word, but he looked at me across the table as if he were looking at someone with whom he had not the remotest familiarity. In his unblinking eyes was no sign either of interest or of recognition. Almost a drugged look was conveyed by his eyes' steadiness and at the same time by the curious impression they gave of being empty. It wasn't so much that they seemed unfocused, but more that they seemed to be looking, steadily and directly, at nothing whatsoever. And yet the nothing they were looking at was *me*—me being looked at directly, steadily, and without the least sign of recognition whatsoever. I remembered my father saying a few moments earlier, "You're no son of mine," and now I found myself paralyzed by a form of panic that I had felt once years before, in early adolescence, at a moment when I thought I was in the process of losing my identity altogether. I felt then as I felt now, as though I could scarcely move, to say nothing of having the ability to seize Eveline and run for our lives. So disoriented was I, so enfeebled, that when my father said in a voice that was very low and seemed to have almost no energy—or interest—in it,

"Who in the devil are you, anyway? And how the devil did you *really* get here?" my pathetic, and inexplicable, answer was,

"Yes."

Slowly, my father turned his head and looked at Eveline.

"Your boyfriend here is quite a fireball," he said. "A real live wire."

Eveline said, "You mean my husband."

My father responded again with what sounded like "mmmph" as he pushed his chair back and went toward the refrigerator.

As for me, smothered by humiliation, fear, anger, sorrow,

paralysis, and despair, I was not able to bring forth so much as a word.

My father's back was turned as he opened the refrigerator and then went to the sink with more bottles. Eveline took both of my hands and leaning toward me kissed me quickly but firmly on the lips.

"Go and get the little journal," she said. "We can show him our list of towns at least."

I quickly kissed Eveline back and stood up, but not before my father turned back toward the table with his bottles.

"Lovebirds. Well, well," he said. He was tall, rakish, handsome—and cold as ice. I pretended not to have heard him.

"Off I go, Pater," I said as I headed for the door. "Quick errand. Back in a trice."

I jumped down the two steps' height from the porch to the ground and loped down the hill to the stock tank, followed the white wooden fence around its corner, and dropped to my knees at the entry to our tent. I knew exactly where the little journal was, in the righthand flap-pocket on my pack, and I went into the tent only halfway, on hands and knees. It was hot inside from the midday sun, even with the overcast sky, and immediately a strange thing happened to me. There were Eveline's things neatly folded and piled carefully on her side of the sleeping bag, and mine on my side, folded also but hardly as carefully. And what happened is that I suddenly thought I was going to fall into a bottomless grief, that I was about to be taken over by the deepest sorrow I had ever known or imagined, that I was about to be gripped by convulsions of sobs that would simply continue without ending. But the instant I tore open the flap-pocket and pulled out the little journal and slipped it into my own inside pocket, something changed. There was no diminishment in the immensity of the overwhelming grief I felt, but I knew, as if simply by having touched the little journal with my fingers, that I wasn't going to be taken over by paroxysms of sobs, that I wasn't going to be convulsed physically by the grief I was feeling—*but that it was absolutely imperative I return to Eveline at once, immediately, in the least possible amount of time.* How it happened that I felt this necessity, I didn't know then and still don't now; perhaps it came by means of some power beyond the physical. In any case, I backed out of the tent, sprang to my feet, and sprinted to the end of the wooden fence, where I swung around the corner post with my feet off the ground and then propelled myself into new and even longer strides going up the hill. When I got to the turn-around, then to the granary, then the tractor shed, a view of the house opened up to me and I saw, just like before, that the walls of the kitchen had disappeared, as had its roof, that the ceiling lamp was hanging suspended from nothing, also as before, and that my father and Eveline appeared to be *dancing* together on the kitchen floor—until one more bound brought me closer and allowed me to see that this was not a dance but, instead, a contest. Eveline and my father were locked together in a struggle. They moved only slightly, but every move, however small, had a fierce intensity and rigidness about it. They turned stiffly, and I saw that my father had raised Eveline's skirt up and that one hand was clamped at the top of her long white leg, while he pushed with his other hand against the back of her head as she resisted fiercely against his pressing face, his ravening lips in search of hers.

Such indignity, absurdity, wretchedness, hollowness, presumption, shallowness, selfishness, vanity, incontinence, insolence, invasiveness, faithlessness, raptorial blindness.

See what you want and take it.

These words, every single one of them, flashed through my mind in the time it took me to leap from the ground to the edge of the porch, and from there in two strides to a position behind my father, insinuate my left forearm in front of his throat, grab my left wrist with my right hand, and pull back against his windpipe with every bit of strength I could summon through the use of both my arms together.

The result was rapid and dramatic. As if he had been scalded or shocked, my father snatched his left hand away from the back of Eveline's head and his right hand from her left buttock. Both of those hands found their way instantly to my own left forearm, where the fingers on them clawed madly, in a sudden insanity of haste and need, at the canvas fabric of my left sleeve.

Eveline, released by my father, stepped backwards a pace or two. For a second or two she held one hand up to her throat. Her dark eyes were enormous. She was, as always, more beautiful than air, water, woods, earth, or sky.

"Be careful," she said. "Don't kill him."

I moved my forearm from my father's windpipe and pinned his arms at his sides with mine, joining my hands in a powerful knot at his front, just below the sternum. I could always knock his wind out by jerking my hands back, hard and fast, into his diaphragm.

As soon as he had his air back he let out a string of threats, insults, and curses.

"You pusillanimous little prick," he said, then added, "whoever the hell you are. Shorty."

"I've told you who I am," I said. "But you're deaf."

More threats, expletives, and denunciations.

"And blind," I added. "And pure evil."

Eveline stood a few paces away, looking on with a frightened and torn expression. Her stance made it look as though she were about to step closer again.

She wasn't in my father's line of sight, but it was as if he sensed her nearness.

"And that girl you've got," he said. "What second-hand used goods shop did you pick *her* up from?"

I pulled back suddenly, and hard, with my knotted hands into his diaphragm. The move made him gasp powerfully.

"You owe her an apology as big as the Ritz," I said.

He was silent.

"We're behaving so elegantly here, you and I," I said. "What happened to the gentleman and officer?"

Silence. Out of the corner of my eye I saw Eveline move a step closer. I didn't say anything more for a moment. Then I said,

"I wish we could have gotten along, you and me."

"I don't even know you," he said.

"You do know me. You know me very, very well. As soon as you've left here and gone off to do your dirty work and then after you've suffered the consequences and find yourself back in 1964 again with the assassination on your hands that you could have helped set things up to avoid, well, you're going to find out then, all over again, how well you know me. And here's another thing. When that time comes, you're not going to remember a single squid's inch of this, here, now, these last couple of days with Eveline and me. How crappily you've treated us."

He gave another wrench of his body against my hold on him.

"I haven't treated you crappily. I don't even know who you are."

"All the more reason to treat us better. You've shown us your worst side."

He gave another wrench, but more half heartedly.

"All right," he said. "I was off base with the girl."

"No you weren't," I said. "You were malicious. Criminal. Monstrous. Beastly. Heinous. Contemptible. Unforgiveable. That's what you were, plus another fifteen or twenty other words as bad or worse. Jesus christ, Pap. Where's your head? Or your heart, for christ sakes? Here you are in this white suit you love so much, all spic and span, spiffy and trim, starched and stiff. Holy shit, Skipper, that's the uniform of the republic. If you want to act like a rapist and a thug you should at least take that thing off and put on some muddy blood-stained rags. She, Eveline, is a prophetess, by the way. That means she's a goddess, visionary, seer, creator, protectress. A saint. Protector of well-being, of all humanity. And here you are, you double-shit asshole, treating her like Mistress Quickly in the Boar's Head tavern or like some other Falstaffian tart or backroom moll."

I was a little bit breathless after all those words. My father gave another twist against the hold I had on him, but, for whatever reason, it was even more half hearted than the last one.

"I don't know what you're talking about," he said.

"Oh, yes, you do," I said. "You're just too good a liar. You know exactly what I'm talking about. You just tell yourself you don't. *There's* the lie. You lie to yourself. *You* could never be a rapist or a thug or a killer, not you, especially not in your nice white suit. That's part of the lie. The nice white suit is part of the lie. Inside the nice white suit you can't do anything bad. Nothing vile or foul or murderous or evil. Just keep on the white suit and anything you do is good."

"Here's what," my father said. He toned his voice down so as to make it seem conciliatory. "How about you just let me go and we talk about this like a couple of gentlemen?"

"I'm not ready for that yet, and I don't think you are either," I said.

"All I can say is this is a hell of a way to treat a man in his own home."

"Listen, Pop. It's *my* home too. You tend to forget."

"Ah, so you say. But I still don't know who you are. Some short guy from Iowa City is all I know."

I let it go. I wasn't done with the white suit.

"Do you want to know something?" I said. "The nice white suit is the nation's boundary, and you're inside that boundary, so *you're* the nation. Do you understand that?"

I could feel him more or less shrug his shoulders. A second later he nodded his head. Maybe that meant something and maybe it didn't.

"All right. So now if you're the nation why is it you're aiming for war?"

"Who's aiming for war?"

"You are. That's what you said last winter, that day in February with Vandenberg and Acheson and the president and those others."

"Nobody said anything about war."

"Oh, no? You were there, for god's sake. You heard Vandenberg say the government had to 'scare the hell out of the American people' and make them believe 'the Russians were coming.' That means turning the Russians into an enemy. And you went along with it. You were for it. And so it began happening."

He didn't say anything. So I said,

"Tell me, when does a country need an enemy? And why? In order for what?"

He still didn't say anything, so I went on:

"And now you're going back to help them firm up the whole deal. You're going back to help them set up the hidden agency that everyone will think is made up of good guys but is really made up of terrorists whose secret business it will be to trigger event after event to get innocent people killed, usually women and children, and arrange it so the blame falls on Russia and the people who support her when in fact it's our own professional killers in white suits, or in tweed jackets and Ivy League ties, who've done it, us, we, this country."

I didn't see her or hear her, but I felt Eveline come up and press herself against me from behind. She rested the side of her face against my back, raised her arms up over my shoulders and clasped her hands loosely in front of my throat. For a moment no one moved. Then my father broke the silence.

"All I want is to go back to sea," he said.

"Oh good jesus, Pop," I answered him. "If that's the only thing there was to it. How simple that would be. But you don't want to go back to sea. You'd be bored to death. A tramp steamer will take you back to sea. No. Maybe you want to go back but only if it's in your crispy white suit. You may want to go back but only if there's real danger and real order and real dignity and real risk, and above all a real enemy. You may want to go back only if there's real glamour and real machismo. No, what you want is the excitement and glory and honor. You want the war back again. That's what you want, you self-centered and deluded son of a bitch."

After a short silence, my father said,

"You're a damned liar."

Eveline unclasped her hands, moved them to the front of my shoulders and put a gentle pressure on them, as if suggesting I should draw back from my father.

No one said anything for what seemed like a long time.

"I wish this could be different," I said. "All of it." I felt as though I wasn't talking to anyone in particular.

"Well, it isn't," my father said. "And you don't know what you're talking about."

So slightly that I could hardly feel her doing it, Eveline put more pressure on the front of my shoulders, drawing me back.

"How about letting me go," my father said. "My hands are falling asleep."

I tightened my grip and leaned back from my waist, drawing him with me so as to lessen the weight on his own feet. Given how much the taller he was, this maneuver meant that my face was pressed into the back of his neck. He smelled surprisingly good, soapy and fresh. My father was a symbol. My father was a clean American.

He weighed less than I'd expected and, although it was clumsy, I was able to move him forward by pushing one of my own knees at a time against the back of one of his and "walking" him. We were only a couple of steps from the edge of the kitchen floor, where the drop to the yard was maybe two feet, closer to three. I maneuvered him forward until he was at the edge. I kicked one of his feet forward and then the other so he was hanging in the air. I don't know how I did it, but I held him there.

"Well, Father," I said. "You're in the airborne now. I'm going to drop you."

"Very funny," he said.

"We're at twenty-thousand feet and you don't have a chute. Out you go."

"Even funnier."

"You know what you're doing is wrong," I went on, gasping a little from holding his weight. "You know what you're doing is more destructive than any just war. You know what you're doing is fraudulent. You know you're legitimizing murder. You know you're capitalizing on death. You know you're tearing apart the fabric of the republic. You say you're waving the flag but you know you're dragging it through mud and shit and dipping it in acid."

I dropped him. He fell straight down and hit hard but kept his knees bent and didn't stumble. Even his white hat stayed on.

As soon as he was down, he turned around in order to look back up at us in the kitchen. I saw him give a start. Eveline was standing beside me, her shoulder to mine, looking down at him. He had forgotten all about her.

He turned and went three or four steps and then stopped. He turned to look at us again.

"By the way," he said. "You can keep your insipid dumb goddamn stupid time-travel. At least what I'm doing is *real*."

And with that he was on his way. Eveline and I watched him go around the corner of the house to cross the front yard toward the driveway.

At the table, I pulled out one of the chairs and sat down. I felt exhausted and hollow. Eveline sat sideways on my lap and put her head on my shoulder, the way she used to do when she came from her chair over to mine up in our corner of the library.

Across the table top were the nine beer bottles in no kind of order at all. One was missing its label and had wads and shreds of paper cluttered around its base. Of the nine, four were still full and a fifth more than half. Another had tipped over and lay on its side. Most of its contents had spilled over the tabletop and dripped over its edge to the floor.

From where Eveline and I sat we couldn't see my father as he passed in front of the house, but when he got to the edge of the driveway he came into sight again. He paused for the slightest moment and then crossed the driveway. From there he walked on a long diagonal across the west lawn toward the road—the reverse of our own path when we first came to meet him. There was no sun—the high haze was gradually thickening—but his white uniform stood out brightly nevertheless against the grass and against the trunks of the elms. From the kitchen we watched him. He parted a branch or two of the dry underbrush at the far edge of the lawn, then crossed through the drainage ditch and climbed up its far side onto the road. He turned to the right and continued walking with his unhurried, long-legged gait.

"How will he go?" Eveline asked. Her voice was drowsy. I could almost have expected a yawn.

"He'll walk to West Tree," I said, "then take a bus to St. Paul. Train from St. Paul to Chicago. Another train to Washington."

In silence, we watched my father going along the road until the corner of our own grove of trees obscured him from view. It would have been easy to go down to the end of the driveway and stand there watching him move farther up the road, his figure growing smaller, going up the incline toward the railroad tracks. Once across the tracks and starting down the other side, he would disappear bit by bit, his feet first, then legs, hips, arms, torso, shoulders, neck, head, and, last of all, the circle of his white officer's hat.

We could have gone down the drive to watch, but neither one of us made a move.

The diminishing speck, my father, a microscopic germ off to do its evil.

I looked vacantly at the table and said,

"I suppose we ought to clear up this mess." Still, neither of us moved. It was getting late, past what we used to call the dead of the afternoon, and sounds were returning. Once again the pigeons scuffled and cooed inside the top of the barn, and out of sight somewhere on the other side of the elms a flock of crows had chosen treetop places for their afternoon gossip. With two or three low-pitched moos the cows announced their return to the barnyard. Eveline and I sat listening. We didn't move. An orange cat hopped up onto the kitchen floor and stood looking at us. It meowed once, then walked across the floor and sat down at the spot where I had dropped my father into the yard. I watched it for a while and then looked away. When I looked back again a minute later it was gone.

In spite of the signs of life, the place felt like a graveyard, empty, hollow, abandoned, forlorn. No one was here. Other than the birds and animals, nothing was here. There was no reason to stay. There was no reason to be here at all.

Eveline must have been thinking the same thing.

"I suppose it might have been nice here once, back when," she said into my ear, hardly more than whispering. "But I want to go back. I really, really want to go back."

"Me too," I said. "Let's leave in the morning. Early. First thing."

By way of answer, Eveline tightened her arms around my neck, then let them go again.

A minute passed without either of us saying anything. It seemed to me that the overcast was growing thicker, the afternoon becoming darker. I missed the slanting rays of sunlight that on a clear day would be falling across the lawn and driveway. I wondered if it was going to rain.

"Do you know what I want to do?" Eveline whispered in my ear. I told her that, no, I didn't know.

"I want to go down to the tent," she said. "Not right away but before too long. I want to be all packed, completely ready to leave in the morning, maybe even before sun-up. I so much want to go back to Iowa City, and to our place, our couch, bed, kitchen, even our bathtub. I want to go back to John's for a sandwich and coffee and to the diner again for supper. I'm going to say something terrible. Forgive me. Promise. But if I don't get out of here very soon I feel as though I might suffocate. I might die. I don't know whether it would be worse to suffocate or to explode, one or the other, or be crushed. Or just shrivel and die. I feel as if *there's nothing here* and we've *got* to escape. There's nothing. We're *nowhere*. Sweetheart, we've got to run for our lives."

I did know. Eveline was right. We had tried and failed. We had failed completely. And now we were the ones left behind. Now we were left here alone, in a dead place, in the center of an immense emptiness with nothing near it or around or touching it. I felt a vast sense of emptiness and dread at once. Sorrow, loss, fear, panic—all at the same time.

I held Eveline. Neither of us moved.

The room gradually began materializing around us again. The roof and ceiling were the first to begin coming back, even though there were yet no walls for them to rest on. The reconstructing took place in a here-and-there manner rather than in the manner of a map being unrolled or a sheet of paper being filled with type, from top to bottom. The middle portion of the ceiling reappeared and gave the cord of the hanging lamp something to be attached to again. Then a portion of ceiling over one of the doors took form, after that another portion on the other side of the room, and so on. The walls took shape in the same non-consecutive manner, although not until after the roof and ceiling were complete. By the time we were enclosed inside the room again—though the doors and windows remained open as before—enough time had passed as to make it noticeable how much the light outdoors had diminished. The room felt narrow and confining in its completed form. Without the need of saying anything to one another, Eveline and I began to separate ourselves from one another and to get up from the chairs we had been occupying. The hanging light wasn't turned on, and the room was dim, though only slightly more so than the outdoors. There seemed no need to talk, or perhaps there was a feeling on both our parts that there could be no benefit in it. Either way, we left the mess of bottles and spilled beer on the table and set out down the hill in silence, although holding hands. We came to the white fence, followed it around its corner, and went over to our tent. Still, we hardly spoke. We lay the sleeping bag down again in front of the tent and finished up what was left of our provisions, two tins of fish, a half loaf of bread—slightly stale but not bad—and the second bottle of our wine from West Tree. The time was now past seven, though I had to look at my watch to know. After so many days of clear sky, the cloud cover was a little bit like the removal of a clock, since there was no way of knowing where the sun was. The high cover changed the feeling of things in other ways, too. The silence, for example, was now so nearly total that it seemed unnatural. It was as if the clouds had a way of absorbing sounds, soaking them up before they had a chance to become audible.

I cleared away the things from the blanket between us, except for the wine, and we drew closer together but didn't touch. After a minute, Eveline said, quietly,

"It's almost autumn."

"Yes," I said. "Two days. It always makes me sad, autumn."

"I know," Eveline said. "In Fremont it was terribly sad. When I was a kid."

It was still just light enough for me to pour more wine without spilling. We drank.

Then Eveline said, "Are you afraid?"

"Not of autumn, I don't suppose you mean," I said.

She gave a tiny laugh, scarcely audible, though there was still music in it.

"No," she said. "Not autumn. Just afraid."

"Yes," I told her. "I didn't want to say anything. But yes. I am."

"Me too."

"What is it, do you think?"

"I don't know," she said, and paused. Then she went on. "Well. I know it sounds crazy. But I've gotten afraid *of this place*. I wasn't before, at all. I mean, when we got here. Actually, it was lovely and beautiful. But not now. I feel as if I know so much more. And now I absolutely *hate* it here. What I said before, about suffocating, or exploding, or feeling crushed if we don't get away. It's all true. It *feels like a trap*, Malcolm, and I'm terrified, like in a hideous dream, that we won't be able to get away. Do you know?"

I dropped my empty cup somewhere on the grass behind me and leaned closer to Eveline. I could just make out her face in the remaining light. She was looking straight at me, her demanding eyes insisting not only on an answer from me, but an honest one. I gave it.

"I do know," I said. "But I also know it's worse for you. I failed you. I failed you miserably. Evie, I should have killed him. I should have murdered him."

"No," she said.

"Yes," I answered. "Because now the crushing fear destroying me is that I've lost you. I'm sure I've lost you. I should have broken his wretched neck."

"*No*. Malcolm, you haven't lost me. I swear. You haven't." Her hand found mine. "But I hate your father. I loathe him. Not just for what he did to me. But for what he's done to you."

"He doesn't deserve to live, Eveline. I failed you."

"Even a worm, toad, snail, spider, rat deserves to live. So I suppose your father does too. I hate him. But he deserves to live."

I could hardly trust myself to speak. And so I kept silent.

"*But*," said Eveline. "I want us to get out of here. And I have a plan." She brought herself closer to me so that we were in all but an embrace. She spoke in an urgent whisper.

"I don't want to get out of my clothes tonight," she said, "because I don't want to lose a split second in the morning, not even to pull on my pants and shirt. I'll hold on to you so tight you can't breathe, I swear, but *sleep* is what I want because *morning* is what I want. In fact, let's get up *before* the sun. Let's be half the distance to West Tree before it even rises. Let's be *on the road, on the road to home,* and then we'll be happy again!"

I found her lips and kissed them gently.

"I swear it," I said to her. "I love you forever and ever, and I swear it."

I crawled into the tent and found the flashlight we'd used on our *Howl* night, hung it by its string from the midrib, and we hurriedly went to work packing up everything that could be packed up now, the night before, which meant pretty much everything except the tent and the sleeping bags themselves. In the morning it would take only a couple of minutes before we could be on our way.

The night was as dark as any I've ever known. When we turned off the flashlight, the feeling was one of being truly blind, of there being nothing anywhere but a velvet, inky, dimensionless blackness, a pure and unalloyed absence of light, something almost tactile. Thank god for touch. Eveline and I, fully dressed except for shoes, lay together for the planned purpose of sleep, and she, as promised, held me tight, though not so tight that I couldn't breathe. Then we turned, nestled like spoons, and the black night took us together into itself. I woke up once, to the sound of rain thrumming quietly but steadily against the roof of the tent. The sound was both soothing and sorrowful, the only rain we'd had since leaving Iowa City. Nestled against Eveline, I fell back asleep.

And that was the end of that. When I awoke, it was not the next morning but another morning. Eveline was gone. I was alone. I had been put into another time, another place.

Lost, o lost, was I then.

Lost, o lost, were we all.

AFTERWORD

1

I won't describe the most indecorous part. My superego fled abruptly, like a frightened bird, and left behind the remaining part of me, an abject animal howling in despair.

•

The date: Friday, September 18th, 1964. The time: Eight o'clock in the morning. The place: My old room in the Quadrangle, number B-90, with its bed, desk, chair, and twin windows.

My first thought was that I had made a terrible mistake, that I had left Eveline in West Tree, in our tent, in the rain, in need of help, and that I must get back to her immediately.

My second thought was a thousandfold more crushing, ruinous, and despairing. I would never see Eveline again, ever. I would never again hear her voice, never again touch her cheek or kiss her moistened eyes. Where was she? I would never know even that, never know where she was, certainly not for sure. She was in another place, in another world, away from me.

I rolled over, buried my face in the pillow, and howled and howled and howled.

•

Descriptives of the life around me now came in negatives: un- reverberative, hollow, empty, colorless, thin. Only a year before—or thirty-one years before—the earth had been enveloped by a living sea of redolent and expressive air filled with an immensity of surprise, variety, and pleasure, with scent, texture, color, aroma. Now, it was as though my sense of smell had been stolen from me, and the experience of the air was narrowed from the breadth of a rainbow to the narrowness of a nylon thread.

•

I was destined to live now in a world and land of emptiness, threat, and fear.

•

Lines, circles, connectives, unifiers? Reading? Protective tendrils surrounding the earth? The republic a multitudinous and varied plenitude of places, peoples, climates, languages, freedoms, songs, ideas, feelings, landscapes, desires, all held together by a million woven filaments delicate and invisible and yet strong as braided steel. . .

Gone. All.

•

"thousands were watching but no one saw a thing"

•

Either the people are blind or nothing was there.

•

Which is worse?

•

Often in the beginning for a place to go I walked over the bridge to the east side, crossed diagonally through the parking lot behind the English-Philosophy building, passed in front of the library, then went from there up the hill on Washington Street to Clinton, past the Bus Depot Diner, on across Dubuque, Linn, Gilbert, and Van Buren, diagonally through the little park and out onto College Street, then up one block farther to Eveline's house.

Nothing was there. I would sometimes stand for as much as half an hour on the sidewalk at the spot where, once, a walkway had led to the three steps up to the front porch and to the big front door with the corridor inside, and, to the right, Eveline's rooms.

Where, once, Eveline had taken me by the hand and drawn me in.

Nothing was there now. Even the growths of the tall plants and shrubs that used to conceal Eveline's bedroom windows were gone. Everything was gone. Even the basement had been filled in. Only a certain sunken area in the lawn suggested that anything might ever have been under it.

Nothing was left. I stood and stood and stood there, thinking of Eveline.

•

Past, present, future—father, nation, Eveline—all lost.

•

When Eveline was taken away in 1947, when she was pushed out from the world of that year, the past was also pushed out of the republic. From that point on, lacking its own past for nourishment, the republic began its long, slow, gradual process of dying.

•

Eveline's voice; the tone, qualities, and scope of her behavior; her attitudes, her imagination, her aims; her desire through each of her abilities to refine, nurture, and protect not some but all things—these attributes were the spirit and manifestation of the past, as was Eveline herself. A young girl going into the Fremont Carnegie library; then walking on the streets of the same town but in the darkness of night; a teacher in the far west of Nebraska, living in upstairs rooms with a wood-burning stove for heat.

•

Once the past was gone, reading also began to sicken and die. This happened slowly at first and then more rapidly. When reading had disappeared altogether, the nation died and was gone.

•

Although most failed to realize it, people also began to follow the nation's pattern, losing the past within themselves, slowly at first and then more rapidly. When the presence of the past inside them became so airy, weak, and thin as to be undetectable, they too died.

This is what has happened now, today, as I write these words.

•

There was no question but that we had been doing the right thing, Eveline and I, in the attempt we made to alter the events of November 1963.

We failed. The reason was that the nation, like my father, had already gone blind and deaf.

Not everything in the past was good, but such good as did lie there was slain.

Thousands were watching but no one saw a thing.

•

After Kennedy was murdered and no one saw it, the others fell like tenpins. All shot in the head; all slain by non-readers; all killed by the same strain of unanointed takers and seizers who had begun their metastatic spreading on and after February 27, 1947.

•

The date of the republic's betrayal; betrayal of its integrity, coherence, harmony, humanity, wholeness. Betrayal, for the final time, of its original purpose, often obscured but never before lost. The myriad tendrils, lines, bands, and threads that had been brought into existence through countless acts of reading—these, having successfully preserved the elements of the republic's singularity that were coherent and humane, went unseen by the newly blind people, became valueless to them, fell, were abandoned to worms.

•

No longer a republic in name, spirit, or soul, the nation since then has been dedicated only to the river of blood.

2

I come now to the task of bringing this book to an end. The date is May 9th, 2028, the time near three in the afternoon. Outdoors, the weather is gusty and unseasonably cold. Through the windows of my apartment I see white clouds, their edges blurred and their bottom-sides dark, being blown across a sky doing its best to be blue.

•

I left Iowa City and arrived in New York in 1969, when I moved into the apartment I still live in, on Manhattan's upper west side, one building off Broadway, on the ninth floor. Modest, old, and comfortable, the apartment has given me a reliable vantage point to overlook the long-gathering and now rapidly approaching death throes of our nation.

The republic itself died long ago: Condemned to death in February 1947; put to death in the atrocities of public execution: November 1963; February 1965; April 1968; June 1968.

In the years since, no President has been a representative of the people nor has any been dedicated to them. All holders of this office have been chosen, cultivated, and elected by what some call "the oligarchy," some "the establishment," some "the shadow government."

All these terms are valid.

It might be called, also, the leadership of a dead hand.

•

Having lived through the death of the republic, and living now through the death of the nation, I can wait only for the destruction of the corpse that has been left behind. Considering my age, it is possible I won't live to see this spectacle. I pray only that it be sparing in the amount of pain, torture, misery, suffering, and anguish that it brings.

•

I sleep less than I did in earlier decades. I sit at the window a good share of the night, gazing out. The avenue is never well lit, but only dimly. For long periods no one passes by; then there may come a pedestrian, walking quickly, as if hastened by fear. Now and then a couple will pass by, arm in arm, moving more slowly, although such appearances are rare. Far more frequently, sometimes each hour after the curfew, come the crisply marching uniformed guards in their ranks of eight, ten, sometimes a dozen. These march arrogantly down the middle of the avenue, heels clicking in unison on the pavement. These soldiers, of both sexes, hold their machine guns in both hands, muzzles pointing to the left and upward.

At other times, unpredictably, the avenue will be turned to daylight by floodlights and flashing red, blue, and white strobes, all amid a deafening cacophony of piercing sirens, crackling radios, angrily shouted threats and commands, the pavement crowded curb to curb with ambulances, police cruisers, firetrucks, and workers in uniforms of varying kinds.

Almost never is it possible to determine what particular reason there may have been for gatherings such as these. Bodies sometimes lie on the ground. Some of these are being attended to while others are covered by plastic sheets.

The urgent pageantry arrives with fierce extremities of haste, noise, and light; remains for a time; and disperses, leaving silence behind.

•

After spectacles such as these, I admit to feelings of loss, sorrow, and fear. I am grateful for having reached the age I have reached, not so much for what I may have achieved, but in gratitude for a future that I will not be required to witness. At the same time, I think also of Eveline, from whose memory, no matter what else might happen, I receive assurance, solace, comfort, perhaps even courage. Permit me to say that I have felt Eveline's closeness with particular intensity during the long months I have spent working on this, her book, the book—once upon a time—of reading.

ABOUT ATMOSPHERE PRESS

Founded in 2015, Atmosphere Press was built on the principles of Honesty, Transparency, Professionalism, Kindness, and Making Your Book Awesome. As an ethical and author-friendly hybrid press, we stay true to that founding mission today.

If you're a reader, enter our giveaway for a free book here:

SCAN TO ENTER
BOOK GIVEAWAY

If you're a writer, submit your manuscript for consideration here:

SCAN TO SUBMIT
MANUSCRIPT

And always feel free to visit Atmosphere Press and our authors online at atmospherepress.com. See you there soon!

ABOUT THE AUTHOR

Born in Northfield, Minnesota, **ERIC LARSEN** graduated from Carleton College and in 1970 took his doctorate from the University of Iowa. For thirty-five years, he taught English at John Jay College of Criminal Justice, CUNY, retiring in 2006. His first novel, *An American Memory* (1988), won the *Chicago Tribune*'s inaugural Heartland Prize. That novel was followed by four others, joined now by *The Book of Reading* to complete a saga of family and nation. For fifty-four years, Larsen was married to the editor Anne Larsen, and the couple raised two daughters, Flynn and Gavin, both active and highly productive in the arts. Larsen lives in New York City and has also authored the non-fiction works *A Nation Gone Blind, The Skull of Yorick,* and *Homer Whole: A Reading of the Iliad.*

www.ingramcontent.com/pod-product-compliance
Lightning Source LLC
Chambersburg PA
CBHW031113160726
47991CB00004B/1356